CARLOS CISNEROS

Arte Público Press
Houston, Texas

The Name Partner is made possible through grants from the City of Houston through the Houston Arts Alliance and the Exemplar Program, a program of Americans for the Arts in collaboration with the LarsonAllen Public Services Group, funded by the Ford Foundation.

Recovering the past, creating the future

Arte Público Press
University of Houston
452 Cullen Performance Hall
Houston, Texas 77204-2004

Cover design by Mora Des!gn

Cover illustration by J. Salvador Lopez
www.deviantart.com/www.redbubble.com

Cisneros, Carlos, 1963-
    The Name Partner / by Carlos Cisneros.
        p.   cm.
    ISBN 978-1-55885-594-6 (alk. paper)
    1. Law firms—Fiction. 2. Law partnership—Fiction.
3. Attorney and client—Fiction. 4. Pharmaceutical industry
—Corrupt practices—Fiction. 5. Texas, South—Fiction. I. Title.
PS3603.I86N36 2010
813'.6—dc22

                                                                    2010000599
                                                                    CIP

♾ The paper used in this publication meets the requirements of the American National Standard for Information Sciences—Permanence of Paper for Printed Library Materials, ANSI Z39.48-1984.

10 11 12 13 14 15 16   10 9 8 7 6 5 4 3 2 1

To Philip,
my brother, my business partner, my amigo.
May we live to remember you, always.

DISCLAIMER

This is a book of fiction. Any resemblance or similarity to people, situations, places and events is purely coincidental.

PROLOGUE

Laredo, Texas, January 28, 2005

MELISSA ANDARZA had been a state employee exactly three years by the time she decided to switch jobs and become a U.S. federal probation officer. Not long before joining the ranks of the gainfully employed, twenty-eight-year-old Andarza had attended the University of Texas at Laredo where she'd graduated with a BA in criminal justice, *magna cum laude*. The daughter of Mexican immigrants, she was a first-generation American and the first member in her family to graduate from college. She was her close-knit family's pride and joy.

Melissa began her professional life as a juvenile probation officer with the Webb County Juvenile Probation Department, where she earned her wings and received accolades from her superiors for her dedication, resourcefulness, unwavering work ethic and the ability to get along with others. But now, after having worked as an adult federal probation officer for almost one year, the "lucky one" (as her colleagues at work called her) was engaged to be married to heart-throb DEA agent, Samuel "Sammy" Guerra, Jr.

The two had met while working on the Victor Montalvo prosecution, a case involving money laundering and drug trafficking. Sammy had been the special agent spearheading the criminal investigation. After a year of contested hearings, bickering, posturing, haggling, debriefings and negotiations between the U.S. attorney and his defense counsel, Montalvo had finally pled guilty. After the guilty plea, Melissa's task was to interview the defendant for the purpose of writing up his presentence investigation report.

1

The district judge had ended up adopting all of the recommendations contained in her report. Montalvo subsequently received a well-deserved life sentence. Unless he escaped from custody, the kingpin was expected to kick the bucket in prison.

This chilly and foggy Saturday morning, Melissa was wrapping up her long-distance run before joining her thirty-year-old fiancé and *mamá y papá* for breakfast at Maria's, her favorite eatery. With their wedding less than nine months away, Melissa had increased her weekend runs from three to five miles. Since she didn't smoke, rarely drank and hated to binge on food, jogging in and around Rio Viejo Estates—Laredo's wealthiest and safest neighborhood—was her way to combat the mounting stress of her "dream wedding." There were guest lists to be updated, invitations to be mailed out, meetings with caterers, setting up wedding registries at several department stores, finding the right photographer, dress fittings, organizing the rehearsal dinner, booking blocks of rooms for the guests coming up from Mexico and elsewhere, even lining up the *mariachis* for the church ceremony.

Melissa looked at her watch and picked up the pace. It was close to eight-thirty. She had four miles to go. Breakfast with her parents had been scheduled for ten that morning. After her early run, she would head to her modest apartment to shower and change before catching up with the family. She smiled as the music from her iPod triggered images of her and Special Agent Guerra making love on the gorgeous beaches of Oaxaca on their long-awaited honeymoon.

She wondered if making love on a sandy beach under the cover of darkness would be considered a crime in Mexico. *Could we get arrested? Could we lose our government jobs over such a minute indiscretion?* The whole idea sounded exciting and irresistible. In her mind, she could picture the tender episode, as the Pacific Ocean lazily pounded the shore and a silver moon straddled the jagged cliffs surrounding the magical bay of Huatulco.

Just then, as the idyllic images became more and more intense, she was startled by a large silhouette standing in a driveway down the street. The man appeared to be barefoot and in his robe. Through the morning mist, she barely recognized Tommy Ray, a prosperous defense attorney known for representing members of the Gulf and Juárez drug cartels. She'd seen the flashy attorney in federal court on many occasions, handling a variety of criminal cases. In fact, it had been Ray who had assembled, coordinated and first-chaired Montalvo's defense team. The millionaire attorney, it seemed, always had a hand in Laredo's high-profile criminal prosecutions. At six feet tall, he was hard to miss.

The Rays were one of Laredo's founding families. They were civic leaders, successful entrepreneurs and pillars in the community. As Melissa came closer, it became apparent that Tommy Ray was holding something in his hand. He looked up menacingly at her. He seemed disheveled, confused and disoriented. He was restless, pacing back and forth like a caged animal. She'd never seen him like this.

Nearby, to her right, Melissa noticed a U.S. mail truck sitting in front of Ray's driveway, the engine idling, blue smoke coming out of its muffler. As Melissa jogged by, she saw the mail carrier slumped over the steering wheel, blood splattered on the windshield. She panicked and began to scream. Melissa spun around and tried to sprint to safety. Tommy Ray cocked his silencer-ready .357 Magnum, locked her in his sights and pulled the trigger. The lethal Black Talon bullet hit Melissa between the shoulder blades and sent her flying like a rag doll, slamming her down on the asphalt. Her iPod came to rest on the grassy sidewalk, Shakira's "Hips Don't Lie" still blaring from the earphones.

She was face down, her delicate frame twitching. Her heart was pounding louder and louder, her head felt like it was about to explode. Choking on her own blood, she started to lose consciousness. "¡Me muero!" she moaned. Her punctured lungs made it impossible to breathe "Sammy, Sammy, "she whispered, "mi amor."

Seconds later as the darkness closed in, she heard the faint wailing of police sirens in the distance. "God, please . . . I don't . . . want to die. Save . . . me. Jesus, let . . . me live," she gurgled, struggling for precious air. More blood spewed out from her nose, mouth and ears, a large pool curdling on the blacktop.

"HERE, TAKE a look at this," said BostonMagnifica's, CEO Salvatore "Sal" Falcone, as he got up from his seat at the end of the large conference table, walked over to a metal cart holding video equipment and plopped in a VHS cassette.

"Must be something really important to drag my ass all the way from D.C.," huffed the other man in the otherwise empty and sterile boardroom.

"It is, Malcolm," complained a furious Falcone as he hit the PLAY button and fumbled with the lights. "My sources got a hold of this tape. It's due to air on Sunday, September 21."

"That's in less than two weeks," volunteered Malcolm Reed.

Falcone played with the TV until he found the right channel to sync with the VCR. "My company doesn't need this right now—a friggin' exposé airing on 20/20 attacking my industry."

The video started to play. The images showing on the large retractable screen inside the pharmaceutical's executive boardroom depicted a gloomy hallway leading into a dimly lit restroom while somber music played in the background. Then, the background music quieted and gave way to audio portions of a terrifying 911 call, the words having been transcribed on the screen for the home viewer to read along.

"This is 911," said the operator, "what's your emergency?"

"Help us! Pleeease help my sister," cried the young caller.

"Who is this?"

"This is Tina," the stressed caller screamed. "Amber, my sister, is trying to kill herself! My God, oh my God, do something!" The young caller was hysterical and seemed to be having a total and complete breakdown.

"Where is your sister?" asked the male operator. "What is she trying to do?"

"What?" asked the caller, sounding confused, sobbing, breathing heavily and then she mumbled into the receiver, "She slashed her . . . wait my dad's home." There was a pause.

A second later an adult could be heard in the background screaming, "For the love of God, no! Please don't take her! Somebody help me! My baby's dying, my baby's dying! Pleeease help me!"

"My sister's bleeding to death!" howled Tina into the receiver. "Help us, please! Hurry!"

"Help is on its way," replied the operator.

The *20/20* documentary played on. The images now on the screen showed the Capitol building in D.C., the shot fading into a large carpeted room buzzing with activity, where hearings on drug safety were being held. Silhouettes slowly came into focus, showing distressed, angry families testifying before forty-five-year-old U.S. Senator Andy Del Toro, proponent of a bill circulating in Congress for the creation of an independent drug-safety panel to monitor the pharmaceutical industry and the Federal Drug Administration.

"Our beautiful little girl Monica," said a mother as she stood up and spoke into the microphone, "died by hanging three days after ingesting 100 milligrams of Zoloft, a psychotropic drug. She was barely nineteen."

"She ended her stay on this earth by slashing her throat," said another tortured father.

"I found our teenage son Victor hanging from a tree in our own backyard," added an angry mother.

As the camera panned over the audience of anguished parents, hugging and comforting each other, the investigative reporter narrating what was to be a two-part series then added, "These families believe the drug complex has known for years that there is a link between suicide, violent behavior and serotonin reuptake inhibitors. They're demanding to know why no one ever bothered to tell them. Why did the FDA allow this to happen? And why hasn't the FDA ordered the drug makers to put accurate black box warnings on these medications?"

The video clip then showed more footage of others testifying before the Texas senator, a vocal opponent of the pharmaceutical industry and its lobby. Not only was Del Toro known to be an advocate for stronger drug-safety laws, but he was also a critic and tireless combatant of the industry's increasing presence and influence on Capitol Hill.

"I'd like to introduce you to my daughter Ashley," said another father. The man was holding up a framed picture of a beautiful, healthy girl with curly black hair and blue eyes. "This is all I have left . . . memories. She committed suicide at the age of eleven, just three weeks after being put on Zoloft and Paxil for social anxiety."

"In the fall of 2003, our daughter Jessica had been excited about starting college after having scored a perfect 1600 on her SAT," continued another mother as tears welled up in her eyes. "Instead of selecting colleges, my husband and I had to pick a casket and a cemetery plot. Instead of visiting Jessica at her campus, we now visit her grave."

A female in her late twenties testified on behalf of her deceased brother. "The doctor had prescribed Xykretza because he said Patrick had situational depression. Patrick complained the drug made him feel like jumping out of his skin. He died by jumping in front of an oncoming train."

"If only a drug-safety panel had existed three years ago, I know my husband Wayne would still be alive today," said Kim Ebel, the founding member of a Washington watchdog group now campaigning to ban SSRIs. "Who are we kidding? The truth is, Congress washed its hands by creating and implementing the 'user fee' program. In essence, they put the FDA in the pockets of the drug companies. So, we have the fox safeguarding the henhouse. How did we let that happen?"

Senator Andy Del Toro then addressed the crowd. "It has always been my position that these drugs do more harm than good. To make matters worse, the drug complex has systematically misled the American public by promoting these drugs as totally safe and highly effective in the fight against mental diseases. Phrases like 'social anxiety,' 'situational depression,' 'seasonal stress,' 'climatic anxiety' and 'temporary collective psychotic dysfunction' have been made up by their marketing departments to convince us that we must suffer from one of these fictitious conditions . . . all in the name of profits."

"These drugs can help some folks, but can also kill," said world-renowned psychiatrist Mark Steely. "The industry must warn the public about the real side effects and must educate the doctors to properly monitor each patient. They need to do better than the current lame black box warnings on the packaging. Why?

Because the warnings being used right now on the packaging do not warn of the seriousness of suicide and aggressive behaviors. They do not warn of fatal interactions with other drugs or of the withdrawal effect. In short, they're worthless. The warnings used right now say nothing of akathisia, which is characterized by agitation, restlessness, sleeplessness and thoughts of suicide. I've seen it firsthand. When I take my patients off these drugs, the fixation with suicide and the akathisia go away within two days. So what does that tell us?

"We've all heard of Columbine and Virginia Tech. Remember Eric Harris, Kip Kinkle, Jason Hoffman, Shawn Cooper and T. J. Solomon? All of them were on serotonin-enhancing drugs or suffering from akathisia. Every single one of them completely psychotic, delusional and suffering from 'command hallucinations' when they killed their classmates.

"Let's be honest . . . depression has always existed, but never before has it been linked to such violence and aggression. Ever since these drugs came on the market, we now see raging bouts of violence, aggressive behaviors and suicide."

When the documentary was over, Salvatore Falcone got up and turned the video player off. He flipped on the lights and stood there, scratching his shiny pate, looking preoccupied.

After a few minutes of dead silence, Malcolm Reed finally spoke. "You and I know that Del Toro has an axe to grind. He's going after the FDA and you guys because his old man croaked after taking Ketek, the antibiotic for respiratory infections."

· "Yes, but that was a friggin' bad drug with horrible side effects, including renal failure."

"And . . . " added Reed, " . . . let's not forget that Del Toro found out that a bureaucrat took money to rubber-stamp the drug's approval when there had been no clinical tests and only minimal research."

"Can you do anything to rein him in? We'll be launching Zerevrea in a month, and I don't want any problems. Doctors' officess across the United States have received our free samples for the national campaign."

"I'll . . . well, I'll see what I can do," said Reed, the dapper chief of staff from 1600 Pennsylvania Avenue. "Del Toro owes my boss some favors. Maybe it's time to call them in."

"Whatever you can do," said the CEO. "We just want a clean launch—no negative headlines, no more attacks from Del Toro or the press."

"I'll help you as much as I can," said Reed, shrugging his shoulders. "But I wouldn't worry if I were you. In the event we can't pull it off the air, no one will remember that slanted documentary anyway. You and I know Americans have the attention span of a tsetse fly."

"Yes, but tsetse flies can turn on you, and they have a knack for putting you to sleep for a very, very long time. Then what?"

"Stop worrying. I doubt that'll happen," Reed reassured Falcone, "I'm on it."

CHAPTER 1

WAIST DEEP IN the tepid waters of the Laguna Madre in South Texas, the old man yelled and waved him over. "Billy, *m'ijo ¡acércate!* Quick! Get the net, son, or this monster will get away! It'll snap the line . . . hurry up! *Se nos va, se nos va . . . apúrale.*" His old man was rejoicing, some thirty feet away, struggling to reel in what appeared to be a huge red fish, possibly a state record.

Billy fought to untangle the net from his gear belt and waded toward his father. He struggled to move as his legs sank underneath him in the soft brown sand. "Hang on," he cried, "I'm coming . . . give it some drag. Careful, don't let him snap the line . . . don't let it get away, Dad."

As he got closer to his old man, his legs grew heavier and his breathing became more labored. Without warning, he suddenly felt a needlelike prick from a stingray. His right ankle began throbbing with burning pain where the ray's barb had pierced his skin, and now his entire right leg felt as if it had been sliced open with a dull blade. Blood started trickling out from the wound. He cursed his luck and tried to move, but the jolts of pain shooting up his body proved to be too much, and he doubled over.

"Dad . . . help. I stepped on a stingray!" Billy cried, as he tumbled headfirst into the water. He managed to pull himself up, but when he looked over to the spot where his old man had been fishing, his dad had disappeared, along with their gear, their fishing guide and their boat.

He was now alone, surrounded by miles and miles of water. The fifty square-mile area straddling portions of South Padre

9

Island was known to the locals as "the flats." With no land near-by and bleeding profusely, Billy was in trouble. Soon the sun would go down, and the distant shoreline would disappear in the moonless night. As the high tide returned, the water level would rise another three feet and the sharks would come to feed in and around the flats. Feeling frantic, he let out a wretched scream that resounded throughout the desolate bay.

"Billy! Billy! Wake up! *¡Despierta!*" said the voice, "*Cariño,* wake up!"

Guillermo "Billy" Bravo awoke from the nightmare as his wife tugged on his shoulders. Dazed and dripping in sweat, the forty-two-year-old sat up in bed and looked at the clock. It was four fifteen AM.

"What happened?" Billy asked, trying to focus. His head was throbbing.

"That thing with the stingray, again."

"Really? I'm sorry," Billy apologized to his wife Yamilé.

"These nightmares have become more frequent in the past two weeks. Is something troubling you?"

"Everything's fine. Get some sleep, princess," Billy said, trying to brush the embarrassing episode aside.

"I don't think I can," she said as she reached under his silk boxers and began to knead him in the crotch.

"Wait! What are you doing, Yami?" he asked, pushing her hand away. "I have an early morning."

"I'm trying to help you relax," she giggled. "I need you, baby, right now, right this minute. *Ahorita.* It's been what . . . six weeks? Don't make me wait any longer."

"It hasn't been six weeks."

"Actually, it's been longer than that," she griped. "I should know. You've been away, traveling, trying cases . . . last week in Brownsville, that week in Corpus Christi, then San Antonio, Edinburg, Victoria, Laredo. What happened to the guy that couldn't keep his hands off me? You couldn't wait to get home. I mean, I had to swat you away, and now?"

"I'm sorry. It's just that . . . "

"And now that you're teaching at the college . . . it's worse. The kids and I never see you."

The irony of teaching was not lost on Billy. Here he was teaching Legal Ethics for business majors, yet he made a living defending malpractice claims and grievances filed against doctors, dentists, hospitals and pharmacists—many of whom were notorious for ripping off Medicaid, Medicare and the insurance companies. How long had he been suffering from what psychoanalysts called "moral hypocrisy"?

"I wish you'd just quit teaching and spend more time with us. *Honestamente*, I don't know why you do it? It barely pays anything."

"I don't do it for the money, Yami. I do it to give back. If I want to make name partner, I've got to show the selection committee my community involvement."

"How about being more involved here at home, *hombre*? Being a good husband and father?"

"Go to sleep, Yami, please. Can we talk about this tomorrow?"

"*¿Cuándo?* You'll be up and gone before dawn."

"Have you stopped to think why that is?" asked Billy, completely annoyed.

"What do you mean?"

"It's called tort reform, woman! Thanks to pretty boy in Austin and his posse of Einsteins, now there are thousands of unemployed insurance defense attorneys out there . . . and it's getting worse. And I could be next. And then, how are we going to pay for all of this?"

"Clients, judges and juries get to see more of you than we do here at home," snapped Yami, equally annoyed.

"Hey! You want a nice house in a gated community? Not to mention a million-dollar beach house and money for the kids' private schools? Well, it takes sacrifice."

"Hey, the beach house in Padre was your idea! I never wanted a beach house. We bought it because you wanted to keep up with the others at your firm. *¿A ver?* When was the last time you set foot in that house? *¿Cuándo?*"

"Last Fourth of July."

"Wrong. Two years ago! Don't you think Mauricio would love for his dad to teach him how to fish? And Alessandra? You promised to teach her how to windsurf, and you haven't done that either. For the last two years, we've stayed out there the entire summer waiting for you to come out . . . *y nada!*"

"So it's my fault?"

"All I'm saying is that it'd be nice if you'd spend more time with us. Do you even remember the last time we made love? The time you went soft on me, eh?"

"I was tired that day! Look, things have been hectic at the office. There are cases coming up for trial, and I've had midterms and grades to turn in. You know that. I'm right in the middle of the fall semester."

"When do you plan on slowing down?" she demanded. "*¿Cuándo?*"

"As soon as I make name partner . . . as I've told you already. Then, I'll relax. My job will be safe, locked in for good. Our future guaranteed. No more financial worries. No more having to keep tabs on knucklehead in the governor's mansion and his tort reform schemes. I'll coast to retirement, sit back and relax."

"*¡Ay, por favor!* You've been an equity partner for over ten years now. Why name partner? What's the difference?"

"Yami, you were born into a family with means," Billy fired back. He sat up in bed, realizing his wife was not going to just roll over and go back to sleep. "You wouldn't understand."

"Try me."

"I never want to be poor again, okay? That's it. Now, drop it and go to sleep."

"Is that it? *No te creo.* That's just an excuse, if you ask me."

"Aggh, *¡chihuahuas!* Look . . . you never had to pick crops for a living and sleep packed like a sardine in the back of an old pickup truck, freezing your ass off, much less travel from town to town during the scorching summers doing backbreaking labor . . . tearing up your hands and arms, getting sunburned to a crisp. Nah, you spent summers playing tennis at a country club, sipping fresh-squeezed lemonade and traveling to fun places, being pampered and chauffeured around while you and your mother shopped at Liverpool, El Palacio de Hierro, Macy's, Harrod's . . . "

Yamilé propped herself up on the pillows and turned on the bedside night lamp. "Why do you resent me and my family so much? Isn't it enough that you've made it? Look at your accomplishments. Best trial lawyer in all of South Texas from Brownsville to El Paso. Your colleagues always nominate you as the top litigator, the most capable, hardworking, ethical, even to a fault. On top of that, you have us. What else could you want?"

"Yes, but all of this can be gone like that . . . POOF! The firm could downsize, especially now. Making name partner would guarantee that won't happen."

"You're an equity partner. ¿Qué más quieres?"

"It's personal, Yami. Making name partner is my American dream, okay? The last notch in my belt."

"Why such a hang up? Is it because you feel like the firm's token Hispanic?" asked Yami matter-of-factly. "Is that it?"

"Ouch!"

"Look, I know it means a lot to you, but it's not worth the heart attack. ¡Por favor, hombre, escucha! You're already living the dream. You've made it, okay? Look at all the nightmares you keep having. There must be a reason for that."

"I'm *this* close. I can feel it," Billy mumbled under his breath as he laid back down and stared up at the ceiling, completely ignoring Yami. "I just need a major win in a big case, and they'll see I'm name partner material. Listen . . . " whispered Billy, slowly, " . . . Bates, Domani, Rockford, Lord and Bravo. Don't you like the sound of that?"

"I hope you know what you're doing."

"Let's get some sleep, okay, princess? Please?" Billy knew that he was not going to win this argument.

"I hope it's not me that has to disconnect you from life support," Yamilé said, pleading with her husband. "Don't you want to be around to give your daughter away in marriage? To see our son graduate from college? Play with our grandchildren?"

"Let me nail this promotion, then we'll all get away . . . go to the beach house—you, me and the kids," Billy muttered under his breath as he desperately tried to fall back asleep. He needed to be at the office in less than three hours. "We'll go to Paris for our anniversary, okay?"

"Don't make promises you can't or won't keep," Yamilé huffed. She turned away, pulled the silver satin sheets over her hundred-and-ten-pound frame and switched the night lamp off.

CHAPTER 2

ATES, DOMANI, ROCKFORD AND LORD'S headquarters occupied the top two floors of the Textron Tower on Allen Parkway near downtown Houston. Bates was the typical insurance defense firm in every respect, except for one little fact: all the name partners (at one time or another) had worked or still served in the Texas legislature. Considered by many to be the premier defense firm in Houston and South Texas, its practice areas included governmental affairs, healthcare defense, pharmaceutical litigation and general negligence defense.

The firm had also built a niche practice in the Rio Grande Valley protecting doctors, medical equipment companies, pharmacists, home health agencies and even dentists in cases involving Medicaid and Medicare fraud. The attorneys based in the Valley also defended other healthcare professionals accused of a wide variety of wrongdoings. Posted on the firm's Web site, Billy Bravo's profile highlighted his local roots and success: *Trial attorney Guillermo "Billy" Bravo in the McAllen office can always be counted on to sway jurors, judges and opponents alike. Born and raised in South Texas, Mr. Bravo has not lost a single trial since 1999. From Laredo to San Antonio, from Corpus Christi to McAllen, all the way down to Brownsville, attorney Bravo has faced the best swaggering trial lawyers the great State of Texas has had to offer, sending them all home with a big fat zero in their pockets. Aside from being a lawyer's lawyer, Mr. Bravo is also a frequent lecturer at legal education seminars. He has written and presented papers on the topics of "Modern Legal Ethics for the Twenty-First-Century Lawyer," "Trends and Developments in the Area of Professional Responsibility," "Conduct*

Unbecoming a Lawyer" and "Morality, Reality and the Law—Just a Formality?"

AFTER A QUICK thirty-minute treadmill run and with less than four hours of sleep, Billy, the loyal workaholic, went in to work at seven AM that Saturday morning in late September. He parked under the only tree in the empty lot in a feeble attempt to avoid getting drenched, courtesy of the remnants of hurricanes Rita and Katrina. At the exact moment he'd taken the keys out of the ignition, the skies had opened up and the rain was now coming down in buckets. He made a run for it, using the Saturday edition of the local newspaper as an umbrella as he fumbled with his office keys, the front door lock and a cup of coffee in the other hand.

As usual, Billy was the only one working that early on Saturday morning. Even Charlie Jensen, the newest hire, never went in on weekends before noon. Billy was sporting jeans, a Franco Tofanetti cotton guayabera, hand-sewn espadrilles and his titanium Raymond Weil diver's watch.

He was now standing in his dimly lit office soaking wet, holding a soggy copy of the paper. In his mind, being alone in his office for a few hours was the only benefit to coming to the office early on weekends. He could drink his venti Starbucks mocha latte while reading the *McAllen Monitor* in peace and comfort.

The cramped office was quiet. The only sounds emanated from his desktop's hard drive, and the rain outside. He sat down at his desk, slowly unfolded the wet newspaper, trying not to shred it in the process, took a sip of coffee and started reading the headlines. One immediately caught his attention: "Midwife Draws Ten-Year Sentence."

The story by reporter Cari DeLuna recounted how FBI agent Art Esquivel had brought to Justice Rosalba Valdez, a seventy-nine-year-old *partera* from Brownsville. The midwife, who was now old and frail and waiting to report to federal prison, had been accused of running a scam for decades, where she charged Mexican nationals a fee to get U.S. citizenship for their Mexican babies.

The investigation revealed that the *partera* and other corrupt midwives from Brownsville to El Paso routinely accepted bribes from Mexican couples to declare that the birth of their children had taken place in the United States. With the midwive's assistance, the parents were then able to obtain fraudulent birth certificates.

Why do they do this? Don't they know they're gonna get caught? figured Billy, in disgust. *And then we all get a bad rap . . . because of a few bad apples. And then we all get a bad name.*

Billy threw the paper in the wastebasket and glanced at his trial calendar. There were five jury trials scheduled for the first Monday of October. The rest of October 2005 was booked solid with depositions, meetings with experts and witnesses, mediations, arbitrations, seminar presentations and even contested discovery hearings. It was already shaping up to be a hell of a month.

He picked up one of the large three-ring binders his secretary had meticulously assembled for him. The trial notebook was labeled "Dr. Myers." As thick as a phonebook, it contained a list of witnesses, copies of subpoenas, sample jury selection questions, discovery responses, motions in limine and lists of marked exhibits and outlines for what would be Billy's opening and closing arguments.

He pulled out the witness list and made a mental note to call Dr. Myers and remind him of what to wear to court on Monday. He looked out his office window. The rain was not letting up. Coffee in hand, Billy leaned back in his chair and looked out into the distance. He now remembered a phone conversation he'd had a couple of weeks earlier. The words still reverberated in his head, as if the conversation had taken place five minutes ago . . .

"I know this comes as a surprise, Billy, but I've been diagnosed with stomach cancer. Doctors say I don't have much time left. I wanted to see if you could raise our fifteen-year-old son, William."

"Excuse me?" Billy had muttered in disbelief, the wind knocked out of him as the room had started to spin. "William who? What? You mean, I . . . we have a son?"

The caller had been Karin Palmer, an Austin lawyer, whom he had met fifteen years earlier at the Advanced Medical Malpractice seminar in the Texas capital. He'd been there for the continuing legal education seminar, a three-day event; but one night after meeting other colleagues from the seminar for dinner and one too many 151 *mojitos*, the unexpected happened. Billy, then a wiry and virile twenty-seven-year-old, and Karin, five years his senior, had ended up back at her home. The only time he'd strayed in his fifteen-plus years of marriage, and he'd caught a bad break.

"I'm sorry I never told you, Billy. But I knew that you were married, and, besides, at the time, I had a thriving practice and thought I could do it all on my own, including raising William, our son."

"And you waited fifteen years to tell me?" snapped Billy, his mind racing as he pictured Yami handing him his severed privates on a silver platter along with divorce papers.

"The doctors say I have a year left, if that much, and I need to start getting my affairs in order," said Karin in a dry cough. "Will you look after our son when I'm gone?"

In his mind, he heard the words "our son" over and over again, teasing him, mocking him, even taunting him.

"But, but . . . " Billy had stuttered, "you need to give me some time, I need to figure out how to break the news to Yami and the kids."

"I understand. I'm sorry I never told you, but as I said, I never planned to get cancer. Get back to me after you've come clean with your family. Please hurry, I don't have much time."

Now, almost three weeks after having received "the phone call," he felt trapped, unable to escape, as if he was running on quicksand, sinking ever so slowly, the sand now up to his neck. The prospect of coming clean with Yami and admitting having had an affair, not even a month after getting married, was simply appalling. The worst part, Billy knew, was that a contentious public divorce would surely nix his chances at making name partner. Mr. Bates would have none of it.

CHAPTER 3

SAL FALCONE TURNED off the TV in his study and felt a surge of excitement come over him. It was the second week of October 2005. Rita and Katrina were all over the news, and the *20/20* exposé had never aired. Malcolm Reed had pulled off a miracle. And just a week earlier, President Bailey had finally declared major portions of Louisiana, Mississippi and Alabama as disaster areas. More emergency aid was on its way.

Experts in the mental health industry confirmed that the majority of victims left homeless by hurricanes Rita and Katrina were exhibiting signs of depression, anxiety and severe debilitating stress. A mental health crisis clearly loomed over the Gulf States. The government needed to respond quickly and provide much-needed housing, restore basic services and help with the cleanup effort. More importantly, the experts predicted the hurricane victims would need counseling, therapy and medication for years to come.

Falcone, the astute businessman, was grinning with delight. He would use the natural disasters as a backdrop to roll out Zerevrea. The timing was perfect to launch his media assault and create nationwide consumer buzz. At the end of the day, the hurricanes would spell billions in much-needed sales for the young pharmaceutical now under his control.

The pieces of the puzzle are coming together nicely, Falcone thought. *Malcolm says Bailey is almost on board. Talk about perfect timing. Two hurricanes . . . one right after the other. Badaboom!*

Falcone was now smiling, thinking of a catchy slogan to go with the launch. *ZEREVREA, The Calm After the Storm. It's perfect.*

Our ad agency better include raging hurricane images in all our commercials. Aerial images of New Orleans under water, floating dead animals, homes leveled, gusting wind, crowds ransacking the stores . . . and then finish with a shot of the entire family on Zerevrea while picnicking in a sunny field, lush green grass, soothing music in the background.

The phone rang, startling the CEO. Falcone walked to the telephone and picked up the receiver.

"Sal?" the voice asked.

"What is it, Melanie?" Falcone answered, recognizing the voice on the other end. "Is everything all right?"

Melanie Hughes was general counsel for BostonMagnifica and Falcone's sounding board. The forty-five-year-old redhead had been at the helm of the legal department for ten years now. "Our registered agent in Dallas, C.T. Systems, just got served with a lawsuit."

"What? BM has never been sued before. Are you sure?" The news knocked the wind out of the CEO. He had to find a chair and sit down.

"Some widow is suing us down in Laredo, Texas. Sounds like her lawyer filed the case back in August but just now served it on us. Our registered agent says it's a wrongful death suit."

"Damn it! I hope it has nothing to do with Zerevrea."

"You think?" asked Hughes, "this soon?"

"Well, marketing has been giving away free samples for a year now . . . saturating doctors' offices and priming the markets, getting ready for the official debut."

"That's true," admitted Hughes, "well, let's not jump the gun. It might not be Zerevrea. It could be something else."

Falcone swallowed hard. "Has it been in the news?"

"No, I don't think the wire has picked it up."

"Well, that's something to be thankful for," growled Falcone. "Let's think about putting a damage-control team in place, just in case it is Zerevrea."

"Okay."

"We'll also need to hire outside counsel to defend this thing. Who do we know in Texas?"

"I'll have to make some calls."

"Let's get on it," commanded Falcone. "We can't afford a smear campaign—not now when the White House is about to endorse us. We need to keep it out of the headlines, got it?"

"Yes," she answered.

"Let's hope we don't end up with a Vioxx nightmare on our hands. Imagine what a flurry of lawsuits would do to BM . . . to our stock."

"It could very well spell the end."

"I don't even want to think about it. We don't have the cash reserves or the insurance coverage to take a hit like Merck."

"Word on the street is that Merck might throw in the towel and pony up five billion to settle all Vioxx lawsuits," added Hughes.

"Damned trial lawyers! Can't have them smelling blood, or it'll start a feeding frenzy."

"Let me call around," said Hughes, "and see about getting us counsel down in Texas."

"All right. Keep me in the loop."

CHAPTER 4

ILLY BRAVO'S SECRETARY announced the early call that Monday morning. It was Mr. Bates, the firm's founding partner, calling from his spread in West Texas. After a weekend of big-game hunting and entertaining clients, Bates was now calling to speak to Billy. It was urgent.

"Billy, what took you so long to pick up the phone, son?"

"I apologize, Mr. Bates. I was on my way to the courthouse. With so many cases set for trial, I got Charlie Jensen covering Cameron County and Brandon Fauntleroy handling the announcements in Starr County. I'm handling the cases here in Hidalgo County."

Bates rarely called on Mondays and never this early. The founding partner had been in the law business long enough to know that his South Texas litigation army was already heading out to the battlefield. Billy knew that if Bates was calling this early, he had good reason to do so.

"Which case are you trying this week?" asked Bates.

"Dr. Myers," said Billy, sounding a bit overwhelmed. "The dentist accused of fondling a patient under anesthesia. It's finally going to trial. We're now number one on the docket . . . judge issued a preferential setting."

With one hand, Billy was signaling Nancy out in the hallway to have Hector, the firm's investigator, load up his car with the boxes of exhibits, projectors, laptop computers, the Elmo and all the file boxes for all of his cases.

"Oh," griped Bates, "too bad we can't delay the trial some more. We could have had one of my partners file a legislative continuance . . . tire the plaintiff out, make her wait four, five years and force her to take pennies on the dollar."

"That may have worked," agreed Billy. "Too bad the legislature is no longer in session. By the way, what are we charging for such continuances?"

"Fifty thousand a pop," said Bates with a chuckle. "We're one of the few firms that can provide that service. The trial lawyers want the law changed, but my partners in the legislature have always quashed the revolt. Hell, we've delayed cases for six, seven years. We've had plaintiffs die while waiting to get into the courtroom. It's a beautiful thing. Listen, Billy," said Bates, changing the topic, "we just got hired to defend BostonMagnifica Pharmaceuticals down in Laredo. Their general counsel tracked me down over the weekend and filled me in on the case."

"The large drug company?"

"Well, it's not a Fortune One Hundred—not like Eli Lilly, Merck or GlaxoSmithKline—but still a Fortune Five Hundred. They're mostly self-insured. Think you can handle it, son?"

"Of course, Mr. Bates."

"Good. We need to take really good care of these folks. If we do a good job, the relationship could mean a lot of work down the road . . . possibly ten million in fees per year, maybe more."

"That much?"

"Sure. A victory could also mean our government affairs section gets hired to lobby for them at the national level and in other states. Landing a client like that could very well guarantee our survival for many more years to come. I don't have to tell you, but you know what tort reform has done to our caseload. The best news of all, however, is that a win would mean a promotion for you, Billy."

"Wow, Mr. Bates. I'm ready . . . I've been waiting a long time to make name partner," Billy replied.

"I know," Bates added. "Listen, Hughes said that it's imperative we get them a defense verdict, okay? Send a clear message to those thinking of suing."

"Got it."

"Very well. They're FedExing the lawsuit to you directly. I want weekly reports on this. Keep me in the loop, got it?"

"Yes, sir."

"Oh . . . before I forget," said Bates, "their in-house counsel made it very clear . . . BM wants to avoid ending up like Vioxx . . . all over the news."

"I'll take care of it and make the 'test case' go away."

"Good. Anyway, do a good job . . . and we can talk promotion afterwards, *comprende,* name partner?"

"Yes, sir."

At counsel's table, Billy punched in the phrase, "Riley Spearman Texas Attorney" on his Blackberry's Internet. Within seconds, the search engine pulled several links to Riley Spearman, the attorney suing BostonMagnifica. One of the links was to a publication called MegaLawyers.com. Spearman's profile read: "The Spearman Law Group, Unparalleled Commitment. Years before forming his law group, attorney Riley Spearman realized there was a need for attorneys who were capable of investing significant time and financial resources in cases that, on the average, take three to five years to resolve. This need became more evident as tort reform efforts in Texas forced litigants out of the court system. Since the number of new filings dropped to record levels, Riley Spearman realized defense firms had started seriously milking their shrinking case loads as well. This new phenomenon pushed the average lifespan of a file from two to four years—and, in many cases, five years.

"In response to these delay tactics, Spearman started a firm that could go the distance. Riley Spearman is uniquely qualified to head such a law firm. He is board-certified as a personal injury trial law specialist. He has also served as lead counsel in Phen Phen lawsuits against Wyeth, has obtained victories for Vioxx victims against Merck, including million-dollar verdicts for Trasylol victims against Bayer. Riley Spearman believes the next big wave in pharmaceutical litigation will concern psychotropic drugs such as Xykretza and Zerevrea. If you feel you have a case, please visit Mr. Spearman's Web site, www.kickassverdicts.com."

Billy had to hand it to Spearman. Even though he was not impressed, Billy knew that it was lawyers like Spearman that kept corporate America in check and defense firms like Billy's gainfully employed. Sure, the critics kicked and hollered that the trial lawyers were abusing and bankrupting the system. But, at the end of the day, it was lawyers like Spearman that uncovered the illegal dumping, the sneaky price-fixing, the defective tires, the bad drugs, the unsafe medical devices and even the fire-prone cruise control modules in certain pickup trucks.

Despite a trial lawyer's intended purpose in society, Billy had, with great pleasure, to say the least, poured out many attorneys like Spearman before. Even some with flashier ads, bigger bankrolls and longer lists of favorable verdicts and settlements. Having been a Valley lawyer for many years, he'd never met anyone who could connect better than him with Hispanic juries and judges. Being local did make a difference, and that was his ace in the hole. Plus, he had no problems relating to and communicating with the average Juan. Of course, it didn't hurt that he still looked like he came right out of the pages of *GQ* magazine and could think on his feet with blazing speed.

CHAPTER 6

JAMES "JIM" BATES was a large Texan. Over six feet tall and tipping the scales at three hundred pounds, he was known behind his back as "Papa Bear." Not necessarily because of his ferocity, cruelty or hot temper, but because of his large appetite for food and knowledge. Those who knew him personally could attest to his extraordinary ability to remember old court rulings, historic dates and even U.S. Supreme Court decisions going as far back as fifty years. He was sitting at his desk reading *Verdicts, Arbitration Awards & Settlements* when Connie called.

"Mr. Bates? The CEO of BostonMagnifica Pharmaceuticals is here and says that he wants to see you. He says it's urgent. He came in unannounced. Can you see him?" asked Connie over the intercom, sounding nervous. She'd been Bates's secretary for thirty years. At sixty years of age, she was as much of a dynamo as the first day she started working for Bates back in Austin in the mid-seventies.

"Of course, sweetheart . . . I can see him. Bring him in."

The senior partner was surprised to have Falcone, the CEO himself, appear out of nowhere. After all, not forty-eight hours earlier, he'd been on the phone with Melanie Hughes, the company's in-house counsel. For Falcone to show up in Houston like this, without an appointment, clearly meant that the drug maker was worried about the trouble brewing in South Texas.

Salvatore Falcone was brought in and invited to sit at Bates's desk. He sported a neatly trimmed gray goatee and wore a tailored wool suit with silk hankie, crisp royal blue shirt, paisley tie and impeccable Ferragamo shoes.

31

"Coffee?" offered Bates, looking over at Connie who was waiting by the large glass doors.

"No, thanks. This won't take long. I just need a few minutes of your time." Connie subsequently dismissed herself quietly from the room.

"Mr. Falcone," started Bates, "you didn't have to travel to Houston. We could have talked on the phone."

"I wanted to meet the lawyers who are going to handle this lawsuit," explained Falcone, "to make it abundantly clear that our company's future hinges on the outcome of this litigation. If I have to fly to Texas to drive that message home, then so be it."

"BostonMagnifica has nothing to worry about. You're in good hands—the best," replied Bates.

"As CEO and majority shareholder of BostonMagnifica, I have to make sure that this case is handled quietly and discreetly. Zerevrea is projected to become our largest revenue-generating drug for the next decade."

"I see."

"The patents on all five of our other moneymakers will expire next year. Every lab from here to Mexico to Bangladesh will be able to produce generic versions."

"Millions in lost revenue," interjected Bates.

Falcone went on without missing a beat. "We're counting on Zerevrea to take us into the future. It's poised to become our cash cow."

"We can help," Bates said reassuringly.

"Good. I was told you're the go-to guys in Texas."

"We'll get it done," Bates replied, "and save your company any embarrassing or damning exposure in the process."

"Just so you know, next week the White House will publicly endorse Zerevrea as the official drug for the mental healthcare initiative aimed at the Gulf States."

"Aah," Bates suddenly understood.

"You see my dilemma? I can't afford to embarrass the White House . . . or for reporters to discover that Zerevrea has been aggressively promoted—that our sales reps have been distributing free samples to doctors for the past twelve months recommending they prescribe it for depression and anxiety as well as other ailments."

"You mean being peddled for off-label use?"

"It's a very competitive business," Falcone snapped back somewhat defensively. "We need to come up with a variety of ways to sell drugs."

"Billy Bravo in the McAllen office has been assigned to handle your case. He'll need to see all the data from the clinical trials," Bates explained, switching topics. "I'm sure he'll want to get intimately familiar with the drug so he can properly defend your company."

"Who is he?"

"Our star defense lawyer down in the Valley office. He will be the first chair handling your case. He hasn't lost a single jury trial in years. I've stopped counting."

"Okay, then," Falcone said. "He will be provided whatever there is on the drug, including testing, research, clinical trials, peer reviews. He'll get everything."

"Good. Listen, I want you to stop worrying. We're dedicated to meeting and exceeding clients' expectations. You want discretion? Well, discretion is our name. You want a win? Billy will find a way to deliver."

"That's why we've come to you," Falcone replied.

AFTER FALCONE made his exit, Bates looked out his window sixty stories high over Houston's Allen Parkway and relived the brief meeting. He started crunching numbers in his head. The BM file could easily fetch his firm three hundred thousand in legal fees and that was even without factoring in one or two appeals. The appeals could easily push the tab close to half a million. Not bad work, if you could get it.

Far away in the distance, the founding partner noticed crowds of young Houston professionals already gathering at the Party on the Plaza. He could see the main stage where the featured band-of-the-week had been setting up, and the roadies were doing the final mike check. The outdoor event signaled the beginning of the fall concert series and the holiday season. To Bates, a satisfied blue-chip client like BostonMagnifica meant an abundant holiday season for the entire firm for many years to come. Billy Bravo, his gunslinger from South Texas, just needed to hit the bull's-eye.

"Connie," shouted Bates into the intercom, "would you track down Billy for me? Last I'd heard he was picking a jury down at the Hidalgo County courthouse. See if he'll answer on his cell."

"Yes, sir. Let me get him on the line." There was a brief pause, and Connie came back on the line. "Mr. Bravo is on the line, sir. He's holding on two."

"Billy," Bates barked into the speakerphone.

"Yes, boss. What can I do for you?"

"Salvatore Falcone, the CEO of BostonMagnifica, just left my office. Did his file come in?"

"Yes, it came in this morning. I've seen it. I told Nancy to start preparing an answer while I do jury selection in the Myers case."

"I see. Listen . . . this guy Falcone . . . he's OCD. He flew in all the way to Houston just to tell me in person how goddamn important this lawsuit is to him and his company. Unannounced. You follow?"

"Well," countered Billy, "he's got to be worried about the other two potential lawsuits."

"What do you mean?"

"Hector just sent me a text message to tell me that Tomas Ray also killed two others before he pulled the trigger."

"Really?"

"Yep. A mailman making the rounds and a young girl—a federal probation officer, no less."

"Two federal employees, eh?" noticed Bates.

"Yes."

"Um," mumbled Bates, "I wonder if the guy knew he was nailing two federal employees?"

"A strange coincidence, don't you think?"

"Just thinking out loud," Bates whispered. "Was it really the drug, or were there other reasons? What was the real motive?"

CHAPTER 5

ILLY BRAVO YANKED his navy-blue blazer from the coatrack in the corner of his small cramped office and started to furiously multitask, picking up his keys, cell phone, reading glasses and a few other items. He was ready to bolt to the courthouse when Nancy walked in holding a package in her hands.

"Boss, everything is loaded up in your Honda. You're set to go. And here . . . this just came in." Nancy handed him a FedEx package.

"Just like Bates said," Billy volunteered as he hurried around the office, trying to decide which tie to wear. In one hand he was holding a red power tie with blue and green stripes and, in the other, a golden paisley tie with French blue accents.

"What do you want me to do with it?" asked Nancy, leaning against the entryway.

"Open it and read the contents to me." He went for the power tie and, in a flash, had it in a Windsor knot, fitting just right around his crisp shirt collar.

Nancy tore the packet open, pulled the stack of pages out, and started speed-reading. "Georgina Ray, Individually, and as Next Friend of Erika Nicole Ray, Tomas Ray, Jr., Claudia Michelle Ray and Cynthia Anne Ray, minor children, and as Personal Representative of the Estate of Tomas Ray, deceased v. BostonMagnifica Pharmaceuticals Corp.

"Plaintiffs believe BostonMagnifica is responsible for the death of Tomas Ray, which occurred on January 28, 2005, in Laredo, Webb County, Texas. At the time of his death, Mr. Ray was under the influence of Zerevrea, a powerful, serotonergic, psychotropic drug manufactured and marketed by BostonMagnifica Pharmaceuticals.

"Mrs. Ray is the widow of Tomas Ray. The couple resided in Laredo, Texas, and she and her children are statutory beneficiaries of the cause of action created by the Texas Wrongful Death Act. They are appropriate parties to allege claims on behalf of Tomas Ray's Estate under the Texas Survival Statute.

"The defendant, BostonMagnifica, is an American-owned, publicly traded drug company with headquarters in New York. It manufactures, markets and distributes a medication called Zerevrea.

"Jurisdiction is based on diversity of citizenship, pursuant to 28 US C. 1332. The monies in controversy substantially exceed Seventy-Five Thousand Dollars ($75,000.00), exclusive of interest and costs. The underlying acts giving rise to this lawsuit happened within the Southern District of Texas. Therefore, venue is permissible in Laredo, Webb County, Texas.

"It was necessary to file this suit as a result of the following facts: Zerevrea is a mind-altering drug designed to alter a person's serotonin. For years, the drug makers have known that serotonin levels are directly related to aggression and violence, whether directed at oneself or others. Thus, selective serotonin reuptake inhibitors (SSRIs) such as Zerevrea have been banned in other countries.

"Zerevrea undoubtedly helps the majority of patients that take it under the appropriate care and close supervision of a doctor. Unfortunately, there is a small cluster of patients who are at an increased risk of violence and suicide as a result of taking serotonin-boosting drugs.

"The industry, including BostonMagnifica, has known about this vulnerable cluster for years. The drug makers have failed to conduct any tests to determine the frequency of this phenomenon or to develop systems to identify and protect patients who are in this risk group. The industry has also failed to warn prescribing physicians, pharmacists and patients about these risks.

"Tomas Ray was born on December 11, 1963, in Laredo, Texas. He married Georgina 'Gina' Yturria, his high school sweetheart. Before his death on January 28, 2005, they had been married for sixteen years. During that time, he never raised a hand in anger to his wife, whom he considered to be his best friend. They had four beautiful children.

"Over the years, Mr. Ray never suffered from depression or other serious psychological ailments. Once in his lifetime, he experienced mild anxiety after seeing combat in the Persian Gulf war. All who knew him considered him to be a loving and peaceful man who loved his family. A week or so before Mr. Ray took his life, he'd complained to Gina of experiencing mild anxiety again. His physician gave him a handful of free samples of Zerevrea. Two days later, on the morning of January 28, 2005, Mr. Ray shot himself in the back of the mouth with a .357 Magnum handgun. Those who knew him believe he had to be out of his mind to commit such an act; that in his right mind he could never have done this.

"BostonMagnifica is liable under two theories of liability recognized under Texas law. FIRST: Defendant is strictly liable under the Restatement Second of Torts 402A and 402B and the new Restatement Third for marketing defects and misrepresentations. SECOND: Defendant's conduct is unreasonable or negligent and was the proximate cause of Tomas Ray's death. The negligence includes the failure to warn, failure to test, failure to implement appropriate patient-screening mechanisms and the overpromotion to the prescribing physician claiming that Zerevrea is the millennium's new 'miracle' drug. All in an effort to get doctors to give away free samples or start marketing the drug.

"Plaintiff herein sues for twenty-five million dollars in actual damages and seventy-five million dollars in punitive damages.

"Plaintiff hereby invokes her right to a jury trial.

"Respectfully submitted, Riley Spearman."

"There you go," Nancy declared, "a garden variety wrongful death lawsuit. Should I start on the answer?"

"Yes, please, get it ready," Billy replied as he rushed out the door, loaded with the trial notebooks and his briefcase. "Mark the file VIP, but don't file the answer yet, not until I've reviewed it."

"You want our investigator to jump on it?"

"Yes, have Hector do research on the plaintiff's lawyer. And on the deceased . . . I want to know everything."

"Got it," replied Nancy as she darted out of Billy's office. Two seconds later, she was back. "Hey!" she said as she poked her head in the door. "Isn't this guy, Tomas Ray, part of the Reyes family that owns the Ray's Appliance store chain?"

"I don't know. I've seen the stores, but I've never heard of him."

"Man, the name sure rings a bell," followed Nancy. "I heard somewhere that it was great-grandpa Reyes that started the chain . . . he later shortened the name to 'Rays' to make it more appealing to the gringos."

"Well," replied Billy, while waving her away, "see what else Hector can find on the Rays or Reyes . . . whatever their last name is. And ask him to get his hands on the police file. Since there was a suicide, Laredo PD probably looked into it."

As always, Billy Bravo would have to rely on Hector Ayala, his loyal, tenacious and resourceful investigator.

BILLY SAT in Judge Moses Ramón's empty courtroom that morning mulling over the allegations in the BM suit. *We need to keep a lid on this one. Who'd want another hot potato like Vioxx?* Judge Ramón, himself a former insurance defense attorney forced to close shop due to all the tort reform, had recently been elected to the 555th Judicial District Court of Hidalgo County. The sixty-year-old judge had not yet taken the bench that morning as he met in chambers with the lawyers from another case. Inside the courtroom, the court reporter and bailiff were off to the side discussing the few cases set for trial on the docket that morning, wondering if Hoffman, the attorney from Austin, would show up to lock horns with Mr. Bravo.

At counsel's table, Billy punched in the phrase, "Riley Spearman Texas Attorney" on his Blackberry's Internet. Within seconds, the search engine pulled several links to Riley Spearman, the attorney suing BostonMagnifica. One of the links was to a publication called MegaLawyers.com. Spearman's profile read: "The Spearman Law Group, Unparalleled Commitment. Years before forming his law group, attorney Riley Spearman realized there was a need for attorneys who were capable of investing significant time and financial resources in cases that, on the average, take three to five years to resolve. This need became more evident as tort reform efforts in Texas forced litigants out of the court system. Since the number of new filings dropped to record levels, Riley Spearman realized defense firms had started seriously milking their shrinking case loads as well. This new phenomenon pushed the average lifespan of a file from two to four years—and, in many cases, five years.

"In response to these delay tactics, Spearman started a firm that could go the distance. Riley Spearman is uniquely qualified to head such a law firm. He is board-certified as a personal injury trial law specialist. He has also served as lead counsel in Phen Phen lawsuits against Wyeth, has obtained victories for Vioxx victims against Merck, including million-dollar verdicts for Trasylol victims against Bayer. Riley Spearman believes the next big wave in pharmaceutical litigation will concern psychotropic drugs such as Xykretza and Zerevrea. If you feel you have a case, please visit Mr. Spearman's Web site, www.kickassverdicts.com."

Billy had to hand it to Spearman. Even though he was not impressed, Billy knew that it was lawyers like Spearman that kept corporate America in check and defense firms like Billy's gainfully employed. Sure, the critics kicked and hollered that the trial lawyers were abusing and bankrupting the system. But, at the end of the day, it was lawyers like Spearman that uncovered the illegal dumping, the sneaky price-fixing, the defective tires, the bad drugs, the unsafe medical devices and even the fire-prone cruise control modules in certain pickup trucks.

Despite a trial lawyer's intended purpose in society, Billy had, with great pleasure, to say the least, poured out many attorneys

like Spearman before. Even some with flashier ads, bigger
bankrolls and longer lists of favorable verdicts and settlements.
Having been a Valley lawyer for many years, he'd never met anyone who could connect better than him with Hispanic juries and
judges. Being local did make a difference, and that was his ace in
the hole. Plus, he had no problems relating to and communicating
with the average Juan. Of course, it didn't hurt that he still looked
like he came right out of the pages of *GQ* magazine and could
think on his feet with blazing speed.

CHAPTER 6

J AMES "JIM" BATES was a large Texan. Over six feet tall and tipping the scales at three hundred pounds, he was known behind his back as "Papa Bear." Not necessarily because of his ferocity, cruelty or hot temper, but because of his large appetite for food and knowledge. Those who knew him personally could attest to his extraordinary ability to remember old court rulings, historic dates and even U.S. Supreme Court decisions going as far back as fifty years. He was sitting at his desk reading *Verdicts, Arbitration Awards & Settlements* when Connie called.

"Mr. Bates? The CEO of BostonMagnifica Pharmaceuticals is here and says that he wants to see you. He says it's urgent. He came in unannounced. Can you see him?" asked Connie over the intercom, sounding nervous. She'd been Bates's secretary for thirty years. At sixty years of age, she was as much of a dynamo as the first day she started working for Bates back in Austin in the mid-seventies.

"Of course, sweetheart . . . I can see him. Bring him in."

The senior partner was surprised to have Falcone, the CEO himself, appear out of nowhere. After all, not forty-eight hours earlier, he'd been on the phone with Melanie Hughes, the company's in-house counsel. For Falcone to show up in Houston like this, without an appointment, clearly meant that the drug maker was worried about the trouble brewing in South Texas.

Salvatore Falcone was brought in and invited to sit at Bates's desk. He sported a neatly trimmed gray goatee and wore a tailored wool suit with silk hankie, crisp royal blue shirt, paisley tie and impeccable Ferragamo shoes.

"Coffee?" offered Bates, looking over at Connie who was waiting by the large glass doors.

"No, thanks. This won't take long. I just need a few minutes of your time." Connie subsequently dismissed herself quietly from the room.

"Mr. Falcone," started Bates, "you didn't have to travel to Houston. We could have talked on the phone."

"I wanted to meet the lawyers who are going to handle this lawsuit," explained Falcone, "to make it abundantly clear that our company's future hinges on the outcome of this litigation. If I have to fly to Texas to drive that message home, then so be it."

"BostonMagnifica has nothing to worry about. You're in good hands—the best," replied Bates.

"As CEO and majority shareholder of BostonMagnifica, I have to make sure that this case is handled quietly and discreetly. Zerevrea is projected to become our largest revenue-generating drug for the next decade."

"I see."

"The patents on all five of our other moneymakers will expire next year. Every lab from here to Mexico to Bangladesh will be able to produce generic versions."

"Millions in lost revenue," interjected Bates.

Falcone went on without missing a beat. "We're counting on Zerevrea to take us into the future. It's poised to become our cash cow."

"We can help," Bates said reassuringly.

"Good. I was told you're the go-to guys in Texas."

"We'll get it done," Bates replied, "and save your company any embarrassing or damning exposure in the process."

"Just so you know, next week the White House will publicly endorse Zerevrea as the official drug for the mental healthcare initiative aimed at the Gulf States."

"Aah," Bates suddenly understood.

"You see my dilemma? I can't afford to embarrass the White House . . . or for reporters to discover that Zerevrea has been aggressively promoted—that our sales reps have been distributing free samples to doctors for the past twelve months recommending they prescribe it for depression and anxiety as well as other ailments."

"You mean being peddled for off-label use?"

"It's a very competitive business," Falcone snapped back somewhat defensively. "We need to come up with a variety of ways to sell drugs."

"Billy Bravo in the McAllen office has been assigned to handle your case. He'll need to see all the data from the clinical trials," Bates explained, switching topics. "I'm sure he'll want to get intimately familiar with the drug so he can properly defend your company."

"Who is he?"

"Our star defense lawyer down in the Valley office. He will be the first chair handling your case. He hasn't lost a single jury trial in years. I've stopped counting."

"Okay, then," Falcone said. "He will be provided whatever there is on the drug, including testing, research, clinical trials, peer reviews. He'll get everything."

"Good. Listen, I want you to stop worrying. We're dedicated to meeting and exceeding clients' expectations. You want discretion? Well, discretion is our name. You want a win? Billy will find a way to deliver."

"That's why we've come to you," Falcone replied.

AFTER FALCONE made his exit, Bates looked out his window sixty stories high over Houston's Allen Parkway and relived the brief meeting. He started crunching numbers in his head. The BM file could easily fetch his firm three hundred thousand in legal fees and that was even without factoring in one or two appeals. The appeals could easily push the tab close to half a million. Not bad work, if you could get it.

Far away in the distance, the founding partner noticed crowds of young Houston professionals already gathering at the Party on the Plaza. He could see the main stage where the featured band-of-the-week had been setting up, and the roadies were doing the final mike check. The outdoor event signaled the beginning of the fall concert series and the holiday season. To Bates, a satisfied blue-chip client like BostonMagnifica meant an abundant holiday season for the entire firm for many years to come. Billy Bravo, his gunslinger from South Texas, just needed to hit the bull's-eye.

"Connie," shouted Bates into the intercom, "would you track down Billy for me? Last I'd heard he was picking a jury down at the Hidalgo County courthouse. See if he'll answer on his cell."

"Yes, sir. Let me get him on the line." There was a brief pause, and Connie came back on the line. "Mr. Bravo is on the line, sir. He's holding on two."

"Billy," Bates barked into the speakerphone.

"Yes, boss. What can I do for you?"

"Salvatore Falcone, the CEO of BostonMagnifica, just left my office. Did his file come in?"

"Yes, it came in this morning. I've seen it. I told Nancy to start preparing an answer while I do jury selection in the Myers case."

"I see. Listen . . . this guy Falcone . . . he's OCD. He flew in all the way to Houston just to tell me in person how goddamn important this lawsuit is to him and his company. Unannounced. You follow?"

"Well," countered Billy, "he's got to be worried about the other two potential lawsuits."

"What do you mean?"

"Hector just sent me a text message to tell me that Tomas Ray also killed two others before he pulled the trigger."

"Really?"

"Yep. A mailman making the rounds and a young girl—a federal probation officer, no less."

"Two federal employees, eh?" noticed Bates.

"Yes."

"Um," mumbled Bates, "I wonder if the guy knew he was nailing two federal employees?"

"A strange coincidence, don't you think?"

"Just thinking out loud," Bates whispered. "Was it really the drug, or were there other reasons? What was the real motive?"

"It's worth exploring," agreed Billy. "Certainly, we'll want to present another plausible theory to the jury to explain Ray's actions if need be. Give them a different nail to hang their hat on."

"I don't mean to tell you how to try your case," Bates replied, "but if we could show he was already suffering from depression or maybe his marriage was in shambles . . . "

"Or he was having financial problems," interjected Billy, "and recently had purchased more life insurance . . . "

"Or he'd recently discovered his wife's affair . . . something like that."

"Then we could explain why the guy went off the deep end. I'll have Hector work on an angle to dig up another explanation to give to the jury."

"There you go. Anyway, I know you're busy. We'll visit later. Take good care of this client, you hear?"

"Yes, sir. Got it."

CHAPTER 7

I T WAS THREE o'clock, and Billy was back in his office after having been down at the courthouse all morning selecting the jury for the Myers trial. He was about to run out the door and drive across town to take the deposition of an expert in another case when his Blackberry started vibrating. He answered reluctantly.

"Billy, I know I just spoke with you less than an hour ago about BM, but we need to visit again," said Bates.

"Don't worry, boss. We don't start our trial until Wednesday morning. Judge Ramón is having a root canal done on Tuesday, and there's nothing going on tomorrow. We only selected the jury this morning."

"Good. Listen, son. I got Mr. Falcone on a three-way call. He's calling from the company jet as he heads back to the east coast. He wanted to hear from you . . . the attorney who's gonna see that his company gets taken care of, understand?"

"Yes, Mr. Bates. I understand," Billy replied.

"Mr. Bravo," shouted Falcone, "can you hear me?"

Billy rolled his eyes. "Yes, sir. Nice talking to you. Please call me Billy."

"Listen, Billy, let's skip the pleasantries. We're now in an attorney-client relationship, so whatever I tell you shouldn't shock you. Besides, we're all big boys here, am I right?"

"Yes," Bates called out from the other end.

"Yes," Billy followed.

"I need confirmation that you're the man for the job, Billy," Falcone announced. "I need a trial attorney who will stop at *nothing* to win this case. Bates assures me that man is *you*—that you will leave no stone unturned, that you will get us a defense verdict. Is this true?"

"I've told Mr. Falcone of your win record, Billy. Haven't lost a jury trial in the last ten years."

"Thank you, eh, Mr. Bates," Billy said nervously while trying to be modest. "I guess we've had luck picking some good juries."

"I've risked life and limb to build this company," continued Falcone, "once our new drug Zerevrea catches fire, it will make the shareholders a ton of money and catapult BM to the top of the charts. You follow, Billy?"

"Got it, sir."

"And once it becomes well-received with the mental health professionals," added Falcone, "we'll find new ways to market it to autistic kids, emotionally-disturbed children and even those with ADHD. That's how pharmaceuticals survive . . . by finding other uses, targeting other consumer groups. Right now, as we speak, we're going to give away millions of samples to all the hurricane victims of Rita and Katrina."

"Billy, you know how it goes . . . ," interjected Bates, "it's no different than aspirin. At first, it was only prescribed to alleviate pain, and now folks take one every day to reduce the risk of heart disease."

"I know what off-label use is," said Billy, "and I also know that the feds frown upon it."

"Billy," Falcone said as he cleared his throat again, "the FDA doesn't scare me. The Prescription Drug Marketing Act doesn't scare me either and the feds have never scared me. What scares me, really, is you losing this trial and then having ten thousand lawsuits filed against BM and getting stuck with a five-billion-dollar cleanup tab . . . money we don't have. Did you read how much Merck is paying to settle the Vioxx lawsuits?"

"Yes, sir."

"Mr. Bravo, our reserves are needed for research in order to come up with new drugs, not to line some shyster lawyer's pockets. Plus, we're mostly self-insured; we don't carry excess insurance coverage. That way, we can catch up to the big boys. Every last penny goes into developing breakthrough drugs. That's where we sink our money."

"Tens of thousands of hurricane victims are having mental issues," exclaimed Bates. "Mr. Falcone's company has volunteered to pitch in, do its part, like a good corporate citizen."

"We're doing our part, Billy," Falcone said. "Can you do yours?"

"Yes . . . sir," hesitated Billy, "you can count on me."

"The hurricane victims, the sick, our shareholders, Wall Street and the thousands of employees whose jobs depend on the outcome of this lawsuit are all counting on you," added Falcone.

"I'll handle it, Mr. Falcone, don't worry," said Billy, suddenly remembering the many grueling childhood trips to Idaho where he had busted his ass picking potatoes. Discussing the Ray litigation in those terms, Billy could suddenly feel the weight of an eighty-pound sack of potatoes on his shoulders.

"We're all counting on you, Billy," said the CEO. "Don't let us down."

AFTER HANGING UP, Billy quickly got on his computer. The discussion with Bates and Falcone regarding the hurricane victims had reminded him that the National Weather Service was now tracking Hurricane Emily, a new hurricane system still stationary north of Venezuela. The weather service projected Emily making landfall near Tampico, Mexico, south of the border, in fourteen days. Billy wrote himself a reminder to check back on Emily. As a Gulf Coast resident, he knew better than to trust the weather advisories. Once Emily got into the Gulf of Mexico, its northbound currents could easily send the hurricane toward Texas, and Billy would have to go and board up the beach house.

CHAPTER 8

ILLY'S BLACKBERRY WENT off, and he purposefully didn't answer it. He hit the "ignore" button without looking to see who was calling. He was in the middle of depositions in a large conference room crammed with other lawyers, paralegals and their assistants. He was going through his direct examination of the plaintiff's retained expert, a thirty-five-year-old hot shot from Florida. The young doctor was considered the world's leading authority on pediatric infectious diseases. The expert had been hired by the plaintiffs in a case involving a small child, now seriously brain-damaged after the infant was misdiagnosed as having trichinosis lesions in the brain.

A few minutes later, without fail, his Blackberry vibrated again, and a text message popped up on the screen. Billy started reading the message as the expert went on and on and on about his education, work experience, medical research, published works and other credentials.

It was Nancy, his secretary. She only text-messaged when it was urgent, and this was a real emergency. Bates wanted Billy to fly out of McAllen that same evening and tour BostonMagnifica's facilities. The development team that had worked on Zerevrea was waiting for him.

Nancy also explained that she had made arrangements to have all his other hearings covered by Fauntleroy and that Mr. Bates wanted him to cut short whatever he was doing and take the first available plane to Boston. There was a flight leaving McAllen at seven with connections in Houston, getting into Boston at one AM. From there, a driver would take them to Worcester the next morning. If he blazed through the deposition, he could still make it. Reservations had been made, the tickets were at the counter and Charlie Jensen would tag along. Charlie would meet him at the airport. Mr. Falcone had offered to fly the pair back to Texas on Tuesday evening on the company jet since he'd heard that Billy had to resume trial on Wednesday.

I can't believe this. Yami's gonna hit the roof when I call to cancel dinner with her and the kids again.

BILLY BRAVO and Charlie Jensen were met at Boston's Logan Airport by Dr. Pierce Drummond, the head of the research and development department.

"How was your flight?" asked Dr. Drummond as he beckoned the limo driver waiting down at the other end of the terminal. The trio was standing at the curb. "I hope you brought some warm clothes. We got our first snow last night."

"This is all I've got," Billy said, sounding ticked off. "I was in the middle of depos when I received the call to drop everything and get up here." He was shivering, uncontrollably. Jensen was rubbing his hands, trying to get the circulation going. Like Billy, he was only wearing a navy-blue blazer and cotton Dockers.

The limo was approaching the curve when Billy noticed Drummond removing something from his coat pocket. "Here," he said with a big proud smile as he shoved a newspaper article into Billy's hand. "The FDA just approved one of our new drugs, Fledkort. Three years of trials and experimental use and finally it's been proven highly effective in the fight against leukemia."

I couldn't care less, he thought as he gave a fake smile to Drummond. "That's exciting," lied Billy. "Did you work on it personally?"

"Yes. I helped develop it. Without it, patients with acute promyelocytic leukemia would certainly die. That's why you, Mr. Bravo, need to nip this lawsuit in the bud. BostonMagnifica can't afford to go under because of greedy plaintiffs' lawyers."

"BM is gonna come out okay," stated Billy. "You'll see, we're just getting started."

"I hope so. We're counting on you," said Drummond. "Here's our ride." The tall doctor was pointing at a black limo. "It'll be a short drive to your hotel. This same limo will pick you up in the morning and take you to our research and production facility in Worcester. Get in."

"Thanks for picking us up," offered Jensen.

"Don't mention it."

"How long have you been the head of R&D?" asked Billy, trying to downplay the enormous amount of guilt he was now beginning to feel. He'd just remembered that Wicho, his son, was supposed to be having an after-school birthday party with his friends at the local Cinemark. Yami had booked one of the theaters for a private screening of *Batman Begins*. He'd promised he'd be there.

"A fellow by the name of Felix Croutoux and I started at the same time after the company was founded, about twenty years ago. I decided to stay and continue working. Felix, on the other hand, took early retirement last year. We were the original members of the R&D department. Now, the department has hundreds of employees."

"Who are we meeting with in the morning?" Billy asked.

"Myself and several members of the team that created Zerevrea. Then, we'll take a tour of our facilities."

"Well, thanks again for picking us up," Billy replied, feeling the warmth inside the car that heightened his mood a little.

PIERCE DRUMMOND was seated at the head of the large conference table. To his right sat Doctors Sudarshan and Neal. Billy and Charlie sat right across from the two doctors, yellow pads and pens in hand. The group had just finished viewing BostonMagnifica's PowerPoint presentation detailing the testing and protocols involved in the development of Zerevrea.

"How is Zerevrea prescribed?" Billy asked, getting right down to business. He took a sip from his cold morning coffee and waited for an answer.

"In pills and liquid form," answered Drummond. "It is effective in the fight against anxiety disorders."

"Any adverse side effects?"

"Patients need to be careful not to mix this inhibitor with any other SSRIs. The combination may cause serotonin syndrome, which consists of agitation or hyperactivity, racing thoughts, restlessness or insomnia."

"Akathisia?" Billy asked.

"Yes," Drummond replied. "It's been described as wanting to jump out of your skin."

The other two doctors were nodding their heads in agreement but did not volunteer any additional information. Drummond was obviously in control.

"Any other warnings?"

"Zerevrea can trigger psychotic disorders and is not recommended for patients who suffer from epilepsy."

"Can it be mixed with other drugs?"

"Not with other SSRIs, St. John's Wort or Tryptophan."

"Any fatal reactions?" Billy asked.

The doctors looked at each other in silence. Drummond quickly answered. "Other SSRIs have been known to cause mental status changes, but not Zerevrea. Zerevrea has been proven to be safe when taken as prescribed."

"What do you mean by 'mental status changes'?" Billy asked without missing a beat. He was determined to find out everything about the drug, good or bad.

"The inability to think straight, confusion, cloudy thinking, hazy judgment," replied Drummond, again glancing at his two colleagues.

"As in an increase in suicidal thinking?" pressed Billy, not wanting to move on until Drummond cleared things up.

"That's the media and the plaintiff's Bar for you," Drummond protested. "There's no truth to that. Our studies on Zerevrea have not shown any increase in suicidal behavior or thoughts, much less aggressive behavior."

Billy made a mental note about Drummond's body language. He'd pushed a hot button. "Has BostonMagnifica concealed any potentially dangerous information that I should be aware of?"

Billy looked straight across the conference table at Sudarshan and Neal, looking for more reactions.

"Of course not," answered Drummond, smiling. "Consumer safety first, Mr. Bravo. Safety first, always. That's our motto."

The pair of doctors were nodding their heads, playing up to their boss, putting on a dog-and-pony show.

"Has Zerevrea been approved for children?" inquired Billy.

"If you've noticed our TV ads announcing the introduction of Zerevrea, the drug is not FDA-approved for anyone under eighteen, if that's what you're asking."

"How many clinical trials were conducted on Zerevrea?"

"Three."

"Were all of these published?"

"One was published in the *Journal of the American Academy of Adult Psychiatry*."

"Which one?"

"The first study."

"And the other two . . . were they ever published?"

"No," replied Drummond nervously. "It was not necessary."

"Why? Were all the findings consistent in all the studies? And by the way, when you get a chance, I'm gonna need to see those studies . . . all of them."

Drummond looked over at the pair sitting to his right, paused for a moment, and finally admitted, "There were some discrepancies, but those could be attributed to the differences in the subject pool."

Unlike Drummond, the pair was squirming in their seats.

"What kind of discrepancies . . . and I am referring specifically to the issue of suicidality," clarified Billy.

"One study showed Zerevrea worked on depression, another study found no significant effect and the last one was inconclusive."

"I am not talking about depression," pointed out Billy. "I am talking about suicidal thoughts. What was the difference in the studies on that issue alone?"

"That . . . Zerevrea is safe. The analysis showed that only 1.2 percent of the test subjects thought of suicide or violent behavior.

This figure is consistent with the same 1.2 percent of the subject pool given the placebo pill. There was no discernible difference to speak of."

"Is that so?"

"Yes, that's what the tests showed."

"When can I see those studies?"

"Next week. I'll need a few days to dig them up. If that's okay?"

"What happens if the patient doubles up on it because of a missed dose?"

"Slight agitation, that's all," Drummond answered, shrugging his shoulders.

"Any other known side effects?"

"Nausea, fatigue, weakness, sweating, loss of appetite and sexual dysfunction."

"And less common side effects?"

"Insomnia, anxiety and, in some cases, shaking or tremors."

"Dr. Drummond," said Billy, clearing his throat, "how do you know if an individual is suffering from an imbalance of serotonin in the brain?"

"No one really knows for sure, Mr. Bravo," explained Drummond. "Remember, there is no test that allows us to get into the brain."

"So, there is no test for this?"

"No."

"Then how do you *think* it works?"

"We theorize that Zerevrea increases the levels of 5-hydroxyindoleacetic acid, which is a byproduct of serotonin. People that commit suicide—most of whom suffer from depression, I might add—have extremely low levels of this acid."

"So, you equate low levels of the byproduct with low levels of serotonin, am I right?"

"That's a fair assumption," Drummond said. "Zerevrea, the tests have shown, increases the level of this byproduct."

"So, an increase of the byproduct signals, in your opinion, an increase in serotonin levels in the brain, correct?"

"Yes," Drummond said, sounding impressed. "Zerevrea prevents the escape of serotonin so more of it stays in the brain where it's needed."

"Well, that's stretching it a bit, correct? I mean, Zerevrea may increase the byproduct, but we don't know for sure that there's an increase of serotonin, do we?"

"We choose to believe there is an increase."

"I see."

"Look, there's no other substance in the brain which produces 5-hydroxyindoleacetic acid!" Drummond said, raising his voice. "Zerevrea shows an increase of the byproduct, which in scientific terms must mean there is more serotonin. So, our drug keeps more serotonin where it should be—in the brain!"

"Okay," Billy replied. "Now, let's move." He realized he'd pushed another hot button.

It was obvious that no one at BostonMagnifica knew exactly how these psychotropic drugs worked. It was all theory, hypothesis, supposition and speculation. What Drummond was saying was that the effects of these types of drugs appeared to act on the neurotransmitters of the brain by increasing or decreasing their levels. And those levels could be measured, arguably, by measuring their known byproducts, their waste.

"Can post-traumatic stress disorder interact negatively with Zerevrea?"

The three doctors did a double-take.

"Come again?" asked Drummond.

"Are you aware or do you know if Zerevrea is contraindicated in patients with PTSD?" Billy wanted to know, since he knew that Tommy Ray had been a Gulf War veteran.

"Eh, well . . . as with any biological abnormality, there is no evidence that Zerevrea interacts negatively with this disorder," Drummond finally answered, apparently trying to confuse the issue.

"Is it your understanding that abnormal biology is always the sole cause of psychiatric disorders?" Billy returned the volley. He could go round and round with the best. After all these years of defending doctors and pharmaceuticals, he'd read a scientific journal or two.

"Ah, I see. You're right," Drummond confessed. "No psychiatric disorder has ever been linked to any biological etiology, with the exception of Alzheimer's disease. I misspoke."

"Did you withhold any other studies from the FDA?" Billy asked, looking straight into Drummond's eyes.

"No."

"I hate to be a pest," Billy apologized, "and I'd hate to be surprised at trial. Was anything, any studies, internal memos, e-mails, results, testing or any data held back from the feds? Whatever you tell me is protected by attorney-client privilege, Doctor." Billy was not about to take a chance. Drug companies were always getting nailed for violating all kinds of federal laws; he was not sufficiently convinced that his client had been totally forthcoming.

"No, everything was turned over," Drummond said, trying his best to sound convincing.

"One last question," said Billy. "Earlier you said Felix Croutoux started this R&D department with you, correct? Was he a scientist?"

"Yes. He left the company a year ago. I guess he retired."

"Could I contact Croutoux as well? Would you mind?"

"Of course. I believe Human Resources can provide you with his info. I'll walk you over there. Come on, let's go. Last I heard, he was living in upstate New York."

Billy and Charlie packed their notepads, shook hands goodbye with Sudarshan and Neal and followed Drummond out of the conference room. It was time for the much-anticipated tour of the facility.

"WHAT DO you think?" Billy asked Charlie as they took their respective seats in the exquisitely appointed company jet. They could see a maintenance worker outside aboard a cherry picker, frantically de-icing the plane wings. The temperature had dropped nearly twenty degrees.

"About?" the associate replied in a clueless manner.

Billy loosened his tie, removed his reading glasses, and rubbed his temples. "Are they telling us everything?"

"I doubt it."

"I felt the same way. It was just a dog-and-pony show. They're hiding something. They're not on the up and up."

"Well," Charlie interjected, "if the plaintiffs drop a bomb at trial, then it's not our fault. You've done your part, Mr. Bravo. You asked them several times to come clean and level with you."

"Charlie," Billy asked as he cleaned his reading glasses with his silk tie, "did I ever tell you the story of the client I defended during my third year of law school?"

"No."

"It just so happened that I'd enrolled in the criminal clinic at the law school my last semester. I wanted to get some real hands-on experience. Try a case with a real judge and jury before law school was over. So, I got handed a misdemeanor assault case to defend."

"I gotcha."

"Anyway, so I'm defending this guy. He'd beat his wife to a pulp. Some redneck named Randy. Um . . . Randy Daniels. That was it, Randy Daniels."

"So, what happened?"

"Well, I asked him to tell me everything, everything that happened that night."

"And?"

"The guy insists he did not lay a hand on his wife. He's adamant. He claims to be innocent and that he's been wrongfully accused and that he wants his day in court."

"One of those that can't admit enjoying wife-beating as a sport," added Jensen.

"Yes, you know the type," Billy said. "Anyway, he claims the cops have it in for him. They're out to get him. It's a conspiracy."

"Don't they always?"

"So, he claims he's told me everything . . . that he only pushed the wife aside as he was trying to leave the house in an effort to avoid another nasty confrontation."

"Was she badly hurt?"

"Oh, yeah! Black eye, bruises on the arms and legs, scratches on the side of the neck—just a mess."

"Did you try the case?"

"Yes, the guy continued to be in denial. I had to."

"So, what did the jury do?"

"Well, the cop is on the stand testifying," Billy paused. "Now, remember, I've asked this jerk repeatedly to tell me everything."

"I know, I know. And?"

"So, the same officer that responded to the call that night is on the stand testifying. The officer tells the jury that by the time he got to the home, the aggressor had fled the scene. So, all he could do was make a report and take pictures of the victim."

"Your client did not get arrested that same night?"

"No, months later, but only after he got picked up on a warrant."

"So, then what happened?"

"Well, I continued my cross-examination, right?"

"Right . . . "

"And I continue to drive home the point that, really, all the cop did in connection with this investigation was just that: make a two-page report and take pictures of the victim. A half-ass investigation, if you will."

"You were trying to make him look bad in front of the jury, right?" asked Charlie, excited, trying to show he had learned a thing or two in trial advocacy class.

"Sure. So, then I ask him if he, himself, did not arrest my client that night, then who was the person who had arrested the defendant?"

Charlie interrupted. "Let me guess. He was picked up later during a traffic stop? I know where you're going with this. I know, I know. You're going to pick the officer apart on the issue of identification, right?"

"Boy, you're good," Billy said, smiling. "They really teach this stuff up at SMU, don't they?"

"I amjured my trial advocacy class," said Charlie, brimming with confidence. "I got the only A in the class."

"You're right. Months later, my client was driving without a front plate, so a trooper stopped him and ran his license, and it came back that he had a warrant."

"Okay, go on."

"So, I asked him, if you've never seen my client, how do you know this person here, sitting to my left, is Randy Daniels?"

"What did he answer?" Charlie asked full of anticipation.

"'My sister is Reba Daniels, the victim of this assault,' said the cop. 'She is married to your client!'"

"Oh no!" cried Charlie. "What did you do?"

"No further questions, Your Honor. Pass the witness."

"Ha! ha!" Charlie laughed.

"If BostonMagnifica wants to hold back, well there is nothing I can do. You can lead a horse to water, but can't make it drink," Billy concluded as he reached for a miniature bottle of scotch and a glass with ice sitting on the tray the flight attendant offered. "Speaking of leading horses to water. What are you drinking?"

"I'll have a vodka tonic."

The blonde attendant handed Jensen his drink and a napkin with lime wedges. "Here you go."

"Cheers!" said Billy as he raised his scotch and gave it a couple of swirls.

"To BM's defense verdict, Mr. Bravo," Jensen said.

"Thanks. And stop calling me Mr. Bravo. Call me Billy."

CHAPTER 9

AFTER SPENDING ALL of Tuesday up in Massachusetts and getting in late from the east coast, Billy was back in his office early on Wednesday morning. He'd slept four hours, showered, changed, shaved and sprinted back to resume his trial. Judge Ramón had scheduled opening arguments at ten in the morning.

Billy anticipated that Hoffman would spend all of Wednesday putting on his case in chief, calling his own witnesses and then possibly going into Thursday. In any event, Billy would get in and out by Friday morning, and hopefully do closing arguments after lunch. He was hopeful that Hurricane Emily would change course, away from South Padre Island, and he wouldn't have to spend his weekend boarding up the beach house.

"Billy, do you have a minute?" Hector interrupted as he poked his head into Billy's office. "I could come back later. I see you're getting ready for trial this morning . . . maybe another time."

Billy looked over the wall of documents and clutter and put his trial notebook down. "I was about to take a break, get a cup of Joe. What's up?"

"They nabbed my dad."

"Who? When? What are you talking about, Hector? Close the door behind you, please. Sit down."

"The feds have him," Hector said, visibly shaken.

"What do you mean the feds have him? Take a deep breath, sit down."

"It's a long story, and I really don't want to take your time . . . I just don't know what to do."

50

"Why don't you tell me why the feds have your old man. Start from there."

"Okay . . . in a nutshell," started Hector, "*Mi jefito* got called to the district office for the Bureau of Customs and Immigration Services down in Harlingen."

"Why?"

"They said there were some issues with his residency," replied Hector, still looking down at the floor.

"What kind of issues?"

"Apparently, when he was a young man, he picked up a conviction for assault. Some white boys jumped him as he and his date, who happened to be white, were coming out of the movies. The three punks beat him senseless, but nothing ever happened to them."

"So he was left holding the bag?"

"Yep. The only one with broken ribs, a broken nose and a black eye."

"And now the Bureau of Customs and Immigration Services and the Department of Homeland Security are using the conviction as an excuse to kick him out of the country, correct?"

"I'm afraid so. Even though he's been a law-abiding resident, retired from the county's public works department, paid his taxes, kept out of trouble and all his family members are U.S. citizens. Is that unbelievable or what?"

"The detention centers are full of people with similar stories," said Billy.

"It's truly, truly sad. I need to help him."

"What's going to happen to him if he gets deported?"

"That's just it. We no longer have family in Mexico. I don't know what's gonna happen."

"What do you plan on doing?"

"Fight the deportation, I guess. My brothers and sisters are pitching in and calling attorneys to see if we can get somebody to represent him. They all want a ton of money, and we just don't have it."

"Do you think he can make bond?" Billy asked.

"I don't know."

"Hire a good immigration attorney. I hear Marlene Goodwin routinely beats the government in deportation proceedings. She's the go-to attorney when in hot water."

"That's good to know. I'll go call her right now, Billy . . . see what she charges. Thanks, Billy."

"Don't mention it." Without missing a beat, Billy pulled his checkbook from the top drawer of his desk and started writing a check. "Wait, Hector, I have something for you. Here's to the cause."

"I can't accept that," Hector said, trying to shove the ten-thousand-dollar check back into Billy's hand.

"Hey," replied Billy, looking at Hector straight in the eyes, "consider it bond money for your dad. Take it. Someday, you'll return the favor or repay it or whatever. Right now, you need it. As your boss, I'm ordering you to take it. You have no choice."

"Okay," mumbled Hector as he scratched his head in amazement and made his way out. "Thank you, Billy."

"Let me know if you need anything else."

IT WAS the end of the first day of trial, and Billy Bravo was pleased with the way things were developing in the courtroom. For starters, he'd been able to inflict some damage while cross-examining the plaintiff. To impeach the plaintiff's assertions that she was still a virgin, pure and virtuous, the judge had allowed Billy to introduce a video showing the twenty-three-year-old female dancing topless on stage during spring break down in Cancun.

Hector had tracked down an ex-boyfriend and managed to score the video for two hundred dollars. Hoffman, the girl's attorney, had hit the roof, crying unfair surprise and trial by ambush. But Billy had replied that he was entitled to impeach the witness on her credibility and that he'd just received the newly discovered evidence.

Since the video had just surfaced, under the rules of evidence and thanks to Hector's uncanny ability to dig dirt at the last minute, the video could come in, if only for impeachment purposes. In the end, the judge allowed the video into evidence, and the jury loved the fireworks.

Now heading home for the day, Billy remembered he still needed to get his hands on the clinical studies for Zerevrea, and Nancy needed to put together an initial Request for Disclosure to the plaintiff in the Ray lawsuit. He stopped at a light and started dictating reminders into his micro-recorder as he made other mental notes. *I also need to get back to Karin and make arrangements to go meet my son. Yami's going to freak!*

With his left hand, he reached into his pant's pocket for change, lowered the driver's side window, and tossed about a dollar's worth into the beat-up coffee can held by an amputee in a dilapidated wheelchair. A minute later, the traffic light went from red to green, and he sped off. He dictated another note to have Nancy line up a hearing down in federal court in Laredo as soon as possible to do a scheduling conference with Riley Spearman.

As he drove away on University Boulevard, he thought about Bates' promise and put all his worries aside, if only for a while. He smiled. In his mind, he could see the firm's letterhead: Bates, Domani, Rockford, Lord & Bravo. He was delighted with the sound of it. It didn't matter that it was probably the longest firm name in the entire Rio Grande Valley—hell, probably in the entire State of Texas! The name was music to his ears.

He sped away down Highway 281 and merged east onto 83 near the Basilica de San Juan exit. His car radio was blaring a familiar song, "Who Are You?" by the British rock band, The Who. He opened the sunroof to his Pilot and stepped on the gas, zooming down the road in and out of traffic.

He took the exit and pulled into the large parking lot belonging to the Catholic Diocese of South Texas. The parking area was quiet and deserted. It was now seven PM. He got out of the car and went inside the cavernous Spanish colonial-style church. The place was empty except for two females praying quietly off to the side. He sat down in one of the pews in the back of the empty cathedral and knelt down, his blue eyes slowly adjusting to the darkness.

"All right, God. I'm here. You got me where you wanted. I know it's been a while since I've been by, probably since the kids were baptized." He felt embarrassed and extremely guilty. "I need your help with the Karin Palmer situation. I can't afford to have a scandalous divorce. Then my promotion will never happen. Help me figure out a way to fix this mess. Please. *Te lo suplico.*"

CHAPTER 10

T
HE LATE *ALMUERZO* was to take place at La Leyenda restaurant in Reynosa, Mexico. The famous eatery was just a skip and a jump south of McAllen. The hacienda-style restaurant was legendary for its fabulous spreads, which included slow-smoked *cabrito* and other succulent dishes prepared with organ meats—*sesos, machitos, hígado, tripitas, mollejas*, calf lung, mountain oysters, even fire-grilled, butterflied slivers of bull's heart.

After the Myers trial broke for the weekend and the jury started deliberations at the close of the evidence, Nancy had managed to schedule the Sunday brunch with Dr. Iván González, one of Billy's childhood friends. The Mexican psychiatrist had suggested they meet at La Leyenda, and Nancy had accepted on her boss' behalf. Little did she know that her boss could not stand the sight and smell of liver, much less eat mountain oysters, organ meats or cow brains.

"HOLA, BILLY," González welcomed him excitedly. "How's the attorney-at-last?"

A startled Billy sprang to his feet, threw the Sunday paper down on a chair and embraced his old friend. The two forty-somethings exchanged pleasantries and finally sat back down at a table. González ordered a glass of Montecillo red wine while Billy had the waiter freshen up his Crown and Seven.

The psychiatrist was sporting blue jeans, a Jack Nicklaus signature golf shirt and New Balance running shoes. He looked to be in perfect shape, smiling from ear to ear, with a noticeable tan and salt-and-pepper hair. The smell of Boucheron floated in the air, as if he'd just jumped out of the shower.

"Ha, ha!" laughed Billy, "attorney-at-last . . . that's funny. *Estoy bien,* Iván. *¡Qué gusto verte!* God, it's good to see ya. It's been what, thirty years?"

"At least," replied González. "When they gave me the message that Billy Bravo had called looking for me, I couldn't believe it. I fell out of my chair. How the hell did you track me down?"

"Well, it wasn't easy. Our firm's investigator tracked down your parents first. The guy's awesome. He can find anybody and anything. He should lead the hunt for Osama . . . the guy would find him. I had no idea you had gone back to Mexico."

"It was one of those rare opportunities. Can you imagine having the presidente himself call you to tell you that he wants you to run Mexico's Ministry of Health?"

"What a difference thirty years makes, no?" Billy said.

"Remember when we used to pick cucumbers in Wautoma, Wisconsin?"

"*Y uvas en* Napa, California."

"Funny how life turned out and I ended up graduating from Harvard Medical School. Who would have guessed it?"

Billy took a sip from his Crown and Seven. "Our families did what . . . eight or nine seasons picking crops together? And now look at you . . . a famous doctor!"

"I hear you're quite the attorney," González said, returning the compliment to his childhood friend.

"I do okay," Billy replied. "Speaking of . . . I called you because I need to pick your brains. I hope you don't mind. I'm involved in a lawsuit dealing with psychotropic drugs, suicide and mental health issues."

"No problem. Whatever I can do to help."

"Okay, then. What's the deal with SSRIs? Can they trigger suicidal behavior? Man to man, I'd like to know the truth."

González took a swig from his wine glass, set it down on the table, cleared his throat and spoke slowly. "Before I answer your question, tell me about the person that died. What was the name?"

"Tommy Ray."

"From Ray's Appliance? That family?"

"Yes," confirmed Billy.

"So, what do you know about the guy?"

"He was about our age, had a wife and four young children. Never before divorced, apparently happily married. Wealthy, too . . . no money problems. Successful law practice, and they also came from old money. Apparently had never suffered from depression. Excellent health. Loved by his peers. Involved in the community. Only one known bout of mild anxiety, after returning from the Gulf War."

"Is that it?"

"Yes. Nothing that screams 'this guy's a ticking time bomb.'"

"Um, have you seen his military chart?"

"No, why?"

"I wonder if he suffered from post-traumatic stress disorder? And if he did, would it have been noted in his military records?"

"I guess I need to get my hands on those," said Billy.

"That might help explain things. Lots of veterans come back from war suffering from PTSD, and they don't even know it. Except somebody like Mr. Ray, with those characteristics and everything going for him, usually would not make a good candidate for suicide. Especially if there was no stress disorder. Something could have made him snap. Was the wife having an affair? Tax problems? Creditors?"

"Doesn't appear so."

"Okay, let's put Mr. Ray aside for a while," González suggested as he took a sip of wine. "The truth about SSRIs is that these drugs sometimes work, but sometimes they can make things worse."

"Really?"

"Sure. The problem is compounded, if, for example, you're already suffering from PTSD, and now you add the akathisia, which is a bad side effect from the drug. Can you see what happens?"

"You've become a stick of dynamite! So, it *is* possible that the guy taking this medication may be worse off?" asked Billy.

"Yes. Imagine . . . you're already feeling anxious, add the PTSD, and now because of the increase in serotonin in your brain due to the drug, you also feel violent and aggressive. That's the problem. It becomes a deadly cocktail." González made the sign of the cross with his thumb and index finger, brought his hand close to the lips and kissed it. "Worse yet, you think you're going absolutely crazy. And of course, nobody warned you of the side effects. And all the while, you just want to end the suffering."

"So why are these drugs so popular? Looks like everyone and their dog is on them."

"Marketing, marketing and marketing, my friend. These drugs are cash cows . . . and in some instances, they do help some folks. In reality, the one single thing we do know is that there's a link between self-destructive aggressive behaviors and these drugs in some patients. It's something the pharmaceutical companies have covered up for years."

"Can I get my hands on those studies?"

"*Va a estar difícil*. These obscure studies are few and far between. Your best bet would be to talk to an insider—a disgruntled ex-employee with firsthand experience who may have been fired or left on his own because of his unpopular views. Those individuals usually prove very helpful."

"I'd thought of that," said Billy. "I told Hector to start digging . . . see what he can find."

"Well, that might be the way to go."

Billy was absorbing all of this by the time steamy bowls of *frijoles charros* and a large platter piled high with smoked *cabrito*, *mollejas*, *machitos* and *sesos* rolled around—frosty mugs of Negra Modelo beer accompanied lunch followed by more cocktails and a sampler dessert platter with *flan*, *chongos zamoranos*, *empanadas de cajeta*, *mangos en almíbar* and different types of *membrillos*.

The three-hour brunch (or "business meeting," for purposes of billing Falcone) was brought to a close with cups of double espressos in the bar area, accompanied by Cuban cigars and snifters full of Kahlua and Bailey's.

Afterward, Billy and González said their goodbyes but agreed to keep in touch—especially now that González was considering relocating his family to McAllen due to the unprecedented escalation of border violence as the drug cartels fought for control of "The Plaza," as the cartel referred to the city of Reynosa. Maybe Billy could line him up with a good immigration lawyer, help him score an investor's visa.

"BRINGING ANYTHING?" asked the U.S. customs inspector manning the aluminum and glass booth at the end of the international bridge.

"No, sir," Billy Bravo replied. He'd been waiting in line at the bridge for almost an hour, but was now almost on U.S. soil. All he needed to do was clear customs.

"The purpose of your visit to Mexico?" asked the young Hispanic agent in the blue uniform.

"Had lunch with an old friend," said Billy, "at La Leyenda. The food was excellent."

The agent said nothing. "Can I see your U.S. passport?"

"I don't have a passport," explained Billy. "I do have a birth certificate in my wallet, though. Here, let me get it."

"You understand," said the customs agent, "next time you come back from Mexico, you will need a passport?"

"Yes, sir, I understand. But, didn't Congress extend the deadline another six months for everyone to get their passport?"

"Yes, they did. My computer shows that this vehicle crosses into Mexico about every six months, so the next time you come around, you better have your passport."

"Yes, sir," replied Billy as he handed the officer his Texas driver's license and his birth certificate. *Man, why must these Hispanic agents be such assholes? They're worst than the gringos.*

Billy took his license and wallet-sized birth certificate. "Thanks, I'll have my wife work on getting everyone their passports."

The agent smirked as he waved the car behind Billy's to come forward. "You do that."

And with that, the short, uncomfortable encounter was over.

CHAPTER 11

ON MONDAY MORNING, Hoffman's assistant and Billy's secretary, Nancy, found themselves clearing out Judge Ramón's courtroom of all the boxes and exhibits from the trial held the previous week. After the attorneys had delivered closing arguments on Friday, the jury had deliberated the remainder of the day. Yet, there had been no verdict.

The jurors were expected to return and continue deliberating all of Monday, maybe even Tuesday. Billy had asked Charlie Jensen to hold Dr. Myers's hand and stay behind with him down at the courthouse while waiting around for the verdict. He had bigger fish to fry, like meeting his adversary, Spearman, in federal court down in Laredo at the initial scheduling conference.

MONDAY AFTERNOON found Billy Bravo, Rick Domani and Hector Ayala sitting at counsel's table inside the courtroom of U.S. District Judge Valeria Allende. Judge Allende wanted to meet the attorneys handling the Tommy Ray lawsuit at once.

In essence, the scheduling conference presented an opportunity for the court and the parties to discuss the type of case now being litigated, the claims and defenses being asserted by both sides, the possibility of settlement, arrangements for the issuance of initial disclosures and for the parties to jointly fashion a proposed discovery plan.

As per Bates's instructions, Billy had quickly informed his boss of the upcoming conference, and Bates had thought it a good idea for his partner, Rick Domani, to appear along with Billy before the district judge. Since Domani, according to Bates, had dated Judge Allende in law school, maybe that little fact could help tilt the scales in favor of the client.

Spearman and Hanslik, his associate, were at the opposite table waiting for the bailiff to announce the arrival of Judge Allende. The attorneys were sizing each other up as they set up their exhibits, yellow pads and pens, trial notebooks and other related documents. There were three loud knocks on a back door into the courtroom.

"Hear ye, hear ye, hear ye!" announced the judge's law clerk as he led the way for the judge. "All rise for the Honorable Valeria Allende, United States District Judge now presiding for the Southern District of Texas, Laredo Division. This court is now in session. Long live the United States of America!"

Judge Allende took her place on the bench, her law clerk sat to her right, and the rest of her staff—the court's coordinator, interpreter and electronic recording officer—sat off to one side at a smaller table fitted with computer screens and recording equipment.

"Good afternoon," announced the judge, who happened to be fifty years old and a portly five-foot-seven. Her black shoulder-length hair was parted down the middle, away from her full cheeks. Her reading glasses sat delicately on her head. "Please, sit down. Announce your names for the record."

"Good afternoon," announced Rick Domani, jumping up. "I'm defense counsel for . . . "

"Let me hear from the plaintiffs first, Mr. Domani," snapped Judge Allende, sounding slightly ticked off.

After Domani sat down, Riley Spearman and Timothy Hanslik slowly stood up and addressed the court. "Good afternoon, Your Honor. Riley Spearman for the plaintiffs. I'm the attorney in charge."

"Tim Hanslik, also for the plaintiffs," announced the associate. "We are present and ready."

"What says the defense?" asked Judge Allende, now looking intently at Rick Domani.

Domani, who was a few shades of red, slowly got up again and spoke. "Rick Domani for BostonMagnifica Pharmaceuticals, along with cocounsel Billy Bravo and Hector Ayala, our firm's investigator. We're ready to proceed, Your Honor."

"Good afternoon," said Billy.

"Good afternoon, Judge," blurted Hector.

"Mr. Ayala," said the judge, addressing Hector, "are you licensed to practice law in federal court?"

"No, Your Honor. I'm not."

"Do you hold a Texas Bar card?"

"No, ma'am," stuttered Hector.

"Have you ever been to law school anywhere? Either here or in Mexico?"

"No, Judge. I have not."

Billy and Domani, along with Hanslik and Spearman, were looking at Hector squirm. They knew where Judge Allende was going with this.

"Then do the court a favor and sit on the other side of the bar," she said, pointing to the twelve rows of pews where the public and the press usually sat.

"Yes, Your Honor . . . I apologize," Hector replied, seemingly embarrassed. As he was getting up to change seats, his cell phone rang. Everybody turned to look at the investigator again, who by now looked half scared to death and was fumbling with the phone trying to shut it off.

"Please give your cell phone to the marshal," ordered Judge Allende from the bench as she signaled to the young U.S. marshal to seize Hector's cell phone. "You'll get it back after you make a five-hundred-dollar charitable contribution to my favorite organization, The Catholic Daughters of America. Once you've made your contribution, come by the clerk's office. Show them your receipt, and they will return your cell phone. Otherwise, the cell phone stays here. You got that, Mr. Ayala?"

"Yes, ma'am," said Hector meekly as he handed his lifeline to the blonde female marshal.

"Let this be a lesson," the judge said and quickly redirected her attention to Spearman. "Counsel, I see you filed an interesting motion for me to step aside. You want me to recuse myself from handling this case?"

"That's right. We need to address that issue first, Your Honor," answered Spearman. "With all due respect, we have filed a motion asking Your Honor to recuse yourself from hearing any matters connected to this case. We believe we have valid grounds to raise the issue at this time. I don't want to discuss the grounds in open court. But it's all in there. It's quite explicit."

"It was not filed in a timely manner, Your Honor, and we have not even seen the plaintiff's recusal motion," complained Domani, quickly thinking on his feet. "We're not prepared to respond to Mr. Spearman's motion. We don't even know what grounds they've raised. I would kindly ask this court to simply entertain issues dealing with the scheduling conference. On the alternative, Your Honor, we would also ask the court to consider, *sua sponte*, issuing a gag order in this case as well. Our client's name and reputation cannot be dragged through the mud. We don't want any of the litigants or anybody else involved in this case, for that matter, speaking to the media."

"Well," the seasoned judge replied, "if the court picks up, *sua sponte*, your request for an ex-parte gag order, isn't that the same as taking the plaintiff's on the recusal motion? You don't want me to address theirs, but you want me to address yours?"

"Well, uh, yes," mumbled Domani, "that's right."

"Just like the court can take up matters on its own, *sua sponte*, the court has ample discretion to take up matters that are relevant to any case at any time," interjected Spearman in rapid-fire form. "This is one of those times . . . the recusal should be heard first."

"From reading the motion, I think the plaintiffs raise a valid issue, don't you think, Mr. Domani?" The judge was looking straight at Domani over her reading glasses balanced on the tip of her nose, appearing visibly upset to be put in such a position.

"This is a very complex and expensive case," volunteered Spearman. "We wouldn't want to commit a reversible error. Imagine spending hundreds of thousands of dollars getting this case prepared for trial, doing discovery for well over a year and . . . "

"Go ahead," Judge Allende said, nodding her head.

" . . . and to have to go through a month-long trial and then have to come back because the Fifth Circuit Court of Appeals orders a retrial on grounds that, with all due respect, Judge, you should have recused yourself."

"But . . . but," said Domani, sounding frustrated as hell, "I doubt the grounds they've raised merit a recusal, Judge."

"Although I agree with you, Mr. Domani, that their motion was not timely filed," indicated Judge Allende, "I do have discretion to take up the issue of recusal at this time. I think it is an important issue. Here . . . read for yourself the grounds the plaintiffs have raised."

The judge handed the motion to the U.S. marshal, who in turn took it and delivered it to Domani at counsel's table. Domani took a few moments and started reading it. After about a minute, he looked up. "But . . . but," Domani blurted out, "What about my client?" He was quite upset and was shaking his head furiously.

"When litigants come to court, they expect to get a fair shot," proclaimed the judge. "The parties expect to start on the same footing and for the judge to be unbiased and impartial. No one wants to be in front of a judge who is going to favor one party over another."

"Okay," Domani muttered in disappointment as he listened intently to his old girlfriend. That's why he'd broken up with her in the first place, he now remembered. She was strong-minded and independent, and once she made up her mind, there was no changing it, even when she was clearly wrong.

"And no litigant would want to find himself or herself in front of a judge who, whether it is true or not, is rumored to lean heavily this way or that way. Wouldn't you agree?"

"Well . . . yes," Domani said, shrugging.

"So, in order to avoid any appearance of impropriety or any hint or innuendo of bias, I would think that, in this instance, recusal might be appropriate," concluded Judge Allende.

"I still think there's no basis for granting plaintiff's recusal motion," argued Domani. "We're all adults here."

Billy jumped up and tried to save Domani any further embarrassment. "Judge, we would kindly ask that another judge be assigned to hear this case. We seriously doubt the plaintiffs will ultimately prevail at trial. We still have a long way to go and will file Daubert motions challenging their experts, including motions for summary judgment. In any event, I doubt they'll even get their case to a jury, but I'd hate to come back and give them another shot just because of this issue. I'd hate for the Court of Appeals to give them another bite at the apple because another judge should have heard the case. Better safe than sorry, I always say."

Billy knew federal judges hated to be reversed by their peers sitting on the appellate court, particularly over something as obvious as Judge Allende having had a romantic relationship with one of the parties or one of the attorneys in a case. Hell, federal judges were even known to recuse themselves if they owned a few shares of stock in a company that happened to be suing or was being sued in their court.

"I agree," indicated Judge Allende. "And believe me, the court does appreciate your cooperation and level-headedness, Mr. Bravo." Then she announced, "Judge Gilmore, the administrative judge for the Southern District of Texas, will assign a judge for the trial. I am sure her staff will be contacting both sides in the next few days to resume the case. We'll be in recess!"

And just like that, the hearing was over. Judge Allende left the bench and proceeded to her chambers. Domani's head was spinning. Hector came over to help Billy collect their materials from counsel's table, as did Spearman and Hanslik, who happened to be grinning.

"This court is now in recess!" announced the young law clerk working for the federal judge. Everyone was sent home without further incident.

THE HEADLINE in the local daily, *The Border Sentinel*, read: "Federal Judge Recuses Herself Amid Allegations of Bias." It was the newspaper's own follow-up after *The Texas Observer* had run a story about the momentous gains the pharmaceuticals had obtained in Austin while the legislature had been in session and how the drug companies appeared close to gaining total control of the legislature with their generous campaign contributors. The *Observer* story briefly mentioned that the lobbyists had failed, however, to convince the Texas legislature to pass a new law prohibiting, outright, all lawsuits against big pharmaceuticals.

The *Border Sentinel* story then quoted Ron Blaylock, a law professor and legal analyst, on the significance of a judicial recusal and what it meant for the drug giant now fighting a lawsuit in Laredo, Texas.

Hector had dropped a copy of the paper on Billy's desk. Santos Chapa, the reporter writing the feature, started the piece by discussing the grounds alleged on Spearman's Motion to Recuse. Since the file was public record, the reporter had obtained a copy of Spearman's recusal motion and copies of BostonMagnifica's request for a gag order. Chapa had published excerpts contained in the motions.

The author had also obtained law student directories and copies of *Tortfeasors & Malcreants*, a magazine published by the University of Houston Law Center, from around the time when both Domani and Judge Allende had attended that institution. Whoever said first-year law students did nothing but study, study, study, obviously had never partied with Domani and Allende.

There were pictures of Rick and a much skinnier Valeria drinking in the law school's atrium standing next to a keg of Shiner Bock beer. Splashed across the feature were more photos of Domani and Allende participating together in mock trial and moot court competitions. There were pictures of the couple partying on the Island of Santorini—looking svelte and tanned—during a school-sponsored summer-abroad program in Greece.

The story then continued with a quick paragraph about the rise of Valeria Allende to the federal bench. It spoke of her work as a young assistant attorney general in the child support enforcement division in Houston soon after having graduated from law school.

The reporter had then attempted to interview Rick Domani to see if he had any comment, but the lawyer had not returned his calls. Chapa had then interviewed Riley Spearman about filing the surprising Motion to Recuse. Although the plaintiff's attorney had refused to disclose his source for the information, once he had corroborated the information, it had been a piece of cake to track down Kate Owen, the judge's roommate in law school.

Ron Blaylock was then quoted as saying that "Defense counsel had gotten home-towned by an out-of-towner. However, the good news was that BostonMagnifica, the defendant, had nothing to worry about the new federal judge being appointed to hear the case, since most federal judges were pro-business. Unless, of course, the new federal judge appointed to hear the case was none other than District Judge Kyle Dorfman."

Dorfman was an old, obnoxious, cranky Marine with a reputation for running the court like the Army. He was known to interrupt the lawyers, toy with them and take over the examinations of the witnesses themselves. This irritated the hell out of the attorneys who got to practice in his court, but the jurors loved him. He was known to put the parties through their paces and routinely wrapped up complex cases in two weeks instead of the average eight weeks.

The story also quoted insiders at the federal courthouse down in Laredo that confirmed that the entire incident had Judge Allende dumbfounded. She just could not believe that Rick Domani had dared appear in front of her.

Finally, the story ended with Gina Ray being quoted. Tommy Ray's widow was now even more determined to "expose the truth about BostonMagnifica's Zerevrea."

CHAPTER 12

"**M**ORNING," SAID BILLY as he walked in the large conference room. After the BostonMagnifica story ran in the Laredo newspaper and Falcone had gotten wind of it, the CEO demanded a meeting with Bates and Billy down in Houston. He wanted answers, and he wanted them fast!

Bates noticed the worried look on Billy's face as the attorney took his place at the conference table, so he immediately tried to diffuse the situation. "Billy, I understand Judge Allende didn't give you all a chance to raise our pre-emptive request for a gag order, correct?"

"Yes, sir," explained Billy. "We were going to ask for a gag order at the scheduling conference, but Spearman filed his Motion for Recusal. The judge had to hear the recusal first. Sorry."

Falcone threw his hands up in the air. "Look, Billy, do you have any idea the predicament I'm in?"

"I do, sir," said Billy, "I can just imagine, trust me."

"No, you don't!" snapped Falcone as he threw a copy of the newspaper across the table toward Billy. "You have no idea. If we go under, do you understand that hundreds—no, thousands—of good, hardworking people will be out of a job?"

"I suppose . . . "

"Half of the folks at Worcester work at BostonMagnifica, Billy. Those jobs are key to the local economy."

"I get the picture," said Billy.

"And thousands of investors will lose hundreds of millions of dollars. Have you thought about that?"

"Yes . . . sir, I've . . . "

"Not to mention we'll be forced to stop making and developing drugs that have been proven highly effective in treating leukemia and other types of cancers."

"I understand, sir, believe me. Dr. Drummond said the same thing. I get your point, really, I do."

"Do you get it? Really? That's why I had you tour our facilities! So that you could get it through that thick, wetback head of yours how significant this lawsuit is. We have to win, Billy. You have to make this go away!"

"No one reads that rag, anyway," Billy replied as he tried to deflect responsibility, "I promise you, sir." He did not appreciate Falcone calling him "thick-skulled." Besides, why wasn't Domani in the same room also getting yelled at? Why only Billy?

"My ass!" screamed Falcone in a combative tone. "You don't think the president reads the Texas papers?!! Not two weeks into the case and already Zerevrea and BostonMagnifica are all over the front page!"

"It was probably Spearman's doing," Bates interjected, trying to save face. "Sometimes plaintiffs' lawyers want to try their cases in the courtroom of public opinion and influence the jury pool."

"It could be," Billy volunteered. "In light of the upcoming pretrial hearing with the new judge, maybe he's hoping the next judge reads the print media so he or she can be swayed this way or that way."

"Well," huffed Falcone, "with the money I'm paying your law firm, I would think that the first thing you'd do is get a gag order in place. That way we're protected from all this horrendous publicity. Haven't you handled these kinds of cases before?"

"Yes, Mr. Falcone, I have, and we expected to get the gag order in place. But, we had no idea Spearman would find out one of our partners had dated the judge." As he said this, Billy looked over at Bates.

"Amateurs!" cried Falcone, slamming his fists on the conference table. "What'cha think? That this is a run-of-the-mill case? One of your usual med mal cases that's just going to go away? Merck has spent a *billion dollars* defending thousands of lawsuits!" Falcone was red around the collar, his carotid quite visible,

becoming louder and louder. "Are all the lawyers down in South
Texas this dumb? Or do I have to spell it out for you?"

Billy did not move or say a word. He was pissed beyond
words. No client had ever insulted him like that. He bit his tongue
but kept looking straight at Falcone thinking of ways to respond
and put the little New Yorker in his place. Actually, Billy wanted
to reach across and punch him dead smack across the nose.
Except his mind went blank, and his limbs felt numb and he was
unable to move.

Falcone continued to ramble on, and Bates did not dare to
stop him. After all, he was paying the bills—big ones. Thousands
and thousands of dollars.

"Can't you see that if we draw attention to this case and the
trial lawyers get a hold of it, we're doomed? Hasn't Vioxx taught
you anything? Phen Phen? Silicone implants? Dow? We might as
well pack our bags, file for bankruptcy, and go home."

"It won't happen again," said Billy, as he pictured those poor
souls in Worcester standing in line at the unemployment office,
himself included.

"How are you going to fix this?"

"We'll shut them up," Bates intervened, trying to diffuse the
situation. "Right away. We'll go to the judge, right, Billy? We'll ask
the judge to restrain the papers, the media from printing stories—
even Spearman and his client—from talking to anyone."

"Yes, Mr. Bates. We'll try," answered Billy. He did not know
what else to say. He was still too shocked to come up with an
appropriate response. The last time he'd been called an ignorant
piece of shit or some similar slur had been as a teenager after his
sister Lucía had been brutally raped. The farm owners—the parents of the rapist—had kicked his entire family off the farm. "Do
you think the sheriff is going to believe a family of dumb migrant
workers? Get off our farm, you fuckin' wetbacks!" the owners had
shouted as Billy and his family packed up their beat-up pickup
truck and made their humiliating exit in the middle of the night.
That had been his family's last trip up north.

"Billy," Falcone said, looking into Billy's eyes, "listen to me,
boy. I want this thing settled, yesterday! You hear? I don't care how

you get it done, but get it done! And I want confidentiality . . . and seal the entire file, *comprende, señor?* You think you can do that? Or do we need to get somebody else in here to deal with Spearman? Do I need somebody else to close the deal? To find another law firm?"

"No, sir. I can do it," Billy uttered. The words still resonated in his head as if it were just yesterday . . . *Dumb, fucking Mexicans. Get the hell off our farm, you fucking greasers.*

"All right, no more screwups," Falcone ordered and gestured to Billy, "I'm through with you. You're dismissed."

Billy quickly gathered his papers from the table as he thought of several different ways to torture and disembowel Falcone. He left the room, feeling a raging ball of mixed emotions in the pit of his stomach.

BACK AT HOME in New York, Falcone's desk was littered with the latest studies, publications and journals discussing the tens of thousands who had been left homeless and the impact Rita and Katrina were having on the nation. In his hand, he held the latest newsletter from the *National Institute of Health.* He'd been reading an article addressing the surge in new mental disorders, including post-traumatic stress cases in the hurricane-ravaged states.

As he stood by the window wondering about BM's future and the Ray lawsuit, the phone rang. He moved away from the window, took his place behind his desk and picked up the receiver.

"Hello?"

"It's me," said Malcolm Reed, "got a minute?"

"Go ahead."

"The president is 100 percent behind Zerevrea for the mental healthcare initiative. He'll announce it publicly on Tuesday in a televised address. He's committed to helping the Gulf States."

Falcone jumped up from his seat, "Perfect! Our marketing campaign is in full swing. And now with the White House officially behind us, we should start posting some really big numbers."

"In his address, Bailey will declare the entire area to be in a mental health crisis," Reed added, "followed by the introduction to FEMA's voucher program for a year's worth of free Zerevrea."

Seeing dollar signs, Falcone pushed his luck. "Malcolm, do you think we can also get the Pentagon to endorse Zerevrea for the soldiers coming back from Iraq?"

"Sal," paused Reed, ignoring the CEO's last request, "before we get ahead of ourselves, I have to ask you one thing. Is this drug safe? The truth. I hate to ask, but . . . I need to know."

"Come again?"

"I mean, we would not want to cause the president any further embarrassment . . . you know . . . with his approval ratings at their lowest level in years . . . "

"You have nothing to worry about," confirmed Falcone. "Zerevrea is very safe and effective. It is habit-forming only in the folks that have had bouts with drug addiction. All others have nothing to be concerned about. It will help the good folks down in the Gulf Coast regain their lives. You'll see."

"Okay, then."

"Talk to you soon."

"Bye."

CHAPTER 13

"THAT'S MY LAST offer," shouted Billy into the phone, "take it or leave it." It was Friday, and the jury in the Myers trial was still deadlocked. They had been deadlocked now for an entire week—something that had never happened to Billy. In the last five years, every time the jurors had come back for Billy and his clients, they had done it the same day. His victories had been clean, swift and fast.

Judge Ramón had finally given the jurors the Allen Charge, a legal instruction designed to make the jurors feel guilty and incompetent for failing to reach a verdict. He ordered them to come to some sort of verdict. Otherwise, the case would have to be tried again with another jury at the expense of all taxpayers, the litigants and precious judicial resources.

But, despite the Allen Charge, there had been no verdict. The jurors were still hung, and now Judge Ramón was contemplating declaring a mistrial. Frustrated with the jury's inability to reach a verdict, the court had called the attorneys and had admonished both Hoffman and Billy to try to get the case resolved. Both attorneys were on the phone trying to find common ground.

"My girl won't take less than two hundred thousand," cried Hoffman on the other end. "She's got her mind set on that number."

"Well, it's one-fifty or nothing. Which would you rather have as attorney fees? Forty percent of a hundred fifty thousand or 40 percent of zero? The video of her dancing topless in Cancun is nothing. I got more surprises for her," bluffed Billy.

"Okay, fine," complained Hoffman. "I'll have to find a way to convince her to take the one-fifty."

"I'll have Nancy prepare the settlement docs. Why don't you make yourself useful and call the court and tell Judge Ramón the case has been settled . . . to go ahead and dismiss the jury," indicated Billy as he hung up the phone. He pulled a large manila envelope from under a stack of files.

Not quite satisfied with Dr. Myers' trial outcome, Billy had experienced, for the first time in years a wave of slight disappointment. Although in legal circles such settlement would have been considered a defense victory and he should have been thrilled—settling what could have been a "home run" of a case for nuisance value, and averting a costly disaster—Billy would have preferred a jury verdict declaring that Hoffman's client take nothing. He was worried. Were his trial skills waning? Was he losing his touch?

As he pondered these issues, he opened the thin envelope labeled "Ray v. BostonMagnifica." He poured out its contents. It contained Hector's latest investigative research: an old folded newspaper, copies of the EMS reports and Hector's typed witness statements. There was also a yellow sticky note from Hector that said, "Billy, I'm trying to find Croutoux. Looks like the guy fell off the face of the earth."

In the middle of the "Obituaries" section, there was the picture of a smiling Tomas Ray in his Marine uniform. The large obituary read in part, "Tomas Ray, 41, a well-known Laredo attorney, passed away Saturday, January 28, 2005, in Laredo, Texas. Known to his friends, business associates, colleagues and family as 'Tommy,' he was born on December 11, 1963, in Laredo, Texas, a descendant of Don Bartolomé Reyes, who was a surveyor for the King of Spain and received land grants in Willacy and Webb Counties for thousands of acres. Tommy grew up in Laredo and attended public schools before joining the Marines during the Persian Gulf War."

Billy stopped reading, put the obituary aside and slowly unfolded a magazine article. His eyes grew wide as he read the story's title: "Massacre on the Rio Grand." It was *Texas Monthly*'s own scathing investigation as to what had transpired that winter morning in Laredo, with interviews of the neighbors, cops, EMS and even Gina Yturria Ray, the plaintiff in the BostonMagnifica litigation.

Billy's heart felt as if it were about to jump out of his chest as he flipped through the pages. The article spelled disaster for his promotion and his client. *Man! What's going on here? Now there's an article in* Texas Monthly? *Falcone is gonna shit. Jesus Christ!*

De La Mota, the reporter writing the feature, started the piece by publishing excerpts of the murder investigation, which, in turn, had led to the lawsuit pending in Federal Court in Laredo. There were pictures of Tommy Ray and his family celebrating Charro Days; of Melissa Andarza, the probation officer; and of Mr. Guerra, the postal worker, in uniform and their mourning families.

The story covered the Ray family and its Laredo roots. It spoke of Tommy's military service, legal career and community involvement. It quoted Gina Ray as saying, "Zerevrea and its maker, BostonMagnifica, were responsible for all the mayhem and destruction. There was nothing wonderful about Zerevrea, the so-called 'miracle drug,' and its manufacturer as well as the FDA knew this . . . they were in bed together. The jury will undoubtedly conclude that BostonMagnifica was responsible for the death of my husband and the deaths of Mr. Guerra and Ms. Andarza as well."

The reporter then interviewed the families of the postal worker and the probation officer. Even their families could not blame Tommy Ray. Tommy Ray had been a wonderful neighbor and a distinguished citizen who would even take time off at Christmas to bake and give away his world famous *choco-flan* and his famous *tamales de dulce*—pink masa delicacies with brandy-soaked raisins, walnuts and shredded coconut. The neighbors loved him. When Ms. Zambrano, the divorcee next door, locked herself out of the house, Tommy Ray was there. When the Homeowners' Association needed free legal assistance, Tommy Ray would cut out of work early and help out at their meetings. And so on and so forth, the praises went on. Everyone that knew him agreed that "he had to be out of his mind to have committed the killings. There was no other way to explain it . . . "

Insiders within the Laredo Police Department and the district attorney's office confirmed that they, too, were scratching their heads in frustration. Why had Tommy Ray shot two innocent bystanders? Why had he then put a gun to his head that fateful Saturday morning? What was the motivation for this gruesome tragedy? It was the mystery of mysteries.

De La Mota then quoted academics for the French, British and Canadian governments in charge of the agencies regulating drugs such as Zerevrea. These foreign governments had grown concerned after the suicide rate and bouts of unexplained violent behavior in their countries had skyrocketed. In particular, Dr. Mark Steely, who had done extensive research on the impact of SSRIs on the brain stated, "the only way to counteract the over-promotion and over-selling of these drugs by the pharmaceutical industry is to properly warn the public and educate the doctors. If Washington and the FDA refuse to ban these dangerous drugs, then the FDA should, at minimum, require bigger, better, stronger black box warnings in all their packaging."

The story had become more and more difficult to digest, but Billy forced himself to finish it. The article ended by quoting U.S. Senator Andy Del Toro, who declared that he had the votes to create an independent agency to scrutinize the FDA and the drug companies. "It is time to reign in the drug makers and look after America's safety."

At that moment, Billy Bravo wished he had enough money in his pockets to pull all the copies of *Texas Monthly* from circulation, pile them high and set them on fire. He was not looking forward to Monday. What was Falcone going to say?

"SO TELL ME," Yami started when Billy answered her phone call, "are you done yet? Are you coming home?"

"I'm wrapping it up as we speak," explained Billy, still reeling from the *Texas Monthly* article.

"How much longer?"

"An hour," said Billy. "Why?"

"Your dad has been calling over here. He's worried about Hurricane Emily. Wants to know if you are going to go board up the beach house or if you want him to go do it?"

There was silence.

"Billy, are you still there? Do we have a bad connection?"

"Yes, princess. I'm sorry. I was just thinking. I'd forgotten about that godforsaken hurricane."

"They say it could very well become a category five. And now, it looks like it's coming this way."

"What a pain!" exclaimed Billy. "This is not something I need right now. I'm gonna have to ask Dad to go handle it. Have him ask Armando, his neighbor, see if he'll help. I'll pitch them some money."

"But, isn't your dad too old? Can he handle getting up on a ladder to board up the windows on the second floor?"

"Armando will do the heavy labor. Dad'll be fine."

"We should have just installed the electric storm shutters when we built the house. We wouldn't be in this predicament," Yami said smugly.

"Let's go to dinner, no?" Billy said, quickly switching topics. He'd rather not talk about the beach house, for it was a source of tremendous displeasure. He and Yami had almost gotten divorced over the choice of flooring. Tile or hardwoods? Saltillo or ceramic? Bamboo or cherry wood? They had gone round and round for two months and even ended up three hundred thousand over budget.

"By the time you get home, it'll be eight o'clock. Are you sure?"

"Why not? I've been craving Terranova's," Billy replied. Having been to church recently, he was thinking of bringing up the Karin Palmer situation to his wife. Maybe it was time to nip the whole thing in the bud and face the music.

"Okay, then. At what time?"

"I'll see you there at eight, okay? I'll just finish up at the office and be on my way, all right?"

"You better not keep me waiting, Billy."

CHAPTER 14

THEY MET AT Terranova's on North Tenth Street, the trendiest Italian trattoria frequented by lawyers, doctors and businessmen. Yami was looking forward to seeing her husband. He'd been coming home when everyone was asleep and was gone to the office before sunrise the next morning, always busy flying to Houston or putting out fires in Laredo and Rio Grande City, or rushing to attend hearings in San Antonio, Corpus Christi, Raymondville and Brownsville. Always on the go, go, go.

Heads turned when the two of them walked in together. Yami was a striking female with emerald green eyes, cinnamon hair and ivory skin. A couple of doctors who were entertaining large dinner parties recognized Billy. His firm had defended them on more than one occasion. The trial lawyers in the crowd, on the other hand, had locked horns with Billy in the past and now knew—after reading the papers—that he'd be defending BostonMagnifica. They would be monitoring the trial closely. A loss would mean a flurry of lawsuits and millions in the pockets of plaintiffs' lawyers. A convincing defense verdict, on the other hand, would probably stop everybody and their mother from suing. The nail in the coffin, Billy knew, would be to have the court order the losing party to reimburse all BM's defense costs and attorney fees. Most always, that was a highly effective deterrent.

Billy and Yami were seated in the back in a small corner booth, away from all the power tables.

"Is everything all right?" asked Yami as she took her place inside the booth, reached for the cloth napkin and placed it on her lap. "You look worried."

"I'm just concerned about federal court, that's all," Billy lied.

"*¿Y eso?* Why are you in federal court? I thought you hated it."

"It's not so much that I hate it," clarified Billy, "but I just don't like federal judges. There's a difference."

"I've always heard you say that the three things you hate the most are billing, defending whiney doctors and Federal Court."

"True," he agreed, "I'd rather be in state court on any given day. When you're stuck in federal court, you're always dealing with judges with egos the size of the Grand Canyon."

"Is that because state judges are elected? Is that why they have to behave . . . so they don't get booted out of office?"

"Yep."

"And federal judges are appointed for life, so they get delirious with power and it goes to their heads?"

"You got it."

"Like?" Yami asked as she squeezed some lemon into her ice water.

"I'll give you an example. There's a federal judge in McAllen, Nelda Cassidy. Ever heard of her?"

"No."

"When you appear in front of her, you have to stand at attention. You cannot cross your arms or put your hands in your pockets. God forbid she notices that your shirt collar is unbuttoned or that you've covered your mouth to yawn."

"Why? What happens?"

"She'll accuse you of being disrespectful and threaten you with civil contempt—or, worse, throw your ass in the holding tank."

"For yawning?"

"Yes, even if you do it discreetly and cover your mouth. You're not allowed to yawn in her court, much less cough or scratch an itch. Even if she's not in the courtroom. . . . She's watching you from her chambers and listening in. She's got cameras and microphones, you know?"

"Don't tell me you have to raise your hand to go to the potty, too?" she asked, giggling.

"*Casi casi,*" he answered, "you're close. One time she asked an attorney who drove in from another county three hundred miles away and walked in five minutes late after his case had been called to surrender his federal license."

"You're kidding, right?"

"You know what happened to the attorney whose cell phone went off?"

"Do tell."

"She had the marshal confiscate it. Then, she handed her gavel to the young marshal and asked him to smash the cell to pieces on the floor in a courtroom full of lawyers and spectators."

"*Eso no está bien.*" Yami agreed with her husband. "No wonder you look worried."

"On another occasion, in a criminal prosecution, she threw the defense attorney in the holding tank because the guy wouldn't take it easy on the government's witness, a Border Patrol agent."

Yami took a sip of water. "What do you mean?"

"The defense attorney had the agent on the ropes, about to get him to admit that he had lied, which would have unraveled the government's case and the judge intervened and accused the defense attorney of being a bully, disrespectful to the witness and even had the marshal—right in front of the jurors—go over to counsel's table and arrest the poor bastard!"

"*No es posible.* Really? She had the lawyer arrested?"

"Yep. She's out of control. And get this . . . a buddy of mine from law school had a huge civil case pending in her court . . . but she dismissed his case thirty minutes before jury selection with all the parties in the courtroom."

"She waited till the last minute to throw him out of court?"

"Yes, even though the case had been pending two years in her court and the parties had spent hundreds of thousands of dollars getting there. Even I, as a defense attorney always looking to get cases thrown out, thought that was wrong. If she was gonna summarily grant judgment for the defense and dismiss my buddy's case, she should have done it at the beginning of the case—not after two years of growing expenses, discovery, depositions and contested hearings. Simply idiotic. You just don't grant a defense's motion for summary judgment thirty minutes before jury selection. It's bullshit. The chic's an absolute *tarada* with nothing upstairs."

"Maybe she's lazy and didn't wanna hear it? Didn't want to be in trial for two months."

"Maybe. Who knows? But it was wrong. Simply pathetic. *No vale madre*. Inexcusable."

"Do you think maybe she was delaying having to issue a ruling, trying to give the parties a chance to settle, get it resolved?"

"I doubt it," mumbled Billy.

"What are you gonna have?" Yami asked, changing the subject. She was grinning from ear to ear, just happy to be with her husband.

"A double-scotch on the rocks," answered Billy as he took a menu from Joey, the waiter, now standing next to them. *I'll need a couple of them to gather some courage and come clean with Yami.*

"I'll have a Bellini," said Yami.

"I'll be back in a minute with your drinks," said Joey as he turned around and left for the bar.

"Anyway, if I win this new case," Billy explained, "Bates said I'll be promoted to name partner."

The waiter was back with their drinks momentarily. He set them down on the table in front of Billy and Yami.

"What are we doing about Hurricane Emily?" asked Yami, purposefully ignoring the name partner song-and-dance. "It appears to be heading this way."

"I've already asked my dad to go board up the beach house," Billy answered as he gulped down his Johnny Walker Blue Label. Having married into Yami's upper-crust family had taught Billy to enjoy, now and then, a good glass of eighteen-year-old scotch whiskey. "With the Ray lawsuit now on my plate, I just don't have time to be dealing with Emily. Not when *Texas Monthly* had my client splashed on its cover and I'm about to get an ass-chewing the size of the King Ranch come Monday morning."

"But you had nothing to do with that," Yami said as she reached and buttered a slice of San Antonio sourdough bread from the hand-woven basket at the table. "How's that your fault?"

"Falcone, the CEO for BostonMagnifica," Billy leaned forward and whispered, careful not to be heard by the other patrons in the restaurant, "is an asshole, okay? The guy doesn't care, doesn't understand. Get this . . . the other day, the moron admits to Bates and me that he's been defrauding the federal government out of hundreds of millions of dollars with price-fixing and double-billing schemes."

"Billy," Yami whispered back as she reached over and grabbed his hands, "the pharmaceuticals are a bunch of rats. Everybody knows that. Just look at the headlines: Fraud, fines, federal investigations, racketeering . . . the list is miles long."

The waiter interrupted the exchange. "Are you ready to order?"

"Eh hem," mumbled Yami. "Yes. All right . . . let me see . . . I'll have the petite escargot in red wine with puffed pastry as an appetizer, and, for my main entrée, the farm-raised jumbo prawns on angel hair al olio aglio."

"And for you, sir?"

"I'll have a house salad and your seafood lasagna with cream sauce, the small portion."

"Any dressing?"

"Your house," requested Billy, "the vinaigrette."

"Anything else?" asked the waiter.

"No, that'll do it," said Billy.

"Very well, if you'll excuse me, I'll be back with your snails and house salad, then," Joey said and scurried along.

"Look," Yami started as she sipped on her Bellini, "you just give it your best shot. If you win and make name partner, well then, good for you. We'll all be very proud. But if you lose, and then the client goes bankrupt from all the new lawsuits, well, too bad. Besides, you yourself just told me the client's a scumbag."

After a few moments, the waiter came by and dropped off Yami's fragrant escargot and Billy's crisp side salad.

"I guess I see what you're saying," Billy replied as he delved into his bib and radicchio lettuce salad dripping in a basil and rice wine vinaigrette.

"Sure," Yami said as she picked a bite-sized snail from her plate. "Maybe some of your jurors already know a thing or two about the drug industry. They might have even heard of Susan Lockus?"

"What about her?"

"She was featured in *Reader's Digest* a month ago," Yami explained, "as part of a series on 'Women Who've Made A Difference.' She's an assistant U.S. attorney in Louisiana."

"Oh yeah? What did she do?"

"Well, she tagged TAP Pharmaceuticals for eight hundred million in fines for paying kickbacks and bribes to doctors to get them to prescribe Lupron."

"Ouch!" Billy said. He reached for his scotch and took a sip.

"And she got Bayer to pay two hundred fifty-seven million dollars for switching labels to disguise the drug's true manufacturing origins—a scheme designed to avoid paying rebates to Medicaid programs."

"I guess you're right. They're no saints."

"You want me to keep going?" she asked, as she reached for another snail.

He buttered a piece of sourdough bread. "Yes, go on."

"She then tagged GlaxoSmithKline for eighty-seven million, AstraZeneca for three hundred fifty-five million and Pfizer for forty-nine million for all kinds of fraud, lying, bribery, false labeling and other stuff!"

"Wasn't this stuff also on *Dateline*?" he asked.

"Yes, they recently ran a story on the villains *du jour*. Anyway, don't be so discouraged. Just do your job."

"No telling what I'll find," Billy declared. "As discovery begins, I'll have to roll up my sleeves and plow through boxes of documents, emails, voice messages, internal memos, videoconferencing transcripts, clinical trials, protocols, spreadsheets, and even sales training manuals."

"Maybe since you teach ethics . . . you're afraid of what you might find," she whispered across the table.

"It could be . . . we'll see." He was now working on his lasagna. He motioned the waiter to bring them both refills on their drinks. *Or maybe it's not such a good idea to come clean with you, not here, not now, in a crowded restaurant, with all these people that know us.*

"Mi amor," she interjected, "*¿otro?*"

He loved her Spanish. It was perfect. Not like his, which sounded like Spanglish half of the time. "*Tienes razón.* I don't need another drink. What I need is a double espresso. I'll be working late. I have to go back to the office." *I don't think I can do it. Karin Palmer will have to wait.*

"Again?" she rolled her eyes.

"Yes, I'm sorry," he said as he waved the waiter to come close. "You want dessert?"

"No, I'm fine. Hey, I forgot to tell you," Yami said.

"What is it?"

"Alessandra's volleyball squad advanced to the district qualifiers. And Wicho is testing for his brown belt this coming week."

"Already?"

"Yep. And I finished clearing your closet of all your old clothes and shoes. Everything is boxed up. The Catholic Daughters will come by this weekend to haul them and drop them off at Comet Cleaners. It's for the victims of Hurricanes Rita and Katrina. Your friend . . . um, what's his name?"

"Rick?"

"Yes," said Yami, "his wife, Noemí, came up with the idea. She's a member of the Catholic Daughters and decided to pitch in. So Comet Cleaners is sponsoring the used clothes drive and relief effort for the hurricane victims."

"*¡Qué bien!* I'm glad we could help," replied Billy. "I wish there was more we could do to help those folks. I can't imagine what it must be like to lose everything." *I wonder if the Catholic Daughters can also help husbands in trouble?*

"I'd hate to be in their shoes. *Una verdadera tragedia,*" countered Yami.

"I can't imagine."

"Are we ready to go? I almost forgot. I need to get back home. Alessandra is out on a date. I want to be home when she returns."

"What?" cried Billy. "With whom?"

"Please, don't even start."

"Excuse me," Billy called out to Joey standing nearby, "bring me a refill on my espresso and the tab. Here, take my credit card. Add 15 percent gratuity."

"Thank you. Be right back," replied Joey.

"When did this happen? When did Ale start dating?" asked Billy, totally surprised.

"She's not a little girl anymore, Billy," explained Yami.

"But, but . . . " stuttered Billy, and, before he could ask more questions, he was interrupted by Joey. The waiter handed him a brown leather check presenter. Billy reached for his credit card, put it away and looked one more time at the bill.

"I don't see where you charged my wife for her second Bellini or my refill. You undercharged us."

"Then it's on the house," the waiter said with a nervous grin. "My mistake."

"No, I want to pay for it," clarified Billy, "ring them up. It's only right. I'll wait, but please go and ring us up."

"Go ahead and ring it up," Yami jumped in. "He's the most honest man in the world . . . otherwise he won't be able to sleep tonight. Trust me, his conscience won't let him."

"Yes, ma'am. Right away. I am sorry about that," Joey said, excusing himself.

"Ay, Billy . . . all these years, and you always insist on doing the right thing for anyone," Yami said. "You're always so honest. I guess that's why I still love you."

"I love you, too, princess. I always have, and I always will . . . I promise." His heart skipped a beat. His thoughts immediately turned to Karin Palmer. Flashing images of Billy and Karin in her Jacuzzi high on top of Westlake Hills, drinking champagne, overlooking Austin's skyline.

The waiter interrupted Billy's thoughts and handed him a pen and his credit card. "Here you go. Top copy is yours, Mr. Bravo. I'll keep these other two copies over here. You folks have a nice evening. Sorry about the undercharge."

Billy signed the bill, put the receipts, credit card and wallet away and said, "You have a good night." He reached for Yami and helped her up from the table.

"I HAVE IT all under control. Don't worry. My promotion is just around the corner," said Billy as he gazed into Yami's eyes. They were standing next to Yami's car in the parking lot, holding each other. "I promise, I will slow down right after the promotion. Just bear with me, *princesa*, please. *Te lo prometo*."

"That's what you've been saying . . . since . . . "

"Shhhh," Billy said as he put a finger on her soft lips. "I love you. You know that. I always will, no matter what. Promotion, no promotion, whatever happens . . . *Saidah Yamilé Álvarez de Bravo, siempre te amaré*. Since the first day I laid eyes on you, I've never stopped loving you."

"*Mi amor*," she whispered back and kissed him passionately. She had to admit, even though her husband was a workaholic, there were moments when he could be the most romantic man in the world. Like one Valentine's Day seventeen years ago when they were both in college up at UT Austin. Billy had shown up at her apartment complex, *mariachi*s in tow, and had serenaded her for thirty minutes until Yami's landlord ran him off.

"*Te amo*," repeated Billy, as he pulled his wife close and kissed her again. "You make my life complete."

"Remember when you were in law school and I was working on my master's in global policy? We'd go to Zilker Park, have a picnic and you'd read poems to me by Pablo Neruda, Rubén Darío, Amado Nervo. Life was so simple then."

"I really miss those days," he sighed, and just then, his Black-Berry went off. "*¡Carajo!*" swore Billy, reaching for it, looking to see who was calling. "I gotta take this call, *princesa*. It's one of the experts we want to hire for the Tommy Ray trial."

"Don't answer it. You can call them back, later."

"I'm sorry, I can't."

Yami threw her hands in the air. She could never talk to Billy, not even for a minute. She stormed off and got in her eggshell-colored Hummer. "I'll be at home. *¡Adiós!*" she said, as she slammed the driver's side door shut.

"BILLY BRAVO speaking." He looked at his watch. It was dinner-time in Texas, but on the West Coast folks were still at work.

"Mr. Bravo, this is Doctor Carl Siegel. I am calling from the School of Pharmacology at UCLA. I believe you left a message regarding a case dealing with BostonMagnifica and its new drug Zerevrea?"

"Oh, yes, Dr. Siegel," Billy answered, "thank you for returning my call. I was calling you to see if you would be interested in coming to our side and helping me defend BM."

"Where was the lawsuit filed?" asked the doctor.

"South Texas. Laredo, to be exact, on the Mexican border."

"Tell me about the case," Siegel requested.

"It's a wrongful death lawsuit. A widow is claiming Zerevrea made her husband commit suicide."

"How old was the guy?"

"Mid-forties," explained Billy, "in good health. So far, nothing that would be considered unusual. Apparently, the guy was in good physical and mental health."

"How long had he been taking Zerevrea?"

"Less than a week."

"Are you sure there's no prior history of depression, bipolar disease, paranoia, schizophrenia or some other mental illness?"

"Don't think so."

"How did he die?" Siegel asked.

"Gunshot to the roof of his mouth."

"Military service?"

"Yes."

"Where?"

"His obituary said he served in the Gulf War."

"Um," Doctor Siegel said, "that's interesting . . . ."

"What? What is it?" asked Billy, sounding excited.

"Lots of GIs that fought in the Gulf War came back with post-traumatic stress disorder."

"And?"

"There's an obscure study out there I ran across several years ago where the author discussed the interactions of these kinds of drugs with PTSD. The research suggested that this might be a really bad combination with tragic results."

"Would the drug companies know?" Billy asked.

"I don't know. The study was done somewhere in Europe . . . published in some obscure medical journal. I think Amsterdam or a place like that. I don't even recall . . . but my gut instinct, however, tells me that the drug companies would probably know of this phenomenon."

"I see."

"Does your client's packaging contain black box warnings?"

"Yes," replied Billy, "but the plaintiff's lawyer claims those warnings are not adequate in light of all the overpromotion. In other words, the overpromotion on the airwaves is neutralizing any meaningful effect the black box warnings are intended to have. Obviously, the same warnings would not be adequate if my client knew or has known all along of the problems with Zerevrea and PTSD. I would probably agree with the plaintiff's lawyer. You follow?"

"Sure, I understand. The question then becomes if the drug maker knows of the fatal interaction with PTSD, or some other risk, and should the black box warnings be more specific in order to address this added danger?"

"Exactly!"

"Well," said Dr. Siegel, "do you have any evidence that BM knew of these added dangers or contraindications? Anything on the mixing of Zerevrea and PTSD?"

"No, nothing I've seen so far," replied Billy.

"Would the plaintiff's lawyer know of evidence that could prove your client knew . . . that your client had knowledge . . . that the present black box warnings they're using are not enough?"

"Like, a smoking gun?"

"Yes."

"I don't know," Billy continued. "I'm afraid that if the info is out there, Spearman, the plaintiff's lawyer, is capable of getting his hands on it. I sure as hell wouldn't discount him yet. It's too early in the game to know for sure."

"The study I read . . . " Siegel remembered, "I want to say it covered victims of natural disasters suffering from PTSD."

"And?"

"The scientists found that folks with this disorder, when pumped with SSRIs, soon heard voices telling them to kill. When the conflict in their heads proved too much, instead of harming their loved ones, they obtained relief by killing themselves."

"I see," Billy said, "so it is possible for these drugs to cause such horror?"

"Sure," Siegel said, "the question here is, can the plaintiff prove it in court? Does the evidence exist to make the case? Can a plaintiff prove that it was actually Zerevrea that pushed the guy over the edge? One thing is to surmise that it must have been the drug, for whatever reason. Another is to actually have proof that it was the drug. What you lawyers call the 'but-for' link or 'proximate cause.' Have you deposed the widow?"

"I plan to meet with her and her lawyer first to see if we can settle this thing without having to fire a single shot, without a trial."

"I see. What does your client say about this? Is there something you should worry about in terms of bad evidence?" asked Siegel.

"I flew up to Boston and met with the scientists that developed the drug and performed the clinical trials. I didn't get a good feeling. But they never came out and admitted anything to me."

"Knowing what we know about the industry, there are probably documents which, in the hands of the wrong party, may expose your client to a great deal of liability."

"We'll see what turns up," Billy said, quickly changing topics and adding, "So, would you be interested in working for us as an expert?"

"Consulting or testifying expert?"

"Testifying."

"Can you afford me?" Siegel said, laughing.

"Name your price."

"I need a twenty-five-thousand-dollar retainer just to review the case. If I am convinced this is something I want to get involved with, we'll sign documents, and I'll bill at four hundred an hour for any work I do on the file. However, you must know that I bill a thousand an hour for in-courtroom testimony and depositions, plus my per diem allowance for work outside of LA, along with travel expenses and incidentals."

Billy's mouth dropped. "Anything else?"

"No."

"I'll have my office overnight the lawsuit and other docs we've gathered."

"Don't forget the retainer."

"Of course. It'll be in the package."

"All right, then, thanks. I'll call you within a week or two to compare notes after I've received the package and the retainer."

"Bye."

CHAPTER 15

FIVE O'CLOCK SUNDAY found Billy eating a cold, days-old *papas-con-huevo* breakfast taco in his dimly lit office. It was one of the many different foods brought to the office by the staff on weekdays. Too tired to go out and fetch some fast food, he'd found it in the back of the fridge behind someone's leftovers from the Luby's down the street. Aside from the little time he took on Friday to take his wife out to dinner, it had been a hectic weekend. He was trying to get his billing done, review discovery responses for other cases, prepare deposition summaries, finish several trial notebooks missing cross-examination questions—all while attempting to organize his office. He and Hector were the only ones working.

As he was finishing his stale taco, Hector came on the intercom. "Billy, are you there? It's your dad on the line. He says it's urgent and that he'd tried to reach you on your cell, but you weren't picking up."

Billy looked at his BlackBerry to find eight missed calls. "Oh man, I forgot I put it on silent after I got in bed last night. Thanks. I'll get him on line one."

"Hey, I forgot to mention," Hector said, "my dad's out on bond. Goodwin is handling his immigration case. Thanks for your help."

"Don't mention it. Glad I could help." He pressed line one.

"*M'ijo*, are you there?" asked Don Guillermo Bravo, almost out of breath.

"What is it?"

"I know you wanted me to board up your beach house, but I need the keys to get in. By the way, have you been watching the Weather Channel?" his father asked, sounding alarmed.

"No, I've been busy. Why?"

"Emily *está azotando* Cancún. She's barreling down on the Yucatan Penninsula. The forecasters predict she'll make landfall along the Texas coast in a few more days."

"So, it's finally moving, eh?"

"Yes. It's a category three hurricane right now. They're saying it will get stronger."

"Are you sure you can handle it?" asked Billy.

"Yes. I've asked Armando to help me. We'll pick up the supplies here in McAllen tomorrow morning, load them up on La Chula and head on out there. Be back on Tuesday evening. You won't have to move a finger."

Billy's old man loved to feel useful. He was always lending a hand and even volunteered to drive Wicho to all his after-school activities. Alessandra, on the other hand, was another story. She felt embarrassed and horrified to be seen driving around in Grandpa Guillermo's beloved pickup truck, La Chula, a bright red 1985 Chevy.

"Thanks, Dad. Please be careful." He hung up the phone and got on the Internet to visit the National Weather Service Web site. It showed Hurricane Emily's latest projected path, and now the forecast called for the storm to land somewhere between Corpus Christi and the Mexican coastal town of Tampico.

CHAPTER 16

"**H**E DID WHAT?**"** Billy Bravo shouted into his cell phone. Officer Puckett, with the South Padre Island Police Department, was calling from Don Guillermo Bravo's cell phone. It was an emergency.

"Come again?" Billy asked as he dropped the box of exhibits on the steps leading out of the courthouse. He'd had an early pretrial hearing scheduled for another case that Monday. The hearing had taken all day, and now he was heading back to the office. "He had a heart attack?"

"Either a heart attack," Officer Puckett repeated, "or a stroke. EMS is taking him to Mercy Medical Center in Brownsville. That's the nearest hospital. It doesn't look good, sir. I'm sorry."

"Is the guy who was helping him board up the house, is he there with you, officer?"

"Yes, he's in custody . . . I've got to call Border Patrol and turn him over to them."

"Could I speak with him? Could you put him on the line?" Billy begged.

"Hold on. Let me put him on, but you owe me, *compadre*. I'm not supposed to . . . it's against department regulations."

Ten seconds went by. It felt like ten minutes. Billy's forehead was covered in sweat, his pulse racing.

"*¿Bueno?*" asked Armando, sounding nervous.

"Armando, *soy yo*, Billy."

"*Ah, sí. Dígame, Señor Licenciado,*" said Armando.

"*¿Qué pasó?*" cried Billy.

"We were working, unloading more of the lumber and supplies, getting ready to start again, trying to hurry and finish up, when your daddy started complaining that he did not feel right. Next thing I know, he's on the floor, clutching his left arm, telling me to call an ambulance. Before he lost consciousness, he also told me to call you. The officer found your number in his cell."

"I didn't know you were here illegally. Let me find you an immigration lawyer and try to get you out of this mess," said Billy as his head started spinning. "Do you want me to call your wife? Tell her what happened?"

"*Por favor, Señor Licenciado.* May God bless you."

Jesus Christ! All these years I've known Armando, I had no idea he was here illegally. Why am I surprised? Our gardener, the maid and even our cook are all here illegally. I've told Yami to get rid of them. It's only gonna get us in trouble. And now this?

THE WAITING area outside the intensive care unit had a TV mounted on the wall, a vending machine and various magazines scattered throughout the quiet room. The TV was tuned to the Weather Channel. The weather projections showed Hurricane Emily making landfall anywhere between La Pesca, Mexico and Corpus Christi. The storm was now over the Yucatan Peninsula, traveling northwest at fifteen miles per hour. Soon, Emily would be in the Gulf of Mexico.

Billy was looking at the monitor, but none of it was registering. He was waiting to hear from the doctors and waiting for Yami to arrive from McAllen with his kids and sister in tow.

He was looking around the room for something to read when Doctor Ahmed Zamir, a staff surgeon with Mercy Medical, wearing green scrubs and a matching mask, approached him.

"Sir?" he called in Billy's direction. "Are you a relative of Mr. Bravo?" There were only two other individuals in the waiting room at that hour.

"Yes," Billy answered nervously as he shot up from his seat. "Is he going to be okay?"

"It's too early to tell," the doctor replied in his heavy Middle Eastern accent. "We've stabilized him, and we're running some tests right now . . . ."

"Was it a heart attack?" interrupted Billy.

"Yes. We want to say he's going to need bypass surgery, but if we do it right now, we don't think he'll survive. He's too weak. We'll have to wait a few days . . . see if he regains his strength. That's the only way we'll be able to operate on him."

"What about his mental functions?" Billy asked.

"We don't know at this point in time. He's stable, though. I would suspect he'll regain some functions. I must ask you, though, just in case . . . did he have his affairs in order?"

"You mean did he leave a will?"

"Yes."

"Yes, he's had a will for years. I prepared it for him, along with his directive and medical power of attorney," Billy said, shaking his head, still dumbfounded.

"Well, let's prepare for the worst and hope for the best," replied Dr. Zamir. "That's all we can do. We'll do all we can for him here, I promise. You can go in to see him, but he needs his rest."

"Doctor?" added Billy.

"Yes?"

"Could we move him to another hospital? You know, with the hurricane on its way and there being a chance the hospital may lose power."

"I'm afraid not," Zamir explained. "He's too weak. I'm concerned that if we try to move him, he won't make it. We'll just have to deal with the hurricane as best as we can. The hospital's equipped with power generators. We should come out okay."

"I see."

"We're just going to have to wait it out."

"Okay," Billy said softly, the room spinning faster and faster all around him.

"*PAPI, SOY YO, Billy, tu hijo,*" Billy said as he rubbed his dad's forehead. "I'm here, daddy. Can you hear me?"

The old man struggled to open his eyes as he slowly turned to face his son. His left arm shook as he reached out. "*M'ijo, . . .*" he said in a soft, trembling whisper. He was hooked up to several monitors and an oxygen machine. Quietly moving about in the background, there was a nurse checking his vitals, looking at the monitors and changing the IV solution bags.

"*No te esfuerces, descansa, viejito.* Don't strain yourself, I'm here. You rest. You don't have to say anything."

With great difficulty, the old man looked up to his son and strained to touch Billy's face. "*Necesitas saber* . . . you, need to know . . . something."

"Please, *viejo*, don't say anything. I know. I know. I love you, too," replied Billy, tears in his eyes.

"*Ya es hora* . . . " mumbled his father, "it's . . . time."

"Shhhh." Billy put his finger on his father's lips. "Rest, Daddy. Don't say a thing. *Por favor, descansa.*"

"For the . . . truth," he said straining himself.

"*¿La verdad?*" asked Billy, thinking his old man was delirious.

"*Cuando naciste,*" struggled the old man.

"When I was born?"

"*Mami y yo* . . . "

"*¿Sí?*" Billy got close to his old man to hear him better, both their foreheads touching together.

"*Pagamos* . . . "

"Okay, you and Mom paid," repeated Billy as he made eye contact with the nurse. She instantly realized what Billy wanted, gave them their privacy and quickly exited the room.

"*Partera* . . . ."

"A midwife?"

"*Sí.*"

"Why did you pay a midwife?" asked Billy.

"For you."

"For me?"

"*Sí.*"

"I don't understand," said Billy, "*¿qué quieres decir?*"

"*Meee* . . . " struggled the old man, "*eeentimos.*"

"You lied?" asked Billy, without a clue. *What does that mean? They paid a midwife. They lied?* He was baffled.

"I'm so sorry," said the old man, "forgive me. We . . . only . . . wan . . . ted the . . . best for you . . . "

"I don't understand?" asked Billy, mystified.

"To . . . say . . . you . . . born . . . in U.S."

"What?" asked Billy, now confused, "I don't understand."

The old man did not answer and just continued to ramble on. "Please forgive me, Billy." His breathing became more labored, and he was now panting. "Please . . . *perdóname.*" He stopped talking.

"Okay, don't worry about it," said Billy, putting his index finger on his dad's lips. "Don't say anything, daddy. *Descansa,* rest, save your energy . . . you'll tell me when we get you home. You're delirious, probably the morphine kicking in."

"*Ah, también,*" started the old man again.

"Shhhh," followed Billy, trying to get him to stop. "You need to rest, please."

"*Tu mamá era . . .* was . . . " He let out a big sigh, and his grip on Billy's arm went soft. The morphine finished kicking in. The old man dozed off.

"What about Mom? *Papi?*" cried Billy in anguish. "Never mind . . . it's okay, *descansa.* Get some rest."

With his hand, Billy pulled the blanket up and covered his old man all the way to his chest. Billy hurt as he had never hurt before. He felt an empty pit in his stomach. What made it ten times worse and almost unbearable was the guilt that accompanied the pain now burning through his heart.

CHAPTER 17

"**L**OOK WHAT I found," said Hector, as he waved some letters in his hand. Grinning from ear to ear, he announced, "Croutoux's son said he'd found it among his daddy's papers. By the way, Croutoux is dead. He's been dead for close to a year. The authorities up in Blue Lake Mountain, where the guy retired, are still investigating his demise. The guy died under suspicious circumstances."

"Yeah?" asked Billy, sounding depressed. Dr. Zamir had called to say that his father had taken a turn for the worse. The doctor was considering the possibility of having to open him up again. Due to his poor condition, they had missed some blockage the first time.

"Yep," explained Hector. "I told his son that I worked for a plaintiff's firm in Texas about to file a lawsuit against his daddy's old employer. I wanted to know if he could pitch in, lend a hand."

"He bought your story, eh? Just like that?"

"If you saw him, you would understand. Remember the movie *Revenge of the Nerds*?"

"Yes."

"*Así*. Like that. I betcha he's got a drawer full of pocket protectors."

"How did you track him down?"

"It was easy. You forget, that's my job. Anyway, the guy works for Dell in Roundrock."

"So, what did you find?"

"Here . . . read it for yourself," said Hector as he handed Billy a two-page letter:

BOSTONMAGNIFICA PHARMACEUTICALS
February 3, 2004

Dear Doctor,

BM Pharmaceuticals wishes to update you in reference to the prescribing information for Zerevrea (stepflaxin HPC). We're doing this to reflect newly obtained safety data—not yet published—on the use of stepflaxin in children, adolescents and people suffering from PTSD.

In recent clinical studies involving children and older patients exhibiting signs of post-traumatic stress disorder, usefulness was not established. There were also increased events among those patients on Zerevrea v. placebo of hostility, suicidal-thinking and related adverse incidents, such as self-harm, aggressive behaviors and suicidal ideation.

Please remember that Zerevrea is not recommended for use in pediatric patients and patients suffering from post-traumatic stress disorder. Therefore, we want to caution you:

Warning! <u>Pediatric Patients/Patients with PTSD. Effectiveness in such patients has not been established. In a number of trials dealing with children and individuals exhibiting PTSD, there were marked instances of increased aggressive behaviors, especially in post-traumatic stress disorder patients, including suicide-related events, along with severe suicidal ideation and self-harm.</u>

Our tests indicate that these common events lead to discontinuation in at least 9 percent of children and adolescents treated with Zerevrea, and at a rate five times that of placebo, were as follows (percentages listed for Zerevrea and placebo, respectively): Anxiety studies, hostility (6%, < 1%) and suicidal ideation (9%, 0%); PTSD studies, abnormal changed behavior (7%, 0%). In these clinical trials there were thirty known attempts at suicide, with increased frequency of abnormal behaviors.

Stepflaxin is in a class of drugs called serotonin reuptake inhibitors. Zerevrea is indicated in adults for the treatment of anxiety, depression and other mental disorders. You should be alert to signs of suicidal ideation in children, adolescents and patients with PTSD, if taking our drug. Always reassess the benefits v. the risks.

If you decide to discontinue the patient from using Zerevrea, please do it gradually. Any reduction should be done under medical supervision.

BostonMagnifica keeps close watch on all its products and is committed to providing the medical community with the latest most updated information.

If you wish to report any adverse incidents associated with Zerevrea, please call our hotline at 1.800.555.5555. Or you can mail any relevant event information directly to BostonMagnifica, Global Safety Committee & Epidemiology, by fax to 1.888.555.5555 or by mail to BostonMagnifica, 600 Market Square, Worcester, MA 02339. We also encourage you to report adverse event information to the FDA's MedWatch Reporting System by phone (1.800.FDA-2004).

BostonMagnifica will send you new labels for your entire stock of Zerevrea. As soon as the FDA approves these improved black box warnings, you should prominently display them, over the old labels. We hope these new labels will be approved to also warn of the newly discovered dangers and negative interactions when used in PSTD patients.

Sincerely,

Felix Croutoux, MD
Head of Clinical Trials and Research, Director of Global Affairs

"Wow," gasped Billy. "So, they knew that Zerevrea interacts negatively with PTSD. Do you think Spearman has a copy of this letter?"

"I don't know."

Billy reached for the cup of coffee sitting on his desk and wondered what else Hector would find. He took a sip and thought about Falcone, Drummond and the meeting up in Worcester, just days before. Here was his firm's investigator using a little elbow grease, the gift of gab and a few white lies and—not two weeks into the case—he had already found a damning piece of evidence. What other surprises were out there?

"Do you know what this means for the hurricane victims?" asked Billy, shaking his head, "particularly if they have PTSD?"

"The end?" asked Hector, eyes wide open.

"Sounds like it!"

"Anyway," continued Hector, "the son said he still needed to go through his old man's things. He'd just gotten himself appointed executor of his old man's estate, and he was in the middle of preparing the inventory."

"Well," Billy continued, as he reread the letter again, "Zerevrea is definitely not for folks with PTSD or children. I wonder if Tommy Ray had PTSD? His obituary said he had fought in the Gulf War."

"It could be. I never met a war veteran who did not have this or that. Maybe he was really screwed up," said Hector.

BILLY'S EYES were glued to the Weather Channel as he drank coffee in his large kitchen at home. He was debating whether to drive to Brownsville to see his old man or attempt to finish boarding up his beach home. Hurricane Emily was sitting stationary, two hundred miles southeast of South Padre Island. The "category four" hurricane was expected to make landfall on the Texas coast in twenty-four hours. Officials had given the island's residents strict orders to start evacuating.

As Billy's eyes remained glued to the TV, the ticker at the bottom of the TV screen read, "Texas Gulf Coast residents hunker down for Hurricane Emily—Drug giant Merck dealt another blow in San Antonio lawsuit . . . jury awards fifty million . . . three thousand more lawsuits filed nationwide following news of SA verdict."

Billy was scratching his head, trying to figure out his next move when the words "Breaking News" flashed on the TV screen. The next take was of a reporter in front of the White House announcing Bailey's mental healthcare initiative for the Gulf States. The White House had finally announced that any hurricane victim that qualified could now receive additional FEMA vouchers to obtain free therapy and counseling for any mental condition for up to two years. The proposal also included vouchers for a year's supply of Zerevrea, a new "miracle drug." The surprising White House initiative was expected to help Bailey in the polls.

THE HOME DEPOT on Bicentennial Boulevard was a zoo. Billy and Wicho were each pulling a lumber cart and a flatbed loaded with inch-thick sheets of plywood, two-by-sixes, power generators, cordless drills, boxes of screws, batteries and flashlights. Meanwhile, Alessandra and Yami were down at the grocery store loading up on ice, canned goods, gallons of water and other non-perishable items. Billy had instructed Yami to top off the gas tank on the Hummer, go by and pick up three large ice chests and find a weather radio somewhere. Any other year, Billy would have just boarded up his McAllen home and had his entire family get the hell out of town, except this year his father was still in the ICU down in neighboring Brownsville. They would have to hunker down and ride out Emily.

"This is exciting," said Wicho with a smile.

"Oh, yeah? You really think so?" Billy asked, sounding worried.

"Sure, dad. I get to board up the house and spend time with you . . . be your helper."

"I just hope we don't take a direct hit from Emily. I was about your age when Hurricane Beulah tore through the Valley and destroyed everything in its path. You're too young to have to experience something like that."

"I know what can happen, Dad. I watched the news during Rita and Katrina. I saw what happened in New Orleans."

"You watch the news?" asked Billy sounding amazed, suddenly realizing how little he knew about his son.

"Mom and I watch the news every evening together, Dad. She lets me watch while I do my homework. I find it easier to get through my work."

"Well, I just hope Grandpa's hospital doesn't lose power, like what happened to those poor folks in New Orleans."

"Is Papo going to be okay?" asked Wicho. "Who's going to be with him during the storm?"

"I'm going to try to go see him after we finish boarding up the house."

"What about our beach house?"

"Papo boarded most of it. It should be okay," lied Billy. He didn't really know. Armando had said that they were almost finished, but he wasn't so sure.

"I'd like to go visit Papo. Can I go with you, Dad?"

"Sure," Billy said. He looked around to see if the lines were moving, but it was the same everywhere. The lines were slowly inching forward, bit by bit.

"I'd sure like to see him. Make sure he's okay. He must feel very lonely," said Wicho as he pushed the flatbed behind his father. "I haven't seen him since he took me to eat wings and watch the U.S.-Mexico soccer game."

"This is all my fault," Billy replied, feeling guilty as hell. "Had I gone down to Padre to board up the house myself, none of this would have happened. Right now, you, Mom, Ale, Papo and Tía Aracely would all be driving to San Antonio to get away for a few days and have a ball. Ride out the storm. Enjoy the riverwalk."

"Oh! I've been wanting you to take me to a Spurs game. That would have been awesome! I love Tim Duncan."

"You do?"

"Yes."

"I had no idea."

"He's averaged 11.5 rebounds per game. He plays center and forward, and he's been the Spurs MVP year after year."

"How long have you been following the Spurs?" Billy asked.

"Three years now."

"Really?" replied Billy as he started handing some of the supplies to the clerk behind the register. "I never knew."

CHAPTER 18

"**Y**OU WANTED TO SEE ME?" asked Billy taking his place at the large conference table. After the news that Merck had been dealt another blow in San Antonio and Hurricane Emily had fallen apart over the King Ranch (which meant the airports had finally reopened), Falcone had demanded a meeting with Bates and Billy Bravo down in McAllen. He wanted an update on the case, and he wanted it *pronto*.

Falcone made a pit stop in Houston in the company jet, picked up Bates and now both were in the McAllen office. Falcone did not care that the hurricane had slammed South Padre Island or that many of the coastal communities in South Texas were barely functioning, much less that the McAllen airport was hardly operational. He wanted to know why his attorneys had failed to keep the case out of the headlines. Why was there now an article in the *Texas Monthly*?

Bates noticed the frown on Billy's face as the attorney loosened his tie and removed his reading glasses. "Billy, I'm sorry about your old man's heart attack. Is he gonna be all right?" Bates chimed in, looking over at Falcone to gauge his reaction.

"He died, boss," Billy said nervously. "We're making funeral arrangements as we speak. We're burying him in the next day or two."

"I'm so sorry," replied Bates, not knowing what else to say. Billy was about to get another ass-chewing by Falcone.

"Billy," interrupted Falcone.

Billy sat up. "Yes, sir?"

"Didn't Hurricane Emily strike the Valley? That just happened, am I correct?"

"Yes, sir. It barreled down on South Padre, but then it veered north toward Port Mansfield and fell apart over the King Ranch."

"That reminds me, Billy. Didn't you have a beach house on Padre?" interjected Bates. "Is it still standing?"

Billy shook his head. "I'm afraid not, boss. The roof flew off, and the inside was completely destroyed—everything's gone. Whatever didn't fly away is now soaked beyond repair."

"How much are you out?" Bates asked. "You did have replacement insurance, right?"

"A million bucks," said Billy, shaking his head. "The insurance company is telling us that there is no coverage for wind-driven rain. We hadn't had a hurricane in over fifteen years . . . so we only had homeowner's."

"Ouch!" grunted Falcone, shaking his head.

"Oh, c'mon!" cried Bates exasperated. "You mean the bastards don't wanna pay?"

"They tried the same thing in New Orleans," Falcone chimed in, "until Bailey stepped in and set them straight."

"No," answered Billy, embarrassed that the same people he defended—the insurance companies—the same people he went to bat for day in and day out, were now socking it to him. Worse yet, he probably could not even sue them because those same insurance companies would stop sending work to his firm. They had him bent over a barrel.

"That's the insurance business," Bates added.

"Okay, let's get back to the business at hand, Billy. So your dad suffered a heart attack and died. Shit happens. On the other hand, Billy, have you seen the headlines?"

"Ehem . . . yes."

"Have you seen my stock?" snapped Falcone as he picked out copies of *The Wall Street Journal* and *Texas Monthly* from his briefcase and threw them across the table in a huff. "Look at the price of stock!" He was now standing, leaning with both fists on the table like a fiercely angry African gorilla, demanding Billy look at the price of stock. "We're taking a beating in the stock market, Mr. Bravo."

"Let me see," mumbled Billy as he tried to find the trade symbol for BostonMagnifica or BMP.

"Here," cried Falcone, yanking the paper out of Billy's hands, "look here!" He was now pointing at the stock quotes, telling Billy where to look. "The price has dropped from fifty-five dollars to just twenty a share since I hired your firm. We've lost over two billion dollars in value . . . in . . . in . . . in . . . less than a month. And we're not even in the courtroom yet picking a jury!"

"That's correct, sir. Actually, we're about six or eight months away from jury selection, but . . . " replied Billy.

"I'll tell you what," blurted out Falcone. "I want you to put together a plan of action. I want you to tell me how you plan to get this thing settled, make it go away. And I want to hear from you in the next twenty-four hours. *Capice*? I want it on my desk before the end of the workday tomorrow. Got it?"

"Hear me out, Mr. Falcone," Billy said. "If you don't like what I have to say, then, fine, I'll give you your fucking plan of action."

"What?" asked Falcone, squinting his eyes.

Bates was looking over at Billy completely mortified.

"Look," said an angry Billy, "let's stop the bullshit and the games, okay? If I got my hands on this letter, then Riley Spearman already has it too." He reached for the letter from his coatpocket and shoved it into Falcone's hands. It was Croutoux's memo warning about the dangers of Zerevrea and the increased risk for suicide.

The CEO picked it up and started reading it. He pretended he'd never seen it before. He put on his best poker face. "What's this?"

"One of your scientists wrote it, sir. I'm surprised you have not seen it."

"This is the first time I've seen it," lied Falcone. "How the hell did you get your hands on this?"

"It came through the mail," lied Billy, "in an unmarked envelope. No return address. Nothing. Perhaps a whistleblower inside your company? They always surface when there's litigation. Maybe he's going public with it."

"But why would he send it to you? The attorneys defending BM? Why not the plaintiffs?" asked Falcone, white as a ghost.

"I don't know," replied Billy. "Why do people lie, cheat, do the things they do? I couldn't tell you. Maybe he's putting us on notice that there's more to come. Hell, it could even be Spearman. I don't know."

"You think?"

Billy loved Falcone's reaction. Now it was he who had the knucklehead on the ropes. Neither Bates nor Falcone needed to know that all this had been Hector's idea and that he, as the resourceful investigator that he was, had run across the memo on his own. It was great detective work. Billy needed to use it as leverage.

"But . . . but," mumbled Falcone, "do you think Spearman has a copy too?" He now sounded truly worried.

"I don't know," Billy said, keeping up the charade, "but it would be safe to assume it's just a matter of time before he gets his hands on it. Maybe, whoever it is, has already sent a copy to the White House. Have you thought of that? But you know something? It doesn't matter. When Spearman starts sending discovery to us, we will have no choice but to produce it anyway. And what do you think will happen when Spearman leaks it to all his trial lawyer friends?"

"Jesus!" cried Bates, who had taken the letter from Falcone's hand and was now trembling as he finished reading it. "This is not good."

"We need to stop him, whoever this bastard is!" yelled Falcone, red in the face. He now looked worried, like a pouting puppy recently smacked with a rolled up newspaper across the snout.

"Well, how about giving me some real authority to settle this chickenshit lawsuit, before this letter or other memos are leaked? Before BostonMagnifica's so-called 'impeccable image' is tarnished forever?" The gloves were off.

"Billy," Falcone said looking into Billy's eyes, "listen, okay. You got two million. I don't care how you get it done, but get it done! And let's try to get confidentiality, okay?"

"I wanna know that I can count on another two million to get you your confidentiality . . . four million, total. Otherwise, I can't make any promises . . . and from now on, you are gonna let me do my job . . . and stop calling at all hours of the day demanding meetings every five minutes. The more time I spend flying to Houston for conferences or having bullshit meetings like this to give you bullshit updates and holding your tiny little stubby hands, the less time I have to properly defend your lawsuit, *capice*?"

Bates' jaw dropped to the floor. He could not believe Billy had found it in him to tell the CEO to go screw himself! It was a risky proposition that could backfire, but he had to admit that Billy finally appeared to have gotten some control over the client. Hopefully, Billy would be calling the shots from now on.

"*Capice*," shuddered Falcone with the copy of the memo in his hands. "I'll go to the board, explain to them we'll need four mil to get out of this lawsuit."

"You do that," added Billy as he got up from behind his desk and pushed the periodicals back toward Falcone. "Good day." The meeting was over.

BUBBA'S BAYOU Draft House was located five blocks from Bates' office in downtown Houston. It was a beer joint with a large, dark, smoky room in the back where art films and vintage movies played all day on a screen the size of a highway billboard. The business crowd would file in at lunch for Bubba's famous sweet potato french fries and blackened buffalo wings served with a tandori yogurt dressing. It happened to be Bates' and Domani's favorite place for winding down on Fridays.

After being dropped off in Houston by Falcone in the company jet, Bates had called Rick Domani and asked him to meet him for a beer. He wanted to catch up, see what had transpired back at the office while he'd been in McAllen. Both name partners were sitting at a table away from the big screen, sleeves rolled up, expensive silk ties flipped over their shoulders. "A Civil Action" was playing in the background.

"So," Domani asked as he reached for a spicy buffalo wing from the paper basket sitting in front of him, "did you hear about the new client Rockford brought in?"

"Who, Dr. Cutter?" asked Bates.

"Yes."

"What about him?"

"He's going to want us to represent him in front of the FDA."

"What did we charge him?"

"Two hundred thousand."

"And he paid?"

"Sure. For every month the FDA shuts him down, he's losing five million. Of course he paid," said Domani proudly.

"What did he do?"

"Well, he ran this company that paid funeral homes to allow him to harvest body parts and tissue and then sell the organs to hospitals for transplants."

"Did he have a license from the Texas Department of Health? This is the guy that owns Lone Star Skin Purveyors, right?" asked Bates.

"Yes. They were harvesting parts from bodies without screening for HIV, hepatitis and sexually transmitted diseases."

"So, they got shut down? Was that it? That doesn't sound too bad. We can help him with that, can't we?"

"It gets sticky because the family members of the deceased were not asked permission," explained Domani. "Thousands of families never knew Grandma, Grandpa, Dad or Uncle got chopped up all in the name of science. They're talking to a plaintiff's lawyer now to see if he'll file a class-action suit."

"Ouch!"

"Maybe we'll get hired to defend those lawsuits as well," Domani suggested.

"Maybe. Anyway, did you hear about Billy's place on the beach?"

"Yes," said Domani, "the poor bastard can't catch a break. I don't know why he hangs around. Doesn't he get it? I mean, catch a clue. After fifteen years with the firm, if you haven't made name partner, chances are you will never make it. To make partner, you need to have served in the legislature." He reached for his Corona with lime and took a swig.

"And I guess he doesn't realize we can't have a Mexican as a name partner anyway. It wouldn't be good for business," added Bates, reaching for the sweet potato fries. "Today he came close to telling a blue-chip client to shove it where the sun don't shine."

"Who?"

"The CEO of BostonMagnifica Pharmaceuticals," grunted Bates. "I felt like firing him on the spot. Too bad we depend on him so much . . . we need him in South Texas."

"Well, the guy is a good attorney and all," started Domani, "but he's no rainmaker or anything. I'll give him credit, though. He can try a hell of a case."

"Yes, and he's dependable," said Bates reaching for another Corona out of the ice bucket in the middle of the table, "but he isn't name partner material. Man, them Mexicans sure make good beer, don't they?"

"I couldn't agree more," said Domani, "my favorite is Tecate Lager. You just can't find it in Houston."

"Well," continued Bates, "Billy . . . he is what he is. We've kept him this long because he's got sway with the Hispanic judges and juries along the border. They like him and respect him, and he gets our clients good results."

"Can you imagine Billy in private practice?" asked Domani, "He'd be making millions!"

"I don't know why he insists on making name partner. Maybe if he got rid of that goatee and changed his name. I mean, what's with the name 'Billy Bravo' anyway? Can you imagine what the clients would say if they found out his real name?" asked Bates as he laughed hysterically. "Guillermo 'Billy' Cuauhtemoc Bravo."

"Shit! We'd be accused of hiring illegal aliens."

"Anyway," Bates said, giggling as he wiped the yogurt dressing dripping from his chin, "I told him we are thinking of promoting him to name partner if he does a good job on the BostonMagnifica litigation."

"And he believed it?"

"Sure."

"Man, what a jerk."

"Let's just have him reel in BostonMagnifica," finished Bates, "have him do a good job for us, land the client its defense verdict and then he can go back to his old cases."

"HEY, Billy, are you still at the office?" asked Bates from his cellular.

"I'm just now heading home," replied Billy. "After the meeting with you guys this morning, I rushed to Brownsville to make arrangements to have my father's body moved to McAllen. . . . We're still working on the funeral preparations. I'm in the car driving home as we speak, just exiting the funeral home parking lot."

"Hey, listen, Billy. I just wanted to go over a couple of things. I know that Falcone had no right to insult you the way he's done at some of the meetings. No one should have to take that. But he's paying our bills, and you know what they say . . . "

"The customer is always right?" finished Billy.

"Right. Wrong. I mean, I don't blame you for putting him in his place. However, next time, let me handle it. Okay?"

"With all due respect, you just sat there. You didn't do a thing."

"You're right. But, next time, let me handle it, got it? Ultimately, he's paying our bills. I'd hate for you not to get your promotion because you let some asshole get to you. It wouldn't be worth it."

"Next time, I'll punch his little Italian ass back to Brooklyn."

"Let it go, Billy. Focus on the task at hand. Help me get the case resolved. Let's reel in BostonMagnifica for good. This is the goose with the golden egg. It can feed a lot of people."

"I'll do my best. I just can't promise you I won't punch him next time he crosses the line. I don't like being called a dumb Mexican and being treated like I don't know what I'm doing."

"Don't make me pick between a client and you, Billy. Please don't."

CHAPTER 19

YAMI'S RICH AND SILKY SHRIMP BISQUE was the perfect way to end a sad day and try to lift everyone's spirits in and around the dinner table. Yami had always said that nothing mattered more than family, a point made abundantly clear now that Papo was gone so suddenly and without warning. The whole family was still in shock. Billy's in-laws had called and expressed their condolences. Yami's mom, Farida, was on her way from the Mexican capital to spend some time with the grandkids and help around the house.

The aroma of slow-roasted shrimp shells and garlic, white wine, cognac, Spanish saffron and herbs permeated the entire house. When Billy walked in, Nano, the family's albino Chihuahua, started barking and jumping with excitement, announcing his Grand Master's welcome.

"Dad's home," shouted Wicho from the dinner table, a warm slice of homemade buttered focaccia in his left hand. No one had seen Nano that excited in months.

"*No lo puedo creer*," Yami said, with sheer delight. "I'm so glad you're home. I didn't expect you this early . . . it's nice." She was sipping a glass of wine as she stood next to the large commercial range, slowly stirring the bisque in a large copper pot.

"I miss you guys. And I need all of you to help me work on Papo's obituary. Plus, I'll be in trial down in Laredo starting soon, and when it picks up speed, I probably won't be around for months. Where's Ale?"

"She's in her room," said Yami. "I already called her to come to dinner."

"Mauricio," ordered Billy, "please go get your sister. Tell her dinner is ready. Tell her I want to see her."

"Sure, Dad. I'll go get her," Wicho said with excitement. "Can we play some chess?" he shouted as he bolted up the spiral staircase.

"*Bueno, pero un juego nada más.* I want to talk to Mom." He walked over to the kitchen sink and started washing his hands. *It's time to come clean. Maybe she'll feel sorry for my ass and will go easy on me now that dad has died.*

"Alessandra has bruises, Billy," blurted Yami out of the blue.

"What do you mean 'bruises'?" *Now what? I just told Falcone to kiss my ass, my promotion is probably out the window, my old man is getting buried, I'm about to come clean with the Karin Palmer situation . . . now what?*

"All over her calves and buttocks. I'm worried. They don't look like the bruises she gets when playing volleyball. Promise me you'll talk to her and convince her to go to the doctor tomorrow."

"I will, *cariño.* I'll take care of it, I promise. I'll call Dr. Pellier, and he'll sneak her in without an appointment. Run some tests. I'm sure it's nothing."

"*Ojalá.* I hope it's nothing."

Billy opened the Subzero, reached in, and pulled out an ice-cold Dos XX. He took a swig. "*No es nada.* I'm sure of it."

"THE BISQUE was incredible," said Billy as he got in bed. "What a treat. *Para chuparse los dedos, delicioso.*" He slid on over to Yami's side and pressed himself upon her back. With his right hand, he reached under her panties and slowly started caressing her.

"Not tonight," said Yami. "I'm worried about Ale. My mind is somewhere else. I'm sorry, I just can't." She pushed him away.

"*Agh, chihuahas,*" huffed Billy as he yanked his hand away. The one night the planets were finally in alignment—including the stars, the moon and heaven knows what other celestial bodies out there—and his wife was overly worried about their daughter.

"I'm sorry," she said.

"I understand, *mi amor.*"

"What do you think it is?" asked Yami, sounding worried.

"I don't know, but we'll find out. Are you coming with us?"

"I can't stand hospitals or doctors' offices, you know that. Unless you absolutely need me there, I'll be waiting by the phone."

"Okay, then. Goodnight."

"Thank you for taking care of my baby, Billy," said Yami. "There's nothing that means more to me. Just knowing that you are on top of it gives me some relief . . . and . . . "

"Yes?"

"I'm sorry about Papo. I know how much it must hurt."

"It's all my fault," said Billy, stifling a sob as the memories came rushing out.

"He would not have listened . . . he loved lending a hand . . . that's what he did. Don't beat yourself up over it. He's in a better place . . . probably watching over us."

UNABLE TO SLEEP, Billy stood silently in the doorway to Alessandra's bedroom and watched her sleep. He remembered a conversation they had had when she was barely seven years old.

"So, you wanna play professional volleyball?" he asked after reading her a nighttime story.

Her eyes had lit up, and a smile appeared from cheek to cheek. "Like Gabrielle Reece. I wanna be like her and play beach volleyball. She's my hero."

"What about dance lessons? Mom would like you to learn flamenco, *folklórico*, ballet. Mom was an accomplished dancer, you know."

"That's boring. I like to be outside, play in the sand. I don't want to be stuck inside a dance studio," she said, sounding very mature for her age.

"I guess you came out like your Papo and me. When I was your age, I could never get enough of the beach. Papo and I would try to get away to go fishing every chance we got. When we came back from picking crops, when school let out or simply to just get away, we would always get away. Just being out there without a single care in the world. . . . I know exactly what you're talking about. Maybe some day we'll own a place out there. Would you like that? Spend summers at the beach on Padre?"

"You promise, daddy?"

"Yes."

She had looked at him with those big, beautiful eyes. Daddy's girl had continued to stare. He'd gotten closer, and she'd gotten closer. Their foreheads touching in a playful manner, eyelashes almost brushing together, their stares locked upon each other. Without speaking a word, their looks conveyed a love impossible to describe—a deep connection, something that happens only between a father and his little girl. It was almost sacred, a sense of complete joy, belonging and fulfillment.

"I'll always love you, Ale. You'll always be my little girl, my baby girl. Nothing can change that, okay? *Nada ni nadie.*"

"You'll always take care of me, daddy?"

"*Yes, m'ija. Claro,*" he'd said as he kissed her on her forehead.

Now, watching Ale sleep, he wondered if he could keep his promise. And how would Ale feel when she found out she had a half-brother?

CHAPTER 20

BILLY WAS STANDING off in a corner holding a bottle of Tsing-Tao beer, trying to get over his dad's passing and worrying about the Karin Palmer situation as he listened to Charlie Jensen and Brandon Fauntleroy argue over the latest disapproval ratings for Bailey on the Iraq war. The entire staff and their spouses had come out to P.F. Chang's on Ware Road to celebrate the holidays. It was the firm's annual Christmas party.

Bates had wanted to do something special for the folks down at the McAllen office, so he had Connie rent the restaurant's party rooms in order to accommodate all of his Valley employees, including the partners coming down from Houston. The founding partner always enjoyed coming down to show off his latest silicone-enhanced girlfriend, call out the *lotería* to his subjects and hand out the presents to the winners of the Mexican-style Bingo. And every year, it seemed, he relished more and more delivering the tiny bonus checks to those attorneys who'd made him and the name partners a fortune.

"And what about the mental healthcare initiative Bailey recently announced," said Brandon Fauntleroy, "where he wants to help the hurricane victims so they can put their lives together? Isn't that a good thing?"

"C'mon, Brandon," cried Jensen, "the guy's trying to help the pharmaceuticals line their pockets. That's all it is. Are you that blind? It was the same with his Medicare Prescription Drug Program. Now, the taxpayer is footing the bill, while the drug companies laugh their way to the bank."

"Boys," interrupted Billy, "one of those pharmaceuticals is our client. Don't let Bates hear you say anything negative about BostonMagnifica." He was pointing at Bates, who was holding court by the open bar at the other end of the large party room. The principal name partner was retelling stories of his early days working at the Texas Capitol. Days of drinking, skirt-chasing and even an occasional fistfight between legislators.

"Giving folks thousands of dollars in FEMA vouchers for free medication is a good thing," whispered Fauntleroy, the gung-ho Republican. "No one can accuse the President of not doing enough for the little people."

Jensen took a swig of his Jack and Coke and replied, "Bailey is going to help his *compadres* running the drug companies. You, Mr. Bravo here, and I know that. Bates knows that. Everybody in Washington knows that. He did the same thing with his buds in the oil industry. In the end, come reelection time, the drug companies will contribute millions to his campaign coffers. The White House doesn't give a rat's ass about the mental health of those poor souls. And neither do the drug companies, for that matter. Big pharma is about money, and all the White House cares about is getting those approval ratings up. That's what this is about. It's good ol' boys scratching good ol' boys' backs. That's all this is."

The discussion was heating up when a female voice said, "Excuse me, boys." It was Yami, tugging at Billy's elbow. "You don't mind if I steal my husband for a second, do you?"

"No, Mrs. Bravo," said Fauntleroy, "of course not."

"No, go ahead," said Jensen, as he and Fauntleroy stood there and watched the Bravos head for the other open bar at the other end of the room. The pair jumped right back and continued discussing the polls and the merits and disappointments of Bailey's presidency.

"WHAT DID DR. PELLIER say about Alessandra?" asked Yami. She looked a little buzzed, too many Cosmopolitans. "You never called me back."

"Uh, I forgot to call him," Billy stuttered.

"You what?!! How could you forget your daughter's well-being?!!"

"I'm sorry. I know, I know, it's just . . . I had to run down to court, put out some fires. And then I got tied up. I'm sorry."

"It's always the same!" screamed Yami.

Everybody at the holiday party turned around and stared at the couple. Billy turned several shades of red.

"It's like pulling teeth with you! I have to chase you around, ask you what the hell is going on. *Es mi hija, ¿no entiendes?* Don't play with Ale's life. I'm walking on pins and needles here, don't you get it?"

"Yami, please," begged Billy, almost in a whisper. "Settle down. You're making a scene." He tried grabbing her by the arm, get her to calm down, "my promotion is on the line. Please, I beg you."

"*No me callo*, Billy," she shouted, "*suéltame*. Let me go. All you care about is that damned promotion. That comes first with you. Not your family, not me, and not even your daughter's health. I've had it!"

Yami stormed off to the ladies' room, leaving Billy by himself, looking like a reprimanded first-grader. Everyone tried to pretend that nothing had happened and picked up their conversations where they had left off. Billy quickly snatched a cocktail from the waiter walking by with the drink tray. He now remembered why he hated office parties.

"WHAT WAS THAT ALL ABOUT?" asked Hector. He was sitting next to Nancy, Billy's secretary. They were at a side table set up for those wanting to play *loteria*. Nancy had been one card short of getting Bingo and winning a set of diamond earrings when she'd heard the yelling and screaming.

"I guess my boss is sacrificing everything to make name partner," said Nancy. "His wife can't take it anymore."

"*Qué pena*. If you wanna know the truth, Billy should have made name partner ten years ago. The whole thing is so sad. These fucking jerks just want to keep the pie entirely to themselves. But if it wasn't for Billy winning all the big cases, the McAllen office would have shut down long ago. That's the truth, and they know it."

"They just can't accept the fact that we're here to stay. If Billy's name was 'William King,' it would have been on the firm's letterhead a long time ago."

"If it was me," said Hector, "I would have left this joint long ago. Go open my own practice and make tons of money. I would have millions in the bank by now."

"Maybe it's not about the money to him," reasoned Nancy. "Have you ever thought about that? Maybe Billy is in it for other reasons. Some people do things to prove a point."

"Yeah, I guess. All I'm saying is that I wouldn't put up with it. *Yo ya los hubiera mandado al carajo*," declared Hector in beautiful Spanish. "They can kiss my ass."

Nancy's eyes grew wide. She figured the margaritas were getting to Hector, just like the Cosmopolitans had gotten to Mrs. Bravo. "Billy is not like that. He's not gonna quit just because he's not getting his way. The guy's persistent—tenacious. *Testarudo*, some would say. How else does he win all his cases?"

"How?" asked Hector.

"He wears you down. He works and works on you and runs you ragged until you are sick and tired of him. He'll wear down Bates and the others too. You'll see."

"Well, I hope he gets his wish. But you know what they say . . . "

"What?" asked Nancy.

"You can't have it all. And that worries me."

"Bingo!" screamed Nancy, jumping up from her chair. Mr. Bates had finally called El Valiente from the stack of cards he was holding in his right hand. She was now the proud winner of a pair of one-carat diamond-studded earrings.

CHAPTER 21

I T WAS EASY TO SEE why Tommy Ray had married his high school sweetheart. Gina Ray was the most striking forty-year-old Billy Bravo had ever laid eyes on. She was tall and slender with flowing curls of light brown hair down to her shoulders. The high cheekbones made her turquoise blue eyes more prominent. Billy could appreciate her tan, even though she was wearing a black pailette tunic with bell sleeves, black crop pants and black suede moccasins. Not an ounce of makeup, and she looked radiant. No one would have ever guessed that a year earlier, this poor woman had lost her husband.

Gina Ray and her attorneys Spearman and Hanslik were waiting in her large dining room, when Billy arrived. The three were sitting at the ornate dining room table for ten, waiting to hear from defense counsel. Spearman had convinced his client to give Mr. Bravo a chance to meet and speak, that BostonMagnifica wanted to talk settlement before the parties really went at each other's throats. Besides, before giving the parties their day in court, most federal judges—at least the ones in the Southern District of Texas—were going to require the parties to attend some type of alternative dispute resolution exercise, whether it was a mandatory mediation or binding arbitration.

Billy introduced himself to Mrs. Ray and greeted Spearman and Hanslik. He then took his place at the other end of the table.

Since there had been no federal judge appointed to hear the case yet, Billy and Spearman had decided to conduct an informal mediation among themselves. It would be their good-faith attempt to try to resolve the case without further court intervention. In the end, the exercise could benefit both sides.

If Billy settled the case, then Falcone could stop worrying about the negative exposure and Billy would certainly land his promotion. A quick settlement, on the other hand, would also mean that Spearman would walk away with close to two million in fees in the event BM pitched the entire four million dollars to the plaintiffs.

"Señora Ray," started Billy in Spanish, clearing his throat, "*lo siento mucho*," and then switching to English added, "I am terribly, terribly sorry for the loss of your husband. My client, BostonMagnifica, its CEO, and my firm all want you to know how sorry we are for the pain you and your family have had to endure. Our deepest condolences."

As any good defense lawyer practicing law in the Valley knew, addressing the plaintiff in Spanish could help the negotiations along. It was a technique used to put people at ease, especially if the parties had deep Latin roots. Gina Yturria's family descended from the original settlers of Laredo and traced their heritage back to Spain. There was nothing wrong with sprinkling a little Spanish here and there and using it as an icebreaker. Whatever it took to get the job done, get the case settled and make it go away, once and for all.

Mrs. Ray was looking intently at Billy as she reached for her sunglasses and put them on. She did not want anyone to see her cry.

"Ehem," Billy cleared his throat, "I spoke with your attorney, Mr. Spearman, and kindly requested a meeting to discuss your lawsuit." Billy expected Mrs. Ray to say something, anything, but Gina Ray did not flinch. She just sat there, stone-cold, with her arms crossed, looking straight across the room as if saying, "Just say what you have to say and get the hell out of my home." The only time she moved was to wipe a few tears rolling down her beautiful cheeks.

"As I was saying," Billy continued, "a lot has been said about Zerevrea, the medication your husband Tommy was on. From reading the lawsuit and the headlines in the media, I understand you feel strongly that Zerevrea may have had something to do with your husband's passing." Again, he paused to see if Mrs. Ray would open up and say something, anything. A response would be a good signal that she was listening, at least acknowledging his presence.

She said nothing.

"*Bien*," Billy said again in Spanish, trying to see if the words were sinking in. "I am not here today to dispute the contentions in the lawsuit. My role is not to be the jury or the judge and decide who is right or who is wrong. Rather, I am here today to explore the possibility of putting this all behind us, coming to some sort of arrangement."

Mrs. Ray shifted positions in her chair and blew her nose, but other than that continued to be quiet. Her arms remained crossed.

"*Creo yo*," Billy added, "I believe that your attorney probably has already mentioned to you what may or may not happen if this case goes to trial. As with all trials, there's risk involved."

Gina Ray reached for her cup of hot chamomile tea and took a sip. She put it down and continued to stare across the dining room out the window overlooking the manmade lake beyond the estate's perfectly manicured grounds.

"My client," continued Billy, "would like to settle this lawsuit and compensate you and your family for your loss. I know that nothing will ever bring Mr. Ray back, and I'm sorry."

Gina Ray said nothing. She remained like a statue. Spearman and his associate, on the other hand, were fidgeting in their seats, pretending to scribble on their yellow pads, but really waiting to hear a multimillion-dollar offer of settlement. They were salivating. The more zeroes, the better. Hell, Spearman was probably already thinking of ways to spend it. And Hanslik, the lowly associate, was probably dreaming of a sizeable bonus to apply toward his student loans.

"¡*Oh, se me olvidó!*" Billy continued. "I almost forgot . . . and let me say this, and by this I don't mean any disrespect, Mrs. Ray. If I could turn back time, give you your husband back and put everything back the way it was before January 2005, I would. Unfortunately, all I can do here today is make a peace offering in a feeble effort to compensate you and your family and offer my deepest sympathies. My client is prepared to pay four million dollars, without any admission of liability and in complete confidentiality, to you today and relieve us all of having to revisit this tragedy at trial."

Billy knew that most people filed lawsuits to make cash. There was no other reason, no other way around it. You couldn't wave a magic wand and bring spouses, children or loved ones back. No one could turn the clock back and prevent accidents, asbestos claims, refinery explosions or medical errors. It was impossible. In the end, it was all about money. How many zeroes and figures were there going to be on the settlement check? Six figures? Seven? Although the critics loved to bash the victims and their lawyers as nothing more than money-hungry vultures trying to hit the lotto, the reason that lawsuits existed was to force somebody to pay money or to try to avoid having to pay for having caused somebody a wrong. That was the way things were. His job was always to pay out as little money as he could get away with and to make cases disappear. The reverse was also true. The function of a plaintiff's lawyer was to try to make the defendant part with his money, and not just a small amount. Spearman's role, his duty and obligation to Gina as her attorney, was to take from Billy's client as much money as was humanly possible.

"Who compensates the families of the mailman and Ms. Andarza, the jogger?" blurted out Mrs. Ray unexpectedly.

"I . . . don't know," Billy replied, a bit uncertain, "they are not part of this lawsuit."

"Maybe they should be" she said.

"Well, er . . . ," stumbled Billy.

"Mr. Bravo," Gina Ray said as she stared out the window, "any settlement negotiations must include the families of the other victims. If I settle my claims with you here today, who is to say that those folks won't come after me or my husband's estate?"

"I see what you're saying," Billy replied, but had no immediate answer. "You raise a valid concern." It was obvious Mrs. Ray could negotiate, probably something she learned from all those years being married to an attorney.

"Also," Mrs. Ray added, further showing she could play hard-ball, "there won't be any confidentiality agreements. The public needs to know what Zerevrea can do."

"But . . . but," muttered Billy, "I cannot entertain settlement discussions, unless there's a confidentiality clause."

"Then we don't need to be having this discussion," snapped Gina Ray as she pulled her sunglasses off and looked straight at Billy. "To you, Mr. Bravo," continued Gina, speaking sternly, "this is nothing more than a file with a number—another settlement agreement with a settlement check attached to it. Once everything is said and done, you'll file your motion to dismiss with prejudice and expect us to walk away. Go home. Call it a day and pretend this thing never happened."

"Mrs. Ray," interjected Billy, "let me reassure you, I only have your best interest in mind . . . " Billy's hands were getting wet with perspiration. Things were not going as planned.

"Let's not kid ourselves," Gina said, cutting him off, "last time I checked, your client was BostonMagnifica, not Tommy Ray."

Spearman and his lowly associate were now looking at each other, eyes wide open, surprised as hell that Gina Ray was showing her true mettle.

"But . . . " mumbled Billy, "my client . . . "

Gina Ray interrupted him. "And what about the stigma? Have you thought about that?"

"I am sorry . . . the what?" Billy asked. "Stigma?"

"The stigma of suicide, Mr. Bravo. Is your blood money going to help my family, my children to live with that?" she demanded to know. "What happens when people ask my children about their dad? What do we say? Do we lie and concoct some story that he died of a heart attack or drowned?"

"Well, uh, no . . . " muttered Billy. He was spinning his wheels, obviously not prepared to handle this discussion.

"Don't you see what people will say?" she asked. "Tommy must have been wacko. He must have gone off the deep end. What made him do that?

"I see . . . "

"And when friends and family ask," she continued, "do I cover up what happened? Do you know how I feel? Do you have any idea? As his wife, I failed to keep him alive, didn't I?"

All that Billy could stammer out was, "I'm sorry."

"Do you know how this is going to affect my kids? What if their friends think suicide runs in the family? As it is, our family is already divided. Tommy's parents and siblings refuse to believe what happened. They say it was no accident."

"Yes, I understand."

"No, you don't understand!" she shouted. "Since this has been in the papers, everyone is looking for skeletons in Tommy's closet! Even you! You don't think I've heard of your investigator coming around and knocking on my neighbors' doors?"

"He is just doing his job," Billy replied, feeling embarrassed.

"The cops want to know. Your investigator is snooping around. The fact is, there are no skeletons! My husband was a good man. It was your client's drug that made him snap! In the meantime, me and my children have been cast out and became pariahs overnight!"

"Eh . . . "

Gina Ray continued to give Billy a piece of her mind. "And now I have to live with the agonizing fear that my children might also want to kill themselves. What happens when they become teenagers and something upsets them? Will they choose to do the same as their dad? Will the idea enter their minds? Do you see what I'm saying? We'll probably be in therapy for years to come! Your money can't fix that! Your money can't make the scars go away."

"I know you feel your life will never be normal again," said Billy, "and I'm truly, truly sorry." He paused for a few seconds. "Suicide has also touched my life, Mrs. Ray. With my sister's death, I changed and I was never the same again."

Gina Rays' attorneys looked up from their yellow pads and started paying attention, shocked to hear Billy's revelation.

"All I can say," he said, "is that I know firsthand what you're going through."

Gina Ray composed herself and began speaking slowly. She took a deep breath. "Let me tell you what it will take for Boston-Magnifica to settle this thing. First, your client will have to settle with us and the victims of the shootings."

"Okay," said Billy as he scribbled on a yellow pad, happy to start moving things along again.

"Second," Gina Ray said, "what kind of sales does Boston-Magnifica ring on an average day, just on Zerevrea?"

"I don't know. I don't have those figures with me."

"Well," said Mrs. Ray, "your client needs to pay each family the equivalent of two days' worth of sales worldwide . . . I believe that's thirty million per family."

It was obvious Mrs. Ray had been talking to Spearman, because only an attorney would want to know those figures. Mrs. Ray's numbers were not too far off.

"I'll have to check on that," answered Billy, "and get back to you."

"Third," added Mrs. Ray, "there will be no confidentiality clause and no confidentiality agreement, no files sealed in federal court. And fourth, BostonMagnifica will have to publicly apologize for all the damage and destruction Zerevrea has caused. Zerevrea is not the first SSRI drug that has come under fire, Mr. Bravo. The British government banned similar drugs because of increased attempts at suicide. In Canada, these drugs cannot be prescribed to children. In France, the government has forced the pharmaceutical industry to educate the prescribing physicians to monitor patients for bouts of aggression and violence. And who knows what other horrors Zerevrea can cause, but your client is not telling! So, those are our terms. My husband was a kind and gentle man, Mr. Bravo. Never before had he exhibited any irrational behavior. Yes, he was a Gulf War veteran, but he was honorably discharged. He was proud to have served his country and to serve his community. He was a lawyer who fought for the underdog, the downtrodden and the underprivileged. He was a hero to me and my children. I will not let his memory or his life's work simply be swept under the rug by you, your client or its millions."

"No, eh . . . " Billy replied, "no one is suggesting such a thing."

"That's all. Those are our terms."

It was obvious to Billy that any sway he had thought he may have over the widow was now certainly out the window, past the manicured lawn, beyond the steam rising from the manmade lake in the back of her estate and scattered in the winter cold. Despite the cold temperature outside, Billy could feel drops of sweat running down his sides and back. His head was full of images of Bates and Falcone. It was not a pretty sight: Falcone growling like a rabid pit bull, ready to take a chunk out of his ass.

"Counselor," Riley Spearman interrupted, "I think my client has heard enough for one day. Why don't you get back to your folks, and we'll resume this conversation at a later date."

"All right. I'll talk to my client and relay the terms Mrs. Ray has demanded. I can't guarantee, however, that I'll get them to move, particularly if there's no confidentiality agreement on the table."

"Then we'll see you in court!" growled Mrs. Ray.

CHAPTER 22

ILLY STARED AT THE COLD PLATE of shish kabobs and rice but could not eat. He'd lost his appetite. All he could think about was his failed attempt at an informal settlement. The last two weeks, he'd been trying to get Spearman to convince his client to reconvene, to give him another opportunity to restate and explain his client's position and to renew the settlement discussions.

Billy had kept the failed attempt secret from Falcone. He needed to figure out a way to get a second try, a second bite at the apple. He also needed a strong incentive to get Spearman and Gina Ray to the table again. The four million that Falcone had given him in authority had meant nothing to the widow. She had not been the least impressed. Maybe Hector could dig up some new stuff—something that would make her reconsider and give him new bargaining power.

"You haven't touched your food," Yami pointed out. They were at Kazra's, a new Persian restaurant in town. Yami was playing with her drink, a frothy concoction made with yogurt, mint leaves and crushed ice.

Billy played with the rice on his plate. "Things aren't so good with the Ray suit right now."

"Why?"

"The case has 'justice seeker' written all over it."

"One of those, eh? A crusader?"

"Yep, one of those."

In all his years as an attorney, Billy had learned one thing when dealing with the type of plaintiff known as a "crusader":

going to trial was always a gamble, nothing more than a roll of the dice, akin to going to Vegas. But if Gina Ray was not in it for the money and all she wanted was justice for her husband or to expose BostonMagnifica, the odds against settling the case or a win at trial went up considerably.

"You think it'll turn into one of those?" Yami asked as she reached for a piece of pita bread.

"It would appear so."

Billy had been on the receiving end in one such case where the widow's mentally unstable husband had died because of hospital neglect. Administrators had known the hospital was routinely understaffed, but they'd had orders to slash costs and increase profits. Depositions had revealed that the deceased—who was under psychiatric evaluation—had been handed a double-edged razor to shave himself. The nurse had never gone back to check on him. The insurer had immediately authorized Billy to tender five million dollars to make the case go away. It had been an offer too good to pass up, or so Billy thought. Unfortunately, the widow had other plans. Andrea Suárez was not going to put up with the notion that a hospital deserved an ounce of compassion just because it was located in one of the poorest counties in the country, and it served mostly uninsured Mexicans, her family included. No . . . instead, Andrea Suárez would make the death of her husband her reason for living. And she proceeded to publicly prod the Texas Legislature to pass laws establishing new patient-nurse ratios and mandatory eight-hour shifts. She had appeared on *Oprah* alongside Texas Senator Andy Del Toro and had testified in Washington before Congress.

"Spearman, the attorney, is not able to control his client," explained Billy. "Gina Ray has all the makings of an Andrea Suárez."

Yami pulled her napkin from her lap, slowly folded it and gently placed it on the table in front of her. She switched topics, sounding impatient. "I'm sorry the case that can make you 'name partner' is full of landmines, but can you tell me when Dr. Pellier is seeing Ale? Did you get her the appointment?"

"Tomorrow. His office called to confirm."

"Good," she replied. "I've been worried sick." She took a sip from her drink. "And the beach house? What's going on down in Padre?"

Billy thought long and hard. He looked extremely uncomfortable with the proposed question. "I've been meaning to talk to you about that. They don't wanna pay."

"What?" Yami asked, eyes wide open. "You work for the insurance companies, and now the bastards don't want to pay? When were you going to tell me?"

Billy looked down at the floor. "The insurance company is saying that we needed to have windstorm coverage or flood insurance. We only had homeowner's insurance."

"So, homeowner's will pay, right?" Yami had never really understood the differences in coverage.

"Well," Billy started again, still looking down at the floor, "there's no coverage under the homeowner's policy for wind-driven rain, so they're denying our claim."

She threw her hands up in the air. "See what I mean? *¿Ya ves?*" Yami had switched to Spanish, she was furious. "*Todo el día matándote para que el seguro no pague un quinto. Ahorrándoles millones y millones. Y ahora que realmente necesitamos el seguro, nos mandan a freír espárragos* . . . and you want to keep working for insurance companies? Save them money? And now when we need them the most, they give us a kick in the crotch? You're an idiot!"

He reached over and tried to calm her down. "Please, Yami, cut me some slack. I'm under a lot of stress. We all are, I know. Just hang in there. I need your support, please. Bates promised to help me fix the insurance mess on our beach home. He's got connections inside. Work with me."

She took a deep breath, crossed her arms on her lap and looked away toward the open kitchen in the middle of the restaurant. She was ignoring his sorry ass. "I want you to take care of yourself and start paying attention to your family. If you don't, then don't be surprised when . . . " She stopped mid-sentence.

"When what? When you leave my workaholic ass?"

"Nothing," she huffed.

"Yami, look. This case will be over soon . . . ."

"This case, that case . . . " she snapped right back as if mocking him, "that's all I ever hear from you. When this case wraps up . . . when that case wraps up. *¡Ya despierta, hombre!* Wake up and smell the coffee. This promotion of yours is never going to happen! Every two or three years, we have this same discussion . . . *¡ya por el amor de Dios, por favor!*" She sprang from the table and headed to the ladies' room, tears running down her face.

Billy stayed behind and sat at the empty table, still pushing grains of rice around his plate.

ALESSANDRA'S APPOINTMENT would finally take place down at McAllen Memorial Hospital. Dr. Pellier, the internist who Billy had defended successfully in court on more than one occasion, had agreed to see her without any formal paperwork or going through the ER. At Yami's insistence and under the threat of divorce, Billy had postponed going out of town in order to drive his daughter to the hospital and consult with the physician. The bruises on her calves had disappeared, but now there was bruising on her elbows, lower back and hips.

"Thank you for squeezing us in this late in the evening," Billy said to his friend, sounding worried. "I've had a hard time getting away from work in order to bring in Alessandra. My wife has been nagging me to convince Alessandra to get the bruises checked. I finally managed to find some time. I've been up in Houston and Laredo with too much work. So, here we are."

"Where have you been getting the bruises, Alessandra?" asked Dr. Pellier bluntly, taking her hand and instructing her to sit on an examination table.

"On my legs, mostly," she said. "I had gotten them before, but they had always gone away. I thought maybe I got them from playing volleyball. We get pretty banged up out there in the court. Who knows? Maybe I got them from bumping into things. You know . . . "

"Alessandra is just like her mom. They both hate going to the doctor," Billy explained. "So it's quite possible that she's been getting them and just not telling us. Last week, I noticed she had them up and down both legs."

"Well, Billy, I'm glad you decided to bring her in . . . I am gonna draw a little blood down at the lab, and we'll know in ten minutes exactly what is going on. I bet it's nothing. You shouldn't worry."

"I really, really appreciate it, Simon," said Billy, "for you to see us like this on short notice."

"I know how busy you are," replied Pellier, "plus, I owe you." Dr. Pellier looked like a disheveled academic—a combination of Einstein and former Surgeon General Koop.

"Please! That's my job. To defend the healthcare industry."

"I mean it. I've always considered you a good friend. You've saved my hide on more than one occasion. I'm glad to be of help."

The doctor turned to Alessandra and asked, "How old are you now, Ale?"

"Just turned sixteen."

"Any illnesses? Anything unusual that you may have noticed with your body these last couple of months?"

"Just some bruises here and there. I didn't think anything of it, because they usually went away."

"Joint pain?"

"No."

"Feeling tired? Without energy?"

"Some. I've been training for the volleyball playoffs."

"Temperature?"

"No."

"Nosebleeds?

"No."

"Do you smoke?"

"No."

"Drink?"

"No!" She looked at her dad. "My dad would kill me."

"Stress?"

"Maybe a little. With schoolwork, volleyball, Honor Society, Homecoming Committee . . . I guess what would be considered normal for a teen."

"I see," Dr. Pellier said.

"How about your gums? Any bleeding?"

"Some, here and there. Mom got me Sensodyne toothpaste."

"Did it help?"

"A little."

"What about your urine?"

"I'm sorry?" Alessandra asked.

"Any unusual smell? Maybe stronger, more pungent?"

"Yeah, maybe a little different, now that you mention it," she said.

"Okay."

"Let me call down to the lab see if they are ready for us," Dr. Pellier said as he picked up the phone and punched in the extension number. As he waited for someone to pick up down at the lab, he turned to Alessandra and said, "Don't worry, Ale, I am sure it's nothing. Everything is going to be all right."

"Thanks," she replied with a worried look.

"Hello," said Pellier into the receiver, "this is Dr. Simon Pellier. I am bringing a patient to the lab for blood work. Can we come down now?" There was a pause. "Okay, we're on our way. Thanks."

DR. PELLIER, Billy and Alessandra were back at Dr. Pellier's office awaiting the lab results. The doctor had started a pot of coffee and was reaching into a small fridge for two water bottles for his guests when his Blackberry went off.

"Yes," the doctor spoke into his Blackberry, "this is Pellier." He signaled over to the Bravos, who were holding hands, to let them know it was the lab calling. The pathologist was on the line.

"Aha," Dr. Pellier could be heard muttering, nodding his head, "Aha . . . okay. I see. Are you sure? All right . . . yes . . . sure, go ahead and do the other screens." He put his Blackberry in his white lab coat pocket and sat down. He faced Billy and Alessandra and spoke slowly.

"You're almost out of platelets," he said to Ale. "That would explain the bruising."

"What are platelets?" she asked.

"A clotting agent in our blood," said Billy, sounding concerned. "It keeps us from bleeding to death. When your platelet count drops, if you get a cut, it becomes very hard to stop the bleeding . . . a person could bleed to death." The room suddenly started spinning around him.

"Your dad's right," added Dr. Pellier. "Now we need to find out what is causing your platelet count to be so low. So, I've ordered other tests. We'll know in a few minutes. I wouldn't worry, Ale. It's probably Idiopathic Thrombosis Purpura, a simple condition we can treat here, locally, with special medication. No problem." He was putting a positive spin on the situation.

"I hope you're right," said Alessandra, squeezing her father's hand a bit harder and looking at him. "I heard of a girl in another school who was bruising and was diagnosed with leukemia. She died six months later."

"It happens," replied the doctor, "but bruising can also be due to a number of other things. And besides, some leukemia is now treatable and very curable with a 99 percent success rate. I wouldn't worry about it." He was hoping to ease her mind by dismissing such possibility.

"There are all kinds of new experimental drugs," continued Pellier, "to treat leukemia. It is no longer a death sentence." The Blackberry went off again. Pellier answered. "Yes . . . I see." There was a long pause. "Are you sure? Fifty blast? Okay. I'll handle it. Thanks."

"It is leukemia, isn't it?" asked Billy.

"Eh, we're not sure," said Pellier, trying to calm Billy's fears. "What we do know is this, Ale. Your white blood cell count is high, your platelets are low and some of those white blood cells are also cancerous. More testing is needed to confirm whether it is leukemia or some other blood disorder."

Alessandra Bravo did not hear Dr. Pellier's last words. She broke down crying and buried her face between her hands while Billy tried to comfort her. She was muttering between sobs, "I don't want to die. Please, God, please. I don't want to die, Daddy!"

"You're gonna be fine," Billy said, trying to reassure her. "We'll get through it, I promise." He then turned to his friend and asked, "Should we go to Houston?"

"As your friend, Billy, I'd have to say yes. Don't waste your time here in the Valley. Get her up to MD Anderson. Get on the next flight out of McAllen. I'll call my colleagues Dr. Menotti and Dr. Kamisch there. By the time you and your daughter show up, they'll be waiting for you. I'm sorry. Now go."

"All right, we'll get going," said Billy, still not really under-standing what just had happened. He was helping his daughter up from the sofa. She was lifeless, like a wet noodle. "Thanks, Simon, we'll call you from Houston."

CHAPTER 23

THE MESSAGE SLIPS on Billy's desk said that Attorney Karin Palmer from Austin had called, to please return the call. It was important. And that another guy named Miguel Celia had called right before five PM, desperately wanting to talk to Billy. There was a callback number, along with a notation that Celia's call had something to do with the Ray lawsuit. Billy looked at his watch. It was ten o'clock at night.

After having dropped by the house to tell Yami of Pellier's findings, he'd come by the office to return some phone calls, print his family's boarding passes and to leave instructions for Nancy and Hector for the next few days.

He dialed the number on the last message slip in his hand. "Hello?" said the stranger on the other end.

"This is Billy Bravo. You called earlier today . . . on the Ray lawsuit?"

"Yes," said the man, clearing his throat. "I'm glad you called back. Listen, I won't take much of your time. I know it's late, but what I have to say may interest you."

"What is it?"

"I used to run cases for Spearman. Last couple of years, the guy has been short on the referral fees he owes me . . . you follow?"

"Yes."

"You could say we had a parting of ways. So anyway, I have some information that could really help you on the Ray lawsuit . . . stuff to pour out Spearman."

"What kind of information?" asked Billy cautiously.

136

"Information from another case. No one knows it's out there . . . it could really tilt the scales in your favor. Stuff I got from my sources inside the U.S. District Clerk's office in Houston. Major shit coming down."

"Listen, buddy," said Billy, "I have no idea what the hell you're talking about, and I don't want to know . . . "

"You just gotta know where to look. It'll put the Ray lawsuit in the bag for ya, and you'll stick it to Spearman—that piece of shit. He still owes me about two million in finder's fees."

"That's between you and Spearman. I'll have no part in it. I have to go, okay?"

"Let me know if you change your mind. You got my number. Once you show Spearman this info, he's gonna shit . . . he won't know what to do. He might just walk away and dismiss his lawsuit."

"Maybe I'll just go to the feds. Sounds to me like you're trying to extort me . . . "

"Have I asked for any money, huh?" asked the caller. "Have I mentioned a price?"

"No, you haven't," admitted Billy, "but listen, I have to go, have to be in Houston in the morning."

"Then it's not extortion. Anyway, things are probably gonna start heating up in court in Laredo. You call me if you change your mind. You got my number. I could even drop by and see you in Houston. I live just south of Houston, in the Baytown area. I run cases for all the big shots, you follow? The refinery workers that get injured . . . I scoop them up, get them to the right attorney. Anyway, where are you gonna be at in Houston?"

"Forget it," Billy uttered, "I'm not going there."

"Suit yourself. Hey, I'm just trying to help."

Click.

CHAPTER 24

FAY HENDRY WAS A PROFESSOR of psychology at the University of Texas, Brownsville Campus. Well respected among her peers, she was one of the few authorities along the Texas-Mexico border on jury psychology.

Earlier in the week, Billy's secretary had set up an appointment for him with Professor Hendry. She had agreed to meet Mr. Bravo at seven AM, before her first morning class. Billy wanted to bring her on board as a jury consultant in the Tommy Ray lawsuit.

"Thank you for agreeing to see me this early in the morning, Professor," Billy said. "I won't take long. Besides, I'm supposed to be on a flight to Houston at noon."

"You better make it short, then." She covered her mouth as she let out a tiny yawn. "Otherwise, you won't make your flight."

"Right. It's an hour drive back to McAllen. I gotta pick up my wife and daughter and make it to the airport by twelve-thirty. It's only seven in the morning, so I'll be okay."

"So, what brings you here?" She gestured for Billy to sit down.

"I'm a trial attorney in McAllen, and I've heard about you. I was wondering if you might be interested in working for us, doing jury consultant work in the event a case goes to trial. At this point, my goal is to get the case settled. But if there's no settlement, we could definitely use a reputable jury consultant."

"When will you know if the case will be tried?"

"Depending on what judge gets assigned to hear the case, in a few weeks thereafter we'll have a pretty good idea if the case will go the distance," Billy explained.

"What kind of case is this, exactly?"

"A wrongful death case."

"Claiming negligence, or a product liability-type?" she followed.

"I'm sorry," Billy said, excusing himself, "the plaintiffs are claiming my client's drug made the deceased turn the gun on himself."

"Don't tell me it's the Ray case?"

"Yes," Billy said, looking into her eyes a bit surprised. "You've heard of it?"

"Everyone has heard of it, especially after the article in *Texas Monthly*. Oh . . . I don't know if I can help you, Mr. Bravo," she drawled. "The summer before it happened, I was a visiting professor at UT Laredo. Melissa Andarza's sister Cathy took one of my classes. I kind of got to know the family."

"I am so sorry . . . I had no idea."

"It's not your fault. I don't think the family would appreciate me getting paid to help the drug company that may have been responsible for their daughter's death."

"I see."

"I am sorry, Mr. Bravo."

"I don't know what to say," Billy said, feeling uncomfortable with the situation. "Who would have guessed it?"

"There's another colleague specializing in jury psychology out of San Antonio, and she might be able to help. Her name's Lilly Pizana."

"Okay, thanks. Sorry to take your time," Billy said, excusing himself. But before he could exit the small office completely, he stopped at the entryway, turned around and said, "Can I ask you something?"

"Sure," she said, looking exasperated.

"What makes them do it? What makes a person want to end his or her life?"

"It can be any of a whole gamut of reasons," Professor Hendry explained proudly, as she removed her reading glasses. "Given the right set of factors in the right combination, even you or I would be capable of such an act."

"Can you elaborate? I am asking you on a personal level, not as an attorney."

"People do it to escape the pain. Sometimes it is physical pain, as in the case of someone with third-degree burns all over their body. But even then, there is a tremendous amount of perturbation or anxieties attendant to the physical pain. Most often, however, it is severe emotional pain—extreme hurt, anguish or feeling like a complete failure . . . "

"I see . . . "

"I've been doing some research to find out how early in our lives we, as humans, first contemplate suicide. Have you ever thought about it?"

"Once."

A lie. Ever since Karin Palmer had come around knocking, he had begun to consider the possibility. It would probably be quicker and less painful than the violent pummeling he was going to get from Yami. The worst part was the thought of losing his entire family.

"How old were you?"

"I guess it was when I was eight or nine," started Billy "We'd gone up to Ohio to pick beets, and after having busted our backs the entire spring, the owner of the operation refused to pay us our wages. He said that he didn't like our work—that we were a bunch of worthless Mexicans . . . to get off his land."

"Really?"

"Yes."

"So you felt worthless, helpless, I suppose?" the professor volunteered.

"Yes."

She continued with her explanation. "When we look at suicide, we look at the cause of the pain. Is it self-hate, feelings of inadequacy—such as in your case being called worthless and useless—or some other irrational fear? Is it loneliness, a tormented soul, rejection, shame or a broken heart, even?"

"Okay, I understand the hurt part. But how do they get from the hurt part to the act itself?"

"The individual is dealing with agonizing pain and trying to cope. The mind wants to stop the suffering, so it considers suicide. The mind wants the pain to end. When the pain surfaces again, the mind again considers suicide. The first couple of times, it rejects the idea. Eventually, the mind accepts suicide as, perhaps, a way to escape the pain and the person moves to the planning stage. We call this 'introspection.'"

"Oh," muttered Billy.

"We usually learn much more if they happen to leave a suicide note."

"That would make sense," Billy said as he looked at his watch. "Anyway, I've taken all of your time. I'm sorry."

It was now almost eight AM. He still needed to drive an hour back to McAllen, pick up his sister Aracely to stay with Wicho and his mother-in-law, now visiting from Mexico, then go by the house to pick up Yami and Ale and rush to the airport.

"It's okay."

"Professor . . . one last thing," Billy said as he was getting up. "Do you believe a prescription drug, alone, can induce you to commit suicide?"

"I doubt it," she said. "There have to be other factors involved, like pain and anguish, perhaps extreme worry, shame, something else. For example, I could imagine the unrelenting pain and other factors already being there, and the drug might just be the thing they need to push them over the edge: sort of a detonator, if you will. There are some bad drugs out there. The profession thinks they work one way . . . and for the most part, it's true; in most of the individuals they work a certain way, but sometimes they can have the opposite effect—they can become the trigger."

"I see."

"There are always exceptions, of course."

"But," Billy followed, "would the drug makers know their drugs can trigger suicide? Be like a detonator?"

"Sure," Professor Hendry said. "Now, getting the companies to admit such a thing is a whole other ballgame. Look at Phen Phen, Vioxx, Zoloft, Paxil, Prozac, etc. For years, the makers fought tooth and nail, trying to avoid having to put even a simple black box warning on their products. They felt such warnings would be akin to an admission."

"They were, I guess, trying to deny and cover up for the longest time, like big tobacco, right?"

"Yes."

Billy came back, and shook Professor Hendry's hand, and excused himself, again. "I'll give Lilly Pizana in San Antonio a call."

"Before you go," called out the professor, "have you asked yourself why Mr. Ray would commit such an unspeakable act?"

Billy paused near the entryway. "Excuse me?"

"Have you asked yourself the key question?" She was playing with her reading glasses, twirling them in her right hand. "That's what you need to be asking. What could have caused this individual to commit the unthinkable? He had the perfect life. A beautiful family, success, money, prestige, so isn't the whole thing a little strange? Did he leave a note?"

"It is very strange, indeed," Billy agreed. "The whole thing doesn't make any sense, and there was no note."

"Maybe we'll never know," concluded the professor.

"You may be right."

"SO, what brings you by the Houston office? Something going on with the Ray litigation?"

"Well," Billy replied, "I'm sure you already heard that Yami and I brought Alessandra to MD Anderson for testing. She was admitted yesterday evening . . . we're thinking it might be leukemia. Anyway, I've been thinking, and—" He took a deep breath.

"What? Spit it out," demanded his boss.

"I need you to take me off the Ray case. I can't do it, not while my daughter is sick. Not like this . . . with everything else going on and so much riding on the case. And Falcone demanding and expecting miracles."

"Are we under any deadlines?" asked Bates.

"No. We're still waiting to see who gets appointed to hear the case." Billy was standing up, looking out the window, over downtown Houston. It looked like "The Romantics," the eighties band, was setting up to play at Party on the Plaza. He turned around to look at his boss, expecting an answer.

"I'll tell you what. Let's do this. How many files are you working on right now?"

"Counting BostonMagnifica?" asked Billy.

"Yes."

"Ninety-five."

"I want you to spread every other file you've got except BM among Jensen, Fauntleroy and the other three associates you got working down there. What are their names?"

"You mean Gault, Wilson and Hubbard?"

"Yes."

"And?"

Bates got up from his desk and walked over to where Billy was standing and looked him straight in the eye. "You just worry about BM and nothing else. Who knows . . . since no judge has been appointed to hear the case, it might be a month before we have to be back in court. By then, your daughter's health will be under control, or maybe it's nothing. You think this could work? Alleviate some of your stress?"

"What about my billings? What files am I gonna bill?"

"I'm waiving that requirement just for you this once for the next eight months. You'll still get the same salary. I want you to take care of your daughter and the BM file, that's all."

"Are you sure? Maybe Domani can take over the BM file."

"Hispanic juries hate his arrogant, pompous ass," explained Bates. "No, I need you to stay on top of it. Besides, I think you've handled Falcone pretty good up till now."

"Thanks for cutting me some slack," said Billy as he stretched out his hand.

"I still want you to make name partner, Billy," said Bates, taking Billy's hand. "You deserve it, but you need to pour out Spearman and get Falcone his defense verdict. Otherwise, I won't be able to convince the partnership committee."

"All right."

"Have you had a chance to sit down and discuss settlement with them?" asked Bates.

"No. I've been busy with my daughter's situation," lied Billy.

"Well, let me know how it goes as soon as you get that lined up. It shouldn't be a problem . . . I mean . . . four million dollars is a shitload of money. Who wouldn't take that kind of money? Hell, we've paid many other widows far less than that."

"I'll try to schedule a meeting with Spearman and his client as soon as I know what's going on with Ale," countered Billy. "I know Falcone is anxious to know what's happened since he got us the four million in authority."

"He is," said a smiling Bates as he led Billy out of his office. "He just called again. He's been calling every fifteen minutes . . . keeps asking if I've heard anything. I told him not to worry, that you have everything under control."

The senior partner was thrilled that he'd been able to convince Billy to stay on the case. At this juncture, his billings didn't matter. Reeling in BM as a client for good did. A win was all that it was gonna take, and Billy Bravo had the Latin magic—the touch, the spice, the mojo, just what was needed. He would deliver the goods. Bates was sure of it. Besides, what jury wouldn't love a guy named Billy Bravo?

CHAPTER 25

ALESSANDRA BRAVO'S HANDS felt cold and clammy in her father's as they waited in the sterile examining room inside one of the wings at MD Anderson Cancer Center. As for Yami, she'd been paralyzed by fear and had stayed outside in the lobby of the massive complex. It was four o'clock in the afternoon, and the place was a whirlwind of activity.

The nurse had just finished installing an IV line and was drawing several vacu-tainers full of blood to send to the lab. She worked quietly without making eye contact with either Alessandra or Billy. After she'd drawn the last sample, she put all her tubes with their labels in a little pink plastic basket and started making her way out of the room.

"Dr. Carlos Menotti will be with you shortly," the nurse said. "He'll come and share the lab results with you. Is there anything I can get you? Water? Coffee? A blanket? Anything?"

"No, thanks," replied the Bravos in unison.

"WHEN IS the doctor coming?" Alessandra asked, sounding worried. "We've been here all day. I want to know what's wrong, daddy." Her eyes were red and puffy from crying. She blew her nose into a ball of tissue she was holding in her right hand.

"Be patient, baby," said Billy lovingly. "They're busy, even if it is Friday afternoon."

"What's gonna happen?" Alessandra asked, looking straight into her daddy's blue eyes. "I don't want to die. What about college? Getting married and having a family? Will I be able to do those things?"

Billy thought back to the promise he'd made to his little girl. Now, nine years later, here he was embroiled in a potential life-or-death situation involving Alessandra. He would do whatever it took, whatever was necessary to help his little girl. Anything to encourage her to fight and succeed, even if it meant staying by her side twenty-four hours a day, seven days a week. Falcone, Gina Ray, BostonMagnifica, Tommy Ray, Spearman, Bates and his promotion included, could all go fly a kite. The question was, did Ale have the will to fight this monster, to vanquish it? Did she possess the *ganas* to take it head-on? Was she a fighter like her father? Did she have it in her?

"Ale," Billy said, trying to be positive, "you're gonna be fine, I promise. We're in the best cancer center in the world. And you have to really believe that you're gonna be fine, too."

Just then, Dr. Menotti opened the sliding glass door and let himself in. He was holding a chart in his hands and looking at it when he spoke. "Hello. Are you Miss Bravo?" he asked. Dr. Menotti was wearing a crisp white lab coat that reached down to his knees. Underneath the lab coat the soft-spoken doctor wore a blue button-down with a paisley tie with hints of brown and blue.

"Yes, that's me," said Alessandra, looking distressed.

"I'm Billy Bravo, her father. Mom is terrified of hospitals . . . she's in the lobby area," Billy said, extending his hand to the doctor. "It's a pleasure."

"I'm Doctor Carlos Menotti," said the man in a South American accent as he reached to shake Billy's hand. He was five-foot-nine, sporting horn-rimmed glasses and looked sharp as a tack—not so much as a single hair out of place. "I'm also a professor here at the University of Texas MD Anderson Cancer Center." He turned to Alessandra. "I have your lab results. How are you all holding up?"

"Worried," answered Alessandra, "if you want to know the truth."

"I'm gonna be asking you a few questions. I want you to relax and take a deep breath. Then, we'll talk about your lab work."

"Okay," she answered.

"How old are you?"

"Sixteen."

"Have you ever been pregnant?"

"No," she said, embarrassed.

"Do you smoke?"

"No."

"Drink?"

"No, sir."

"Any health issues?"

"Not really. A yeast infection once, but nothing else."

"Why did you go to see the referring doctor . . . ?" he looked at his chart, "Dr. Pellier?"

"My mom and dad noticed some bruises on my legs in the last couple of weeks. They got concerned, and mom ordered my dad to take me in for a checkup. He's friends with Dr. Pellier."

"Other than the bruising, had you noticed anything unusual?"

"No."

"Were you tired?"

"A little."

"Joint pain?"

"No."

"Heavy bleeding?"

"Yes, now that you mention it. I noticed my last two periods were heavier than usual. Also, my gums had started bleeding a couple of weeks ago."

"Mom bought her Sensodyne toothpaste thinking that would do it," interjected Billy.

"Okay." Dr. Menotti said, "What did Dr. Pellier tell you?"

"That he thought it could be leukemia."

"Is that it? Anything else?"

"No."

"All right. Let me tell you about your lab work. The results seem to confirm that you have Acute Promyelocitic Leukemia, or APL. The good news is that APL is the most treatable and curable of all leukemias."

"I told you," said Billy, trying to keep his daughter's spirits up.

"And the bad news?" Alessandra asked.

"Well, we won't be able to confirm if it is indeed APL until tomorrow when we squeeze you in for a bone marrow aspiration."

"If it is not APL, then what?" she asked.

"It could be another type of leukemia, either ALL or AML," said Dr. Menotti. "The type of leukemia will determine the best course of treatment. That's why we first must know what type of leukemia it is."

"Am I gonna die?" Alessandra asked, point-blank. The question shocked Billy.

"No, you're not gonna die. The patients that do die of leukemia die of complications because their immune systems have been compromised. You are young and healthy, and there's no reason why you couldn't be in remission in thirty days."

"Remission in thirty days?" asked Billy with eyes wide open.

"Sure, assuming there are no complications."

"God bless you, doctor," cried Alessandra.

"Do you want to know what APL does? Why you're bruising?" the doctor asked.

"Please tell us," said Billy, being polite.

"Think of an assembly line in a factory. Inside your bones, within the marrow, there are workers making platelets, plus red and white blood cells, okay?"

"Okay."

"Well, the worker in charge of making white blood cells goes nuts and starts making defective white blood cells . . . these are cancerous cells. They start attacking everything else, including your platelets, thus your reduced platelet count. Your platelets help you stop from bleeding. Your bruises are the result of internal bleeding, since your platelet count is very low."

"I see," she said.

"What we do here is give you medication to bring the worker around and have him start making healthy white blood cells again. We also kill all the defective cells to prevent them from causing more damage. Are you with me so far?"

"Uh huh," she mumbled bravely.

"If we confirm that you have APL, then you will be given a new cutting-edge drug called Fledkort, developed by an up-and-coming drug company called BostonMagnifica. You will also take arsenic through your IV line in a combination therapy. It's a new, experimental protocol we are following here at MD with very good results."

"What are her chances of beating this thing?" Billy asked.

"Thanks to Fledkort, APL is 99 percent curable and treatable. If after a year of taking Fledkort you have not relapsed, then the statistics tell us you'll be 95 percent out of the woods. If, after you go off Fledkort, you go another three years with no relapse, you'll be 99 percent cured."

"I'll take those odds," joked Billy.

"So, I'll be on chemo for a while?" asked Alessandra.

"Yes," answered Dr. Menotti, "but you should be able to resume your normal life. We'll keep you here until we get you in remission . . . then we'll send you home and you'll continue treating at home. You'll come up here for check-ups, though."

"What do you mean by 'new protocol'?" asked Billy.

"There are what we called different 'treatment tiers,' ways to combat cancer. This drug combination with Fledkort and arsenic is a first-tier treatment. If it doesn't work, then we give you some other type of chemo until we get to the old radiation, and then, if all else fails, we do bone marrow transfusions . . . last tier."

"Wait," said Billy, "you mean arsenic as in the poison?"

"Yes. The Chinese have been using arsenic for thousands of years in very, very small quantities. And now we know why . . . because it works."

"Are there any side effects?" Alessandra asked.

"Some," Dr. Menotti answered, "some side effects like bloating, fever, diarrhea, clotting and dry skin. But we have everything here to take care of that."

"How old are you, Dr. Menotti?" asked Billy. "You're too young to be a doctor. And, I mean that as a compliment."

"I'm thirty-nine. Married, with three young girls."

"Where are you from?" Billy asked.

"Chile."

"For a moment there, I thought you were from Argentina," Billy said, trying to lighten up the mood in the room.

"No. We're neighbors, though."

"You like soccer?"

"*Claro.*"

"One last thing," Billy said.

"Yes?"

"When can we expect Ale to be in remission? In a couple of days?"

"Oh, no," explained Dr. Menotti, "It just depends. We have to keep Alessandra here to see how she'll react to the chemo and how she tolerates its side effects. It could be two weeks . . . maybe a month. But if there are complications, then it could be much longer."

"Really?" Billy said, taken aback, now rethinking his options in the BM case. Now more than ever, Billy knew he needed Spearman to come to the table and get the case settled. Because not getting the case settled opened up the possibility of a trial that could lead to disaster. And if BM went under, Fledkort would no longer be available and Alessandra could very easily end up dead.

Dr. Menotti noticed Billy's concerned look. "Mr. Bravo, the social worker will meet with all of you in the morning after Alessandra has had her bone marrow aspiration."

"Okay."

"She'll get you situated as far as housing, counseling, religious services—everything and anything you might need. We cater to people from all over the world. We've been doing this for a long time. We're pros."

"Thanks. We came with enough clothes for the weekend. We barely had time to catch a plane out of McAllen yesterday."

"You're gonna be fine, Alessandra. In a little while, they'll move you to your room. I will see you in the morning after the aspiration. Your mother can stay in the room with you. There's a fold-out bed. Goodnight."

"Goodnight, doctor," Alessandra replied.

"*Hasta mañana,*" Billy added.

CHAPTER 26

EARLY THE NEXT MORNING, Billy darted to the Houston office before heading back to MD Anderson to be with his daughter. Ale's bone marrow aspiration was scheduled for ten AM. It would take him less than fifteen minutes to make it from Milam Street, where the principal offices were located in the downtown area, to the medical center. It was a straight shot down Main Street, two streets over from the Houston office. Nancy had called and left a message that Falcone had called a meeting with his lawyers.

When Billy walked in the large conference room, Falcone and Bates suddenly got quiet and ordered Billy to sit down. There was a third gentleman sitting next to Falcone whom Billy did not recognize.

"Billy," said Bates, "this here is Rodney Millar. He's a publicist, or what we call here in Texas, a PR guy. He's here to help us get a handle on this thing."

"A pleasure," said Billy as he reached over the table and shook Millar's hand.

"How do you do?" asked Millar, the spin master. The guy had a slight Caribbean accent and appeared to be in his mid-fifties. He was rather trim, about five-foot-eleven and 175 pounds. He sported short, cropped hair, was clean shaven and had brown eyes and a friendly smile.

"Fine . . . just fine," said Billy as he took his seat.

"Billy," Falcone said, jumping in, "explain to Mr. Millar your take on the potential jury pool down there. How can we influence them? Now that Zerevrea is being aggressively promoted and has made its debut, we're thinking of putting on a marketing campaign targeting the Hispanic population in Webb County."

"Excuse me?" Billy replied, somewhat confused.

"Well, since we're under attack with the story in *Texas Monthly* and the articles in the local paper, we want to counteract. Start thinking ahead, maybe using TV commercials or print and radio advertisements touting Zerevrea's benefits and BostonMagnifica's accomplishments . . . sway the jury pool, if you will."

"You mean *taint*," Billy corrected Falcone. "Taint the jury pool—that's what it's called."

"You call it tainting, we call it educating the public," intervened Millar in a firm but affable tone.

"Well," Billy said, clearing his throat, "if you must know, the population is mostly Hispanic, and of the 250,000 inhabitants, only about 10 percent have a college education . . . with about 20 percent barely having finished high school."

"What else?" asked Millar. He was jotting everything down on a yellow pad.

"I want to say I read somewhere that about 70 percent of the population was born in the United States. The other 30 percent came from somewhere else, mostly Mexico."

"Good," replied Millar. "What else comes to mind?"

"Oh, yeah," remembered Billy, "Spanish is spoken by 91 percent of the population . . . and out of the entire population, only half speak proficient English."

"This is good," added Millar. "Have you tried many cases down there?"

"I'd say about twenty-five jury trials in state court . . . but only one previously in federal court. We've won all of them."

"Were you the first or second chair?"

"I first-chaired all the cases."

"So, you've had a lot of hands-on experience with the folks down there?"

"I'm a trial lawyer, Mr. Millar. I've tried cases in every county from Cameron to Webb, to Bexar, all the way to Nueces. Different courthouses, different judges and different juries."

"What was the jury makeup down in Laredo?"

"They are 90 percent Hispanic, one or two retired Anglos, from what I remember. There were always a couple of teachers, nurses, the occasional winter Texan transplant, some engineers or managers that work in the *maquiladoras* across in Nuevo Laredo. One college student usually squeaks by, a couple of laborers, even small business owners. That's always been my experience."

"And lawyers, doctors, heads of industry?"

"They always get stricken from the panel. Doctors hate plaintiffs' lawyers, so the plaintiffs' attorneys always cut them loose. Lawyers don't have a chance with either side for some reason or another. And most heads of large corporations have had to face litigation. They think the plaintiff is just trying to hit the lotto, so they get knocked out, too."

"This is all very interesting. Now, tell me about Gina Ray. Have you met her?"

"Eh, no," stuttered Billy. "I've spoken with her attorney, though. He's trying to squeeze me in to see her, to start talking settlement, hopefully soon. Maybe next week."

"Have you heard anything from her attorney, what kind of client he thinks he's dealing with?"

"Yes. According to Spearman, she doesn't want money," Billy lied some more, putting words in Spearman's mouth. "She wants a public apology. She wants to hear BM publicly admit that Zerevrea kills."

After the failed informal settlement conference, that had been Billy's impression. Except, he was not about to admit to Falcone that the feeble attempt at resolving the lawsuit had been totally unproductive so far and that the whole exercise had been a complete and utter waste of time. Gina Ray, in essence, had kicked his ass. And if Falcone knew exactly what had transpired, he would probably can his law firm right there and on the spot. Then, of course, Bates would turn to Billy and inform him that his promotion was out the window. Maybe he would even get fired and lose his health insurance, which his family desperately needed right now more than anything else in the world.

"A justice seeker, huh?" Millar asked.

"Ah, yes. You could say that," countered Billy, sounding distracted, thinking of Ale. He looked at his watch. "From talking to Spearman, the impression I got was that she's not in it for the money."

"What's a justice seeker?" Falcone asked.

"A plaintiff that wants to right a wrong, send a message. Somebody on a mission to bring a corporate giant to its knees and get them to admit they were wrong. These types don't care about the money . . . they want their day in court to show the world what kind of piece-of-shit the defendant really is," Billy explained.

"In my experience," interjected Bates, "those are always the most difficult cases to get settled."

"Exactly," added Billy. "She's going to be a tough nut to crack. Add to that the fact that her attorney has deep pockets and can hang in there for a couple of years."

"That could be a problem," Millar said. "Sometimes a lawyer who is running out of money while financing the litigation can help turn things around by helping convince his own client to settle."

"This is not such a case," added Billy. "The guy has the cash reserves to go the distance."

"What do you propose we do now, then?" Millar asked.

"Give me another sixteen million in authority right away, just to make it an even twenty," Billy said.

Falcone protested, "But I already approved four. That's a lot of damn money!"

"Yes, but," replied Billy, "four million to a justice seeker is nothing. I need twenty million. Spearman will put enormous pressure on Gina Ray to settle. The guy is a lawyer, but he's also a businessman. With all this money on the table, I doubt he's going to want to try this thing on principle simply because Gina Ray wants justice and wants to prove a point."

"Billy is right," added Bates. "Wave those bills in front of Spearman, and he'll start leaning heavily on the client. I've seen it happen dozens of times. The incentive to try the case will go out the window once the lawyer sees the piles of cash on the table."

"That's one way," added Billy, "or once we get our new judge and the case starts moving, we start pounding Spearman. We don't give him any breathing room, not an inch. We hit him with discovery, depositions, motions, investigate their witnesses, experts, the plaintiff—we leave no stone unturned until we tire him out or he convinces his client to come to her senses and come to the table prepared to negotiate."

"The old 'scorch-the-earth technique,' eh?" added Bates.

"We go for the throat," finished Billy.

"I don't follow," said Falcone.

"We put them through their paces," Billy said. "We outspend them, outwork them, outrun them, outsmart them and wear them down until they make a mistake or give up. And if we get lucky, we land in front of another federal judge who is lazy as shit, leans in favor of corporate defendants, doesn't want to hear cases and is known to grant the defense's motions for summary judgment. Which means the plaintiff gets poured out, loses his shirt and we all go home."

"Or you land in front of a judge that loves the preemption doctrine," interjected Bates. "That's the easiest way to send a plaintiff home packing."

"Could happen," followed Billy. "Plaintiffs' lawyers have been on the losing end of that argument for years in federal courts."

"What is that?" asked Millar.

"Our lawyers argue that because the FDA approved Zerevrea," Falcone explained, showing a basic understanding of the doctrine, "the FDA must have found that Zerevrea was safe. And if the federal government has already said that the drug is safe and has given the company permission to sell it, then you can't come into court and say that under state law, the drug is considered 'unreasonably dangerous'."

"So, federal law overrules state law?" asked Millar.

"Exactly," replied Falcone, happy to see Millar catching on.

"Mr. Falcone is right," followed Bates, stroking the CEO's ego.

"Ninety-nine percent of all Republican appointees to the bench side with the defense on such motions," said Billy. "Except we don't know what kind of judge we're going to get."

"So, we could end up with a Democrat judge?" Millar pointed out.

"It's possible, but don't forget," Billy said, looking at Falcone, "even if we get a judge that abhors the preemption doctrine and the case is allowed to reach the jury, we will win in the Fifth Circuit Court of Appeals. They'll reverse for sure."

"Yes, but in the meantime? What about all the bad publicity? Isn't there an easier way?" Falcone asked.

"I wish there was, Mr. Falcone," Billy answered. "Let's just face this thing square in the eye and deal with it. Either give me a bunch of money to make Spearman salivate, get this thing settled and get you the confidentiality that you want . . . or let's beat them at trial. I haven't lost a case. Now, I'm still willing to try to resolve it without much fuss, but if that doesn't work, then let's just take them head-on."

"Billy is right," interjected Bates. "I've seen hundreds of cases where the plaintiffs eventually give up or just settle for pennies on the dollar. They end up accepting nuisance value, if you will."

"Or," Billy continued as he looked straight over at Millar. "We can try to taint the jury pool—as has been proposed here this morning. Personally, I think tainting the jury pool is the stupidest thing I've ever heard. When the new judge hears from Spearman that we're manipulating the media, he'll find a way to sock it to us. I don't even want to think about it. Hell, if you had a remote chance to get the gag order, that'll be out the window, too."

Millar, Falcone and Bates looked at each other, surprised at Billy's comments.

"So, then?" Falcone asked.

"Look," Billy said, "it's just a matter of time before Spearman gets his hands on Croutoux's smoking memo or heaven knows what else. Get me twenty million in poker chips so I can get this thing settled and make it go away for you. The last thing you want is for Spearman to make that memo available to every plaintiff's lawyer across the nation."

"Why don't we," Millar started, "try to nip this thing in the bud before more stories are published or before the nation's media jumps on the bandwagon."

"What do you propose?" Bates followed.

"Let's do all those things Mr. Bravo is proposing, but let's also launch our Zerevrea campaign for the Laredo market. Educate the public just in case we have to try it," explained Millar.

"It's Mr. Falcone's call," replied Billy, turning toward Millar. "Listen, I have to run to the hospital. My daughter is having a procedure done. I'll be in touch."

"I forgot you need to go. Sorry to keep you, Billy," said Bates. "Bye."

CHAPTER 27

ILLY WAS SIPPING coffee, watching *Live, with Larry King* down in the hospital cafeteria while waiting on Ale's lab results. Larry King was doing a show on Army wives and their husbands coming back from the war, recently diagnosed with PTSD. It seemed in the last twenty-four months, with the escalation of suicide bombings in Iraq and the increasing IED (improvised explosive devices) attacks, the rate of PTSD in soldiers returning home was at an all-time high.

The Pentagon had finally admitted the existence of a high incidence of PTSD in the ranks—38,000 diagnosed cases to date—but had issued a statement maintaining that the Joint Chiefs of Staff and the president truly cared for the servicemen and servicewomen of the United States of America. Consequently, millions of dollars had been approved for their mental treatment, rehabilitation and medication. To show its patriotism and its support for the troops, BostonMagnifica, now known as "The Transparent Pharmaceutical," the only drug company to step up to the plate, had pledged to provide a year's worth of Zerevrea at no cost to all Iraq veterans that needed it.

"This is Larry King," said Larry, sitting across from three Army wives. "We're talking to Maggie Johnson, Victoria Hammond and Jana Petrides, all married to husbands who fought in Iraq. When we come back, we'll talk to their husbands, all suffering from PTSD, and how they're coping with this mental disorder. We'll also have Tim Keebler, the father of Jim Keebler, on the show. Tim recently testified in front of the House Committee on Veteran's Affairs regarding his son's suicide. A native of Houston, Jimmy was with the Texas National Guard and had just recently returned home from his tour of duty. We'll talk to Senator Andy del Toro, who thinks five hundred soldier suicides in 2005 alone were too many and thinks that no matter how many new mental health professionals are hired to teach soldiers to recognize the symptoms, more needs to be done—including the ban on drugs such as Paxil, Prozac and Cymbalta. Also, on the show, Colonel Erica Ritchie, a whistleblower from inside the office of the Army Surgeon General who claims the military is downplaying the number of suicides and reported cases of PTSD. Don't go away . . . we'll be right back after this brief message from our sponsors."

BostonMagnifica's TV commercial came on, complete with scenes of the devastation in New Orleans, huge waves pounding the Gulf Coast, beach homes on stilts crashing down into the waters, hurricane winds yanking the roofs off several gas stations and warehouses. Then, there was a scene with a happy family enjoying a gorgeous, sunny day at the park. The five of them were laughing, playing touch football and wrestling on the picnic blanket. Dad was even playing airplane with his baby boy.

The announcer said, "Zerevrea, the Calm After the Storm. Talk to your doctor if Zerevrea is right for you. In clinical trials, Zerevrea has been proven effective in eliminating symptoms of depression and anxiety. Zerevrea, Calming Relief For You and Your Loved Ones."

Larry King was back, and he wanted to know if the wives had noticed any changes in their husbands since their return home. The military wives—indoctrinated to tow the line—had replied that they supported their husbands, supported the war, supported President Bailey and were confident that with the proper treatment and BostonMagnifica's Zerevrea (the show's producers had insisted they had to plug Falcone's company), their husbands' PTSD could be brought under control. Their husbands would be normal again. They were not that concerned, for Zerevrea was a promising new drug: it had no side effects and it was free.

"ARE THE LAB results in?" Billy asked, looking at his watch. It was seven o'clock in the evening, and he was now standing with Yami next to the nurses' station right outside Ale's room. Both were exhausted and ragged. Yami looked as if she was about to have a nervous breakdown, her eyes vibrant red from crying. Billy was disheveled with beard growth and dark circles under both eyes.

"Yes," replied Yami, "Nurse Denise, Menotti's assistant, dropped by a few minutes ago and said that the lab confirmed it is APL leukemia. She said Menotti will drop by in the morning and talk with the three of us. She sounded upbeat."

"That's good news, right?" muttered Billy. "Menotti said that is the most treatable and curable kind, right?"

"Supongo que sí."

"It is," said Billy, trying to comfort his wife. "Menotti said it's the easiest leukemia to treat and that Fledkort is 99 percent effective in treating it. By the way, I don't know if you know this, but Fledkort is manufactured by my client. I didn't want to be the one to have to tell you this, but if I lose the Tommy Ray case and the floodgates of litigation come unhinged, then BostonMagnifica could go bankrupt. If that happens, there's a chance that Ale's medicine might no longer be available."

"What?" Yami's jaw dropped to the floor. She looked panic-stricken.

"I'm sorry," said Billy as he looked down at the floor.

"You mean," started Yami, "a loss in Laredo could hurt Ale?"

"Yes."

"My God. Oh my God, Billy!" cried Yami. "You have to win! My baby must live!" Billy hugged his wife, who by now was sobbing loudly.

"I will," whispered Billy in Yami's ear, "I will win, I promise. One way or another. I'll do my best."

IT WAS seven-thirty AM, and Billy was sleeping, curled up on a sofa in the visitors' sitting area down the hall from Ale's room. Yami had been unable to sleep and was now poking at her husband, trying to wake him up.

"Billy," said Yami, looking and sounding worried, "they've started Ale on the chemo."

"Is she okay?" asked Billy as he rubbed his eyes.

"She's running a fever. The arsenic makes her throw up, and the Fledkort gives her the runs. Plus, she's all *picoteada* with IVs on both arms because they're pumping her full of hemoglobin, platelets and medicine. The nurses come in every two hours to draw blood. She can't get any sleep. Plus, the room is freezing. Why, God? Why is this happening to my baby?"

Billy did not know what to say. All he could mumble was, "Has Dr. Menotti dropped by?"

"You just missed him, but he'll be back around ten this morning," she said, shrugging her shoulders. "He explained that Ale should be in remission in six weeks or so. She'll have to stay here until then."

"Oh." He was now sitting up, running his fingers through his bed hair trying to fix it.

"I'll stay here with her. Why don't you fly home and bring me more clothes," Yami asked, trying to be strong.

"We'll have to figure out where to stay. This is rough, sleeping on this little sofa. There have got to be places around here with weekly and monthly rates," Billy countered, "within walking distance."

"Mary, the social worker, said that Rotary House across the street is a good place to stay. Maybe I can look into that tomorrow."

"Let me know what we need to do," Billy said. "I can take medical leave if I have to."

"No," said Yami, "now is not the time to jeopardize your employment or the health insurance. You need to keep working, and you need to win in Laredo."

"I know," agreed Billy.

"You can drive up with Mauricio on weekends and visit until we figure out what's gonna happen next," Yami said decisively. "I need to stay with Ale."

"I understand. Are you sure it's okay for me to go back to work? I mean it."

"Let's stick with the game plan. *Yo me quedo.*"

"Okay," he said, nodding his head in agreement.

They hugged in silence, the two of them alone in the sitting area. Yami cried in Billy's ear, "I pray to God nothing else goes wrong. I don't think I could handle it." She used the crumpled tissue she'd been holding in her right hand to wipe away the moisture from her eyes.

CHAPTER 28

ILLY'S BLACKBERRY went off, and he intentionally disregarded the call. It was Karin Palmer calling from Austin. He was exhausted after having spent the prior night and most of the day pacing the hallways at the hospital, worrying about his daughter. He would have to call the Austin attorney at a later time.

With his life quickly spiraling out of control, Billy decided to pay a much-needed visit to the hospital chapel. Located deep inside the massive research complex, the nondenominational chapel was next to the cafeteria and the business center in the compound's basement. The place was open twenty-four hours a day, seven days a week for those needing spiritual comfort.

Once inside the chapel, Billy fell to his knees and started praying. He'd been praying for a while when his cell phone started vibrating again. He looked at his watch; it was already nine-fifteen in the morning. He ignored the call. Without fail, a few minutes later, the phone vibrated again and a text message popped up on the screen. It was Nancy, his secretary, wanting to know if he was going to attend a status hearing with Judge Kyle Dorfman, the new judge appointed to hear the BM lawsuit.

The text message added that a guy named Roland Hernández, Dorfman's law clerk from Harvard, had called early that morning and advised Nancy that Judge Dorfman wanted to get the Ray lawsuit off his docket. The judge wanted to finish the case in three months, four months max. Judge Dorfman would allow each side to do one round of discovery, take two expert depositions a piece, with each deposition lasting no more than three hours. When that was done, the case would be turned over to the jury.

It was time to get the show on the road.

BILLY HAD NEVER HEARD of Judge Kyle Dorfman or his obsession with speed. With all of his personal complications boiling to the surface, Billy was not sure that three months would be enough time to get the BM case ready for trial. It was one thing to have an entire year to prepare a case and then try the actual case in one or two short weeks. But it was completely insane to try and work up a pharmaceutical case in three months and then try it in the fourth month. The whole thing was preposterous.

"You look like hell," said Hector. He was sitting across Billy's desk holding a cup of coffee. "How are things going?"

"Worried about my daughter . . . haven't been sleeping much. I've got all kinds of shit running through my head. I think I'm going crazy. And now Judge Dorfman wants us to drop everything and try this thing in three months. I hate federal judges."

"Is Ale going to be okay?" asked Hector, a serious, concerned look on his face.

"We don't know yet." Billy stood up and looked out of his office window. "Doctor says there's a new drug that can make her well. She might have to be on it for the rest of her life, though . . . we don't know. They're running all kinds of tests, doing everything they can to put her in remission."

"Well," Hector said, "I'm glad to hear her doc in Houston is going all out for her, Billy. I guess that's what they do. Try everything to make sure the patient beats cancer. Make sure the patient lives to fight another day."

"Yeah, I guess," sighed Billy, shaking his head. "Have you spoken with Croutoux's son again? Anything new?"

"The guy said he'd gotten himself appointed executor of his daddy's estate and that he was gonna start going through his things and selling the house on Blue Mountain Lake and his place in the city. He'd said he would call if anything else turned up."

"Okay. Hey, do me a favor."

"What do you need, boss?"

"Nancy has the number for a guy that called from Houston the other day. The guy used to run cases for Spearman . . . says he's got some info on the Tommy Ray case. Talk to him and see what he's got to say."

"All right, Billy. I'll get right on it. Call me if you need anything else. I'm just down the hall." Hector could see Billy's thoughts were hundreds of miles away and not on the scheduling conference less than twenty-four hours away.

"Thanks, Hector. *De veras. Gracias.*"

DRIVING up over the Queen Isabella causeway on his way to South Padre Island, Billy had rolled down the windows, stuck his arm out and felt the cool, February sea breeze whizzing by. He looked north, way out in the distance and could see the area of the bay where his nightmares always occurred. He felt shivers down his spine. There it was—the exact spot, wedged between the marshes and the flats, where in his dreams his old man would disappear, vanishing along with the godforsaken red fish.

Eric Clapton's "Tears in Heaven" was playing on the radio. Maybe it was the song or the fact that guilt overcame him, but he suddenly remembered that he still needed to go visit his father at the cemetery and check to see if the headstone had been delivered.

He drove down South Padre Island boulevard. Except for a few work crews rebuilding the island's hotels and residences, the place looked like a ghost town. He made a right on Jupiter Street and followed it to the end. On Gulf Avenue, he made a quick right and then a quick left onto the empty lot where his million-dollar beach house once stood. He turned off the car but left the radio on.

Would you know my name . . . if I saw you in heaven? He was humming the words in his head, thinking of what life would be like without Alessandra, without his family, when it hit him.

Hector had said it that morning when they were talking. It was like a hammer to his head, and it all came back to him. Everybody up in Houston was doing their part to save Alessandra. Everybody! Not just Menotti or her nurse. Everyone was pitching in to give her a fighting chance, so his daughter could live another day. These were folks on a mission, coming together to beat cancer, no matter the price, however long and painful the treatment was, just so the patient could continue to live, if just for another year, a month, even a few more days. And what was Billy doing? What the hell was Billy Cuauhtémoc Bravo doing to help his own daughter?

"YES, MR. BRAVO," said Nancy, "what is it?"

"I need you to track down Spearman. Call his office, his house, whatever it takes. I need to talk to him. It's urgent."

"And what do I tell him?"

"I need an hour of his time. I don't care if he's trying a case out of state. I'll go see him. I need to talk to him concerning Gina Ray."

"You don't want to wait to talk to him at the status conference in Laredo? It's just a day away."

"No. This can't wait. I need to see him or talk to him before then."

"Okay. I'll see if I can track him down."

"Thanks," said Billy, "I'll see you in a bit. I'm driving back from Padre. Call me as soon as you locate him."

"Okay."

"One last thing . . . set up a conference call with Bates and Falcone . . . for let's say . . . four o'clock. I should be back in the office by then."

"Is everything all right?" asked Nancy. "You sound out of breath, too excited maybe?"

"I'm fine. I just thought of a way to get BostonMagnifica its defense verdict. That's all."

"I'm sure Falcone will be glad to hear that."

"We'll see."

Billy punched the accelerator on his Pilot and drove west over the Queen Isabella Causeway through Port Isabel, Laguna Vista and past the speed trap known as Los Fresnos, whizzing by until he reached Highway 77. Then he veered northwest toward the city of McAllen. It took a little under an hour as he hit speeds in excess of ninety miles an hour and then he made his way north onto 281 until he exited on University Boulevard and arrived at his office on Clossner Avenue.

"YOU CAN'T BE SERIOUS!" cried Falcone over the speaker-phone.

"Look . . . if you want this thing to work, you've got to give me some real money, Mr. Falcone," demanded Billy. "I need some real authority here, not chicken feed. Or do you want to end up like Merck . . . having to dish out billions of dollars to settle thousands of lawsuits?"

"What are we talking about?" Falcone asked. "I already gave you four, then twenty—that's plenty of authority. Plus, whatever coverage there is from the limited insurance policy."

"There's only a million in coverage under the insurance policy, Mr. Falcone. That, plus the twenty you gave me won't be enough. I need seventy-five to make this thing work."

"Seventy-five million? That's crazy! How can I justify it to the board members? If the plaintiff's Bar finds out we're paying seventy-five mil a pop, we're screwed!"

"Look!" said Billy quite exasperated, "you tell the board that we need the money to pay the Andarza and Guerra families their 'hush' money. Otherwise, 'justice seeker' won't go along, according to Spearman, and we will have a real problem."

"But, Billy, seventy-five million is a lot of dough."

"I'm not gonna pay seventy-five, Mr. Falcone. I just need to know that I have that kind of authority in case I need it. Besides, isn't President Bailey's healthcare initiative due to be amended to include the Iraq War veterans, too?" asked Billy, putting more pressure on the CEO. "You wouldn't want this thing to embarrass the president, would you?"

"Billy's right," Bates chimed in, "it would be stupid to embarrass the White House. Better nip this thing in the bud. What's a few more million? Besides, you'll make it right back once the initiative catches on fire; BostonMagnifica will be raking it in."

"I'm already spending a boatload of money on Millar and the new campaign," complained Falcone. "This is getting expensive."

"Look," said Billy, "last year BostonMagnifica contributed to numerous political races for members of Congress and state officials, a combined total of forty-five million dollars. And you want to nickel-and-dime Spearman? You're scrounging, fighting with me over pennies, when the fact remains that BM has worldwide sales of over thirty million dollars a day. If we don't make this thing go away, BM could end up mortally wounded. I, too, can't afford for BM to go under, Mr. Falcone. Did you know that? My daughter needs your Fledkort. That's the only chance she's got to survive leukemia. Doctors are telling us she'll have to take it for the rest of her life. So, I'm telling you—no, I'm begging you—please get me more authority. I'll make the case go away. I will."

"All right," said a reluctant Falcone, "give me twenty-four hours, and I'll have an answer. Let me see how much money we can come up with."

"That won't do. I need to know now," said Billy. "I have a meeting with Spearman later on this evening. The guy is trying a case in Starr County next door. I've got to get this done before our scheduling conference with Judge Dorfman tomorrow. I need to know now . . . today."

"Okay," said Falcone, sounding out of breath, "I'll need an hour. You'll have an answer in an hour."

"I'll be waiting," replied Billy.

CHAPTER 29

JUDGE DORFMAN WAS already sitting on the bench going over the criminal docket and taking care of a couple of sentencings that had been scheduled for eight-thirty that morning. As a visiting judge now handling the Tommy Ray case, Judge Dorfman liked to pitch in and do other things around the courtroom. This morning, Dorfman had convinced Judge Allende to let him call the criminal docket and even handle some of the sentencing hearings.

Billy walked in, took his seat and waited for the judge to call his case, scheduled for nine AM. A few minutes later, Spearman walked in with Hanslik in tow, and the two of them took their place three rows behind Billy. Like boxers waiting in their corner for the bell, they gave each other menacing looks.

Judge Dorfman was a chubby sixty-year-old with curls of white hair on the sides and back of his head. His shiny bald pate was accentuated with a strawberry birthmark the size of a half-dollar, dead front and center above his forehead. His reading glasses were hanging on a chain from his neck.

"The court will now call the civil docket," announced Judge Dorfman, sounding angry as he reached for his reading glasses. "In the matter of Gina Ray v. BostonMagnifica Pharmaceuticals. Announce your name and who you represent for the record."

"Good morning, Your Honor," announced Spearman, making his way to counsel's table. Hanslik followed him with a briefcase in each hand. "Riley Spearman, along with Mr. Hanslik. We represent Gina Ray, the plaintiff in this case."

"Billy Bravo, Your Honor," interjected Billy. "My firm represents BostonMagnifica Pharmaceuticals, the defendant. Present and ready." He was now taking his place at the other counsel's table, straight across from Spearman.

"What's going on with this case?" asked the judge. "Please bring me up to speed."

"Nothing, Your Honor," explained Billy. "Judge Allende recused herself at the last meeting, and nothing has been done since a couple of months ago. Then the holidays got in the way."

"Well, that's all about to change," growled Judge Dorfman as he looked at Spearman. "Mr. Spearman, is that true?"

"Yes, Your Honor. I'm afraid that's true. Nothing's been done."

"So, there's been no discovery? Nothing for two months?" asked Judge Dorfman, rubbing his hands.

"We've exchanged standard requests for disclosures, judge," said Billy, "but that's about it. We're trying to come up with a joint case management and discovery plan."

"The plaintiffs," added Spearman, "if we could, Your Honor, we'd like to get to trial in twelve months from now. We'd like to have about nine months in which to do discovery and take depositions, a final pretrial conference and then trial."

"Judge," said Billy, "if plaintiffs want to have nine months in which to do discovery, that's fine with us, except we would then require the court to issue a gag order, instantly. The widow, Ms. Ray, has been talking to the media and the press and she's been tainting the jury pool. She needs to stop. Frankly, we're worried our client won't get a fair trial down here in Laredo."

"That's a crock!" cried Spearman. "If somebody's been trying to taint the jury pool, it's Mr. Bravo's client, judge. Have you seen their TV commercials? They're all over the airwaves. Never before has the Laredo market witnessed such overpromotion by a drug company. Not until this case, anyway—until this defendant."

"Judge," cried Billy, "my client has the right to advertise its products. This is part of a nationwide campaign that has been in the making for quite some time now. Besides, not only does the U.S. Constitution guarantee freedom of speech to individuals, but it also extends the same rights to businesses and corporations. My client has the right to advertise and promote. It's not illegal."

"Gentlemen," interrupted Judge Dorfman, looking exasperated, "take note. I don't see anything complicated about this case. And certainly, the court is not going to issue a gag order on either side. Now, either the drug made the guy do it, as plaintiff claims, or it didn't, as BostonMagnifica contends. So, you'll have a month to do written discovery and another month to take all the depositions you want, with the exception of the experts. I will only allow two experts per side, and no expert will be deposed for more than six hours. Jury selection will be May 4, and the trial will commence promptly on May 10, 2006. Between the weeks of April 16 and the end of April, you can mediate, arbitrate and have hearings on your summary judgments, Daubert challenges or do whatever else you like. I'll be available. You want your day in court? Listen, I'll promise you this . . . I will give you your day in court, but I'm not going to play games or get bogged down with gag order this or gag order that. If Gina Ray wants to speak her mind, let her. If BM wants to advertise, let them. Just be warned that I'm not like other federal judges who sit on motions for an entire year, making everybody wait and spend money and then the day of trial decide to find a lame excuse not to work and reach for defense counsel's motion for summary judgment and grant it at the last minute. No sir, not this court. I won't make everybody spend money, waste time and resources, get stressed out and in the process give the entire federal bench a bad name. People have lost confidence and trust in the judicial system, and that, my friends, won't happen in my court. I might be tough, loud or even offensive to some of you, but no one can say I'm not fair. Both sides will get a fair shake when in front of me, guaranteed. Now, get to work. This court will be in recess."

Both Billy and Spearman called out to the judge requesting more time. Three months to try a multimillion-dollar case was simply not enough.

"Judge," cried Billy, first, "I have my daughter at MD Anderson being treated for leukemia . . . three months is not enough time . . . I'm having to—"

"I agree," said Spearman, interrupting and joining Billy at the same time, "it will take me at least two months to interview, screen and hire the two experts, judge. Three months is just not enough time."

"Mr. Bravo," said Judge Dorfman, "if you can't try the case, then I suggest somebody else in your firm should pick up the slack. Maybe you should be worrying about your daughter and let somebody else worry about BostonMagnifica."

"But . . . but . . . " mumbled Billy, feeling like a trapeze artist dangling on the high wire. *I was handpicked to try this case. My promotion is riding on it, not to mention my daughter's medication.* "I'll figure something out, judge. We'll find a way to be ready in three months."

"As for you," said Dorfman, pointing at Spearman, "maybe you should have lined up your experts first, way before thinking of filing this lawsuit. You should have made damn sure your client had a viable case. The law gives you two years in which to file a wrongful death case. You know that, and I don't have to tell you. That time is supposed to be spent investigating, getting your ducks in a row, making sure the evidence does exist so you can prove your case once you get into the courtroom. If you jumped the gun before doing your research, well, then you'll have to explain that to your client. I will not delay the case because you failed to do what any other reasonable, prudent attorney in the state of Texas would have done before filing or because you failed to find an expert who is willing to say what you need him to say to support the theory of your case. Sorry."

"But . . . " replied Spearman weakly, " . . . it's just that—"

"Gentlemen, I suggest the both of you get to work. We're running out of time," instructed Judge Dorfman, "I'll expect you both to submit a joint case management and discovery plan tracking my deadlines before the end of tomorrow. I'll see you back here in April. This court is now in recess." And with that, the scheduling conference was over.

CHAPTER 30

THE HEADLINE READ "Suicides Spike Among Victims of Hurricanes Rita and Katrina." It was a bleep of a story in the back pages of the *Houston Chronicle*. Billy was reading the paper in the waiting area right outside Alessandra's hospital room. *It's started*, thought Billy, sadly. *Not even three months since the folks started getting Zerevrea, and now there's a spike in suicides. What's next, the soldiers returning from Iraq?*

Billy was back up in Houston for two reasons. The first was to visit his daughter and wife. It had been a couple of days since he'd last visited. He missed his daughter terribly. The second was that after the scheduling conference in Laredo, and as per Judge Dorfman's instructions, Billy and Spearman had talked. They had agreed to meet in Houston to put together the joint case management and discovery plan and hopefully also talk settlement again. The day Billy had visited Spearman in Rio Grande City, both of them had talked frankly, and both had expressed an interest in continuing to entertain settlement discussions. Billy had promised Spearman that at the next meeting, he would show up with more settlement authority, and Spearman had taken the bait. Never once did Billy reveal that he had seventy-five million in poker chips in his pocket or that he now had the intentions of settling the Andarza and Guerra cases and that he needed Spearman's help to accomplish such a task. Although desperately needing to get the Ray case settled, quietly, too, Billy was not about to throw away close to a hundred million dollars. Not where liability was being disputed and Tommy Ray—unlike Andarza and Guerra—could have died from different reasons.

173

To Spearman, the fact that Billy had driven to the neighboring county to see him in the middle of a trial in an effort to resume the negotiations could only mean one thing: the defendant wanted to pack his bags and go home and was ready to throw in the towel. And that was always welcomed news. The only problem was Gina Ray. Would she go along? Obviously four million had not been enough. Would Billy Bravo show up with more money? Hell, there was no dishonor in wanting to put millions of dollars in a plaintiff's pocket, especially when a defendant feared the damning truth about its drug being exposed.

"I THOUGHT you were having a follow-up meeting with Spearman?" asked Bates as he pointed for Billy to take a seat at his desk.

"My meeting is at two," explained Billy. "I've been down at MD Anderson visiting my daughter. I flew up last night."

"How is she?"

"They've got her on Fledkort. They expect her to be in remission in no time."

"Well, that's good news, no?" asked Bates.

"Yes. Great news. Who would have known, eh? Our own client making Fledkort."

"A strange coincidence," remarked Bates.

"Yep, and what about Zerevrea? Now, there's another story. I believe it's beginning to cause havoc down in Louisiana and will only get worse when the servicemen come back from Iraq," said Billy.

"What do you mean?" Bates asked, looking up from his computer monitor.

"Remember the memo?"

"The one Croutoux wrote?"

"Yes. Hector also got his hands on another obscure study that backs up Croutoux's memo. There's already a spike in suicides in the Gulf States. It was in the headlines this morning."

Bates got up from his desk, walked over to the other end and made himself a drink at the wet bar. "And?"

"It's happening. Folks with PTSD are beginning to crack. Not a couple of months into President Bailey's healthcare initiative, and the suicide rate has spiked in some areas. A cluster here, a cluster there."

"Why are you so concerned?" Bates asked, taking a sip of his Jack on the rocks.

"I'm just saying, on one hand, our client makes this miracle drug that leukemia patients need in order to survive. And, on the other, they throw caution to the wind, all in the name of profit, while trying to grab a slice of the market share and now potentially thousands will die. That's all. It's just an observation," mumbled Billy.

"Life is give-and-take, Billy. You know that. You, of all people, should know better. You're a lawyer. That's what we do—we compromise, settle, negotiate, prod and cajole and try to come up with solutions to make sure it's a win-win for everybody. We give and take, day in, day out. Unfortunately, that's not always the case. That's when justice requires a trial. When there can't be any give and take and there can only be a winner . . . that's when we let a jury decide."

"What about the veterans coming back from the war? They're next to get on Zerevrea, and then what? They're walking time bombs. Eighty percent are suffering from PTSD. Doesn't that bother you?"

"No, it doesn't. The only thing that concerns me," snapped Bates, "is for you to win the lawsuit down in Laredo. This firm needs BostonMagnifica as a client. Think of all the work Falcone will send us if we do a good job for them. As long as there's work, you and I, our employees and their families will be able to eat, take trips, put our kids through college. Your own daughter will continue to receive the medication she needs to live, Billy."

"But . . . "

"It's about keeping the lights on," cried Bates. "Don't you get it?"

"I get it. I do, really. It's just that . . . "

"Look," interrupted Bates, "just do your job. Get the case resolved and stop worrying about things we can't control. Who gives a crap about those poor bastards? The veterans are already screwed up to begin with, so let them whack each other, commit suicide, whatever. You want your promotion? Then get the job done. If you don't like it, then tell me and I'll put somebody else on the case. It's that simple. Maybe the work we do here at this firm is not for you. I thought I was helping you by just letting you work exclusively on the BM file. Give you an opportunity to prove to us that you're name partner material. But now, I just don't know. I'm getting worried."

"That's not what I meant," apologized Billy.

"Just go to your meeting with Spearman, Billy. Go take care of it. Remember, if you can't do it, tell me, and I'll put someone else on the case. That's all."

Billy got up and headed out the door. He had never seen Bates act that way. The guy was turning into a complete asshole.

"BILLY," said Yami, "we need to talk. It's important. Can you come by the hospital before flying back home?" She sounded desperate.

"Is Ale okay?" asked an alarmed Billy as he parked the rental car outside Spearman's office building. Spearman's office was located inside the Transco Tower right next to the Galleria Mall, Houston's shopping district. It was a sixty-four-story skyscraper that had been built two decades earlier. Spearman's office occupied all of the space on the fifty-fourth floor.

"She's okay."

"Then what is it? I'm getting ready to go into a meeting."

"The billing office at MD Anderson is telling me our insurance won't pay for Ale's treatment anymore. They're demanding cash. What do we do?" Yami sounded frantic.

"Use the credit cards. The hell with it . . . max them out until we figure something out, or I'll cash in my retirement. Do you have the name of the person you spoke with at the hospital?"

"Yes," Yami cried, "her name is Ruth, at extension 3579."

"Let me call her and see who she spoke to at the insurance company," Billy replied, trying to reassure his wife. "Maybe this is all just a mistake. Let me handle it, okay? You just worry about Ale and let me worry about the insurance company. I'll call you after I get out of my meeting. I'm sure it's a mistake."

"Okay, then," Yami gulped.

"Keep your chin up, baby," Billy said, putting up a strong front, although he felt the walls slowly closing in. "We'll get through it. I love you. Be strong for Alessandra. She needs you to be strong. Call you in a little while."

"*WHAT AM I gonna do? My damned luck!*" Billy mumbled under his breath. He was pissed. He pounded his fist on the steering wheel, turned the ignition off and flung the driver's door wide open as he got out. *What else can go wrong, eh? C'mon, God, stop screwing with me!*

He slammed the car door shut, pulled out his cell phone and, before heading into the meeting, he started dialing the number and extension 3579 at MD Anderson. He was going out of his mind and needed some answers *pronto*. This was not something he needed right before the meeting with Spearman. Being pissed off and angry as hell was not conducive to a meaningful settlement negotiation.

"WICHO, how are you holding up, son?" asked Billy. He was dialing from inside the plane as everyone else finished boarding the aircraft. He was coming home after spending most of the afternoon with Spearman, trying to find some common ground, trying to bridge the gap and get the case resolved. Part of the afternoon had also been spent trying to resolve Ale's health insurance coverage crisis without any success. In a few minutes, the crew would give the command for everyone to turn off their cell phones and electronics as the plane pushed off the gate.

"Fine, Dad. Grandma Farida has been taking good care of me," said Mauricio. "She's been cooking her famous *bascha* patties, my favorite."

"I love that dish," said Billy.

"Where are you?" asked Wicho.

"I'm on a plane at Hobby Airport, heading back to McAllen."

"How's Mom and Ale?"

"Good, real good," Billy said, downplaying the situation. "The doctor said your sister is responding well to the chemo. She should be coming home soon."

"I've missed you guys. I wish I could go up there and visit my sister."

"I miss you, too, son. Listen, you wanna go to dinner? My plane comes in right at six. I'll just stop by the office, pick up my mail and swing by the house to get you. We'll go eat dinner somewhere. Give grandma a break so she won't have to cook. Does that sound okay?"

"That'll be great!"

"All right. Tell Grandma Farida and Tía Aracely not to worry about making dinner. We'll bring them something to eat or ask them if they want to join us."

"Okay, I'll ask. I'll see you in a little bit," said Wicho, sounding excited.

"All right, son. I gotta go. They're telling us to turn off our cells. I'll see you in a bit."

"Bye."

NANCY KNEW to open all the legal correspondence addressed to "Hon. Billy Bravo." She routinely opened his mail, made notes of any hearing dates scheduled by the courts and updated Billy's discovery and response deadlines on his desk calendar and computer. This evening, however, there were two distinctive-looking letters addressed to Billy Bravo that remained unopened. The envelopes were marked "Personal and Confidential." One of the letters was from the State Department, the other in a light blue envelope from the Bureau of Customs and Immigration Services (BCIS).

Billy's heart skipped a beat when he grabbed the State Department letter and opened it. The letter said that a passport to Guillermo Cuauhtémoc Bravo could not be issued because he had been born with a midwife. Since many-a-midwife along the Texas-Mexico border had been prosecuted for falsifying birth records on behalf of foreign nationals, the new policy at the State Department was for these individuals to provide additional documentation to establish that their birth actually took place in the United States.

The letter added that Mr. Bravo could produce a minimum of two affidavits from disinterested witnesses of his birth back in 1963 or a complete set of medical or hospital records evidencing his birth. If none of these documents were available, then Mr. Bravo could contact the midwife that gave birth to him, confirm that she was not one of the midwives prosecuted for falsifying birth records and have her provide an affidavit, along with supporting documentation that Guillermo Cuauhtémoc Bravo had actually been born in the United States.

Finally, the letter advised that failure to produce proof that he had actually been born on U.S. soil and that he was here in the United States illegally would subject him to removal proceedings as per BCIS rules. The second letter addressed the consequences of being illegally here in the United States or without permission. It explained how the criminal justice system worked and, in great detail, the range of punishment for the crime of illegal entry, along with other punishment options. Of course, the accused, or Billy Bravo in this case, could avoid a potential jail sentence by simply signing voluntary deportation papers. The letter also suggested that Mr. Bravo should consider saving money on a criminal defense attorney and not attempt to fight the potential illegal entry charge. A voluntary deportation was always recommended. It was cheap, fast and painless.

Billy cursed his luck as he tossed the letters in the waste basket. "*Qué mamones.* This has got to be the most ridiculous thing I've ever heard. American Dream? This is a fucking nightmare."

Billy googled the words "Board-certified Immigration Attorney" and the name of a Houston attorney, Jimmy Díaz, came up. He clicked on the link to the attorney's Web site. He double-clicked on Contact Us and scribbled the firm's phone number down. He dialed the number. After about three rings, a woman answered.

"Law office of Jimmy Díaz and Associates. How can I help you?"

"Yes," said Billy, clearing his throat, sounding out of breath, "this is attorney Billy Bravo from McAllen, Texas. I was wondering if Mr. Díaz is available? Can I talk to him?"

"Are you referring a case, Mr. Bravo?" asked the woman from the answering service.

"Yes, I guess you could say that."

"What's the name of the client?"

"It would be me. I think I might need his services, if not a consultation."

"Well," the operator replied, "you said you were calling from McAllen, down in the Rio Grande Valley."

"Yes. Why?"

"Mr. Díaz sees clients down in the Valley once a week. He is going to be in the Brownsville office on Thursday. Would you like to make an appointment to see him then?"

"Yes. Is there anything available on Thursday? Friday's out; I got to be in Houston."

"I'm showing he has a four-thirty available. Will that work?"

"Yes."

"Very well. You're confirmed to see Mr. Díaz this coming Thursday at four-thirty. We're at the corner of Seventh and Ringold, Suite A. It's a hundred seventy-five dollars per visit, just so you know. He's board-certified in immigration and naturalization law."

"Okay," said Billy, "that won't be a problem. Thank you." He hung up the phone.

BILLY BRAVO was writing the appointment with Díaz on his desk calendar when Hector barged in. "Did you watch CNN last night?" Hector asked as he handed him a packet of documents with his latest findings. Billy's office was littered with blowups, exhibits, boxes of documents and deposition transcripts since he was getting ready to hand over two cases that were going to trial in three weeks. He'd decided to go through each of the boxes in order to organize them for his replacements, Gault and Hubbard.

"No. I did not have a chance. I took Wicho out to dinner after I got back from Houston and then came back to the office and did some more work. I didn't leave the office until three in the morning. I've got to deliver this joint discovery plan to Dorfman before noon today. As it is, Spearman and I should have submitted it two days ago. It's late as hell . . . the bastard gave us three months to get ready to try the Ray lawsuit."

"Oh," muttered Hector.

"So, what about CNN?"

"There's been a recent spike in suicides all along the Gulf States," Hector said.

"You don't say?"

"Yep. The authorities are beginning to look into it."

"I was afraid of that."

"And," Hector added, "my sources tell me there's a guy in Beaumont, a plaintiff's lawyer named Dykeman, that thinks there might be a link to Zerevrea. The guy's discreetly monitoring the Ray lawsuit, keeping things under wraps. Has thirty families with suicides signed up already . . . waiting for Spearman to hit a home-run."

"Shit," Billy exclaimed as he sat down and loosened his tie.

"Maybe the guy got a hold of Croutoux's memo," Hector said, "and thinks where there's smoke, there's gotta be fire. Anyway, I called that guy, Miguel Celia."

"And?"

"He's supposed to call back. He said that he was rushing to Mexico to sign up the parents of a roofer who fell to his death off a Staybridge Suites Hotel currently under construction. Said he'd call me back."

"Well," Billy started, "let's find out what it is he wanted. He said he had the goods on the Tommy Ray case, or something like that."

"Do you think Spearman will get his hands on Croutoux's memo?" asked Hector. "Or find his son, like I did?"

"I don't doubt it. Did you see how he recused Judge Allende?"

"Yes. Talk about getting lucky."

"The guy," said Billy, "did his homework. He's going to be a formidable opponent."

"Anyway, get this . . . Lantrex Pharmaceuticals is being sued over Triax, a drug that's supposed to turn bad cholesterol into good cholesterol. The drug giant plans to cut seven thousand jobs and close eight manufacturing plants around the world. The latest estimates are that Triax will end up costing the giant up to three billion dollars in verdicts and settlements. There are allegations the drug causes non-reversible erectile dysfunction."

"I'm afraid," said Billy, "the same could very well happen to BostonMagnifica."

"Hey, did I mention that a Dr. Haverti prescribed the Zerevrea that Tommy Ray was taking?"

"How did you find out?"

"I paid the garbage collector to go through the Ray's garbage."

"Good work!"

"There were a couple of bills from Haverti's office. I later found out he's a family practitioner, so I called his office pretending to be from the insurance company requesting some information on Tommy Ray in order to approve payment."

"And?"

"The woman at the front office said his last visit was on Monday, exactly five days before the incident. She also said that his chart showed the doctor prescribed Zerevrea."

"Anything else?"

"Well," Hector continued, "I think we need to get those records from Dr. Haverti."

"I'll have Spearman have Mrs. Ray sign a release . . . we'll get those records. Don't worry. Hey," said Billy, switching topics, "I've been meaning to ask you about your dad. Whatever happened with the removal proceedings?"

"*En eso andamos*," Hector answered. "We're working on it. His attorney seems to think we'll be able to defeat the removal proceedings and stop the deportation. She thinks he has an excellent case. Why do you ask?"

"Do me a favor. Close the door and take a seat. I want to tell you something. Can I trust you?"

"Sure, Billy. When have I spilled the beans?"

"This cannot get out, you follow me? No one knows, not even Yami, get it? She's going through a lot with Alessandra up in Houston." Billy had a serious look on his face. Hector had seen that look before, but only when Billy sliced and diced the opposition's retained experts on the witness stand.

"I gotcha, brother. I'll take it to my grave, okay? What is it? What's bothering you?"

"I tried getting a passport and found out there's something wrong with my birth records."

"What do you mean?"

"I got this letter . . . they're saying that because I was born with the help of a midwife, for some reason, they can't give me my passport."

"Are you sure?"

"Yes, I think it might have something to do with all those *parteras* they prosecuted years back, remember? The ones taking bribes from foreign nationals to lie and say their kids had been born in the States."

"You think?"

"I'm pretty sure," Billy said, "but there might be more."

"More?"

"Yes," said Billy as he leaned forward and whispered. "Just before my old man died, he said something that scared the shit out of me. It completely blew me away . . . "

"What?"

"That he and Mom had done the same. They had also bribed a midwife . . . that they had done it for me, for my benefit. That they had lied about me being a citizen."

"*¿Estás seguro?*" Hector's jaw was suddenly resting on the carpeted floor.

"I'm afraid that's what it is."

"You mean . . . you're not a U.S. citizen?"

"I don't know . . . I guess I'm not."

"What are you going to do?"

"I don't have the slightest clue. I'm thinking I'm going crazy. I'm losing it. Can you imagine growing up your entire life thinking you're a U.S. citizen and you're not? Hell, I'm not even Mexican. What the hell am I?"

"I'm sure it's gotta be a mistake, Billy."

"It gets worse, though," admitted Billy. "There's more."

"Huh?!"

"This could very well be the end of my marriage. Should I just come clean? Tell Bates? Will they back me up? What if I'm prosecuted for being here illegally and end up being deported? Am I gonna be around when Ale needs me the most?" Billy was crying, holding his face in his hands.

Hector had never seen him like that. It was unimaginable. The greatest kick-ass lawyer South Texas had ever seen, reduced to tears. *Qué tragedia.*

"What if you just forget about the stupid passport? Can you just go on? Why must anybody know? No one has cared for forty-two years, right? Never before did you need a passport. The hell with them! I'd keep quiet," suggested Hector, "just keep using your birth certificate and driver's license."

"I can't just sit and do nothing. BCIS will come after me. Dad decided to confess, clear his conscience, but didn't realize he'd screwed my entire existence. Turned my world upside down," cried Billy. "I'm losing it, Hector . . . I think I'm even having panic attacks. And then, to top it all, as if dealing with Ale's leukemia wasn't enough, I got a call a few months ago, and the caller said that I have a teenage son living in Austin."

"What?" asked Hector, completely dumbfounded. "How old?"

"Fifteen, sixteen. I don't know."

"Does Yami know?"

"Of course not. I don't even know how to tell her," he said as he popped his neck left and right to relieve the stress.

"When did that happen?"

"A few months after I got married. I went to a Continuing Legal Education seminar in Austin. A few of us went out to dinner afterward and started drinking. There was an attractive local attorney in the group. One thing led to another, and there you have it. Now, the attorney is dying, and I get a call out of the blue to see if I want to start being the young man's father."

"Jesus! Are you sure? I can't believe it. I would have never guessed. Billy, you had the perfect life! *No es posible, no lo puedo creer.*"

"Anyway," Billy said with new resolve, slowly getting up from his desk, "thanks for listening. I gotta get back to work."

"I'm here for you. Anything you need. *Lo que sea.*"

"Thanks," said Billy as he reached to shake Hector's hand.

"Don't mention it. *No es nada,* brother," said Hector as he scurried out of the office. "Your secrets are safe with me."

BILLY WAS SITTING AT HIS DESK licking his wounds and still feeling sorry for himself when Nancy announced, "Boss, Roland Hernández with Judge Dorfman wants to talk to you. He's holding on line three."

"Thanks," replied Billy as he picked up the phone and said, "This is Billy Bravo."

"Are you prepared to spend time in jail for being in contempt of court?" asked Hernández bluntly.

"What do you mean?" asked Billy with a frown on his face.

"You know what I mean," said the law clerk. "Or are you, like Spearman, deaf, dumb, blind and stupid?"

"Excuse me?"

"Look, Judge Dorfman wants to know where the joint plan is. Is it on its way? Or how much longer are you and Spearman gonna keep him waiting?"

"It's being filed electronically," snapped Billy, "as we speak. You should have it before lunch this morning. It's coming."

"Don't keep the judge waiting," admonished Hernández. "Neither you nor Spearman are gonna like it if you keep this up. The judge doesn't know I'm giving you a heads-up. You better get that stuff to me before lunch today . . . otherwise, don't be surprised if the marshals show up at your office after lunch, Mr. Bravo."

"You gotta be kidding me," complained Billy, popping his neck back and forth, left and right. "I'm getting arrested because the plan is a day late?"

"Two days late," corrected Hernández. "And, yes, both of you will get arrested for contempt of court if the joint case management and discovery plan is not on the judge's desk before noon. Judge Dorfman doesn't screw around. One call to the marshals in Houston, one call to the marshals in McAllen . . . that's all it'll take. You and Spearman will be spending the night in the can, so bring your toothbrushes."

"Shit!" cried Billy. "I'm hitting the Send button right now. Tell Judge Dorfman I apologize. No need to send the men in blue. It's on its way."

"I'll give him the message," replied Roland Hernández. "Anything else?"

"No."

CHAPTER 31

IMMY DÍAZ'S BROWNSVILLE OFFICE was located inside a five-story brick building owned by a local trial lawyer named Tod Ramírez. Billy had heard the name since Ramírez was awash with cash and contributed millions to the local judicial races and, rumor had it, he also had the state Bar in his pocket. This, apparently, gave him free reign to solicit and snatch all the big cases in South Texas.

Billy walked down the bright hallway leading to the immigration attorney's suite on the first floor. It was lined with framed copies of settlement checks Ramírez had collected on behalf of his injured clients. The smallest check was for four hundred thousand dollars; some were as big as twenty million. The attorney had also framed and displayed copies of the front pages to several confidential settlement agreements with heavy-duty giants such as Ford, GMC, Firestone, American Airlines, Enron, AT&T even Lehman Brothers, among others. His clients' names had been carefully blacked out, along with the settlement amounts. However, the message was clear: "I don't care who you are. Tod Ramírez will make you pay, rake you over the coals, waterboard you once or twice and maybe even take your firstborn. You better not lock horns with this tough *muchacho*, or he'll have you and your five-hundred-dollar-big-firm-sissy lawyer for lunch."

He knocked on the door with the sign "Jimmy Díaz Immigration Lawyer" on it. A loud voice said, "*Adelante*. Come on in. Take a seat in the reception area. I'll be right there."

Billy let himself in and took his place in the empty reception area in front of the office, The staff was apparently gone for the day. It was almost five o'clock. He'd been delayed due to traffic, but at last he'd made it to his appointment in Brownsville.

"Hey," Mr. Díaz greeted Billy as he came out of his back office, "I didn't think you were gonna make it. I told my receptionist to shut it down. She left about ten minutes ago. She's got night school."

"I'm sorry," apologized Billy. "With all the highway construction between here and McAllen, not to mention rush-hour traffic, I just got delayed. I should have known better and left earlier. I apologize for keeping you waiting."

"No problem," said Díaz, "come back here to my office. Just let me lock the front door. We can talk at our leisure."

Díaz walked past Billy and proceeded to lock the front door to his suite. The lawyer looked young, maybe in his mid-thirties. He was wearing pressed khakis, a blue button-down with the letters "JD" monogrammed on the right cuff and brown leather loafers. He motioned Billy to follow him to his back office. Díaz took his place behind his desk, and Billy sat down on one of two client chairs across from the attorney.

"I think I might be in trouble," started Billy, "big trouble."

"¿Y eso?" asked the attorney, "How so?"

"I suspect my dad bribed a midwife years ago to lie and say that I was born in the United States. As my old man was on his deathbed, he came clean, but I couldn't ask more questions. At first, it didn't register. I doubted the whole thing. Maybe I was in denial. But when we tried to get my passport some weeks ago, the State Department sent notice that I couldn't get it because a *partera* generated the birth record. The officials say I need to jump other hoops to prove my citizenship. They said they are leaving my file open until I can provide additional documentation. I finally put two and two together . . . what if they're after me?"

"You think?"

"All my life, fighting to be treated the same, equally. You don't think I've known all along that I'm the token Mexican at my law firm? I've known that from day one. But I've kept quiet. I've busted my ass to show these bastards that we're just as good, if not better or at least the same . . . equal," Billy continued.

"I hear ya."

"So, for fifteen-plus years," continued Billy, "I've worked my fingers to the bone, trying to make name partner, prove a point to the gringos that own the firm and break glass ceilings for others. And now it turns out that not only am I not the same, but I am not even American, not even a citizen. And I've been living a lie for forty-some years."

"I understand," said Díaz. "The whole thing can be very traumatic, not to mention scary."

"Can you imagine getting your ass deported?" asked Billy. "What that must feel like? The embarrassment and humiliation? To have to leave your family, your loved ones?"

"What would your peers think, right?" added Díaz.

"I can't even comprehend," wailed Billy. "Leave everything you ever knew . . . behind. And then have to start a new life from scratch, middle-aged, in another country—a foreign country—with no prospects, not knowing a single soul. *La verdad no entiendo.* All I ever wanted was just to feel accepted, respected, valued, fulfilled."

"The nightmare you're talking about happens every day. It happens more than people care to know, Mr. Bravo," explained Díaz. "I see it on a daily basis. Families are being split apart, innocent people are going to prison and even U.S.-born children are being left behind as their undocumented parents are yanked from their jobs in order to boot them out. I've had folks here in my office, right there where you're sitting, from doctors, cops, even Border Patrol agents, all the way to bankers and school teachers, who have nervous breakdowns, painful meltdowns when their parents fess up about why they can't get a passport or why they thought, at the time, it was a good idea to bribe a midwife."

"Of course Washington doesn't give a rat's ass," protested Billy, "and Austin?"

"*Menos,*" replied Díaz, then added, "To the politicians it's all a game, nothing but posturing and using immigration as an issue to remain in office one way or another."

"I guess you're right."

"Of course I'm right. History has taught us that when a country's economy is going to pot, the first ones to get blamed are the immigrants. It happened in Germany, France, England and now it's happening here again. We're the scapegoats. It's easy . . . lynch the bastards, lock them up and throw away the key. Instead of focusing on the bastards that really pushed the country to ruin."

"Can my situation be fixed?" asked Billy hoping for a miracle. "Quickly?"

"Yes and no. It just depends."

"What do you mean? I need to know because I'll be out of pocket in three months. I'll be starting a trial down in Laredo on a big case."

Díaz loosened his tie, removed his Rolex watch from his left wrist and set it on the desk in front of him. He played with its ceramic bezel. "Remember who we're dealing with. Bureaucrats, government agencies, immigration court, aging judges, red tape. However, the biggest hurdle we face is trying to cross-examine an affidavit that some midwife gave in the eighties, seventies or in some cases even as far back as the sixties. In other words, the midwife may no longer be around to cross-examine her on her affidavit or the statements she gave to federal investigators."

"Oh," muttered Billy. Again, he popped his neck, left, right, left, right. It was becoming a habit, and his neck muscles were increasingly tense and felt like new guitar strings.

"But if we find two witnesses to say that they knew that you were actually born here . . . "

"But my dad did admit he bribed a midwife. . . . This is not a case where we're saying we got thrown in the mix by accident or wrongfully included on some list that was put in front of the *partera* to sign and confess to."

"Well," explained Díaz, biting his lower lip, "that's what I'm saying. If your name got thrown in the mix by accident, then we can fight it. But if the facts are what they are . . . like you say . . . then there's nothing I can do for you."

"Nothing, eh?" Billy let out a big sigh. He was looking up at the ceiling trying to contain his anger, his frustration, including his obvious disillusionment, confusion and everything else he was feeling at that moment.

"There's one thing we might be able to do," offered Díaz.

"What?" Billy perked up.

"I can delay your removal trial . . . your deportation proceedings for a couple of years. Maybe the law will change by then . . . you could be granted amnesty. Maybe we'll elect a new president, somebody that wants to take the country in a different direction."

"That's no way to live."

"Or, if your children are U.S. citizens, they can petition for you when they turn twenty-one," suggested Díaz.

"My oldest is barely sixteen."

"And your parents?"

"They're both dead."

"Well . . . " added Díaz, trying to come up with an alternative. "I would certainly recommend delaying your removal. It's a compromise. I've helped clients delay their deportation six, seven years. Something is better than nothing. You could at least stay here with your loved ones. Who knows? Maybe by then Congress will pass immigration reform."

"Can I get a passport in the meantime?" interrupted Billy.

"No."

"Are you sure?"

"I'm sure. But send me your family history . . . parents' birth records, baptismal certificates, your siblings, everything you can get your hands on. Maybe there's a loophole somewhere."

"I'll have my assistant get you all that stuff right away. In the meantime, what do I do?"

"Don't get arrested and stay out of trouble . . . the stuff you've been doing all your life . . . go to work, *como si todo estuviera normal.*"

"Do I tell my wife?"

"It's up to you," Díaz said.

"All right," Billy said as he got up and reached for his wallet to pay for the consultation.

"Put that away, Billy," demanded Díaz in a friendly tone. "I won't accept your money, not from a colleague."

"But," stuttered Billy.

"Just refer me clients . . . if you know somebody who's in hot water, send them my way. Anyway, we'll be in touch. Send me the info. Here's my card." Díaz grabbed a couple of cards from the card holder on his desk and handed them to Billy. Then he went to shake Billy's hand.

"Thanks, partner," remarked Billy. "I'll let myself out. Oh, one last thing . . . "

"Yes?"

"I knew I was forgetting something. There's a guy named Armando Ruiz, he's incarcerated at the Bay View Detention Center. He's a friend of the family. I need you to help him and see if you can stop his deportation. It's been a few months since his arrest . . . I promised him I would look into it and then forgot about it."

"I can try if it's not too late . . . maybe he's already in Mexico," said Díaz.

"I'll have my assistant email you the guy's personal info, along with my credit card info. Charge me whatever. I'd like to help him if it's not too late."

"Okay, I'll look into it."

"Thanks," said Billy.

"*Ándale,* be careful."

THE DRIVE from Brownsville to the city of McAllen on old Military Highway 281 can be best described as a scenic one. The narrow two-lane roadway runs parallel to the Rio Grande and slices through tiny farming communities with names such as La Perlita, San Sebastian, Los Indios, Las Prietas, San Pedro, La Paloma and Progreso. All along the deserted highway, one can see miles and miles of fields planted with okra, soybeans, sugar cane, sorghum, corn, onions and cotton. Traveling that evening on the old highway, Billy now remembered his dad's words as the family got ready to go north to work the fields.

"We need to stick together, be there for each other on this our last trip *al norte,*" his old man had said. "Next year, your mom and

I plan to find work here at home. In the meantime, we stick together—that's what families do. We help each other, sacrifice for each other, forgive each other."

How is bribing a midwife to say I was born in the U.S. helping me now, Dad? Billy wondered. *How is coming clean with Yami and telling her the truth gonna help us? What were you and Mom thinking? Me arruinaron la vida. My life is now completely screwed, flushed down the toilet. How could you let me live this lie?*

He dialed Yami at MD Anderson in Houston. The call went through. "*¿Bueno?*" answered Yami.

"Hey, princess," mumbled Billy, "how's Ale?"

"Doctor says her blood work is looking real good. Her platelets are up, but they still want higher numbers. Doctor says Ale should be in full remission in two weeks. She's tolerating the chemo really well. How's everything with you?"

"Not good. I have something to tell you. Are you sitting down?"

"Yes."

"I'll understand if you decide to divorce me after what I have to say," Billy mumbled. "I'm not proud."

"I'm confused. What do you mean? You're scaring me, Billy. What is it?"

"I'm a *mojado*, a wetback, an illegal alien, Yami. *Un ilegal.* And I never knew it, until recently . . . I don't know what we're going to do."

"What are you talking about, Billy Bravo? Where's this coming from?" Yami now sounded alarmed.

"I was never a U.S. citizen. *No soy americano. Soy mexicano . . .* I think. When Dad was on his deathbed," explained Billy, "he wanted to say his piece. He revealed to me that I had been born in Mexico and that he had bribed a midwife to lie and say that I had been born in the United States. Before I could ask any questions, he dozed off and, days later, he slipped into a coma . . . and then died. I didn't want to believe what he was saying, but it's been confirmed. The State Department won't even issue a passport to me."

"Are you sure?"

"Yes. They're telling me I have to prove that my birth occurred here on U.S. soil. I've been living a lie!"

"There's gotta be a way to fix it."

"There's not. I just left an immigration attorney's office. If what Dad said was true, then I have to face this thing head-on. If I'm not a citizen, then I'm not a citizen. Two wrongs can't make a right. I can't fix a lie with another lie. There's nothing I can do."

"What does that make me, then?" asked Yami, horrified. Sixteen years earlier, Billy Bravo had petitioned his soon-to-be bride to make her an American citizen. The process had been done under the assumption that Billy was a citizen. Her paperwork had gone through without any glitches. She had apparently derived her citizenship from her husband, who now, as it turned out, had not even been a citizen to begin with.

"An illegal alien like me," replied Billy. "*Somos dos mojados.* We're screwed!"

"What do we do?"

"Keep living a lie, I suppose. The immigration lawyer said that we're not the only ones in that boat. There are thousands of folks in our same shoes. There are even federal employees in our same predicament. In the meantime, they keep to themselves and go about their daily lives without making any waves. That's what we'll have to do."

"This is not what I signed up for, Billy," said Yami, fuming, "first Alessandra, then your stupid promotion, then we lose our beach house, problems with our insurance and now this? I can't handle any more surprises! What's next? You telling me all these years you've had a lover?!"

"Yami, pleeease," begged Billy, "*escucha, amor* . . . I'll figure out a way out of this mess. Yami? Are you there? Yami? *Princesa*?" The cell went dead.

CHAPTER 32

AFTER JUDGE DORFMAN sent Hernández to deliver the message that the attorneys were heading to the slammer for not complying with his mandate, Spearman and Billy got busy. During the first two months, discovery had been exchanged, depositions had been taken and experts had been designated, all without a glitch or any hint of trouble. In fact, Billy and Spearman were working splendidly well together. Spearman had made all his witnesses and experts available, and their depositions were taken. At first, it appeared as if Spearman would enlist world-renowned expert, Dr. Andrew Steely. But a week before his deposition, the world's leading authority had died in a horrific, mysterious hit-and-run accident in New York City, right outside the United Nations building.

Billy produced his witnesses, Falcone, Drummond and Sudarshan, plus his two additional retained experts, Siegel and his own expert in economics. Immediately after the last deposition was taken, Billy filed summary judgment motions in an effort to get Spearman's claims thrown out of court. Spearman promptly replied with his response to Billy's motion, explaining why summary judgment was improper and why Gina Ray should be allowed to have her day in court.

Billy was back at his office trying to figure out how he was going to pay his latest Visa bill—a whopping one hundred sixty thousand dollars resulting from the month of uninsured treatment for Ale. After a month of haggling, numerous phone calls and even repeated threats of litigation, his health insurance had finally approved partial payments for Ale's treatment (albeit a month late), but not for all of it.

A portion of the payments involving Fledkort—an experimental treatment and doubtful protocol in the eyes of Billy's health insurance company—were still being reviewed. He threw the Visa bill on the pile of bills that were not getting paid anytime soon when he noticed an opened envelope with the return address of the U.S. District Clerk's office in Laredo. He reached for the piece, pulled out its contents and unfolded the documents. It was the court's signed order and opinion in connection with Boston-Magnifica's Daubert challenge and summary judgment Motion No.1, Raising Federal Preemption Grounds.

In step with his dictatorial style, Kyle Dorfman, the judge assigned to the case, had decided to take up the motion without live testimony or argument from either side. By invoking an obscure provision of the local rules for the Southern District, the court, *sua sponte*, had decided to read the parties' motions and responses and issue a ruling without further delay. It was time to rule on the pending motions since the case was less than two weeks away from trial.

"*¡Carajo!*" complained Billy, "*pinche juez loco.*" He'd been around long enough to know that it had been the judge's law clerk that read the parties' motions, reviewed the exhibits, researched the law and prepared the opinion for the judge's approval. *He must have a hell of a law clerk. I hope that Hernández kid is as smart as he sounds. Imagine? Two days to read, research, and prepare the court's opinion that Dorfman ultimately, just rubber stamps. Amazing!*

In many instances, the outcome of multimillion-dollar cases rests solely on the shoulders of some pimply faced, twenty-six-year-olds, barely out of law school, with no real-life experience, their only distinction being that they graduated either summa cum laude or magna cum laude. In other words these *mocosos* are considered brilliant legal minds.

"Talk about perfect timing. Not what I needed right now," Billy repeated quietly under his breath as he began to read the court's opinion:

Came for consideration BostonMagnifica's Daubert Challenge and Motion for Summary Judgment based on Federal Preemption Grounds, including Plaintiff's Response and Exhibits. After careful review, the Court issues this opinion and order.

Background

This case deals with the suicide of Tomas Ray. A week prior to his death, Mr. Ray was prescribed Zerevrea by his physician, Dr. Haverti. In the past, Mr. Ray had suffered from mild anxiety (perhaps some slight PTSD) and had taken valium, once, but had never ingested a psychotropic drug like Zerevrea. It's undisputed that Mr. Ray never before suffered from depression.

On Saturday, January 28, 2005, after fixing his family breakfast, Mr. Ray walked outside on his robe carrying a handgun and shot dead two strangers. He then placed the handgun in his mouth and pulled the trigger.

Plaintiffs contend that Zerevrea was the detonator that made Mr. Ray go off and that the defendant knew there was a link between Zerevrea and suicide but failed to warn the public. Defendant argues that the reason Tomas Ray pulled the trigger was probably due to something else. That there is no proof that the ingestion of Zerevrea, alone, made Mr. Ray kill himself. Defendant suggests that something else could have also pushed Mr. Ray over the edge. That without more proof, Plaintiffs cannot prove specific causation.

In the alternative, Defendant argues, since the FDA approved Zerevrea, then the drug has been deemed safe for public consumption and Plaintiff's lawsuit should be dismissed. This, in a nutshell, is the federal preemption argument.

The Food, Drug and Cosmetic Act (FDCA) requires the FDA to approve medicines that are "safe and effective" before they may be sold. To obtain approval, the maker must submit a new drug application (NDA) containing test results, results of clinical studies and trials, along with other information.

These applications can routinely be disapproved if the FDA finds 1) a lack of adequate testing, 2) the data shows the drug is unsafe, 3) the available information is insufficient, 4) there's no evidence showing the drug works as the maker claims 5) the labeling proves false or misleading.

If the application is approved, the FDA continues to monitor the drug's safety. If new information surfaces indicating the drug is no longer safe or other data suggests the labeling is false or misleading, then the FDA can pull its approval. This was the case with Vioxx, Ketek, Baycol and other drugs. At the time the FDA approved their use, little did the public and the FDA know that ultimately those drugs would be pulled from the market because they turned out to be unsafe, even though the FDA initially approved them.

Drugs can also be unsafe if the labeling or warning used to inform the physicians is incorrect or inadequate. All print matter used in marketing and labeling the drug is regulated by the FDA. In this case, the FDA approved the following black box warning for Zerevrea. <u>Suicide: The possibility of a suicide is inherent in individuals with depression and may persist until remission. Close supervision of high-risk patients should accompany drug therapy. Prescriptions for Zerevrea should be dispensed consistent with good patient management.</u>

Analysis

The Supremacy Clause, article VI, clause 2, of the United States Constitution, preempts any state law that conflicts with the exercise of federal power. Federal law will always override state law under the Supremacy Clause when (1) Congress expressly preempts state law; (2) Congressional intent to preempt may be inferred from the existence of a pervasive federal regulatory scheme; or (3) state law conflicts with federal law or its purposes.

Here, Plaintiffs sued in Federal Court because there is diversity jurisdiction in that Plaintiffs are from Texas and Boston-Magnifica is from another state. The Plaintiffs invoked Texas tort law alleging that Texas requires more stringent warnings and that the labeling should say that Zerevrea "does" trigger suicide. Defendants argue that using Texas law conflicts with the FDCA and FDA's own regulatory scheme. This court disagrees.

The FDCA and FDA are merely "minimum standards" a "low ceiling" with which the drug makers must comply. Nothing prohibits a drug company from strengthening a warning label. Since federal law contemplates that a drug maker will improve its labeling practices, then we must logically conclude that the FDCA and FDA impose minimum requirements. Therefore the regulatory scheme does not prevent the drug maker from issuing stronger warnings if there is "reasonable evidence of a link of a fatal hazard."

Defendant's arguments are misguided in that there are now ample reliable, scientific studies which have linked a higher risk of suicide to the use of SSRI drugs. And given the recent hearings spearheaded by U.S. Senator Andy del Toro and the FDA's numerous recent inquiries regarding suicidality and SSRIs, it would be inconceivable to this Court to accept BostonMagnifica's argument that an additional, stronger, better, warning regarding suicidality would be false or misleading or would contravene federal law or its purpose.

This Court next addresses Defendant's contentions that there is no link that Zerevrea actually triggered Tomas Ray's suicide. Under a purely scientific analysis, this Court is of the opinion that Plaintiff's allegations that Zerevrea caused Tomas Ray's suicide are sufficiently supported by the latest studies regarding suicidality and SSRIs. Even the FDA, after years of mounting pressure, announced recently the implementation of black box warnings regarding suicidality in children and adolescents. Experts worldwide have also concluded that there is a connection between SSRIs and suicide.

Plaintiffs provided the Court with copies of the actual prescription for Zerevrea obtained by Tomas Ray just days before, along with photos of the thirty-pill-prescription-bottle with his name on it. Defendant has failed to controvert this powerful evidence or disprove that Tomas Ray did not take those pills.

Finally, the Plaintiff's also produced affidavits, and medical records from Mr. Ray's treating physicians and friends to establish that Tomas Ray was a peace-loving man and would have never contemplated suicide. On the other hand, Defendant failed to show that Tomas Ray was suffering from an incurable illness, severe depression or that he'd witnessed his wife having an affair to suggest there were other causes for his suicide. In short, Defendant failed to show other reasons which may have led to Tomas Ray's death.

Just like the FDA recently found that there is a link between a risk of suicide and these drugs, this Court must also find that there is, at least, a "scintilla" of evidence that Tomas Ray was on Zerevrea the day he pulled the trigger. Even though the Defendant invoked the Daubert doctrine and has challenged Plaintiffs' experts' reports and opinions as to, both, specific and general causation, this Court has determined that the reports and opinions carry with them a scintilla of reliability and relevance to support Plaintiffs' causation elements.

Conclusion

The Court finds that BostonMagnifica's Daubert Challenge and Summary Judgment should be denied and this case should proceed to trial in accordance with the court's previous scheduling order.

SIGNED ON THIS THE 16th day of April, 2006.

Kyle Dorfman, U.S. District Judge

"I'll be damned!" exclaimed Billy.

CHAPTER 33

A N ENTIRE CHILDHOOD spent traveling to *el norte* to pick crops had taught Billy Bravo how to deal with most, if not all, of life's curve balls. When life's surprises knocked the wind out of him, he stood right back up, unfazed. When life played dirty and got him thrown off his horse, he dusted himself off, composed himself and got back on the saddle. Time after time, he'd made it a habit to keep his chin up and work harder and longer, while always keeping his eye on the prize.

Now Judge Dorfman and the State Department, along with Karin Palmer, and all the other shit piling up on his marriage, had dealt him another humbling blow that appeared to have landed him face-down on the canvas, bruised and bloodied, his one good eye blankly staring out into space. With nothing left to lose, either Billy regained his composure, his wits, *el ánimo, las ganas* and got right up before the standing ten-count, or he threw in the towel, called it a day and marched right back to where he'd come from —Mexico—with his voluntary departure court papers in hand.

"Dorfman denied all of our motions," growled a resilient Billy, sounding disgusted at the whole situation. "I don't think the jerk even took the time to read them. It's time to go on the warpath. Get ready to try this damned thing."

"What do you mean?" asked Hector. They were talking in the small office kitchen while Billy made a fresh pot of coffee and Hector microwaved a half-dozen leftover tamales he'd brought from home.

"We're gonna win the Ray lawsuit, whatever it takes," assured Billy. "My daughter's life depends on it."

"I'm here to help, *jefe*. You can count on me."

"Just so you know, Hector," said Billy as he poured himself a cup of freshly brewed coffee, "I'm not doing this for BostonMagnifica or because they're such good clients or because they deserve to win. I'm not going balls-to-the-wall because of my promotion, either. As a matter of fact, I don't give a flying fuck about my promotion anymore or Bates or this country or this fucking firm, for that matter."

"Why are you talking like this?" asked Hector, in shock. "I've never heard you cuss like this."

"I'm fed up, Hector. Remember our conversation?"

"Yes."

"Well, there's nothing I can do about it. In time, the gig will be up, and I'll probably have to go back to Mexico. My American Dream has turned into a hellish nightmare."

"Ouch!" yelped Hector as he yanked the plate of hot tamales from the microwave.

"In the meantime, I'm going to focus on the things I can control. I know I can win this lawsuit. A win means Ale continues to get the medication she needs so she can have a normal life. I couldn't have the American Dream, but *she can*. Both my kids still have a full life ahead of them. They were born here; they're both citizens. My parents couldn't give me that gift, unfortunately. They tried. Even lied about it. That's water under the bridge now. I will not let my kids down. I will win this case for my children. That's what I'll do."

"Okay," said Hector, aware of Billy's new resolve, "I'm behind you."

"All right. You got the temp agency lined up to send us the mock jury for next week, correct?"

"It's all set to go."

"Okay, then. Let's set up in the mock courtroom and help Nancy get our exhibits ready."

"I'm on it."

WICHO WAS playing video games on the big-screen TV in the family room when Billy walked in and sat down next to him. Billy was physically, emotionally and mentally bankrupt. After ranting and raving to Hector in the office kitchen earlier in the day, he'd felt a little bit better. More in control, if only on the surface. At least he had a plan. He had also spoken to Karin Palmer, and they had agreed to wait until the Ray suit was over for Billy to escape to Austin and meet his son.

Right after the discussion with Hector in the office kitchen, Yami had called wondering if he had been able to resolve the medical insurance crisis. She had maxed out all of the credit cards, and the folks in the business office at MD Anderson were now threatening to file hospital liens on any and all properties under their name. She had wanted to know how that would affect them. After Billy explained to her the legal significance, Yami had snapped and gone on a rant. She was clearly cracking under the pressure.

"Long day at the office, Dad?" Wicho asked tenderly.

"Yes, m'ijo. It's been crazy busy."

"Are you doing okay? Do you miss Grandpa?"

"Yes, m'ijo. Not a day goes by that I don't think of him. I now regret not having spent more time with him," said Billy as he removed his tie, kicked off his shoes and put his feet up on the leather ottoman.

"You know what I'll miss most?" asked Wicho.

"What?"

"Helping Papo make *paella* right before the games on Sundays."

"Wasn't that good? I never asked him where he learned to make it," said Billy. "Shrimp, clams, chorizo, chicken . . . having come from Spain, maybe it was in his blood."

"You forgot the *azafrán*," added Wicho. "Spanish saffron was always the key, according to Grandpa . . . and a good *sofrito*. I remember going with Grandpa to all the specialty stores looking for saffron. It had to be just right. Only the brand from Los Massa-Goñi from La Mancha would do."

"He was picky, that's for sure," answered Billy, suddenly remembering the aromas wafting throughout the house as his old man labored over the large copper *paella* pan making *sofrito* and sautéing the small but flavorful Spanish *chorizos*. "Hey, did he have a favorite team?"

"Yes."

"Which one?"

"Chivas. Chivas USA was his favorite team."

"I didn't even know there was a Chivas USA," Billy said, seemingly embarrassed.

"There is. Anyway, I spoke with Mom today," Wicho added with a smile. "She said Ale might be coming home in two weeks."

Billy sat there staring at the TV. He felt anxious, tired and worried. In his lifetime, he'd always managed to take things in stride, not really worrying about certain mundane things, but now he felt any control he'd had was gone, up in smoke. The high he'd felt earlier while talking to Hector back at the office had now turned into the lowest of lows.

"I'm flying up to see Mom and Ale this Saturday," muttered Billy. "Do you wanna go?"

"Really?"

"Yes. After this weekend, I don't know when I'll be able to get away again. I have a big trial coming up in federal court. Jury selection is in less than two weeks."

"Are you gonna win?"

"I'm afraid even if I win," said Billy in a serious tone, "I'll be losing, no matter what."

"What do you mean?"

"It's hard to explain, *m'ijo*. I'll explain it to you another day."

"Okay," Wicho said and shrugged his shoulders. "Thanks for letting me come to Houston with you, Dad."

"Be packed up and ready to leave Friday as soon as I come home from work, all right? We'll catch the last flight to Houston."

"Okay. Are we taking Grandma Farida and Tía Aracely?"

"No. We're just going up real quick and coming right back. I don't want to complicate things. Besides, Grandma Farida needs to rest. She's been here all these weeks taking care of you."

"Okay," Wicho replied as he punched the buttons on the wireless controller for the video game.

"I'm going to take a shower," said Billy. He reached over and planted a kiss on Wicho's head.

"I'll go to bed in a minute."

"Are Tía Aracely and Grandma in bed already?" asked Billy.

"Yes, they went to bed at nine o'clock."

Billy looked at his watch. It was ten-thirty PM. "You need to go to bed, too, *m'ijo*. Make sure that by the time I come out of the shower, you're in bed. *¿Entiendes,* Mauricio?"

"Yes, Dad."

"Okay, then. Good night."

CHAPTER 34

L IKE MANY PARENTS WITH CHILDREN being treated at MD Anderson, Yami had become a regular at the prayer chapel inside the research hospital. It was late at night, and she was on her knees praying for Alessandra to make a full recovery and for a solution to the problems now piling up in her marriage.

Yami prayed in silence as tears streamed down both her freckled cheeks. She prayed like she'd never prayed before. She prayed for God to give her daughter strength to fight, to want to keep on living, to want to see another day, to let her graduate from high school and then go to college. After all, Ale was such a terrific student that after the sixth grade she'd advanced straight into the eighth grade. If Ale made a miraculous and speedy recovery, she could still graduate from high school at sixteen and maybe even finish college by her twenty-first birthday.

Yami prayed the rosary. She prayed the Our Father and prayed to the Holy Spirit, to Mary the Blessed Mother, to the saints and she even recited the powerful novena she had not prayed in years. She prayed for strength and understanding. Finally, she prayed that God would keep her family together, intact, at whatever the cost, whatever the price and to watch over Billy and Wicho as they were flying back to the Rio Grande Valley. Their visit had been brief, but much needed.

"LOOK WHAT I found," said Hector, as he waved a stack of sheets recently printed from his computer. "Croutoux's son just emailed me these . . . more stuff he found inside his old man's storage shed."

"He scanned them and emailed them to you?" asked Billy, impressed.

"Yes," explained Hector, "and among the things he sent me, I got his old man's death certificate. The coroner wrote the cause of death as 'homicide.'"

"Really?"

"Yes. He also sent me what appear to be the 'missing' clinical trials for Zerevrea."

"Perfect," said a smiling Billy, "just what I need to seal the deal. I had asked Drummond for these months ago, and the guy never produced them. . . . Now they'll come in handy."

"I didn't think they were ever going to give us these, Billy, honestly. This is not the first client we've had that hides documents."

"You're right," Billy mumbled.

"Anyway," followed Hector, as if chasing down clues, "what do you mean by 'seal the deal'?"

"Something I've been working on. I'll tell you later when it's all said and done," said Billy. "Leave those here."

"*Muy bien*," replied Hector as he handed over the stack of papers and made his way out of Billy's office.

"Hey, wait up," said Billy.

"What is it?"

"How did you manage to convince Croutoux's son that you worked for a plaintiff's firm?"

"I gave him my old card from when I used to work and run cases for a major well-known plaintiff's firm out of Corpus. The firm's Web page still lists my name as one of the investigators. Plus, the business card only has my cell number and my personal email address. And the receptionist at my old firm, who still happens to be my friend, takes my messages when people call looking for me. She just tells them I'm out working in the field and then calls me with the message."

"Very clever," said Billy, "very clever."

"*Hay que ponerse águila, maestro*," replied Hector. "We investigators have to be creative, right?"

"Right."

CHAPTER 35

"Dime, mi amor. ¿Qué te pasa?" asked a panicked Billy. "Why are you crying, what's happening? Please get a hold of yourself."

"It's Alessandra!" screamed Yami over the phone. "She's taken a turn for the worse."

"What do you mean? I thought she was supposed to be in remission."

"Aaay," Yami sobbed uncontrollably, "she is, but it's not that."

"Get a hold of yourself, Yamilé, cálmate, por el amor de Dios. Take a deep breath, please. Así, just like that. Keep it up. Nice and easy, just like that."

"She's got a blood clot near her heart. The arsenic sometimes has that side effect, forming blood clots. That's why she's been on blood thinners."

"But . . . but," replied Billy, "when did this happen?"

"She just started complaining of chest pain. They rushed her to get an X-ray, and that's what came up. They're trying to dissolve it with blood thinners but if that doesn't work, they'll need to operate . . . and there's always a risk and with the blood clot being so close to her heart and all . . . "

"I'm on my way," snapped Billy. He looked at his watch. It was barely seven o'clock in the evening, already too late to catch a flight to Houston. "I'm leaving the office right this minute and getting in my car. I should be there a little past midnight, okay? I'm coming. I'll see you in a few hours."

"Be careful. I can't handle an accident right now. I just can't, please, Billy."

"I'll ask Hector to drive up with me."

"Okay," Yami agreed. "Hey, if the blood thinners don't work and Ale needs the operation, do you know how we're gonna pay for it? Did you straighten out the insurance mess?"

"Yes, I already took care of it with the business office," lied Billy. He hated to lie, but at that precise moment, he did not possess a better answer. "It's been resolved."

"Okay."

THE CHECKPOINT on Highway 281 North is, for the most part, manned by very young Border Patrol agents and their drug-sniffing dogs. The checkpoint itself is a structure built much like a large airport hangar, open on opposite ends so that the highway traffic flows quickly through it. Traveling north, the vehicles are ordered to form two lines and inch forward slowly until they're met by agents.

Off to the sides but within the large structure straddling the highway sit three double-wide trailer homes retrofitted into functional office space for the agents. Travelers leaving McAllen wanting to go north to Houston or San Antonio have to go through the checkpoint south of Falfurrias. This is true of all commercial traffic, including eighteen-wheelers, produce trucks, RVs, school buses, Greyhound buses and everything in between.

It was eight o'clock in the evening, and Billy and Hector had been on the road for about an hour, when Billy began slowing down to join the line now creeping forward toward the checkpoint, still a good quarter mile away.

"I can't believe there's this much traffic," said Billy, "on a Wednesday night."

"This is the one thing that sucks about this checkpoint," complained Hector, "there's always a bunch of traffic . . . plus, the checkpoint is manned by a bunch of jerks. You hear all these complaints about the daily harassment and abuse."

"Those goons better not mess with me. I'm not in the mood," said Billy.

"Did you ever ask your relatives if they knew anything about that?"

"No. There are no relatives on my father's side, remember? He was an orphan. On my mother's side, most relatives are also dead or in nursing homes. Their memories are shot to pieces. The last one to know anything was Dad . . . and, well, you know the surprise he sprang on me. My mom died ten years ago . . . you weren't working at the firm yet."

"I can't believe it's been that long since your *jefita* passed away. I guess since I always heard you talk about your old man, I assumed she was also still around."

"My dad was all I had left," explained Billy.

"So, you gonna lie if they ask if you're a citizen, Billy?"

"What else can I do, Hector? I guess I've lied about it all these years. Trust me. I've had nightmares about it. Each time you falsely represent yourself to be an American citizen, it's a new and separate federal offense. Each carries a five-year jail term."

"Oh," mumbled Hector, scratching his head and suddenly realizing the gravity of the situation.

"I went from being 'the hottest, kick-ass trial lawyer in all of South Texas' to this," huffed Billy, "an unwanted, persecuted illegal alien . . . all in a matter of minutes." Billy turned to Hector and caught him doing the sign of the cross. He was also praying quietly under his breath. "What are you doing?"

"Praying for you, me, us, Billy," answered Hector, looking worried. "I had completely forgotten about your situation."

"Pretend you don't know a thing if they ask."

"I'll stick to my story and you stick to your guns, Billy. Use the birth certificate in your wallet . . . if they ask."

"I was planning to . . ."

"Then, it should work."

They were getting closer to the checkpoint. Billy and Hector could now make out the gender of the agent running the checkpoint. It was a female U.S. Border Patrol agent.

"*Qué todo salga bien por el amor de Dios*," said Hector, "it's in God's hands."

At that precise moment, the pair got quiet and thoughtful, concentrating on calming their nerves. They needed to act as normal as possible, whatever "normal" was.

Deep in the confines of his mind, Billy realized, *So this is how undocumented people feel when they come up on the checkpoint? Like true criminals.*

TWENTY MINUTES had elapsed by the time the pair came face to face with the Border Patrol agent. She appeared to be in her early thirties, Anglo, her blonde hair up in a ponytail, sticking out through her green cap, tight smile, her uniform perfectly crisp.

She nodded at Billy and Hector.

Billy lowered the driver's side window and waited for the officer to address them.

"U.S. citizens?" Officer Sullivan asked as she ran the vehicle license plate numbers in a small computer station next to her.

"Yes, ma'am," Billy blurted out, grinning, his stomach churning with anxiety.

"American citizen," Hector added.

"You all have any proof of citizenship?" Her questions were short, fast and to the point.

"Ah, eh, sure . . . let me pull out my wallet," Billy replied as he reached into the console in the middle of the bucket seats and found what he was looking for. "Here it is," he said as he pulled a wallet-sized birth certificate and presented it to the female agent.

"You got a picture ID?" she asked as she read the document and looked at her computer screen. She had a slight frown on her face.

"Something wrong?" Billy asked, after noticing the agent's facial expressions.

"Let me see your picture ID," she demanded without responding to Billy's question. "Pull it out from your wallet and show it to me." She appeared to have forgotten that Hector even existed. Her focus was now solely on the driver of the vehicle.

Billy promptly complied and pulled his Texas driver's license from his wallet. "Here you go, ma'am."

The agent did a double-take between her computer screen, the driver's license, the birth certificate, and the driver of the Honda Pilot. "What do you do for a living, sir?"

"I'm an attorney down in McAllen."

"Really?"

"Yes, why?"

"Where you heading?"

"MD Anderson Hospital in Houston . . . see my daughter . . . she's being treated for leukemia."

"How often do you visit Houston?" she asked with a stone-cold face.

"My law firm has its principal office in Houston. I'm up there quite a bit," Billy countered. "Is something wrong?"

She did not answer, but kept inputting information into the computer, concentrating on the screen. "I'm sorry. You're gonna need to pull into that second office building," she said, pointing at one of the trailer homes. As she said this, she scribbled something on a red Post-it pad and pasted the bright sticky under one of the windshield wipers. "Here are your documents. You're gonna need them."

"WHAT DO YOU MEAN there's a warrant out for my arrest in Houston?" Billy screamed in shock. "That can't be! It's gotta be a mistake!"

"I'm sorry, sir," the fifty-something, male supervisor behind the counter said with a snicker. "You can tell that to the judge."

"The judge? What do you mean?"

"From what I can tell," explained the agent, "looks like you have something pending in Harris County . . . that's why there's a warrant. Could be a speeding citation or unpaid parking tickets . . . anything, really. You'll have to clear it up over there."

"Can you call the Harris County jail and see if they'll tell us why the warrant was issued?" interjected Hector. He had plenty of friends that ran criminal cases out of the jails down in Hidalgo and Cameron counties, and he'd heard that the last thing anyone wanted was a federal detainer showing up in the system. Since Billy had immigration issues, an immigration detainer could mean they were going to hold him in custody until his deportation. If, on the other hand, the warrant resulted from some outstanding minor infraction, then Billy would be able to post bond and quickly bolt from jail once he set foot in Houston.

"Our systems are connected," said the agent with the Texas-sized moustache. "I can pull it up myself and see why Mr. Bravo has a warrant. Give me a minute."

Billy was sweating bullets. Hector had never seen him looking so pale. He looked as if he was about to have a heart attack or pass out.

"Here it is," said the agent looking at his computer screen. "It has something to do with some hot checks."

A lightbulb went off in Billy's head. "My stolen checkbook! It happened during Border Fest! Remember they broke into my car and stole my briefcase? That's gotta be it!" A wave of relief came over Billy. "I'll just have to hire a lawyer and clear it up with the Harris County DA's office. That wasn't me writing those hot checks."

"Is there anything else?" asked Hector.

"Nah. That's it," replied the agent, "just a hot check case, nothing else."

Hector followed up. "Can we just fax you an incident report from the Hidalgo County Sheriff's Department where Mr. Bravo reported the theft . . . clear this up? Let him go?"

"That's between you and the Harris County District Attorney. Let me know what they say," answered the agent.

"So what happens next?" Billy asked. Having been a civil defense attorney his entire career, he had no clue what was going to happen next. The stuff he'd learned at the criminal clinic while in law school had been quickly forgotten.

"I have to take you into custody . . . call the sheriff's office to come pick you up. This is a warrant out of Harris County. That's where you're going . . . I guess you'll have to get a bond from a judge up there, post it and get out."

"Look," Billy started, "you don't have to take me into custody. I'll self-surrender in Harris County, please! My wife and kid are waiting in Houston. They're waiting for me. They're at MD Anderson Hospital. My daughter has cancer, for the love of God! Please. I'll take care of the hot checks. I'll have a lawyer look into it."

"Give me all your belongings," instructed Hector. He knew his boss had the gift of gab and could convince judges and juries, but he was not getting out of this one. "I'll go on to Houston and explain to Yami what just happened. I'll get you lined up with a bondsman and get you out as soon as you set foot in the Harris County jail."

"How long will that take?" asked Billy, eyes about to jump out of their sockets.

"A couple of days," said the agent. "I doubt the Harris County sheriff is going to drop everything to come pick up a hot-check writer. If it was a murder warrant, well, things would be different. They would be on their way, faster than an alien trafficker trying to outrun a posse of federal agents giving on its tail."

"I'll get you out," Hector explained as he demanded that Billy turn over to him his wallet, cell phone and car keys. "Let me get out of here, get to Houston and explain to Yami what just happened. Hopefully, they'll fetch you in the morning and by early afternoon, tomorrow . . . poof! I'll have you out of jail. I'll call Rick Solís, an old buddy of mine, criminal defense attorney . . . the guy's well-connected, and he owes me some favors. He knows his way around Harris County. He'll make some calls and have somebody come fetch you . . . I promise."

"But what about Ale?" cried Billy, "She needs surgery. I need to be there. Yami needs me there. And I'm due to start the Ray trial down in Laredo in a few days!"

"We'll get you out in time," promised Hector, "you'll see. Hand over everything."

"Here," said Billy reluctantly. He finished handing Hector his billfold, belt, watch, wedding ring, reading glasses, money clip with five one-hundred-dollar bills and the car keys. "Please don't mention it to Bates. I'll never make partner."

"Step right over here, sir," the agent said, pointing at a makeshift holding cell inside the office trailer. "You'll have to wait here until we hear from the sheriff's office. Then we'll know what to do with you." The agent escorted Billy to the holding cell, pushed him in and locked the steel door behind him. It slammed shut.

"Get me out of here, Hector!" shouted Billy from inside the cell as he pounded on the door.

YAMI WAS sitting in Dr. Menotti's office, and the doors were closed. She was sitting across from the kind doctor, tissue in hand, her eyes obviously irritated from all the crying, the worry and desperation. It would take an additional day for Billy to get out of the Harris County jail. Hector and Mr. Solís had been busy tracking down a friendly judge to set bail on Billy. In the meantime, Dr. Menotti wanted to update Yami, since the blood thinners had failed to dissolve the blood clot, and Ale was running out of time. They needed to remove the clot.

"Where's Mr. Bravo?" asked Dr. Menotti. "I expected him to be here."

"It's a long story," said Yami, totally embarrassed, looking down at the floor. "Let's just say he's been unavailable . . . as usual." Her tone began to change, and she now sounded upset, frustrated just thinking about her husband.

"I see."

"Is Alessandra going to be okay with the surgery? She's all that matters right now. Will she pull through? Please, I beg you, don't let anything happen to her."

"We won't let anything happen to her, Mrs. Bravo, I promise. I've assembled the best team possible. First thing tomorrow morning, we'll surgically remove the blood clot. It'll be a three-hour procedure, assuming there are no complications."

"Promise me there won't be any complications. Promise me you will give her the best treatment possible. *Se lo suplico, Doctor.*"

Dr. Menotti got up, went around his desk and stood behind Yami. He placed his hands on her delicate shoulders and in a calm, soothing voice said, "*Todo saldrá bien*, you'll see. Ale will pull through."

"Promise me you will take care of my Ale," Yami pleaded, sounding desperate, her voice cracking.

"We will, we will" assured Dr. Menotti. "We're getting Deban-sky to do the surgery. He's the best in Houston."

"I'll go crazy if anything happens to my baby. I mean it, Doctor. Please."

"Get a hold of yourself, Mrs. Bravo. We'll do everything we can for your daughter. You need to be strong for her. It won't help if she sees you like this. You understand?"

"Yes, yes. I'm sorry. I'll be strong."

"Good. That's better."

CHAPTER 36

ECTOR HAD PULLED some strings, and between him and Defense Attorney Solís, they'd found a friendly judge to call the Harris County jail and intimidate a young officer running the booking station into allowing Mr. Bravo's newly hired attorney to post a two-thousand-dollar attorney-surety bond. Once Solís had turned the paperwork in to the jail, Billy had been released instantly.

The pair was back at work in McAllen getting ready for the trial, after having spent the last two days up in Houston with Billy's daughter. Ale's operation had been a complete success, and the threatening clot had been removed by the able hands of Dr. Debansky. She was now making a speedy recovery.

Of course, Billy had not been that lucky. Upon his release from the Harris County jail, he'd gotten a scolding and ass-chewing from Yami, with the intensity of an F5 tornado. She was so angry at him that she'd come close to pummeling him. And because Billy had gotten himself arrested, he'd also forgotten their wedding anniversary on April 30! For the second time in all his years of marriage, the word *divorce* had come up. Either he made things right and got his messes straightened out, or he would be moving into his office permanently.

"Did you make the travel arrangements for our experts?" asked Billy, "do they know when to get to Laredo?"

"Yes, I've emailed them the confirmation numbers for their flights, car, and hotels. They've all emailed me back saying they received their itineraries, and all of them are aware of when the trial will start and when they're expected to testify."

"Did the subpoenas go out for all the other witnesses? The Laredo PD officers that responded to the call and the EMS first responders?"

"Done."

"How about the subpoena for the doctor that prescribed the Zerevrea?"

"That too."

"All right, then. Tomorrow we'll do our mock trial, and depending on what they come back with, I'll tweak the case over the weekend, and we're done. We're ready to try this thing. I wanna be done with this case once and for all. It's brought me nothing but misery."

"Hey, but if you win, you'll get your promotion, right?" asked Hector, "It will be worth it, ¿verdad?"

Billy scratched his head and thought about it for a while. "I don't know about the stupid promotion anymore, Hector. To get it and keep it would mean I would have to keep living a lie. So, who knows? I tell you what I do know. My daughter needs me to win this case. Yami needs me to win this thing, too. Now, more than ever, Ale needs a lawyer who will do whatever it takes to win this thing, whatever the price. Ale and other patients need Fledkort, and they'll need it for the rest of their lives. I need to make sure BostonMagnifica continues to exist and keeps on making the drug."

"I see the old Billy is back," remarked Hector with a smile. "Let's show them big-city trial lawyers from Houston how we try cases in South Texas!"

"HEY, GINA?" said Riley Spearman into the speakerphone. He was going over the last-minute details, getting ready for the trial. "I'm calling you because I'm coming in on Saturday. Timmy and I are flying down in my plane and should land in Laredo in the early afternoon. I'd like to work with you all of Sunday to get you ready for the witness stand, rehearse your testimony, fine-tune your delivery, prep you for Bravo's cross-examination and teach you a few techniques to connect with the jury. We also need to review your prior deposition testimony."

"I'll be available all weekend, Riley," Gina Ray replied. "You know I've been waiting for this day. It's been over a year."

"Good, then," answered Spearman, "our final pretrial hearing is Monday, jury selection on Tuesday and we'll probably start putting on our case on Wednesday morning. You'll have to be ready to take the stand by Thursday. That's the anticipated schedule."

"Do I need to be there on Monday?" she asked.

"No. Not until we start jury selection. Starting on Tuesday, you'll need to be there by my side every day."

"Okay."

"One last thing," said Spearman, "on jury selection day, I'll need you to bring your children to court. The jurors need to see all of you."

"That won't be a problem. I'll pull them from school."

"Did you get the photos I asked for?"

"Yes, I found some good ones of Tommy and the kids and some from our wedding, the birthdays, family gatherings."

"Fantastic. Okay, I gotta run. I'll give you a call as soon as we land in Laredo."

CHAPTER 37

"HOW DID THE mock trial go?" Yami and Alessandra asked at the same time. Billy had rushed to catch the last flight out of McAllen to Houston right after the mock trial exercise. He'd decided to fly and avoid the pesky checkpoints. When one flew out of the Valley, all one needed was a boarding pass and a picture ID.

The Border Patrol agents standing next to the TSA screening employees did not have immediate access to computers in order to run a criminal history or check someone's immigration status. In case they asked, all the travelers needed to do was flash his or her passport or a birth record, along with a picture ID. For now, he would continue to use his now "bogus" wallet-sized birth certificate—the same one he'd carried since he'd graduated from high school.

Billy wanted to see Alessandra and Yami one more time before heading to Laredo to start the Ray trial. He needed to show Yami that he really cared and that he would never divorce her, no matter what.

"They felt the plaintiff's evidence fell short, so they sided with us and said Zerevrea did not cause Tommy Ray's suicide," Billy lied. In reality, the mock jury had found that Zerevrea, indeed, had triggered Tommy Ray's suicide. They had also ruled that Zerevrea was an extremely dangerous drug and that the black box warnings were totally inadequate.

Billy was not about to reveal this piece of information to his wife. If the Laredo jury came out feeling the same way, his client and Ale were truly screwed. A plaintiff's verdict meant thousands of other lawsuits would be filed within weeks all over the country.

With the recent spike in suicides in the Gulf States, plaintiff's lawyers were already putting two and two together. Soon it would be game over. BostonMagnifica would easily end up mortally wounded. It would not be a pretty bankruptcy, by any means.

"What else did they say?" asked Alessandra from her hospital bed, thrilled that her father was about to win the most important lawsuit of his career. Growing up with a trial lawyer in the house, she'd had the chance to spend many hours in the courtrooms of Hidalgo County, watching her father spank plaintiff's lawyer after plaintiff's lawyer.

"That Mr. Ray probably had other reasons to end his life, but that they did not see how my client's drug would have pushed him over the edge," Billy lied again.

"How long are you staying with us?" interrupted Yami from Ale's bedside.

"Tonight only. I have a meeting with Melanie Hughes at Bates' office in the morning."

"Who's she?" Yami asked.

"She's in-house counsel for BostonMagnifica. She's flying in to discuss last-minute details. The mock jury could have it all wrong. Maybe we'll take a hit, I don't know. It could be a huge verdict. We need to do damage control, prepare for the worst-case scenario."

"But that won't happen, right, Dad?" Alessandra asked.

"Of course not, baby," said Billy. "Anyway, I'll come back and see you before I fly to McAllen. Hector and I will drive the next day to Laredo to start the trial."

"Dr. Menotti says Ale should be going home very soon," interjected Yami. "She'll have to continue receiving her chemo down in McAllen. We'll need to find an oncologist willing to follow Menotti's protocol."

"I'm sure we'll manage."

"I know. Good luck in Laredo. I hope your client appreciates everything you've sacrificed to get them a win," said Yami as she sized up her husband.

"I hope so, too," replied Billy.

SITTING AT the huge conference table inside the Houston office dressed in her tailored suit, Melanie Hughes was text-messaging headquarters when Billy Bravo walked in. The in-house counsel for BostonMagnifica was a striking forty-five-year-old redhead with blue eyes and shapely long legs. The entire room smelled of Tiranami, a sensuous fragrance Billy had smelled on Yami the last time they had made love almost a year ago.

"Are you ready, Mr. Bravo?" asked Hughes.

"Everything is set to go. I'm ready to pick that jury."

"Everything's lined up, then?"

"Yes," replied Billy. "We're on."

"Good," replied the in-house counsel. "I was concerned Sal would disapprove. But your trial strategy, I have to admit, was genius."

"I had to think of something. My daughter's life also hangs in the balance," said Billy.

"I would have done the same thing for my son. I remember when he was just a little guy. Now, he's getting ready to finish college. He's what's kept me going all these years."

"I finally learned my lesson," confessed Billy. "It took me a while though."

"It's easy to get sidetracked," Hughes replied, "when one gets caught up at work."

"One can lose sight of what's important, for sure."

"Well, I hope things turn out all right. Otherwise, we might as well close up shop."

"According to the mock jury," Billy lied in an effort to put the general counsel at ease, "your company has nothing to worry about."

"I hope so," said Hughes.

"*Veni, vidi, vici,*" Billy said as he got up from the table and walked over to a window. He was looking out over downtown Houston and what the locals called Buffalo Bayou. "For you, me, my family, BostonMagnifica, its employees, shareholders and even my law firm."

"Our future is resting on your shoulders, Mr. Bravo. We're all counting on you."

"I know. Believe me . . . I know."

CHAPTER 38

I T WAS SUNDAY, and Billy and Hector were back in McAllen waiting on Charlie Jensen inside the courtyard of La Fonda del Sabor, a new restaurant touting a unique concept in Latin fare. It had opened near downtown off Pecan Avenue in a quaint neighborhood called Parque Antiguo. The whole area had a Bohemian feel to it. There were coffeehouses, restaurants, bookstores and art galleries. Local artists also kept workshops and studios there. This would be the pair's last meal in McAllen for the next two weeks. The Ray trial in Laredo was due to get underway the next day, with the pretrial conference scheduled to start promptly at nine.

Billy looked relaxed. He was drinking a glass of homemade sangria, twirling the chunks of fresh fruit in his mouth when he said, "Didn't Charlie say he was coming?"

"He was packing his bags, last I spoke with him. He said something about following us in his car. That he'd meet us here, outside in the parking lot."

"Oh, okay," said Billy.

"Are you ready to try this damned case?"

"¡Claro!" Billy said with renewed confidence. "It's time to put this case to rest."

"I'm glad to see you so pumped up. What happened in Houston? Did you get that mess straightened out?"

"Somebody was writing hot checks from one of my bank accounts."

"Is it done, then?"

"Well, your buddy Rick Solís got the cases dismissed. Hopefully the check writing has stopped. Otherwise, I might get picked up again. What a pain in the ass! Nancy had already put stop payments on all the checks, even closed the account. *¡Hijos de su pinche madre!*"

"And the birth certificate situation? Have you straightened out that mess? Or should I expect the feds to pick you up in Laredo?"

Billy started laughing. "You're too much, Hector."

"Hey, it could happen."

"Well," admitted Billy, "I'm still in hot water, if you must know. Díaz is trying to find a way to fix the problem. In the meantime, I'm a *mojado*. I still might end up being deported back to Mexico."

"That's impossible!" Hector exclaimed. "What are you going to do in Mexico? And your family? What's gonna happen?"

"*No sé*," Billy said, sounding frustrated. "I may just tell this great country of ours to kiss my . . ."

"Those bastards in Washington have no clue, do they? You don't hear them deporting Canadians, Indians or Pakistanis. It's only us—the Mexicans! When did this country go from 'let's secure our borders from terrorists' to 'keep all the Mexicans out'? What are they afraid of, that we're gonna take over the country?"

"*Ya, hombre, basta*, drop it," demanded Billy. "Let's order some lunch."

"How did you find this place?" Hector asked, switching topics, still shaking his head as he imagined his old man being deported and sent to live in Mexico, away from his loved ones. Separated from family by some draconian immigration rule that some moron in Washington ill-conceived and left to be enforced and arbitrarily interpreted by some flunkie Border Patrol or customs agent without a legal education.

"Believe it or not, Yami read about it. She had asked me to bring her here for our anniversary. Who would have thought we'd end up spending our anniversary apart from each other. . . . Hopefully, we can come back with Ale and Mauricio and celebrate."

"Well, I'm surprised you took time off to do lunch. With the trial starting tomorrow and stuff . . . you never eat lunch. What gives?"

"Being locked up and getting knocked around a few times can have a profound effect on the way one sees things, Hector. Since Ale got ill, I've been taking stock . . . "

"You gonna slow down?" asked Hector, surprised.

"I don't know what I'm gonna do. But I'm gonna make some changes, that's for sure. For starters, I plan to spend more time with the family."

"*Qué bueno.* Yami will like that."

"If my ass doesn't get deported or she doesn't divorce me after I fess up."

"You haven't told her about your son?"

"I've been waiting for the right moment. It hasn't happened yet."

A busboy wearing black mariachi pants and a white, short-sleeve guayabera and leather huaraches stopped by to fill their glasses with water and to refill the breadbasket with more chile-spiced *pan de campo*.

"*Qué problemón, ¿no?*"

"*Sí,*" Billy muttered. "But as soon as this trial is over and I dispatch Spearman, I'm gonna do two things."

"What?"

"I'm gonna ask Bates for my promotion straight up. Tell him to his face that it's time for me to make name partner. And then, after that happens, I'll take an entire month off—stay home with my wife, spend time with the family, maybe even take them to Austin and introduce them to William Palmer, my son."

Hector reached for a piece of warm bread and spread some *cilantro-habanero* butter on top of it. "If there's somebody at that firm that deserves to be name partner, it's you, Billy. I hope you get it."

"I think it's time."

"Damn right," answered Hector, "it's been long overdue . . . I'm sure you will, I mean, you've won so many cases for them. I don't see why not."

"Are you gentlemen ready to order?" interrupted the waiter. "Do you want to hear today's specials?"

"What is it?" asked Billy.

"Today," started Victor, "we're featuring boneless, skinless breasts of free-range chicken rubbed in a *mojo de chile guajillo* and *tamarindo*, char grilled and seared over red-hot mesquite charcoals. It comes with *chorizo*-sprinkled potatoes, tender *chayotitos* au gratin with *queso manchego* and for dessert we have the *canela*-spiced sweet potato pecan pie served warm with homemade ice cream."

"I'm sold," blurted Hector, "that's what I'll have."

"I'll have," Billy said, "the saffron-infused *paella pescadora*, with a spicy shrimp cocktail *al estilo* Mazatlán and another sangria."

"I'll be back shortly with your food and drinks. Thank you." The waiter turned around and was gone.

"What if Bates doesn't make you name partner?" asked Hector. "What are you going to do then?"

"That's option number two . . . I'm out of here. Maybe it's for the better . . . time for a change. I'll go and become an immigration lawyer, assuming I get to stay."

"Well," Hector said, "I'm sure the wife's gonna be thrilled when she hears that you are cutting back at work. To change," toasted Hector raising his sangria.

"*Por el cambio*," toasted Billy, "*¡salud!*"

CHAPTER 39

I T WAS MONDAY, and Jim Bates was back from the Harris County Bar weekly breakfast when he noticed a pile of mail waiting on his desk. The one piece that caught his eye had a return address from the Washington office for the Department in Washington. He sliced the envelope open and unfolded its contents. It was a letter addressed to Billy Bravo's employer.

Dear Managing Partner:
Our records indicate that Guillermo Cuahutemoc Bravo is an attorney working at your firm. Please be advised that the above-named individual recently applied to obtain a U.S. passport. However, the individual may be a Mexican national using fraudulent documents in order to obtain gainful employment in the United States.

His birth record has been flagged as one originating with a border midwife who has been convicted for accepting bribes to lie on birth records. The above individual has been identified as one whose birth record was generated by said midwife in the early 1960s. Therefore, the individual's citizenship status is now being scrutinized and investigated by the Bureau of Customs and Immigration Services.

You are formally being advised that under Section 8 USC 1324 (a) (1) (A) (iv) (b) (iii), any person who encourages or induces an illegal alien to reside, knowing or in reckless disregard of the fact that such residence is in violation of law, shall be punished as provided for each illegal alien in respect to whom such a violation occurs, fined under Title 18, imprisoned not more than five years or both.

Section 274 felonies under the federal Immigration and Nationality Act, INA 274A (a) (1) (A), also include:

A person(s) (including a group of persons, business, organization or local government) commits a federal felony when she or he:

- assists an illegal alien she/he should reasonably know is illegally in the U.S. or who lacks employment authorization by transporting, sheltering or assisting him/her to obtain employment, or
- encourages that illegal alien to remain in the U.S. by referring him/her to an employer or by acting as employer or agent for an employer in any way, or
- knowingly assists illegal aliens due to personal convictions.

Penalties upon conviction include criminal fines, imprisonment and forfeiture of vehicles and real property used to commit the crime. Anyone employing or contracting with an illegal alien without verifying his/her work authorization status is guilty of a misdemeanor. Aliens and employers violating immigration laws are subject to arrest, detention and seizure of vehicles or property. In addition, individuals or entities who engage in racketeering enterprises that commit (or conspire to commit) immigration-related felonies are subject to private civil suits for treble damages and injunctive relief.

"Holy shit," yelled Bates as the letter dropped to the floor. He pushed the Intercom button on his desk phone. "Connie, summon the partners. We need to have a meeting . . . *Right now!*"

"WHAT DO we do?" asked Rick Domani. "I gotta say, I'm really disappointed." He was reading the letter one more time, making sure he had not missed a thing.

Fred Rockford came to Billy's aid. "Well, the letter doesn't say that Billy is, in fact, an undocumented worker. All it says is that BCIS is *investigating* to see whether or not this was one of those birth records that may have been obtained by illegal means. That's the way I read it, anyway."

Drew Lord spoke next. "I don't see why we should be worried. Even if it turns out the guy is here illegally, we didn't know a thing. We, as a firm, did not engage in any knowing conduct. We just did not know, period!"

"I never liked the guy," sneered Domani. "I always suspected something . . . I just couldn't put my finger on it."

"What's the first thing you learned in law school?" asked Rockford, turning to Domani.

"Everyone is innocent until proven guilty," replied Lord, without giving Domani a chance to answer. "I think it's premature to do anything at this point. Let the guy finish the trial down in Laredo, and then we can have a meeting with him."

"We need to get to the bottom of this," Bates interjected. "This would not be good for business. Not now, with all the anti-immigration sentiment gripping the nation."

"I agree with Rick, however," Lord volunteered, "this takes him out of contention for the promotion to name partner."

"Yes," said Rockford, "I would have to concur with that assessment. It doesn't rise to the level of firing the guy. Let's have the meeting and see what he has to say. Give him a chance."

"Let him finish the Zerevrea trial. Right now is not a good time to fly him up here. Let him get the client its defense verdict, then we can talk to him," Lord said as he got up and started heading out of Bates' office. "The guy's been loyal to this firm for close to two decades, and you're ready to can his ass just like that? Where's your loyalty to the poor bastard?"

"I agree," said Rockford as he headed out the door. "I'm sure there's an explanation. Maybe it's all a mistake. Billy's been the most honest, dedicated, respectable attorney I ever met. More than I can say about some of us."

BILLY FOUND a parking space on Matamoros Street right across from the federal courthouse in Laredo. It was nine in the morning on Monday, the day of the final pretrial conference and the temperature was already hovering in the hundreds. He, Charlie and Hector got out of their respective vehicles, unloaded several boxes from the Honda Pilot onto a dolly and headed for the main entrance.

Billy was smartly dressed in a navy-blue pinstriped two-piece suit and was carrying a new black leather briefcase with gold "GCB" initials engraved on the side. Hector was wearing khakis with a long-sleeved Oxford button-down and a tie and Charlie Jensen, the two-year associate, was wearing a charcoal-gray, double-breasted wool suit.

Billy was feeling butterflies—the jitters he'd always felt right before trial. Although to the outside world he appeared calm, cool and collected, the pent-up adrenaline always continued to mount until it was time to deliver opening arguments. Once his opening had been delivered, his nerves would subside and the pesky butterflies would go away.

"I'm gonna try to get us counsel's table near the jury box," Billy indicated. "Judge Dorfman's courtroom is on the third floor."

"All right," Charlie said, "we'll catch up with you."

WHILE CHARLIE held the elevator door open, Hector made his exit, dolly and boxes in tow and started walking down the hall to Judge Dorfman's courtroom. Inside, the pair found Billy sitting at counsel's table, the one nearest the jury box. He was deep in thought, going over some notes scribbled on a yellow pad.

"Where do you want the boxes?" Hector asked.

"Set them over here, under the table, next to me."

Hector unloaded the dolly and removed the boxes. One by one, he picked them up and placed them at Billy's feet under the large wooden table. Charlie set his briefcase on counsel's table and removed two duplicate trial notebooks that Nancy had prepared for the attorneys trying the case.

"Where is everybody?" Hector asked.

"I guess they're on their way," Billy answered without taking his eyes from his notes. "They'll be here, trust me. It's only 9:25 AM."

"Where did you go last night?"

"I couldn't sleep. I kept thinking of my wife, so I decided to go to Denny's next door and work on my opening argument."

"How much sleep did you get?"

"Three hours."

"You feel all right?" Hector asked.

"It's always like this for me when I'm in trial. I rarely sleep more than four hours," Billy answered. "It's what we trial lawyers call being in 'trial mode'."

"How long do you think it will take Spearman to put on his case in chief?" asked Jensen.

"A week. You figure he'll put the widow on the stand first. Then, he'll call the cops that responded to the scene of the suicide, followed by the investigators, the EMS personnel and the coroner. Then, they'll call some of our scientists that worked on developing the drug, plus their retained experts and then Tommy Ray's parents—maybe a son or daughter, too."

"Aren't his kids little?" asked Hector.

"One of the girls is eleven. I think Dorfman will let her testify. Not that the kid can add anything to the trial itself. If Spearman has her on the stand, it'll be to gain sympathy from the jury."

"So, it'll be a short trial?"

"Yep. Five days for the plaintiffs, two days for us to put on our defense witnesses and experts, then closing arguments."

"Is Domani coming down to help you try the case?"

"No. Charlie and I are going to try this sucker. I asked Falcone to fly down and sit by my side at counsel's table for a few days. We'll see if he shows up by ten."

"Do you want me to set up the Elmo?" Hector asked.

"No, we'll use the court's Elmo and projector, should we need it. We'll wait and see what kind of setup the plaintiffs bring."

"All right," said Hector, "let me borrow the car keys so I can go return the dolly."

"Here you go," Billy said as he tossed him the keys. "See if you can find me and Charlie some bottled water. Thanks."

"Be back in a few."

CHAPTER 40

THEY MARCHED INTO Judge Dorfman's courtroom single file in two groups, numbered one through forty and forty-one through eighty. The first group huddled together over on the right-hand side of the courtroom. The second group sat on the left side of the room.

Judge Dorfman welcomed the groups and gave them instructions as to the different stages involved in jury selection—what the lawyers called *voir dire*. He explained that he liked for the attorneys to do their own questioning of the panel—that Billy Bravo and Riley Spearman would be asking questions of them, for it was their job, even though there were other federal judges that asked the questions themselves and did not allow the attorneys to question the potential jurors. He explained that this was an attempt by said judges to play king or God and reminded everyone that a trial was not the judge's case—but the attorneys'. And, if those judges wanted to play lawyer, well, then they should tender their resignations and go hang their shingle.

He talked about their duty as jurors and the importance of the jury system. How it was imperative that as Americans, they take time to participate in the process. How slowly but surely, developments in the law were chipping away at one's right to a jury trial. Dorfman did not come straight out and say that it was big corporate interests that were now abusing the arbitration process (including the legislative process), but the implication was there. The fact of the matter was that the jury trial was vanishing, quickly disappearing. Courts everywhere were ordering folks to arbitrate rather than litigate, and in record numbers. Initially, the concept of arbitration had looked good on paper, but now it had become ridiculously expensive and corrupt and had been turned into a racket by arbitration societies and the lawyers themselves.

Judge Dorfman spoke of how in recent years, there had been a shift, a trend, a push by legislatures across the nation to prevent good, able juries or judges from determining the outcome of the litigants' civil dispute and instead letting panels of expensive legal experts render a binding decision. This shift was affecting the profession, and, he, as a judge who believed in giving all litigants that came before him a fair trial, was seriously concerned. It was imperative to the integrity of the entire judicial system to keep the jury trial alive—to let the everyday person, folks like themselves, those being selected to hear the Ray case, to bring their knowledge and experience into the courtroom.

He explained to the panel that the Ray case dealt with claims that a certain drug taken for anxiety had made the deceased turn the gun on himself and that the plaintiff had the burden of proving that it had been the defendant's drug that made the deceased pull the trigger.

This was going to be a difficult case, perhaps even sad as it dealt with a violent suicide. The jurors should anticipate being in trial between one to two weeks, that both attorneys would be asking questions of them and to please answer the questions truthfully, honestly and openly. If for some reason, they felt uncomfortable answering a particular question, they could refrain from answering and, at the break, approach the bench and address their concerns.

"Mr. Spearman, the attorney for the plaintiffs, will now be asking you some questions," instructed Judge Dorfman. "You have forty-five minutes for *voir dire*. You're up, counsel."

ONCE SPEARMAN used his forty-five minutes for questioning, Judge Dorfman signaled Billy that it was now his turn to address the panel.

Billy got up from counsel's table and walked over to the podium in front of the jury box. He placed his yellow notepad on it, cleared his throat and addressed the members of the *venire*. "Good morning. *Buenos días*."

"Good morning," replied the bunch.

"My name is Billy Bravo, and this here," said Billy, pointing at Jensen, "is my cocounsel, Charlie Jensen. Charlie will be helping me try this case. Charlie and I both represent BostonMagnifica Pharmaceuticals of Worcester, Massachusetts. While my client's business office is in New York, they do all their research and man-ufacture product in Worcester."

The entire panel looked at Charlie. Charlie smiled back and greeted them. "Good morning."

Billy then pointed at Hector, sitting off to one side. "This is Mr. Hector Ayala. He works with our firm and will be assisting Charlie and me during the trial." Hector nodded to the panel. They nodded back.

"How many of you have heard of my client?" asked Billy.

Half of the group raised their hands.

"*Muy bien*, a lot of you. Okay, let me see . . . you ma'am, Juror Number Twenty, fourth pew in the back, what have you heard?"

A young female in her mid-twenties replied, "I've seen the commercials . . . they make medicine for depression and anxiety."

"That's correct. They make Zerevrea. Let me ask you, first, before we go any further, has anyone here among you ever lost a loved one to suicide? A relative, a spouse, sons or daughters, a friend?"

Panel Member Number Fifty-One raised his hand.

"What's your number, sir?" interrupted Judge Dorfman. "There in the back."

"He's Fifty-One, Judge," said Billy. "Mr. Cody Jones, correct?"

"Yes, sir," said Mr. Jones, looking up at Judge Dorfman.

"Mr. Jones," continued Billy, "would you mind telling us a lit-tle bit about that? Is it okay if we talk about it?"

"Yes, sir," the man said. He looked to be in his late fifties with white hair and full sideburns.

"What happened?" followed Billy.

"After seeing combat in the Gulf War, my nephew came home all messed up. He was never the same. Doctor said he was suffering from post-traumatic stress disorder and depression. They tried all kinds of things—therapies, medications, counseling. . . . I think he finally just gave up. He was in his late twenties."

Billy knew it was not necessary to prod anymore; he would not go any deeper than that, not at this time, anyway. "So, your nephew had been depressed. Is that a fair assessment?"

"And his wife had left him," volunteered Mr. Jones.

"So, do you think it was a combination of things: coming home messed up from the war, his wife leaving him, not seeing his kids, struggling with depression all those years?"

"That's about right," Mr. Jones said. "He was probably fed up."

"If you get selected as a juror, do you think the fact that your nephew committed suicide and that this case also deals with suicide will affect you in your deliberations, Mr. Jones?"

"No, sir. I'll listen to the evidence and decide the case on the evidence, nothing else," answered Mr. Jones.

"Anybody else?" asked Billy.

Panel Member Thirty-Three raised his hand. He was a young Hispanic male with a shaved head and a goatee, probably in his late twenties. "My oldest brother, Robbie, committed suicide, too . . . about ten years ago."

"I'm sorry to hear that," replied Billy

"He'd been struggling with a cocaine addiction for over ten years. He'd lost his wife, his kids, a great job with the federal government, his house . . . in the end he stole a stash belonging to some bad dudes . . . I think he knew they were not going to overlook his wrongdoings, so rather than face them, he popped some sleeping pills, downed them with bourbon and never woke up again."

"So, his suicide was no mystery," added Billy. "It came as no surprise, and there appeared to be a reason behind it . . . like in the case of Mr. Jones' nephew, right?"

"Right, there were many other factors."

"Exactly," retorted Billy. "Did you all hear that? There was a divorce, a severe drug addiction, action in combat, depression . . . something, *algo*, no? Something that pushed them over the edge, wouldn't you agree?" asked Billy, looking for a response.

They all nodded their heads, appearing to be completely in agreement with Billy Bravo.

"Let me move on, now. Anybody here taking Zerevrea, my client's drug?"

There were no hands. The panel members were looking around to see if anybody raised a hand.

"How about Paxil? Zoloft? Prozac? Anybody here taking any of those medications? What we call serotonin reuptake inhibitors?"

About twenty hands went up.

"You, sir, in the first row," said Billy, "which one?"

"Paxil," said the guy in his early fifties.

"Does it help?"

"Yes. It's helped me with my social anxiety. Before, I would not have raised my hand. I was extremely shy. Public speaking gave me the heebie-jeebies, but now . . . look at me!"

Everybody laughed. Even Dorfman was laughing and smiling.

"Anybody else? Either taking those medications or taking other antidepressants?"

A bunch of hands in the back of the room went up.

"You, sir," said Billy, pointing at Number Seventy-Six.

"I'm on Prozac . . . it helps me function. I'm able to go to work, provide for my family. Something I could not do before because of panic attacks."

"So, it has helped you?"

"Yes, big difference. Thank God for these wonderful drugs."

"Well, I took Zoloft," interjected Number Fifteen, a middle-aged female, "and it gave me the jitters. I quit taking it, didn't like it. I felt wired all the time."

"Thanks for your response," said Billy. "As you can see, these medications affect people differently. In many instances, they really help, but in some other instances, they might not. In our case, the plaintiffs are saying that Zerevrea is a dangerous drug and that it can make people snap. That the warnings that come with the box, here on its side . . . " Billy picked up a box and pointed at the black box warnings printed on the side of the packaging, "are not enough. That manufacturers should do more. That BostonMagnifica should do more. That because the warnings are inadequate, then the average user cannot understand them."

"But," interrupted Panel Member Number One, shaking his head, looking somewhat confused, "are the plaintiffs saying that Tommy Ray, a lawyer by training and profession, a guy with more education than most of us, wouldn't have understood the warnings on the side of the packaging?"

Billy looked over at Spearman. Never once in the fifteen years of trying cases had he seen such a panel of potential jurors. He turned back and tried to answer the question. "The plaintiffs allege that BostonMagnifica's warnings used with Zerevrea are not adequate and don't do enough to inform the average user. That's it, in a nutshell."

"But, those black box warnings," interrupted Panel Member Number One again, "weren't they approved by the FDA?"

Billy wanted to turn around and look at Spearman again, even stare at him, but forced himself not to. There was no way in hell that Spearman was going to win this trial if other members of the panel felt like Panel Member Number One. By the way the guy had asked the questions, it was as if he was ready to hand Billy a defense verdict. "Yes," answered Billy, "the FDA says when to put those warnings on the packaging, what language to use, what dangers to warn against and even dictates the size of the warning. Should it be half-inch-by-half–inch, one-inch-by-one-inch, etc."

"Really?" asked Number One.

"Yes," said Billy.

Number One raised his hand again. "I'm trying to understand this, Mr. Bravo. Please excuse my ignorance. So, if the FDA approved the drug in question, and they're the federal government, logically, it follows that the drug has been deemed safe, no?"

"Did everybody hear that?" Billy asked, happy the way things were turning out.

Most of the panel members were nodding their heads in agreement, acknowledging Billy.

Billy went on. "There's one last thing I want to talk to all of you about. What were some of those instructions Judge Dorfman gave you when you first walked in? When he was explaining to all of you the purpose of having jury selection? Remember?"

"To leave our biases outside," replied Number Twenty-One, the housewife with the husband that worked for the Laredo Fire Department.

"And what does that mean?"

"Your attitudes and beliefs," said the housewife, "saying that BostonMagnifica must have done something wrong because it's a drug company, and drug companies are always busted for breaking the law or because they have tons of cash and are always trying to buy influence in Washington."

Everyone laughed again.

"That's good. In other words, you come in here, and your mind is already made up one way or another," followed Billy, "even before you've heard a single piece of evidence, because of something you believe. Whether there's any truth to it or whether you're wrong or right. Your mind is already made up, right?"

He pointed to another housewife, Number Sixty-Six. "What else did Judge Dorfman say?"

She got embarrassed, but managed to utter, "To leave our prejudices outside too."

"That's right," answered Billy, "did all of you hear that?"

Everybody raised their hands, all nodding in agreement, looking at each other.

"What's the one thing we don't want you to leave outside? The one thing we *do* want you to bring with you to the courtroom?" asked Billy. "The one thing the judge never said for you to leave outside or forget to bring with you. Anybody?"

This time there were no hands—nothing. All the members were looking around to see who would answer.

"Give up?" asked Billy.

"Common sense?" asked Number One. "We bring our common sense, is that it?"

"Yes, your common sense," answered Billy, smiling. "That's it. In this trial, you are going to hear a lot about science and formulas and fancy-schmancy medical terms and chemistry . . . but we are going to ask you to apply your common sense as you plow through the evidence and come to your own conclusions and findings. That's all we want. Use your common sense and apply it to the case. Listen to the witnesses, evaluate their credibility, look at the evidence and use your common sense. I can tell by the way you answered questions here this morning that you all are very smart and observant. This is not going to be a difficult case. Surely, it's got some gory details, and there will be discussions about brain matter, bullets, blood and violence, among other things, but in the end, you will have to answer this question: 'Did Zerevrea make Tommy Ray snap and turn the gun on himself?' And when you come to that fork in the road—when you have to decide which way to go and you have to pick either 'yes' or 'no'—I sincerely hope you'll apply your common sense. That's all I ask, and that's all BostonMagnifica asks. *Usar el sentido común.* In the final analysis, we do ask that you leave your biases, prejudices and negative attitudes and feelings outside of the courtroom. But the one thing we do ask you to bring, what the defendant reminds you to always carry with you when listening to all the evidence, without fail, is your common sense. So, please, don't forget to bring your common sense to the table and apply it to your deliberations. *Eso es todo.* That's all. I look forward to trying this case in your presence. Thank you."

CHAPTER 41

THE TWELVE JURORS and two alternates were already sitting in the box when Judge Dorfman nodded to Riley Spearman to start delivering his opening argument. "Forty-five minutes, counsel. You're up."

"Thank you, Judge. Thank you, members of the jury," said Spearman as he got up from counsel's table and, without skipping a beat, jumped right into his opening argument.

"As you already know, this is the only chance I get to talk to you directly about the evidence in the case. Throughout the trial, the attorneys are prohibited from talking to the jury. We can say 'hi' or 'good morning,' but that's about it. So, I want to discuss with you what I believe the evidence in this case will prove or show. By the way, today, you also get to go to science school. During the course of this trial, you'll get to hear a lot about SSRIs. Zerevrea, the drug in this case, is a selective serotonin reuptake inhibitor, just like Prozac, Paxil and Zoloft. You will also hear the word 'suicide' or 'suicidality' a lot. And you will also learn how, since the late eighties, drug companies have known about the connection between these drugs and suicide and aggressive behaviors.

"Now, the evidence will show that in the late eighties, the first SSRI drug, Prozac, was introduced by Eli Lilly & Company. Prozac quickly became a hit and turned out to be a cash cow for the company. The 'all-time best and biggest seller' in the history of antidepressants. So, in 1990, SmithKline Beecham jumped on the bandwagon and came up with Paxil. Right away, however, there were clinical studies that suggested that these kinds of drugs were safe for most people—the majority of us. Nevertheless, there was a small fraction—what we call a small 'vulnerable subpopulation' of patients—that experienced aggressiveness and suicidal thinking.

"Are you with me so far?" Spearman asked.

The jurors nodded in agreement.

"Perfect," Spearman continued, "now, just as Eli Lilly developed a chemical substance called fluoxetine, what you and I know as Prozac, SmithKline Beecham developed a substance called paroxetine, which later became Paxil. Pfizer, another drug company, then invented sertraline, and that became Zoloft. Many years later, BostonMagnifica developed a chemical called stepflaxin, which is now known as Zerevrea. That's what we're dealing with here.

"Let me tell you what you will learn from the few studies that have been conducted about Zerevrea. First, 36 percent of the patients who volunteered to participate in BostonMagnifica's clinical trials dropped out because of horrendous adverse side effects, mainly in the first or second week. I believe you will find this significant as you consider the fact that Tommy Ray had only been on this medicine for a mere two days. As the studies dealing with SSRIs have shown, the adverse effects happen mainly in the early period of treatment. If something terrible is going to happen, it usually happens in the first two weeks, while the human body and the brain are adjusting.

"Now, here's where it gets interesting. We are going to be talking a lot about studies done on Prozac, Paxil and Zoloft, but guess what . . . as I said, there are a very few studies done specifically on Zerevrea—they're almost nonexistent, in fact. There is one very short paper detailing some adverse reactions to Zerevrea, and there's BostonMagnifica's one or two clinical studies. No more than that. What's important is the fact that BostonMagnifica's own paper seems to suggest that the adverse experiences were either caused by Zerevrea or possibly by Zerevrea and a combination of other factors.

"Also, you will hear that these drugs cause something called 'akathisia,' what the medical community defines as having 'a great deal of inner turmoil.' Some patients have described the akathisia as being pricked with pins and needles on the lower extremities or being wired, wanting to jump out of their skin. The condition may also be accompanied by sudden bodily movements like jerking, restlessness and being unable to sit still. Others have described this condition as the brain being 'on' and you can't 'turn it off' or get it to go to sleep. A few subjects have described the feeling as being highly irritable, wanting to punch and pummel the day-lights out of people.

"So, let's go back to 1990, when a key event happened. Harvard published an article prepared by a psychiatrist and a psycho-pharmacologist. These guys discovered ·that a small group of patients immediately started thinking of suicide while on Prozac. The drug company didn't like it one bit!

"Fast forward to October of that year. The FDA asked SmithK-line Beecham to submit its comments or findings regarding the suicide issue and Paxil. The FDA wanted to know if Paxil had the same problems as Prozac. Now, you will hear evidence that all this time, more specifically the nineties, the pharmaceuticals continued to hide the ball. A decade went by and, finally, in the years 2003 and 2004, our Congress stepped in to investigate. And the FDA, reluctantly, but due to mounting pressure, *finally* ordered the drug makers to put black box warnings on all SSRIs advising of the danger of suicide.

"Okay, let us fast forward to Laredo, Texas, and the case in question. Mr. Tommy Ray, it is alleged, was suffering from anxiety and depression, and I just want to tell you that we're disputing the existence of the alleged depression. He certainly had one or two episodes of mild anxiety, but not depression. Perhaps even a slight case of post-traumatic stress syndrome after Tommy returned from the Gulf War, but nothing else. Tommy Ray was never treated for depression by a psychiatrist or a licensed professional counselor or any other such professional. His physician, Dr. Haverti, saw him about five days before he took his own life. You will see from his medical records and the testimony that he was not a violent man and that he had no previous suicidal thoughts or tendencies. He did, however, express that he had been feeling a little anxious. So, his doctor prescribed Zerevrea, a so-called new 'miracle drug'."

Spearman turned around and pointed at Falcone, now present in the courtroom. He then faced the jurors again, "Now, why is this significant? Because as the years went by, the pharmaceuticals got smart and started marketing their SSRIs for other things rather than just depression. You see, the market became so competitive, so saturated with all these drugs that in order for them to stop losing their market share, they had to come up with new ways to sell their drugs. They had to find other uses and new customers. So, in time, they asked the FDA to give them permission to peddle their drugs for other things—such as anxiety, seasonal affective disorder, even hyperactivity. That's why Tommy was prescribed Zerevrea, for his mild anxiety.

"Now, we believe, even though BostonMagnifica has a black box warning about suicide and violence, that in this day and age, this is not enough. What do we mean? What we mean is this: When you have the pharmaceuticals promoting their drugs over the airwaves, on TV, radio, in the print media, even on the Internet, with the biggest advertising budgets in the history of the United States—bigger even than budgets for the beer companies—this overpromotion cancels the effect of the meager black box warnings. That's why we're saying they are defective. They don't do enough. Just turn on the TV. They're everywhere . . . in your *Reader's Digest* or the *Parade* insert in your Sunday paper. In Europe, they cannot advertise, just as we don't allow the tobacco companies to advertise here in the U.S.A. Ask yourself, Why do we advertise these drugs?"

"Objection!" cried Billy Bravo, "Judge, this is not closing argument. That last comment was improper, and I'm asking the court to instruct the jury to disregard. This is not the right time to start deliberating or asking questions."

"Sustained," replied Dorfman and then turned to the jury. "Members of the jury, you haven't heard a single piece of evidence yet. It would be incorrect to start your deliberations now. Please disregard." Then Dorfman turned to Spearman. "Counsel, I remind you, this is opening argument."

"We believe, and the evidence will show," continued Spearman, "that had Dr. Haverti been better warned by the sales reps working for BostonMagnifica, if they had presented the warnings in a manner which would have brought home the message to the prescribing physician (in other words, get his attention), then Dr. Haverti could have better warned Tommy Ray about what side effects to watch for. Then, the moment Tommy Ray felt agitated, all he had to do was call his doctor and ask him to change his medication and try something else. That being said, you will hear deposition testimony from an ex-Zerevrea salesman that called on Dr. Haverti, a Mr. Aaron Tillman, and you will hear him talk about his lack of training and education in either emphasizing or reemphasizing warnings to doctors.

"You will also hear from Dr. Freemont. His professional life has been spent studying people that commit suicide and teaching how to prevent it. He's a psychiatrist, a clinical professor in Canada and a suicidologist who has studied the drug industry and has researched SSRIs. He is another expert in our case, and he will testify as to why the black box warnings on Zerevrea fall short of their mark.

"Also, please remember that we will be talking about serotonin, a chemical neurotransmitter in the brain. This substance takes messages from one cell to another. The evidence will show that this same substance, serotonin, has been linked to aggression, violence and suicide. Dr. Freemont will tell you that SSRIs are supposed to work on the serotonin system. By the way, serotonin is referred to as '5HT,' which is the way serotonin is written in scientific terms. With different receptors in the brain, serotonin works on this via different pathways. Now, why do we say reuptake inhibitors? Let's talk about that and what the evidence will show.

"This inhibitor mechanism, and the experts will explain it better, allows less serotonin to escape and keeps more of the serotonin in a little area of the brain called a 'synaptic cleft.' Scientists believe that an increase in serotonin translates into less depression. But we also know, and the companies know this, for it's common sense, that more serotonin would also mean, logically, more juice for purposes of aggression and even violent behaviors such as suicide or self-harm. So, the more serotonin one has or is carrying in the synaptic cleft, the more the likelihood for aggression and violent behaviors.

"Now, let me wrap up my opening by talking about Tommy Ray. Tommy Ray was a peaceful, loving, law-abiding, God-fearing man who adored his wife and children. He was a successful businessman, a dedicated attorney, war veteran, adjunct university professor, volunteer and a well-respected community leader and friend to many. Up until the day he died, he had never suffered from any illness or debilitating condition. Those who knew him will tell you that in his right mind, he would have never hurt a fly. *In his right mind.* The day Tommy Ray went on a killing rampage and then turned the gun on himself, he was not 'in his right mind.' Something made him snap. Something increased his aggressiveness and turned him violent. That something, the evidence will show, was Zerevrea, BostonMagnifica's so-called 'miracle drug.' And we know it was Zerevrea because he was not on any other medication. As a matter of fact, Tommy Ray rarely took medication—not even aspirin, much less illegal drugs. However, days before he pulled the trigger, his physician had prescribed him Zerevrea.

"When the coroner tested Tommy's spinal fluids, he found increased levels of 5HT acid. The evidence will show, and our experts will tell you, the presence of high levels of this acid translates into the presence of high levels of serotonin in the brain. Dr. Freemont will tell you that drugs such as Zerevrea increase the amount of serotonin. It is our contention that the high levels of 5HT acid found in Tommy Ray's spinal fluid prove he'd been on Zerevrea for at least two days prior to his death. And it was Zerevrea that triggered the violent episodes, including his suicide. The defense will try to say it must have been something else. But the coroner will tell you there were no other substances. There was no aspirin, codeine, nicotine, marijuana, cocaine . . . nothing. He lived a clean, healthy life. Tommy Ray loved life, his family, his many clients, his business associates and his community. Tommy Ray loved his country, but his country failed him. His government failed him, and the FDA failed him. BostonMagnifica failed him. So I beg you, ladies and gentlemen of the jury, I beg *you* not to fail him. Return a verdict for Tommy Ray. See that justice may be done in this case."

Riley Spearman gathered his notes from the podium in front of the jury box, walked back to counsel's table smugly and took his place. Spearman knew it was going to be hard for Billy to play "catch up." The plaintiffs always went first, and that meant dibs on making the first impression with the jury.

"YOU'RE UP, Mr. Bravo," Judge Dorfman said. "You've got forty-five minutes, but you don't necessarily have to use all of your time."

Billy stood up from counsel's table and looked at the jury. He focused on the foreman and on the Hispanic jurors. It was time to bring them back from the emotional to the rational. It was time to diffuse Spearman's inflammatory accusations. It was time to take the wind out of Spearman's sails, steal his thunder.

He pulled a bottle of pills from his pant's pocket. It was labeled "Fledkort," and he set it on top of the podium where all the jurors could see it. He then walked away from the podium, planted his feet firmly in front of the jury box and, without notes, started speaking softly, naturally. Pointing at the bottle on the podium he said, "This case deals with Zerevrea, a drug made by my client. And this gentleman right here," said Billy, pointing at Falcone, sitting at counsel's table next to Jensen's left, "is the proud CEO of BostonMagnifica Pharmaceuticals, Mr. Salvatore Falcone."

Dressed in a conservative, brown business suit, Falcone stood up, smiled and acknowledged the panel. He nodded his head and quickly took his seat.

Billy continued, "That pill bottle on the podium is another one of the many useful, safe drugs that my client makes. It is called Fledkort. The evidence will show that BostonMagnifica Pharmaceuticals makes drugs that save lives. Like many other of BostonMagnifica's helpful drugs, Fledkort is used to fight leukemia, a type of cancer that affects the blood.

"Believe it or not, my daughter takes this drug. She was diagnosed with leukemia several months ago. As we speak, she is up at MD Anderson Hospital in Houston taking her chemo in pill form, Fledkort. She survived her leukemia thanks to the good folks working at BostonMagnifica." Billy turned and looked at Falcone and nodded his head in gratitude. Falcone nodded back.

"And just like Fledkort, BostonMagnifica makes Zerevrea to help people like you and me and Alessandra, my daughter. Because of Fledkort, my daughter is now in remission and getting ready to come home."

"Objection," shouted Spearman, "Judge, this trial has nothing to do with Mr. Bravo's daughter. Who cares if she's got leukemia? This trial is about Tommy Ray, not the daughter of Billy Bravo."

"I don't hear an objection," interjected Billy in a very calm and soothing voice. His strategy apparently was working. He had stolen the spotlight from Spearman. Just minutes earlier, the trial had been about Tommy Ray, the suicide victim and Zerevrea, a dangerous drug. But now, Billy was turning things around by talking about Ale and the amazing breakthrough drugs his client was developing to help fight cancer.

"What's your objection?" asked Dorfman.

"Relevance," shot back Spearman.

"With all due respect," said Billy, politely, "this is opening argument, Your Honor. I should have a little leeway to show this good jury who my client is. Mr. Spearman has demonized my client during his opening argument, and I didn't object, although it was totally improper. I just want this good jury to know that BostonMagnifica makes very safe and effective medicines. That's what the evidence will show."

"Continue," said Dorfman, dismissing Spearman's objections with a hand gesture.

"The evidence will show that BostonMagnifica makes medications that help people, and in many instances, even save people's lives. The same cannot be said for Tommy Ray, who took the lives of two innocent bystanders in a senseless killing before taking his own."

"Judge," shouted Spearman, as he sprang from his chair, "I resent Mr. Bravo calling my client a killer. I would like the court's instruction to the jury to disregard that last comment by Mr. Bravo and for said comment to be stricken from the record."

"All I said was that Mr. Ray had taken the lives of two innocent bystanders," replied Billy. "I never called him a cold-blooded killer or a murderer, Your Honor. Mr. Spearman, himself, called his own client a cold-blooded assassin, Your Honor." *Touché.*

"Approach the bench!" Dorfman yelled, "the both of you."

"Yes, Judge," replied Billy, innocently.

"If you don't stop this nonsense," instructed the judge, addressing both attorneys, "right now, right this minute, I'm going to throw your asses in the slammer. We won't finish the case in a week, if the both of you keep objecting for no reason other than to annoy the hell out of each other and this court. The next frivolous objection or meritless interruption by either one of you will carry a five-hundred-dollar fine. You've been warned. Let's get on with the show."

Both Spearman and Hanslik returned to their tables while Billy took his place, again behind the podium directly in front of the jury box. Jensen had remained seated during the exchange at the bench. Falcone seemed to be enjoying the spectacle immensely.

"Now, let's switch gears," continued Billy, "and let's talk about what the plaintiffs need to prove. First, they need to prove to you, ladies and gentlemen, that Zerevrea is unreasonably dangerous. Judge Dorfman will later give you an instruction as to the legal definition of those two words 'unreasonably dangerous.' They also need to prove that Zerevrea is an unreasonably dangerous drug because it is defective in some way, shape or form. When we deal with drugs or a consumer product, we say the product is defective because of a problem in the way it was manufactured, designed or marketed. Thus, if there's a problem with the manufacture, design or marketing, then the product can be considered defective or unreasonably dangerous.

"In this case, the plaintiffs will try to say that the reason Zerevrea is unreasonably dangerous is because it was marketed for anxiety and depression without better, stronger, more specific warnings. They will try to argue that Zerevrea is defective because we failed to warn the public about other known dangers and that we failed, in spite of all the overpromotion, to better educate the treating doctors."

Billy paused, looked down and played with his wedding ring, making sure the jurors were still paying attention. He then looked up and reminded them, "Now, let's get real. This case isn't about Zerevrea or over- or under-promotion. This case is about how Tommy Ray's pressure-cooker life caused him to snap and commit these horrible crimes back on January 28, 2005. BostonMagnifica understands, as do I, that you may feel bad for the Ray family. Such feelings are natural. My own heart goes out to Mrs. Ray and her children. But as you will learn from Judge Dorfman and as the case moves along, your final decision, your verdict in this case, must be based on the science and the cold, hard evidence before you—not on sympathy or pity.

"So, let's look at what the evidence will show. Tommy Ray had a slight history of anxiety. Why do people get anxiety? Because of stressful events surrounding their everyday existence. Tommy Ray was a lawyer, and, as a lawyer myself, I know that there are clients to take care of, hearings to attend, trials to prepare for, phone calls to return, emails to reply to, depositions to take, mediations, arbitrations and so on. Plus, there are families to feed, bills to pay, and then, on top of that, all the boards and everything else Mr. Ray was involved with. Mr. Ray even taught college, for goodness sake.

"We believe the evidence will show that Tommy Ray failed to be totally honest with his treating physician, Dr. Haverti. We believe the evidence will show that he concealed the full extent of his anxiety and perhaps even his post-traumatic stress disorder. This is not unusual. Some patients think this would be considered a stigma, an embarrassment—especially for a man like Tommy Ray who was a pillar in this community. What would people think if they found out he had mental issues? Who would hire him? Would you go to such a lawyer?

"Now, taking two Zerevrea pills—if he took them at all—did not cause Mr. Ray to kill himself. That's going to be a highly contested issue in this trial. But we'll get into that later. Be advised that we are disputing that fact. So, there will be no evidence that anybody saw Mr. Ray take those two pills.

"The facts, the evidence, the science, and your common sense will lead you to that conclusion. Anxiety, unfortunately, if left unchecked, can also lead to suicide in some cases. Research suggests that most suicides occur when patients are undertreated or not treated at all. Zerevrea is an effective drug treatment. It reduces anxiety, depression and saves lives—not only the lives of the patients taking it, but also helps improve the quality of life of those who have to care for the patient, such as spouses, parents or children. BostonMagnifica is proud of Zerevrea's record in helping folks suffering from anxiety and those who are also affected by the illness.

"So, even though Tommy Ray reported to Dr. Haverti feeling 'slight anxiety' on two occasions, you will see that his military chart makes mention of severe anxiety, perhaps even post-traumatic stress disorder, going back as far as 1990. You will have those records in evidence, and you will be able to look at them. The doctors that made those entries when Tommy was being honorably discharged after serving his country have since died, so we don't have a deposition or a recorded statement obtained from those doctors to present to you. However, we do have the medical records. And you will be able to see for yourself and draw your own conclusions about Mr. Ray's anxiety, PTSD and its severity.

"This is very important, and this is key. As the evidence will show, had Mr. Ray been forthcoming with his doctor, then Dr. Haverti may have been in a different position to better monitor him or may have chosen to prescribe him a different medication or even prescribe Zerevrea at a lower dosage. So, that exchange, that level of communication between patient and doctor, never took place, but should have. And you will have to ask yourselves, 'Why didn't it happen?'.

"You will not see a long history of visiting doctors, psychiatrists, psychologists or licensed professional counselors. It's just not there. There are one or two visits to his doctor, his annual checkups and the military charts. That's it. We also do know through Father Piper Trabulsi, the priest at the church where Mr. and Mrs. Ray worshipped, that Sister Lourdes Marie, also doing double-duty as professional counselor, saw Tommy Ray on one occasion when something was troubling him. Unfortunately, Sister Lourdes Marie died, and her records were misplaced, so we don't know the full nature of their exchange during that period of time. We do know, and Mrs. Ray will tell you, that two or three nights before the episode, Mr. Ray had been unable to get a good night's sleep. He seemed preoccupied.

"You will learn that Mr. Ray was a proud man. We believe the evidence will show that he would not have wanted people to think he was suffering from mental ailments, whether it was anxiety, PTSD or anything else. He needed to be strong and in complete control of his life. His clients, his family and his business associates demanded it. As a result, he was not totally honest with his treating physician, and this had some bearing on him choosing to exit life. He simply did not give a complete history of his past episodes of anxiety to Dr. Haverti, and Dr. Haverti will tell you this would have made a difference in the prescribed course of treatment. Dr. Haverti didn't even know Tommy Ray had seen action in combat.

"You will also learn from Mrs. Ray that she knew very little about her husband's cases or clients. Mr. Ray was a very private person when it came to sharing or disclosing the family finances or the family business. True, it is difficult to know what goes on behind closed doors, but Mrs. Ray never knew if the appliance stores were making or losing money. Mr. Ray handled the family's finances, and if the businesses were in trouble, she would not have known it.

"Now, Mrs. Ray refuses to believe that something was troubling her husband. So, like us, like you, she's grasping for answers. So she chooses to file a lawsuit claiming Zerevrea made her husband commit this crime. In fact, the plaintiffs say only two Zerevrea pills did it—drove him over the edge. There's no question that Mr. Ray filled a prescription for Zerevrea and that low concentrations of serotonin's waste product were found in his blood. The question in this case is whether Mr. Ray's suicide was truly caused by Zerevrea, or something else.

"Mr. Ray's personal demons overcame him, whatever those were. Those demons, coupled with the increasing anxiety, the

PTSD, the science, the evidence and your common sense, will all play a role in your deliberations."

Billy Bravo then paused and got ready to make his final point. He looked at the foreman and the Hispanic jurors and, as he leaned into the jury box, he said, "One final note . . . at the end of the day, the evidence will show that there's a huge problem with the plaintiffs' case. You'll notice they did not address this issue in their opening argument. But, *I* will address it. Their case has more holes than a spaghetti strainer. They will not be able to show you one shred of evidence that Mr. Ray's tissue tested positive for Zerevrea. There's not going to be any evidence that Mr. Ray even had Zerevrea in his system. Sure, there was an increase in 5HT, but that can be caused by a number of things, as our experts will explain to you.

"At the end of the day, after all is said and done, if the plaintiffs allege that Zerevrea made Mr. Ray do something, should they not be prepared to show evidence that Tommy Ray actually had traces of the drug in his system the day he died? Without that, the plaintiff has no case. Common sense, my friends. Just common sense."

Spearman, who the entire time had been listening to Billy Bravo, finally lodged an objection. "Judge, my burden of proof is preponderance of the evidence, not beyond reasonable doubt! Counsel is mischaracterizing plaintiff's burden. All we have to prove is that it was more likely than not that Tommy Ray had the drug in his system. That's what the law requires."

"Overruled!" cried Dorfman, as he gave Spearman an icy stare. "Carry on, Mr. Bravo."

"Thank you, judge. So, when all is said and done, we are going to ask you to render a verdict for BostonMagnifica. Ask yourselves this question: How can you say a certain drug made you do something if you don't even have proof that the drug was ever in your system?

"Finally, I want to address one last issue in my opening argument. A few years ago, more particularly, all through the eighties and nineties, when large corporations got hauled into court— especially to courtrooms all across South Texas—the thinking was that jurors in the Rio Grande Valley could not be fair. The thinking was that jurors in South Texas were not educated, easy to manipulate and easy to convince to award large sums of money. *Que éramos unos tontos*; a bunch of dummies. They referred to us as 'jurors running amok.' Folks complained that the plaintiffs' lawyers went to great lengths to find ways to file their lawsuits in courtrooms all along the Texas-Mexico border, even here in Laredo, where Hispanic juries could be had. *Porque éramos fáciles de convencer* . . . because we were gullible and easy to convince.

"Hell! South Texas was even called a 'judicial hellhole,' and corporate defendants hated it. Even my client, BostonMagnifica, was concerned about the kind of jury it was going to face down here in Laredo, truly worried. And I said, 'NO. I'm not worried. I know my people. *Mi gente.* And we're going to try this case, and we're going to let them decide, and we're going to trust they do the right thing. We're not going to run away because of the things that have been said. I know that a South Texas jury is going to do the fair thing. If Zerevrea is a good drug, then we don't have anything to worry about. No one will be able to change that fact. If the evidence shows that Zerevrea helps people and doesn't trigger suicide, then it won't matter how the plaintiffs try to spin their case. The truth is the truth. The facts are the facts. Hispanics, Whites, Blacks, whatever, I don't care. A South Texas jury will always do the right thing, the correct thing, the 'just and fair thing.' I even told my client that a South Texas jury will give us our day in court and that it would be a good day. Now, I know that all of you will listen carefully to all of the evidence presented in this courtroom this week. And I know that you will use your common sense. That's all we're asking. Let us silence the critics and show them what a South Texas jury can do. *Gracias.*"

CHAPTER 42

"**T**HE PLAINTIFFS CALL Dr. Paxton Freemont to the stand," announced Spearman. Doctor Freemont got up from his place behind counsel's table and walked to the witness stand. He was quickly sworn in. He was a distinguished-looking gentleman in his sixties with white hair and impeccable style. It was obvious his dark blue suit had been tailor-made, maybe even hand-stitched.

"Your Honor," interrupted Billy before Mr. Spearman carried on, "I'd like the record to reflect our running objection based on the grounds raised in our previously filed Daubert motion. We know the court ruled already; however, we'd still like to preserve BostonMagnifica's right to examine Dr. Freemont on the issue of scientific reliability raised in that motion, when our time comes to ask questions. I don't want to interrupt Mr. Spearman's direct examination by having to take the witness on *voir dire*."

What this meant was that—even though Judge Dorfman had ruled against BostonMagnifica's Daubert challenge and had found a hint of evidence that Zerevrea may have caused the suicide—BM still felt there was no cold, hard scientific evidence linking Mr. Ray's suicide to Zerevrea. And despite having been dealt that setback, BM wanted to preserve its right to go over those issues with Freemont, again, in open court, if need be.

"It will so be noted," huffed Dorfman. "Carry on, Mr. Spearman. You may proceed."

"Would you please introduce yourself to the ladies and gentlemen of the jury?" asked Spearman.

"My name is Paxton Freemont."

"What kind of doctor are you, sir?" followed Spearman.

"I am a medical doctor. My specialty is psychiatry, and I have a PhD in neuropharmacology."

"Where were you born and raised?"

"I was born in Paris but grew up in Canada. I studied in Montreal and did my research at Harvard here in the United States."

"What came first, your medical degree or your doctorate?"

"I was first a medical doctor, then I got my PhD."

"Did you pursue a residency in psychiatry?"

"Yes."

"Do you do research or focus on any one particular area?"

"Yes, my research has focused on serotonin, the reuptake mechanism and the way SSRI drugs work in the brain."

"Can you tell us how serotonin works in our brains?"

"Serotonin is one of many neurotransmitters in our brains. There may be hundreds of these, but this one we discovered first, when LSD was first introduced. LSD acts on serotonin. In the seventies in particular, people were conducting studies on mood. They wanted to see if drugs could act on this brain system to treat nervous disorders."

"What's the difference between neurotransmitters and receptors? Or are they the same?" asked Spearman.

"No, a transmitter is one thing, the receptor is another. Think of serotonin as a key and the receptors as a row of locks on other nerve cells. Serotonin can fit into a number of different locks, but not all of them. That's the simple version."

"Has any of your research on the serotonin system ever been funded by BostonMagnifica Pharmaceuticals?"

"No, none by BM, but I've done this kind of research for Eli Lilly and others in the early eighties."

"So, you were an employee of Eli Lilly?"

"Not exactly. I worked in a psychiatric unit, and we gave a pool of depressed patients an early SSRI being developed by Eli Lilly. We were doing some testing. Then came Prozac."

"Anything else? Other studies?"

"Yes, in the mid-nineties, I was in charge of testing Prozac in individuals exhibiting obsessive-compulsive behaviors. Then we compared Prozac and Paxil."

"Were the studies completed?

"Yes."

"Was the data from these studies made public?"

"No . . . all the trials were sealed and confidential, and they have never been published."

"Dr. Freemont, how long have you been writing and speaking about the dangers of SSRI-induced suicide or violence?"

"Started around 1997."

"Why are they called 'SSRIs'? Who coined the term, do you know?"

"Objection . . . no foundation," cried Billy, "and calls for speculation."

"I'll rephrase, Judge," answered Spearman.

"Rephrase," replied Dorfman.

"Do you know the people in the marketing department that invented the term SSRI?"

"Yes."

"Did you know them at the time when these events took place—the same time when the name was created?"

"Sure. I knew them then, and I know them now. They're my friends and my colleagues."

"And these folks in marketing, were they the source of the information regarding the term SSRI?"

"Yes," answered Dr. Freemont as he turned and looked at the jury for the first time.

"Okay, then. Tell us, why 'SSRI'?"

"The folks that created drugs after Prozac were already miles behind. Prozac had cornered the market. And, the folks making Paxil needed a catchy phrase. They were trying to find a marketing angle to help push sales. Some genius decided that Paxil should be a more selective reuptake inhibitor than Prozac—kind of saying that it worked better. In the end, it backfired; all the other drug companies also claimed that their drugs were selective serotonin reuptake inhibitors, too. Then, we came to find out that

Paxil and others were really not more selective, in that it not only affected serotonin, but also affected other brain systems, like the noradrenergic system, the whole thing ended up being pretty dumb."

"Would you say that's part of the problem with these drugs?"

"Objection!" shouted Billy, "Counsel is leading the witness."

"Sustained," ruled Judge Dorfman.

"Are these drugs safe?" rephrased Spearman.

"Objection! Improper and no foundation," interjected Billy.

"Sustained," Dorfman said.

"Withdraw the question. Let me ask it this way . . . " said Spearman. "In your practice, Dr. Freemont, do you prescribe SSRIs?"

"Yes. I think SSRIs can be very helpful in *some* individuals. Certainly, I use them on my patients. I regularly prescribe Zoloft and Celexa, but other SSRIs can have negative interactions with other drugs. I've stayed away from Paxil because some European countries have raised concerns about patients becoming dependent on it."

"Okay," said Spearman, "we're almost done, Dr. Freemont. Have you written articles about the link between suicide and SSRIs?"

"Yes. Over fifty peer-reviewed articles."

"Have you ever conducted research involving SSRIs and folks that were not depressed?"

"Yes."

"What happened, can you tell us?"

"I recall a study with twenty subjects. Three became suicidal, all women."

"Really?" followed Spearman as he turned to look at the jury. "Doctor, were these results published?"

"Yes, they were."

"Let me switch gears here, Dr. Freemont," indicated Spearman, "I want to cover your expert opinion regarding general causation, okay? In your expert opinion, Dr. Freemont, do SSRIs cause some patients—not all—to become homicidal or suicidal?"

"Objection!" shouted Billy, trying to distract the jurors. "Improper question."

"Overruled," replied Dorfman.

"Yes, they do, Mr. Spearman."

"What about Zerevrea? Can it also push some patients to kill or commit suicide?"

"Same objection!" cried Billy.

"Overruled," said Dorfman.

"As with all SSRIs, Zerevrea could drive folks to kill, become violent and even take their own lives. As these drugs continue to be tested on different subject pools, with different pathologies, we're now beginning to see high numbers of adverse events in folks also suffering from PTSD"

"From everything you've seen about this case—all the documents, the trials, the research, including the black box warnings and packaging regarding Zerevrea—do you, Dr. Freemont, believe in your professional expert opinion that BostonMagnifica has properly educated the treating physicians with respect to patients suffering from anxiety or some probable form of PTSD?"

"No."

"Do you believe in your professional expert opinion that BostonMagnifica has properly warned the medical profession or others regarding the risk of homicide and suicide, considering their overpromotion of Zerevrea?"

"No," said Freemont, again looking over at the jurors. "When you consider the black box warnings, again, those warnings refer to suicide happening to people who are depressed. There are no warnings for those also suffering from anxiety, or maybe even PTSD. Not everyone who takes these drugs is suffering from depression, Mr. Spearman. We've heard of doctors prescribing these drugs even to people suffering from migraine headaches."

"Finally," sighed Spearman, "with respect to specific causation, in your professional opinion, did Zerevrea cause Tommy Ray to shoot Samuel Guerra, Sr., Melissa Andarza and then turn the gun on himself?"

Billy jumped to his feet, "Excuse me, Your Honor. I'd like the record to reflect that Mr. Spearman has 'opened the door' regarding the events and circumstances surrounding the demise of Melissa Andarza and Samuel Guerra."

"It will so be noted," answered Dorfman.

Spearman continued, "You were saying, Doctor?"

"In my professional, expert opinion, yes, Zerevrea made Tommy Ray do it."

"Are you sure?"

"Yes. I am 100 percent sure . . . absolutely positive."

"One final note, Dr. Freemont," said Spearman. "In your expert opinion and to a reasonable degree of scientific certainty, is there a clear dose-response link between Zerevrea and suicidality?"

"Yes."

"Pass the witness," announced Spearman.

"Let's take a twenty-minute break," countered Judge Dorfman and then addressed the jurors. "Please be back at eleven-thirty."

DR. FREEMONT was already sitting in the witness chair by the time the twelve jury members returned to the courtroom and took their respective places in the box.

"Please continue," said Dorfman, looking over at Billy.

"Thank you, Your Honor," said Billy with a short nod of the head. "Dr. Freemont, I remind you, you are still under oath."

"Yes," said Freemont, clearing his throat.

"May I approach the witness?" asked Billy.

"You may," answered Dorfman.

"Dr. Freemont," continued Billy, I'm handing you a notebook with studies that either you have reviewed or you, yourself, have conducted. Please take a look at them."

Freemont took the binder from Billy and flipped through it. "Yes, I've seen these documents before, sure."

"In 1993, you wrote an article entitled 'Prozac and Suicidality.' It's marked as Exhibit 255. Is that correct?"

"Yes, I wrote that article."

"Now, in that report, you discussed the findings of other researchers in connection with SSRIs, correct?"

"Yes."

"Those researchers were Bromely and McClure, correct?"

"Yes."

"Your mentors, correct?"

"Yes."

"Now, in your 1993 report, you mention that Bromely and McClure had scrutinized the Eli Lilly database for evidence of increased suicide in subjects using Prozac, but they found no such evidence, right?"

"Correct," said Dr. Freemont as he loosened his tie.

"And in that same report, you believed their statements to be true, correct?"

"Correct, I had no reason to doubt their findings."

"Dr. Freemont, you said in that same paper, and I quote, 'reactions to Prozac are rare and if blown out of proportion, this may lead to more suicides by virtue of patients staying away from the necessary treatment.' Did you say that, Doctor?"

"Yes, I did say that," Freemont confessed.

All eyes were on Freemont as the jury was now watching the expert start perspiring.

"And," Billy continued, "did you say, 'since such reactions are rare, the risk compared to the cost dictates that patients continue treatment, particularly since 99.9 percent of suicides are triggered by depression when compared to perhaps only a .0001 percent caused by SSRIs'?"

"Yes, I said that."

"Finally, in your report you said that 'this slight concern wouldn't be a problem if a warning was communicated to the patient,' correct?"

"Agreed," conceded Freemont.

"All right. Then could you please turn to page ten of Exhibit 255, bottom left-hand column, next to the last paragraph. It says, 'all available post-treatment studies have not conclusively established that SSRIs are prone to cause suicidal acts.' Did you write that?"

"Yes, but look at the context upon which it was made," explained Freemont. "We were talking about post-market surveillance studies, and those have never been effective in picking up adverse events."

"Were those not your words then, Doctor? Words from your 1993 article published in a peer-reviewed journal?"

"Yes, they were."

Billy looked over at Spearman, then over to the jurors. He was enjoying himself too much. It was payback time. "Thank you. Now, when you prepared that report, Dr. Freemont, and I'm talking about the 1993 report, who sponsored that study?"

"You mean, who paid me?"

"Yes."

"Eli Lilly."

"How much?" asked Billy.

"I don't recall. It's been too long, almost thirteen years."

"Would you like me to show you the 1099s that you received from Eli Lilly that year?" asked Billy as he waved some papers in his hand.

"No, uhm . . . " stuttered Freemont, "that won't be necessary. I remember now. It was a hundred twenty-five thousand dollars for the six-month study."

"Now, how much are you charging Mr. Spearman for your testimony here today?" asked Billy as he pointed a finger to Spearman.

"Objection!" cried Spearman. "I resent Mr. Bravo's comment. He's suggesting we're buying our expert's testimony, Judge. That's just wrong."

"Sustained," said Dorfman.

"So, how much are you charging, then?" Billy asked again.

"It's eight hundred an hour for courtroom testimony and depositions and six hundred an hour to review documents."

"Did you charge a retainer just to get involved with the case?"

"Yes, but only a five-thousand-dollar fully refundable retainer," answered the doctor reluctantly.

Billy turned and looked at the jury, trying to gauge their reaction. The college students were already shaking their heads. Freemont was nothing more than an expensive gunslinger.

"So, how much have you billed Mr. Spearman so far?"

"Well, give or take, I'd say thirty-five thousand dollars."

"Now, Doctor, I want to show you Joint-Exhibit Number 265, the affidavit you prepared in connection with the Lancaster matter."

"Ah, yes," said Dr. Freemont, relieved that they were no longer discussing how much he was costing Spearman.

"Was that a civil or criminal matter?"

"Criminal."

"You prepared the affidavit offering your view as to whether or not an SSRI may have been involved in triggering the crime, correct?" asked Billy.

"Yes. The defendant had been accused of murdering his spouse. That's correct."

"But you said, and I quote, 'It's possible that at least one SSRI may be associated with higher rates of suicide in certain individuals, but there's never been a link between SSRIs and a patient wanting to hurt others.' Do you remember writing that?"

"Yes, I remember that case. The whole thing was tragic, very tragic."

"Now," Billy continued, "have you done any testing specifically on Zerevrea, and can you tell us if Zerevrea affects some people one way and others another way?"

"No, I have not."

"You can't tell us either way, can you?"

Spearman shot up from his chair. "Objection! Counsel is badgering the witness, Your Honor."

"Overruled," said Dorfman, rolling his eyes.

"What I can tell you," replied Freemont, ready to pounce on Billy's open-ended question, "is that the limited data available on Zerevrea seems to suggest that there's also a link between its use and suicide. And, knowing what we know of SSRIs, common sense would dictate that Zerevrea is no different."

Billy fired back. "Then, common sense would dictate that your testimony is for sale to the highest bidder, too, Dr. Freemont."

"Objection!" screamed Spearman. "Sidebar, Your Honor."

"Approach the bench, Mr. Bravo," called the judge. "Now!"

Both Spearman and Billy met Dorfman at the bench. "Mr. Bravo," whispered the judge, "I don't know where in the hell Mr.

Spearman found this expert, and frankly, I don't care. But I will not allow you to trade punches with him like that. It's inappropriate and unnecessary. Please refrain."

"Yes, Your Honor," said Billy.

"Your Honor," called out Spearman as he walked back to his seat, "can you instruct the jury to disregard Mr. Bravo's comment and also strike it from the record?"

"It will be so noted," replied Dorfman, gesturing the pair to take their seats. "Continue, Mr. Bravo."

"Thank you, Your Honor. Now, Dr. Freemont," Billy added, "let's keep talking about common sense, okay?"

"Okay."

"Have you seen any documentation—anything that you've reviewed in order to prepare for this trial here today—that establishes that Tommy Ray indeed had Zerevrea in his system?"

"Well, I've reviewed about one hundred boxes of documents, but all I've seen are the lab results that would show increased levels of toxicity."

"So your answer is 'no,' then? Very well," Billy countered, and before Dr. Freemont could answer, "We pass the witness, nothing further."

"Mr. Spearman," called out Judge Dorfman, "redirect?"

"No, Your Honor. The witness may be excused."

"Very well. Let's go to lunch and be ready with your next witness after lunch. We'll be in recess," declared the judge.

GINA RAY was the next witness after the lunch break. She was administered the oath by Judge Dorfman and quickly sat down in the witness chair. She sported black pants with a beige blouse and very little makeup. Her hair was up in a bun. Her attorney, Spearman, addressed her from counsel's table.

"Please introduce yourself to the ladies and gentlemen of the jury," instructed Spearman.

"Georgina Ray," she replied, looking at the jurors.

"Do you go by any other names?"

"Everybody knows me by 'Gina.' My friends and family all call me Gina."

"Where were you born?"

"Here in Laredo, Texas."

"Where did you grow up?"

"In Nuevo Laredo, on the Mexican side of the border. I attended elementary school in Nuevo Laredo, then high school on the U.S. side and had two years at Laredo Junior College."

"How old are you?"

"Forty."

"Who was your husband?"

"Tomas Ray, but everyone knew him as 'Tommy.' Tommy Ray."

"How long were you married to Tommy?"

"Fifteen years."

"How long had you known him before he died?"

"All my life. We practically grew up together. He was my best friend, my confidant, my partner. I knew him from the time he'd go visit his *tías* in Nuevo Laredo. His aunts were our neighbors when we lived in Mexico."

"Any children?"

"Four, three girls and a boy. The oldest is eleven, and the youngest is six."

"Take us back to the morning of January 28, 2005. Do you recall that day? What happened?"

"I recall waking up alone in bed that Saturday morning and wondering where Tommy was. On Saturdays we would traditionally lounge in bed until nine or ten. That is, when Tommy was in town and not away trying cases. Most of the time, our little ones would come and get in bed with us and we would all sleep for a couple more hours . . . but not that Saturday."

"Do you remember what time it was when you first noticed Tommy missing from bed?"

"Yes. I'll never forget. The clock on our nightstand said seven-fifteen AM."

"How would you describe your marriage to Mr. Ray?" Spearman asked.

"Beautiful. Solid. We were high school sweethearts. When Tommy returned from the Gulf War in 1990, we got married the next year. We loved each other very much . . . if that's what you mean."

"So he was a war veteran?" Spearman asked and turned to look at Billy. It was going to be a fight to the death. He would evoke every last bit of sympathy for his client, every last drop.

"Oh, yes. He was awarded the Medal of Valor for saving the lives of his men during an enemy ambush. He was his platoon's commander."

The jurors' eyes were glued to Gina Ray. The foreman, however, would occasionally turn to look at Billy and Falcone as the witness delivered her answers, to see Falcone's body language and whether or not Gina's answers were inflicting damage on him.

"He was also an attorney, correct?" asked Spearman.

"Yes. His clients loved him. He had an extremely successful criminal defense and personal injury practice. He was the go-to attorney if you needed representation in federal court, whether it was a white-collar crime or anything else."

"Was he involved in the community?"

"Very much so. And he was a firm believer in giving back. His law firm sponsored several 'Little Ms. Kickball' teams, he was on the board at the Boys and Girls Club, and he served on various other boards. When the local high school students needed money for trips, they always came knocking on Tommy's door. Of course, he also served on the board of Ray's Appliance Stores."

"Tell us a bit about that."

"Tommy's family comes from old Spanish settlers that first came to the area because of Spanish land grants. His grandpa, Don Victoriano Reyes, opened the first appliance store in the thirties, sometime after the Great Depression. Eventually, the name got shortened to 'Ray's.' Sixty years later, there are over one hundred stores all along the Texas-Mexico border from Brownsville to El Paso."

"I understand the stores do very well, is that correct?" asked Spearman.

"They used to," answered Gina.

The answer surprised the jury, even Spearman. The lawyer had never bothered to ask her about that nor had he considered the possibility. He simply had assumed, like everyone else in South Texas, that the store chain was a cash cow.

Gina continued with her testimony, "But now, the competition is brutal. I mean, there are Sam's, Sears, Home Depot, Lowe's, Conn's and others . . . even K-Mart sells some appliances. In recent years, it has been getting tougher and tougher to keep the profit margins up."

"I see," Spearman said.

"Tommy was on the board at Ray's Appliance Stores, but he made his money from his law practice. He earned every penny."

"What do you mean?"

"He worked all the time. He had cases in federal courts all across the country. I'd say he was gone three weeks out of the month."

"Was he a good husband?"

"Yes, absolutely. When he was home, he was a devoted father and husband. He loved his children, and his children loved him."

"Going back to that Saturday morning . . . after you noticed he was out of bed, did you do anything?"

"I got out of bed and reached for my robe. At first, I thought Tommy must be down in the kitchen making breakfast for the kids. I mean, the whole house smelled of *chorizo* and biscuits. As I was putting my robe on, I looked out my bedroom window . . . and was blown away by what I saw. Out on the driveway, I saw Tommy's lifeless body next to a pool of blood . . . holding something in his hand," she said, sobbing.

"I'm sorry," Spearman said, "are you okay?"

"Yes," she said, wiping her tears.

"Are you telling the ladies and gentlemen of the jury that you did not hear the gunshots?"

"That's correct."

"Do you know why?"

"Later on, I came to find out that the 357 Magnum was silencer-ready," she explained.

"Did you see your children that morning?"

"Yes. They heard my screams and ran into our bedroom. They were horrified. They had no clue. I dialed 911 at first because I thought somebody had driven by and murdered my husband. I thought that's what had happened."

"Did he have enemies to your knowledge?"

"I don't think so, no. Not to my knowledge."

"Disgruntled clients?" followed Spearman.

"No."

"Have you heard the 911 tapes?"

"No."

"Your Honor," said Spearman, addressing Judge Dorfman, "at this time, we would like to play the 911 recordings from the morning of Saturday, January 28, 2005."

"Objection," declared Billy. "I don't see the relevance, Your Honor. Plaintiffs' counsel is trying to inflame the jury. It has already been established that Tommy Ray died of a gunshot blast. What can the tape recordings possibly add?"

"I'll allow it, Mr. Bravo," ruled Judge Dorfman. Spearman plopped the tape into a tape recorder and hit the Play button.

"911 operator, state your emergency."

"Please! Please, I beg you! Somebody shot my husband," cried Gina in hysterics.

"Can you see your husband? Is he breathing?"

"I'm inside the house! He's out in the driveway in a pool of blood! Please send somebody!"

"Can you see the shooter? Are you safe inside?"

"No! No! Maybe, I mean . . . I don't know. Please, hurry! Please, send somebody."

"What's your address?"

"543 Jacaranda, Río Viejo Estates. Please, hurry! I beg you!"

"All right, ma'am. Stay on the phone. The police are on their way."

Spearman hit the Stop button. "Is that what happened?"

The jury was riveted to the testimony, every single one of them looking intently at the witness. Gina Ray was sobbing uncontrollably. Replaying the 911 tape had brought about a torrent of emotions. She dried her tears with tissue the court reporter sitting next to the witness chair provided, and after regaining her composure, she answered, "Yes . . . that's what happened, pretty much."

"Let me switch gears, Mrs. Ray," followed Spearman. "Was Tommy also an adjunct professor at Texas A&M, Laredo Campus?"

"Yes."

"What did he teach?"

"He taught Introduction to Criminal Law and Procedure as part of the curriculum for the Criminal Justice Program."

"So, he was very involved, even in academics? Is that a fair statement?"

"Yes."

"Is it true that one of Tommy's greatest accomplishments was being awarded a Fulbright Scholarship to live and teach Comparative Law at the Universidad Autónoma de Nuevo León in Monterrey?"

"Yes," said Gina, "he did that for a year and enjoyed the experience immensely."

"Did he also start an exchange program between A&M Laredo and the Universidad Autónoma de Nuevo León?"

"Yes. He always had an interest in international and cross-border issues. But, most importantly, he was a staunch supporter of equal rights and equal protection under the law."

"It sounds to me like your husband Tommy Ray was a great humanitarian. Do you know if he had 'groupie clients'—ones that might have wanted him all to themselves?"

"Of course not! His clients loved him . . . everybody loved Tommy."

"A scorned lover?" asked Spearman.

"No, he was loyal to his wife and family. We rarely had any disagreements, if ever."

"Financial troubles?"

"Not at all. Now, I did not handle the home's finances, but I'm sure I would have known if something was going on. No, I don't think so."

"Did he suffer from depression?"

"No."

"Any other medical ailments?"

"No."

"What medications was he taking prior to pulling the trigger?"

"He'd been on Zerevrea for two days. I later found out that his doctor had prescribed it on a Monday, but he didn't pick up the prescription until Thursday. That's when he started taking it. He'd been on it a couple of days."

"Are you sure?"

"Positive."

"Why had he started taking it, if you know?"

"He'd gone to see his doctor, and from what I understand from something Dr. Haverti said to me after the funeral, Tommy had told the doctor he was feeling a little anxious, nervous. So he was prescribed Zerevrea."

"Why was he feeling outwardly nervous? Do you know?"

"No."

"Did he ever say?"

"No."

"Did you notice him to appear extremely worried, preoccupied or anxious?"

"No. My husband was not one to wear his emotions on his sleeve, you know?" she elaborated while looking at the jury. "He was tough. He had to be. He sometimes had to defend the indefensible."

"Was he on any other medication at the time he was taking Zerevrea?"

"No."

"May I approach the witness?" asked Spearman.

"You may," said Dorfman.

"Before I forget, Mrs. Ray," said Spearman as he handed an orange prescription bottle containing small tablets to his witness, "is this the bottle of pills that Tommy was prescribed? Do you know?"

"Yes, that's the one. It has my husband's name here, and this is the doctor that prescribed Zerevrea."

"Move to admit," Spearman requested.

"No objection," answered Billy from counsel's table.

"It'll be admitted," said Dorfman.

"Thank you, Mrs. Ray. That's all I have. Pass the witness."

"Mr. Bravo," said Judge Dorfman, "your witness."

"Yes," said Billy, clearing his throat. He fixed his reading glasses and looked down at his notes. "Mrs. Ray, did you actually *see* Mr. Ray taking the Zerevrea pills?"

"Uh," she started, "well . . . weeks later, after the dust settled, I noticed that the prescription box said it was a thirty-count bottle, and two were missing."

"Oh," said Billy, "you counted them?"

"Yes, sir. Two were missing."

"Very well," replied Billy, "but going back to my question, did you *see* your husband, Mr. Ray, actually take the pills . . . one on one day and the other on the other day?"

"Actually, no, sir. I did not."

"No further questions, Your Honor," said Billy Bravo. "She may be excused."

"Mrs. Ray, you're excused. You may step down," instructed Judge Dorfman. "Mr. Spearman, call your next witness."

"We call Laredo Police Officer Daniel Marks, Your Honor," indicated Spearman.

SGT. DETECTIVE Daniel Marks took his place on the witness stand. He was in his late forties, chubby and sported a thick, bushy moustache. He was wearing an old and faded navy-blue blazer with gray polyester slacks. His law enforcement badge was clipped to his belt but was barely visible under his bulging belly.

"Sgt. Marks, what's your rank within the department?"

"I just got promoted to Sgt. Detective."

"Congratulations. How long have you had this promotion?"

"Two months."

"How long have you been a detective?"

"Ten years. I did two years with the sex crimes unit, three years with narcotics investigations and the last five years in homicide."

"Did you process the scene in connection with the suicide of my client's husband, Tommy Ray?"

"Yes."

"And when you responded to the call that Saturday morning, what did you encounter? Please, tell the ladies and gentlemen of the jury."

"I saw the body of a young female lying in the middle of the street."

"Your Honor," interrupted Billy, "may we approach the bench?"

Dorfman rolled his eyes, "What now?"

Spearman and Billy, along with Hanslik and Jensen, met at the bench. Billy whispered, "Your Honor, I don't know where Mr. Spearman is going with this line of questioning, but he's opened 'the door'. I don't want to be accused later of violating any motion in limine should I decide to ask a question about the murders . . ."

"Mr. Spearman," whispered Dorfman, "counsel's right. Where are you going with this? This is not buying your client any sympathy from the jury, what are you doing?"

"I disagree, Your Honor," said Spearman in a hushed tone, "the jury needs to see the horror and the mayhem these drugs cause . . ."

Dorfman shrugged his shoulders while looking at Billy, "Okay, then Mr. Spearman . . . suit yourself . . . go ahead and continue with your examination."

Except for Spearman who remained standing, Billy and the others took their places back at counsel's table.

"Was she alive?" continued Spearman.

"No, sir."

"Did you ever come to find out the name of the young lady that died that morning?"

"Yes."

"And what was her name? Can you tell the ladies and gentlemen of the jury?"

"Melissa Andarza," answered the Sgt. Detective.

"And what else did you see?"

"The postal worker making the rounds that morning was slumped over the steering wheel of his delivery truck with the engine still running."

"Was he alive?"

"No. He was also dead."

"Did you later come to find out the name of the postal worker?" asked Spearman.

"Yes. The postal worker was Samuel Guerra, Sr."

"How did they die?"

"Gunshot wounds. The young female was shot in the back, and the mailman was shot in the face."

"Did you come upon a third individual that morning?"

"Yes."

"Who?"

"The individual's name turned out to be Tommy Ray."

"And how did Mr. Ray die, if you know?"

"Self-inflicted gunshot wound," said Sgt. Detective Marks, "to the back of his mouth."

"What else did your investigation reveal?"

"Our investigation revealed that Mr. Ray exited his garage carrying his silencer-ready .357 Magnum that morning. We think he shot the postal worker first. We speculate that Ms. Andarza, the jogger, did not hear the shots because she was wearing headphones. There was nothing to indicate she struggled to get away or that there was a physical encounter with her attacker."

Judge Dorfman was shaking his head as he listened to the exchange between the plaintiff's lawyer and the witness. There was no way that the detective's testimony was helping Gina Ray's cause.

"What else?" asked Spearman.

"A neighbor thought she heard something—a scream, maybe. She couldn't tell, really. When she went to check and looked outside from her second-story bedroom window, she saw Tommy Ray turning the gun on himself."

"Was Mr. Ray on his driveway?" Spearman asked, pointing to a blowup exhibit depicting the wealthy neighborhood and the Rays' home.

"Yes. Tommy Ray died on his circular driveway," replied Marks, as he pointed to the exact location on the exhibit.

"Were you the first one to arrive at the scene that morning?"

"No. By the time I arrived, two other units had responded and had secured the scene."

"Did your investigation reveal any motive as to why Mr. Ray may have killed the others and then turned the gun on himself?"

"That's one of life's greatest mysteries," said the detective as he looked over at the jury. "There was no rhyme or reason to the killings or the suicide."

"Had Mr. Ray ever had any dealings with Ms. Andarza? Did he know her?"

"Other than the fact that she jogged in the same neighborhood, there was no meaningful connection to speak of . . . no link, really."

"What about Mr. Guerra, the postal worker? Did Mr. Ray have an axe to grind with him?"

"No. No one reported anything unusual. Apparently, Mr. Guerra was well-liked in the neighborhood . . . almost a permanent fixture. The only connection I was able to come to was that Mr. Guerra's son was engaged to be married to Melissa Andarza, the jogger that also lost her life that morning."

"So," started Spearman, "what do you think made Tommy Ray turn the gun on himself?"

"Objection!" called out Billy from counsel's table. "Calls for pure speculation, Your Honor."

"I'll rephrase, Your Honor," answered Spearman. "As a detective who's been involved in hundreds of murder investigations, do you have an opinion as to why Tommy Ray killed two victims, seemingly at random, and then turned the gun on himself?"

"Other than maybe he snapped, no I don't."

"What do you mean 'snapped'?" asked Spearman.

"I mean nothing made sense. He had no enemies, he did not know, to speak of, Ms. Andarza or Mr. Guerra. Grant you, both of the victims were federal employees, but we felt that was just a coincidence. He had no financial troubles. There were no motives. He appeared to have a great loving relationship with his wife and children. No scorned lovers, no blackmailers. Nothing . . . zero to go on. To this day, we're still scratching our heads, if you really want to know the truth. Maybe a medical condition, maybe the drug he was taking, I really don't know."

"You mean depression?"

"We looked into that, but there was no history of depression or mental illness."

"But wasn't he a war veteran?" asked Spearman.

"Yes, but even after fighting in the Gulf War back in 1990, no one ever reported anything unusual. Not his wife, and not his friends or family. He appeared normal."

"So, then you think he 'snapped'?"

"Something had to make him snap, at least that's what I believe," said Marks as he turned to the jurors. "Ask yourself, why would somebody with a perfect life want to screw it up like that? It doesn't make sense."

"Thank you, Sgt. Detective Marks. Pass the witness," said Spearman.

Without wasting a single second, Billy Bravo jumped into the cross-examination. "Detective, did you go to medical school?"

"Excuse me?" asked Marks, as he played with his moustache, eyes wide open.

"Did you go to medical school?" repeated Billy.

"No, sir, I didn't."

"Did you study psychology?"

"No, I did not."

"Did you study counseling?"

"No, I did not."

"Have you worked in a mental institution?"

"No, I have not."

"Are you a psychiatrist?"

"No, sir."

The jurors were turning their heads back and forth like an oscillating fan set on high speed.

"Are you a licensed professional counselor?"

"No, sir, I'm not."

"Have you read Freud?"

"Objection!" cried Spearman, "Relevance?"

"I'll allow it," barked Judge Dorfman even before Billy Bravo had a chance to reply to Spearman's objection.

"No, sir, I have not," answered Marks meekly.

"Have you read Jung?"

"No."

"Have you ever performed an autopsy?"

"No."

"Have you ever seen the brain of a person who has, as you put it, 'snapped'?"

"No, sir, I have not."

"The truth is," Billy Bravo said, "you really don't know why Tommy Ray did the things he did that morning, isn't that correct?"

"Well . . . yes, I suppose. That is what I said already."

"No one knows, isn't that correct?"

"Correct."

"This thing about snapping, as you put it, is pure speculation because you really don't know. Is that a fair statement?"

"Right."

"I mean," continued Billy, "Tommy Ray could have had a mental defect, right?"

"It's possible."

"Maybe he was suffering an anxiety attack?"

"Maybe . . . "

"Or had a chemical imbalance, right? You've heard of chemical imbalances, haven't you?"

"Sure."

"Were you in Tommy Ray's home when he allegedly took his two Zerevrea pills?"

"No, of course not," replied the officer.

"So, you don't even know if he was on Zerevrea when he committed those unspeakable acts against the innocent bystanders, do you?"

"That's correct. I would have no knowledge of that."

"Maybe . . . you'd like . . . "

"Mr. Bravo," interrupted Judge Dorfman and looked over to the jury, "I believe you've made your point. Move on."

"That's all I have, Your Honor," said Billy, reading between the lines. "Wait . . . one last question."

"Ask your question," instructed Dorfman, rolling his eyes. "And make it quick."

"Did you know or had you heard if Tommy Ray was the target of a federal investigation for conspiracy to launder drug proceeds?"

"Objection!" cried Spearman. "Improper and meant to inflame the jury. What's the relevance?"

"Counsel," asked Dorfman, looking over at Billy, "what's the relevance?"

"Goes to show motive, Your Honor," replied Billy, "and it's another plausible explanation for Tommy Ray's suicide. It's quite possible that if Mr. Ray knew he was the target of a federal investigation and/or an indictment was coming down, he may have chosen to exit life instead of facing a long prison sentence."

Judge Dorfman seemed satisfied with Billy's response. "I'll allow it."

"I renew my objection!" cried Spearman after being blindsided by Billy's question. Gina Ray was looking at Spearman and his associate, Hanslik, with a confused stare, not really understanding what was happening.

"Overruled!" said the judge.

"You may answer," continued Billy.

"Well, uhm," started Sgt. Detective Marks, clearing his throat, "for many years, there have been rumors going around that Mr. Ray helped the Gulf cartel launder drug proceeds through his appliance stores chain. Again, that's been the rumor. If the feds were onto him or others, I wouldn't know. There could be a federal indictment out there somewhere under seal, and we wouldn't know about it—not until it is unsealed."

"Do some folks commit suicide rather than face a long prison sentence?" followed Billy.

"Objection!" shouted Spearman, "Totally improper and highly speculative, Your Honor."

"Judge," replied Billy, ready with a response. He'd been anticipating Spearman's objections. "It's common knowledge that inmates commit suicide all the time in their cells because they don't want to be there. I'm sure Sergeant Detective Marks has witnessed some of these events. He would even have personal knowledge. There's nothing speculative about that."

"I don't know," answered Marks without giving Judge Dorfman time to rule on Spearman's objection or acknowledge Billy's well-thought response.

Billy did not wait for a ruling either. "Well, let me ask it this way . . . have people committed suicide in your city jail, while in your custody?"

"Yes . . . it's happened."

"Why is that? Do they want to be there? Do they enjoy being incarcerated?"

"No, they don't."

"So," continued Billy, "could that have been a motive for the suicide, knowing that there might be an indictment coming down, and if true, knowing that you will lose your businesses, your assets, your livelihood and your good reputation in the community? Knowing that you've failed your family, your friends, your business associates, even your spouse?" Billy was now looking at Gina Ray.

"I suppose it could be a strong motive. Yes."

"Pass the witness," said Billy.

Immediately, Spearman began trying to rehabilitate Sgt. Detective Marks. "To the best of your knowledge, Detective, was Tommy Ray ever indicted either at the state or federal level for whatever reason?"

"No."

"This 'rumor' you're talking about, that's all it is, correct?" asked Spearman, "just a rumor?"

"Yes. That's all it is. Nothing else."

"And people spread rumors about other people all the time, don't they?"

"Yes, they do. Lots of *chisme* going round."

"What was that word?" asked Spearman, "*Chisme?*" He'd never heard the expression.

"Gossip," explained Marks, "it was just rumors, gossip. Nothing ever came of it."

"So, it would be accurate to say that in all these years you've known or heard of Tommy Ray, you have never seen criminal charges leveled against the man?"

"Correct."

"You've never seen an indictment with his name on it?"

"No."

"Anything whatsoever alleging wrongdoing of any kind?"

"No, sir, I have not."

"Pass the witness," said Spearman.

"Nothing further," replied Billy, "except I'd like to keep the detective under subpoena in the event I'd like to recall him."

"Very well. The witness may step down," said the judge.

At that very moment, Roland Hernández, Dorfman's law clerk, approached the bench and handed the judge a small piece of paper. Judge Dorfman réad it, made a frown and announced, "Ladies and gentlemen of the jury, I've been called away to handle a hearing next door for Senior Judge Kent McFarland. That means you get to go home early today. Please don't discuss the case with anyone. Be back at nine-thirty in the morning. We're in recess until then."

CHAPTER 43

"HEY, MR. BATES, can you talk?" Billy Bravo decided to call his boss after wrapping up the first day of trial. Falcone had been in Laredo only for opening arguments and the initial part of the trial, but after the first break, he'd scurried away to go back to work at the home office and remain as far away from Laredo as possible.

Billy, Jensen and Hector were now sitting at a booth inside the Taco Palenque restaurant located within walking distance of the courthouse. They were watching the dinner crowd arrive as the place filled up with courthouse employees, bailiffs, marshals, assistant U.S. attorneys, clerks, security guards, even Judge Valeria Allende was sitting in the back surrounded by her staff.

"Yes, Billy. How's the first part of the trial going?" asked Bates.

"Pretty good. I don't think Spearman has done any real damage. For a moment there, I thought he was trying to inflame the jurors with gory details of the two other killings."

"Did you object?" interrupted Bates.

"I pretty much decided to let it go," Billy explained. "We had a brief bench conference, but decided not to keep objecting. That way the jury wouldn't think I was trying to keep something from them. Besides, maybe the jury will think twice about giving money to a killer."

"Yes. I've been there. It's important to pick your battles. The converse is also true. I've seen good attorneys object to everything and anything. Pretty soon, the trial starts dragging, and the jurors start hating the attorney making all the objections . . . what was supposed to be a three-day trial is now a two-week ordeal. Sometimes, as attorneys, we forget that the jurors just want to get it over with. They just want to go home and get on with their lives."

"You're right, anyway, we'll see how it goes."

"When do you think Spearman will be done putting on his case?"

"Thursday."

"So, you'll need your experts on Friday?"

"Well," started Billy, "I think I can stall with my cross-examinations and force Spearman to go until Friday. I would like to call my first witness next Monday."

"Good move," said Bates. "The jury will have the entire weekend to forget everything they heard the past week."

"Yes. I can start with a clean slate on Monday. Plus, if we fly down our experts on Friday or Saturday, we can have a full day—somewhere in there—to go over their testimony and get them ready to testify."

"Are the plaintiffs going to call Falcone during their case?"

"Not live, no. They don't have him under subpoena, so no, I don't think so. If anything, Spearman will play excerpts from Falcone's deposition we took up in Boston last month. We'll do the same when we present Mr. Falcone's testimony, if needed."

"Well, sounds like you have it under control."

"I just wanted to give you a heads up," explained Billy. "I might fly to Houston Saturday morning to go check on Ale. I can work with the experts on Sunday and have Hector and Charlie entertain them on Saturday if I decide to go see my daughter."

"You're the lead attorney, Billy. Do what you have to do," Bates said.

"All right. I'll call you toward the end of the week to give you an update."

"I'll be expecting your call."

CHAPTER 44

THE JURY WAS quickly seated in the jury box the following morning. Riley Spearman called the coroner as his next witness. Dr. Chester Dahm was a key witness for the plaintiffs, and Billy Bravo planned to score some key points with him to blow even larger holes into the plaintiff's case. Dr. Dahm was an imposing figure. At six-foot-two and in his late fifties, his presence filled the courtroom. While under direct examination by Spearman, he testified for a full hour as to his credentials alone before getting into the facts of the case. His curriculum vitae and all his awards and published papers comprised a stack three inches thick, like a college textbook.

"Dr. Dahm," Spearman asked, "is this fifty-plus page document your latest, most updated curriculum vitae?"

"Yes," replied the doctor, full of bravado. He was smiling and looking straight at the jury. He looked to be enjoying himself, like a professional actor who'd routinely performed in front of live crowds and happened to have a great stage presence.

"Judge," said Spearman, "we'd like to tender Dr. Doctor Dahm as an expert in the area of forensic pathology."

"Mr. Bravo?" asked Judge Dorfman, eyebrows raised, "any objections?"

"No," replied Billy, "no objection, Your Honor."

"The record will so reflect," finished Judge Dorfman and, looking at Spearman, said, "Move along, counsel."

"Did you perform an autopsy in connection with Tommy Ray's passing?" asked Spearman.

"Not exactly," explained Dr. Dahm.

"Why was that?"

"Well, in this case, when the shootings occurred, I was out of town at a conference. But after I got back to town and had a chance to talk to the investigators and the others that processed the scene, it became obvious that the cause of death was a self-inflicted gunshot wound to the roof of the mouth."

"And?"

"Also, the Justice of the Peace who pronounced him dead at the scene did not request one, nor did Mrs. Ray," the doctor replied. "I guess the JP thought there was no need."

"So, what did you do then, if anything?"

"Well, we still examined the body and did various tests. The results are contained in the Certificate of Death, even though there was no autopsy, per se."

"Is this," began Spearman, "the report you prepared in connection with this case?" He was waving a stapled two-page light blue document.

"It should be. I would have to look at it just to make sure it belongs to Mr. Ray."

"May I approach the witness, Judge?" asked Spearman.

"You may," said Judge Dorfman.

"Yes," answered Dr. Dahm as he took the document from Spearman's hand, "this is the report I prepared in connection with Tommy Ray's suicide."

"Let me stop you right there," said Spearman. "How can you be certain it was suicide?"

"There's nothing else that would indicate it was a murder."

"Is that it?"

"No. Tommy Ray's upper extremities tested positive for gunpowder residue also."

"Is that it?" Spearman asked again.

"No. When considering Sgt. Detective Marks' investigation and the neighbors' reports, along with the gunpowder residue and the type of gunshot wound we were dealing with, it became evident we had a suicide on our hands."

"What else did you do?"

"We took tissue samples, along with blood samples, and test-ed them for any foreign substances," said Dr. Dahm. "We did some blood screens."

"Like?"

"Illegal drugs, prescription drugs, poison—anything foreign that should not be in a person's blood."

"Did you find anything?"

"Nothing unusual. Tommy Ray came back normal. There were no traces of cocaine, heroin, marijuana, amphetamines or ecstasy. Not even alcohol."

"So, you're saying that none of those substances could be blamed for the suicide or for making him crazy, is that right?"

"We certainly can't blame them if they're not present."

That had been the exact point Billy had been trying to make from the beginning, straight from his opening argument and now Dr. Dahm himself had touched on it lightly. Hopefully, the jurors had picked up on it.

"Are these the photographs of Tommy Ray you took back at the morgue?" asked Spearman, waving a packet of photos for the jury to see.

"Yes."

"Move to admit the photos and the doctor's report, Your Honor," Spearman said, addressing Judge Dorfman.

"Have they been marked?" asked the judge.

"Yes," replied Spearman, "these are plaintiff's Exhibits 300 through 360."

"Very well. Any objections, Mr. Bravo?"

Billy Bravo was busy scribbling down questions on a yellow pad for his cross-examination and replied without looking up, "As to them being marked 300 through 360 and to the doctor's report, we don't have an objection, Your Honor."

"Very well," said the judge, "then 300 through 360 will be admitted."

"May I publish them to the jury?" asked Spearman.

"Yes," replied the judge.

"I will object, however, to the autopsy photos being published to the jury," Billy interjected as he got up from his seat. "First and foremost, these photos are highly inflammatory. Secondly, they're irrelevant under Rules 401 and 403 of Federal Evidence. Everybody in this courtroom already knows that Tommy Ray died of a self-inflicted gunshot wound. These photos don't add anything else that could be considered remotely probative under the circumstances or under the Texas and Federal Rules of Evidence."

"Anything else?" asked Judge Dorfman over his reading glasses hanging on the tip of his nose.

"That's it," said Billy.

"That'll be denied," the judge said, "Exhibits 300 through 360 will be admitted."

"Thank you," Spearman said, gloating, as he strutted over to the jury box and handed the gruesome photos and the report to one of the male jurors. "Pass the witness."

"Your witness, Mr. Bravo," said Judge Dorfman.

"May I wait for the jury to finish looking at the photos before I start my cross-examination, Your Honor?" asked Billy. He knew the jurors would be distracted for the next several minutes while they glanced at the photos. It was better to wait, let them finish and then resume the cross-examination of Dr. Dahm.

"All right," huffed Judge Dorfman.

The entire courtroom fell silent as each of the jurors got to see the fifty-plus cadaver photos. All in all, it must have taken about ten minutes for the jury to put down the photos. During that time, Billy Bravo scribbled more questions on his yellow pad.

"You may continue, Mr. Bravo," announced Judge Dorfman from the bench. "We're ready to proceed."

"Dr. Dahm," started Billy Bravo without missing a beat, "have you and I ever met?"

"No, sir. We have not."

"Prior to you testifying here today, had you met Mr. Spearman?"

"We spoke on the phone and discussed my findings."

"Is that it?"

Dr. Dahm was no longer smiling and playing up the jury. In his twenty years of testifying in trials, he knew one side would be out to pick him apart. This time, the pleasure belonged to defense counsel, Billy Bravo.

"Well . . . yes."

"I mean, have you ever met Mr. Spearman in person? That's what I meant," clarified Billy.

"Yes, that too," said Dr. Dahm, clearing his throat.

"When was that?"

"This last weekend, he invited me to dinner twice."

"Here in Laredo?"

"Yes."

"Where did you go?"

"To a restaurant, of course," Dr. Dahm answered while the jury laughed along.

"No, I mean . . . " said Billy, "did you go to McDonald's or to a fancy steakhouse? What restaurants did you go to?"

"We had dinner at Pelican's Wharf."

"What? Australian lobster tail? King crab? Filet mignon?" asked Billy. "Expensive wine?"

"We had some wine, steak and lobster. It wasn't that good, really," explained the doctor, trying to downplay the whole incident.

"Who paid?"

"Mr. Spearman's firm picked up the tab."

"Did you talk about the trial? Your testimony?"

"Five minutes maybe. Not more than that," the doctor answered as he looked over at the jury. The entire jury was no longer making eye contact with him. Instead, they were focusing on Spearman.

"Are you Spearman's retained expert?" Billy asked point-blank. "Is he paying anything for you to testify here today?"

Billy Bravo knew that Dr. Dahm could not be hired by either side in that he was Webb County's official coroner. However, as a witness who had some participation in the case, either side could call him to testify. By suggesting that he was on Spearman's dime, the jury surely could decide to overlook and disregard his entire testimony. Obviously, he could be considered to be biased toward

Spearman, the guy that fed him fancy, expensive steak and lobster dinners.

"No, of course not," he said, sounding embarrassed, "that would be unethical."

"I object," cried Spearman from his table. "Since when is it a crime to take a witness to dinner, Your Honor?"

"What's your objection?" countered Billy.

"Relevance?!" cried Spearman. "How are Dr. Dahm's eating habits relevant to this trial?"

"Move on, counsel," the judge admonished.

"Did you go out to dinner a second time?" Billy pressed forward.

"Yes, at Lagasse's on the Border."

"Who picked up the tab?"

"Mr. Spearman," answered the coroner.

"I want to go over your report, if I may. Would that be okay with you?" asked Billy as he switched gears.

"Go ahead," the coroner said, sounding relieved.

In all his years defending healthcare claims, Billy Bravo had reviewed hundreds of autopsies and witnessed some autopsies himself. In reading the coroner's reports, he'd learned to skip all the preliminary stuff contained therein—like the stuff dealing with measurements, weights and actual procedures—and instead get to the meat and potatoes, right away. The summary was the key, always.

"I'm looking at the summary in your coroner's report, and I see that you wrote that the cause of death was a gunshot wound to the roof of the mouth, is that correct?" asked Billy.

"Yes."

"Powder residue was found on Tommy Ray's hands and around the face, correct?"

"Yes."

"Is that because he pulled the trigger with his right hand and the gun went off in and around his face?"

"It appears so."

"Now, the drug screen . . . did that come back negative?"

"That's correct."

"No alcohol in his system, right?"

"Right, as I've said."

"Now," said Billy changing tempo, "it says here that you found two sets of circular burn marks in the testicle area, correct?"

"Yes."

"Can you describe the circles for the jury?"

"They were small—the size of dimes, perhaps a bit smaller."

"Any idea how they got there?"

"I can guess . . . "

"Speculation!" objected Spearman.

"I'll allow it," ruled the judge.

"Doctor Dahm," insisted Billy, "please tell us."

"Well, I did some tissue sampling in and around the area surrounding the circular burn marks. The cell counts were different on the burned, scarred tissue than on the rest of the scrotum. So, to me, that indicated that those marks were done days earlier than the day he pulled the trigger. They were recent."

"What could have caused those marks?" asked Billy, "and how long have they been there?"

"In my line of work, I've seen similar markings before. I concluded the marks were probably made by a stun gun, like the one used on cattle . . . they appeared to be a week old . . . ten days maybe."

"A stun gun?" asked Billy as he gauged the jurors' reaction. The jurors were wide-eyed as well.

"That's my opinion."

"Very well," said Billy. "So, you've seen this type of marking before . . . these circular marks. Is that a fair statement?"

"Yes."

"Your Honor, may I see Exhibit 26 again?" asked Billy.

"Go ahead," indicated Dorfman.

"Judge," cried Spearman, "I'm gonna object. Mr. Ray committed suicide. Mr. Bravo is trying to confuse the jury by suggesting Mr. Ray was allegedly tortured. This is totally improper, inappropriate and for Mr. Bravo to show those images, frankly . . . I'm offended. We're offended," he said as he turned and looked at Gina Ray.

"Mr. Spearman," countered Judge Dorfman, "I think Mr. Bravo is trying to show that there might be an alternative explanation why your client may have wanted to exit this life. Your objection is overruled."

"Thank you," said Billy as he reached for the exhibit from a pile of stacked documents next to the court reporter and quickly put it under the court's Elmo. The grotesque images of Tommy Ray's shaved privates quickly filled the large retractable screen hanging on the opposite wall across from the jury box.

"Dr. Dahm, Exhibit 26," started Billy as he pointed to the images on the screen, "What is that?"

"The deceased's privates," answered the witness.

"Now, are those circular marks," Billy carried on as he pointed them out to the jury with his laser pointer, "consistent with the use of a stun gun?"

"Yes," said the doctor as he squinted his eyes, trying to look at the image on the screen.

Billy pressed forward. "Is that consistent with someone who may have been tortured?"

"Objection!" shouted Spearman, "The witness doesn't know . . . it's all speculation."

"Overruled," said Dorfman. "You may answer."

"It would be consistent, yes," replied the coroner.

"It would appear so, right, torture?" asked Billy, planting in the jurors' minds the idea that maybe Tommy Ray had committed the unthinkable for other very good reasons. Perhaps the Gulf cartel had warned him not to point fingers at anyone in case the rumors were true.

"Objection!" shouted Spearman. "Where is counsel going with this? Torture, no torture, old torture wounds, whatever. That's irrelevant to this trial, Your Honor."

"These are Spearman's own expert's findings, Judge," replied Billy as he nodded over to the jury.

"Object to the sidebar!" cried Spearman. "Dr. Dahm is not my retained expert. I'm asking for an instruction to the jury to disregard counsel's last comment."

"These are Dr. Dahm's findings," countered Billy. "It's in evidence already. With all due respect, Mr. Spearman himself introduced the coroner's report and the pictures, if the court would recall?"

"Overruled," the judge said. "Carry on, Mr. Bravo."

"Thank you. Now, Professor Dahm, where were we?"

"Dr. Dahm," corrected the coroner, "it's *Doctor* Dahm."

"Yes, doctor," apologized Billy. "In your experience, have you ever seen other cadavers with torture marks to the testicles?"

"Oh, yes. It is prevalent. Like the old Colombian necktie. In recent months, we've seen that many of the enemies of Montalvo's drug ring that have been killed had also been tortured with stun guns—and not just in the testicles or genitals, some even had those markings in their eyeballs."

"Could you explain to the ladies and gentlemen of the jury what a Colombian necktie is?" asked Billy.

"Objection!" shouted Spearman. "What does a Colombian necktie have to do with this trial, Judge?"

"I don't hear an objection, Judge. What's the objection?" asked Billy.

"Relevance! This information has no relevance to the case, Your Honor. That's the objection."

"I'll allow it," said Dorfman. "I want to know what a Colombian necktie is. Please tell us, Dr. Dahm."

Spearman sat down visibly upset. He was whispering something to Tim Hanslik, probably calling the judge a name or two.

"Sure. The assassin slits open the victim's throat, and through that opening in the throat area, they yank the entire tongue out to make it look like a necktie," continued the coroner.

"Ouch," said Billy as he rubbed his own neck. "So, different torture methods are commonly applied to the man's testicular area, is that a fair statement?"

"Yes."

"And stun guns are one way to torture a poor soul, right?"

"Yes. That's one way . . . probably the most civilized I've seen."

"Now, to be fair, you don't really know if Tommy Ray was tortured or not, is that correct?"

"That's correct. We'll never know. All I'm saying—as my report indicates—is that I found those markings in the scrotum sack. They're consistent with a stun gun. Birthmarks are common, skin tacks are common and piercings are now pretty common, but small circular burn marks are not that common."

"We're almost done, Doctor," announced Billy. "Do you remember making this statement a few minutes earlier when Mr. Spearman was asking you questions: 'We certainly can't blame them if they're not present?'"

"Yes, but . . . we were talking about illegal drugs," clarified the doctor, figuring out where defense counsel was going with the question. He was trying desperately to stay one step ahead of Billy Bravo.

"Well, what about Zerevrea. Was Zerevrea or traces of it found in Tommy Ray's body, blood or tissue?"

"Eh, uhm . . . well, no. I didn't find any, no. But then again, I did not test for it, but there was 5HT acid."

"I understand, but that's not my question. Did you find traces of Zerevrea?"

"No, but as I said, I was not testing for it. To be fair to Mrs. Ray, at the time we did our testing, no lawsuits had been filed. We worked with what we had, the spinal fluid. We then extrapolated that information and concluded that Zerevrea could have increased the serotonin, thus the high readings of 5HT. Mr. Ray had been prescribed that medication by his doctor, and two pills were missing, so why would he not have taken them? Why would he instead throw them away? It didn't make sense. And further-more, why would he have a high concentration of the acid?"

"I hear what you're saying, Doctor, but to a reasonable degree of medical certainty," asked Billy, "can you tell this good jury that Tommy Ray had Zerevrea in his body at the time he pulled that trigger?"

"No, I can't. I was not asked to test for it," replied the doctor. "There's no way of knowing that. We'll never know."

"Can anybody then blame Zerevrea for Tommy Ray's death if we don't even know if it was present?" asked Billy, looking over to the jury to see if they were following along.

"Objection!" said Spearman, pounding his fist on counsel's table. "Calls for speculation . . . plus, Mr. Bravo is mischaracterizing the testimony."

"Judge," said Billy, "those were Spearman's expert's words: 'We certainly can't blame them if they're not present,' Your Honor. Professor Dahm . . . "

"It's *Doctor* Dahm," clarified the witness from the stand.

Everybody in the courtroom knew it was Dr. Dahm, even Billy. He was just pushing the witness's buttons.

"Judge, Doctor Dahm said those words as he testified to the presence of illegal drugs in Mr. Ray's body. We can have the court reporter read back Dr. Dahm's testimony if you'd like."

"The jury will remember the testimony," instructed the judge. "Your objection is overruled, Mr. Spearman. Are you almost done, Mr. Bravo?" The way the judge asked the question, it appeared as if he was telling Mr. Bravo that he had done enough damage. No sense beating a dead horse. It was time to wrap it up.

"Didn't you testify earlier, Doctor Dahm," said Billy, "and I quote again, 'we certainly can't blame them if they're not present,' end quote, when you were asked by Mr. Spearman about the presence of illegal drugs?"

"Yes, I did say that, as I now recall."

"Well," continued Billy, "can you really blame Zerevrea if it wasn't found, if it wasn't present? Let's be honest."

There was a pause. Everybody in the courtroom turned to hear the answer. Finally, after a few moments, Dr. Dahm finally caved and said flatly, "No."

"Pass the witness," Billy said as he looked over at the jury and locked eyes with the foreman.

"Redirect?" asked Judge Dorfman of Spearman.

"None," barked Spearman, shaking his head. "The witness may be excused."

AFTER DR. DAHM testified, the order of witness on the subsequent days included the local doctor that prescribed Zerevrea, the EMS technicians that responded to the call on January 28, the

Rays' next-door neighbor, another expert on the usefulness and effectiveness of black box warnings printed on the packaging, a marketing and media consultant who testified that the overpromotion of drugs on national TV in essence neutralized the effectiveness of the so-called black box warnings on the packaging and excerpts of videotaped testimony of Salvatore Falcone, CEO of BostonMagnifica Pharmaceuticals. Even Tommy's parents were called to the witness stand. Billy Bravo continued to hammer his simple, yet effective message. This he did with all of the witnesses, even though the question was—in some instances—clearly outside their area of expertise. No one, according to Billy Bravo, had been able to prove, much less show, that Tommy Ray had traces of Zerevrea in his system. And no one had seen Tommy Ray consume the two missing tablets of Zerevrea. Thus, Billy countered —and even got Spearman's labels and warnings expert to agree— not only was Zerevrea safe, but there was no discernible link between Zerevrea and Tommy Ray's suicide. The missing link was indeed missing.

CHAPTER 45

"**H**OW ARE YOU holding up?" Billy asked as he placed a call to his wife at MD Anderson Hospital. The first week of testimony was almost over, and now he was back in his hotel room getting ready for the next day.

"I'm tired, baby," said Yami, "really tired. The nurses had to come in here four times last night to change Ale's soaked sheets and her robe. Even though the doctor says her blood readings are good and that she's in remission, the arsenic she's taking makes her sweat and her gown gets soaking wet. Then, she gets the chills. It's impossible to get a good night's sleep. The only good thing is that she's no longer having those horrible side effects she was having in the beginning. And there haven't been any more blood clots, praise the Lord."

"Tell her," said Billy, "that come Friday at five o'clock, I'm catching a plane to Houston to go see you both."

"Can you get away?"

"Yes. We might even be finished by then. It's going by pretty quick."

"Is it going well?"

"I think so. Of course, I would love to get into the jurors' heads . . . see what they're thinking, you know? But, so far, I think it's going pretty well. My heart goes out to Mrs. Ray, but I just don't see how they can win."

"Why do you say that?"

"None of Spearman's witnesses have been able to show that Tommy Ray had the drug in his system."

"So, no causal link?"

"No link so far," Billy confirmed. "Judge Dorfman shouldn't even let the case get to the jury. We'll have to wait and see how it all plays out. I might even get the case dismissed, get a directed verdict, although that's not what we really want."

"Okay, baby. Let me let you go. I'm tired and want to get some sleep before the parade of nurses starts again."

"I love you and Ale," Billy said. "I'll see you all on Friday."

IT WAS the end of the first week of trial, and Hector and Jensen were loading up boxes of documents into Billy's Honda Pilot to take back to the hotel. Upon Billy's return from Houston, Jensen, Hector and Billy had agreed to meet back at one of the hotels on Sunday and spend the evening preparing BostonMagnifica's experts. Billy was getting in the courthouse elevator, carrying exhibits, going over everything needed to prepare his experts, making sure nothing was forgotten in the courtroom. Then out of nowhere, Hector jumped into the elevator.

"*No lo vas a creer*," Hector said.

"*¿Qué?*"

"They think they solved Croutoux's murder."

"Really?"

"Yep. My buddy in New York emailed me two days ago, but I just now checked my Hotmail account. He sent me the paper clippings as an attachment. You wanna hear what it says?"

"Yes."

Hector cleared his throat, "'A longshoreman found murdered, slumped over the steering wheel of his car behind a warehouse on the city's dry docks, appears to be the lone killer of Dr. Felix Croutoux, police said. DNA on a cigarette butt found at the scene where Croutoux's badly decomposed body was found last year matched the longshoreman's DNA in a national criminal database. However, the investigation was not closed and remained open pending the tying up of some loose ends. The district attorney, Elliot Molaneri, had said earlier that they were looking into who ordered the hit on the longshoreman. Another spokesperson would not comment on whether there would be more arrests in connection with Croutoux's murder.'"

"Interesting," said Billy. "I wonder who ordered the hit on Croutoux?"

"Obviously," said Hector, "somebody who didn't like him very much."

CHAPTER 46

ON MONDAY MORNING Billy Bravo, Hector and Jensen, along with Doctors Drummond, Sudarshan and Neal ate an early breakfast at the Denny's restaurant next to their hotel. As planned, Billy had spent all of Saturday up in Houston, and on Sunday, he and his crew had worked with the scientists from BostonMagnifica, reviewing their anticipated testimony. After breakfast, Billy and the doctors drove down to the federal courthouse. Hector and Jensen followed with all the exhibits, documents and other trial materials.

On Friday, before breaking for the weekend, Spearman had indicated he would be calling as hostile witnesses—as part of his case in chief—the scientists from BostonMagnifica who had worked on developing Zerevrea. Billy's job, then, would be to bolster their testimony or rehabilitate them (in the unlikely event Drummond, Sudarshan and Neal took a hit).

"Are we ready to proceed?" asked Judge Dorfman of Riley Spearman. The jurors were all sitting in the box, anxious to get started. They looked refreshed and ready to go after the long weekend.

"Yes, Your Honor," replied the plaintiffs' attorney.

"Call your next witness," instructed the judge.

"We call Doctor Pierce Drummond as a hostile witness," announced Spearman.

Drummond was sworn in by the court reporter and ordered by Judge Dorfman to take his place. He was quickly turned over to Spearman.

"Good morning, Dr. Drummond," said Spearman. "And how was your flight into Laredo?"

"On time," replied Dr. Drummond as he looked the jury over, grinning from ear to ear, "no delays. Thanks for asking."

"Doctor," Spearman asked, "do you recall having your deposition taken up at headquarters in Worcester approximately two months ago?"

"Yes."

"And at that time, you swore to tell the truth, remember?"

"Yes."

"You understand that you are under oath here today?" continued Spearman.

"Yes."

"As a matter of fact, during that deposition, you and I entered into an agreement, do you recall?"

"Yes."

"Our agreement was that if I asked you a question and you chose to answer it, it would be fair to say that you clearly understood the question, correct?" Spearman was holding up in his right hand the deposition transcript of Dr. Drummond for all the jurors to see—just for show, of course.

"Correct."

"And if you didn't understand a question, you would have an opportunity to ask me to rephrase the question or ask it again in a different way, correct?"

"Yes."

"So, we're clear that if you answered a question at your deposition while under oath, that meant that you understood my question and you would not try to change your answer later on, am I right?"

"Yes, that was the agreement."

"How's Zerevrea prescribed?" Spearman asked.

"It comes in pills and liquid form," answered Drummond.

"How is it packaged?"

"Small boxes, two variations of either twelve of twenty-four tablets. The boxes all have a black box warning printed on the side, as required by the FDA. We're in compliance."

"Is it always packaged like that?"

"Not necessarily. If you're filling a prescription, the pharmacist will put x amount of tablets in small round plastic containers with enough pills for the number of days needed, as per the treating physician's recommendation."

"Isn't it true that Zerevrea is a selective serotonin reuptake inhibitor?" asked Spearman.

"Yes."

"How does it work?"

"You want the long or short explanation?" asked Drummond, looking over to the jurors.

"Short."

"It enhances the concentration of serotonin in the brain."

"So, it is designed to help the patient keep more of the serotonin in the brain, correct?"

"Yes."

"Why is that important?"

"We . . . and by 'we,' I mean 'the scientific community'," explained Drummond, "believe that people that suffer from depression have a chemical imbalance in the brain. Too much of this or not enough of that, to put it in simple terms."

"What chemicals do humans have in their brains? Can you tell this good jury?"

"Serotonin, dopamine and norepinephrine, among others. These are what we call neurotransmitters."

"So, Zerevrea is supposed to help the patient keep certain levels of serotonin, correct?"

"Yes. It's supposed to regulate those levels."

"Isn't it true that serotonin is linked to aggression, irritability and impulsivity?"

"That's what the research suggests," answered Drummond.

"What is Zerevrea prescribed for?"

"Depression, including obsessive-compulsive and anxiety disorders."

"Is that it?"

"Yes."

"Are you sure?" pressed Spearman.

"Yes, I'm sure."

"Did you testify differently at your deposition?" asked Spearman, trying to trick and confuse the witness.

"I don't think so."

"Do you recall testifying that your pharmaceutical sales reps are also trained to push Zerevrea for attention-deficit disorders and migraines?"

"You're right," admitted Drummond. "It also helps children with ADHD and migraines. It is a wonderful drug with many uses and many benefits. We believe it will also help patients with bulimia. We've applied to the FDA for approval for those other uses."

"Any adverse side effects?"

"Yes."

"Such as?"

"The patient needs to be careful not to mix Zerevrea with any other serotonin reuptake inhibitor."

"Is that because it may cause serotonin syndrome?"

"Yes."

"And what is serotonin syndrome?"

"It consists of agitation or hyperactivity, racing thoughts, restlessness or insomnia."

"Like akathisia?" Spearman asked.

"Yes."

"Would you agree with me that akathisia, if left unchecked, can lead to suicide?"

"There are many reasons why people may want to commit suicide, in my professional opinion. I don't believe akathisia is one of them."

"But isn't it true that your so-called 'miracle drug' can trigger certain psychotic episodes?"

"Zerevrea may trigger psychotic disorders and is not recommended for patients that suffer from epilepsy. It should always be taken while under the supervision of your treating physician. May I remind you and the jury that Mr. Ray was under the care of his local physician?"

"What do you mean by 'may trigger'?" asked Spearman.

"*Can* trigger," Drummond corrected himself. "I'm sorry. It *can* trigger psychotic disorders."

"How often can these psychotic episodes be triggered?"

"Very rarely. One episode in every 10,000 patients."

"But isn't it true that if mixed with other drugs, it can be fatal?"

"Yes, if mixed with certain other SSRIs, St. John's Wort, or Tryptophan."

"Why is that?"

"Because the patient may have a slight reaction."

"You mean a fatal reaction?" corrected Spearman.

"I would not call it fatal," clarified Drummond, "but the interaction of these types of drugs with other SSRIs, St. John's Wort and Tryptophan have been known to cause mental status changes in *some* individuals."

"What do you mean by 'mental status changes'?" Spearman asked without missing a beat.

"Studies with other SSRIs have shown that the patient's thinking or judgment becomes cloudy or confused," replied Drummond and quickly added, "but not with Zerevrea."

"Let's be honest. What you're trying to say—and correct me if I'm wrong, Doctor—is that there's an increase in suicidal thinking with these types of drugs. Studies have shown that folks that take these drugs suddenly start thinking about suicide, isn't that correct?"

"Yes, but not with Zerevrea," Drummond replied, clearly attempting to deflect any bullets.

"So, you're telling this good jury, then, that other similar drugs can cause an increase in suicidal thinking, but not your Zerevrea? Is that what you're saying? Is that what you want this jury to believe, even though your medication also has to carry black box warnings as required by the FDA?"

"The black box warning on the side of the box is just a precautionary measure. The FDA wants it there, so we put it there. We're in compliance. All it says is that some reuptake inhibitors may increase suicidal thinking. It doesn't say that Zerevrea necessarily causes suicide."

"So, you expect this intelligent jury to believe that other similar medications do trigger suicidal fixation, but your medication—which is in the same category—doesn't? Is that what I'm hearing?"

"Zerevrea is safe and effective when taken as prescribed and under the supervision of your treating doctor. In my expert opinion, Zerevrea does not cause suicide or bouts of aggressive behavior," countered Drummond. "There's no clinical data to suggest such."

"Okay. Let me see if I understand," Spearman, the seasoned trial lawyer said, rolling his eyes, while at the same time looking over at the jury. "Other drugs in the same category as Zerevrea—we're talking selective serotonin reuptake inhibitors here—have been known to increase suicidal thinking, correct?"

"Yes, studies have shown that in drugs like Paxil, Zoloft, Prozac . . . those drugs—"

Spearman continued to try to shake Drummond, "But Zerevrea, another serotonin inhibitor, according to you, does not increase suicidal thinking."

"That's correct. Zerevrea is 100 percent safe when used as prescribed. Our studies have not shown an increase in suicidal thoughts, much less aggressive behavior."

"But you would agree with me, would you not, that other SSRIs have been linked to an increase in suicidal thinking and aggressive behavior?"

"Yes, like I said before, other similar drugs have been linked to those behaviors. However, there's no study that has linked Zerevrea to those behaviors."

"Has Zerevrea been approved for children?" inquired Spearman, tired of kicking a dead horse and ready to move to a different topic.

"Objection! Relevance?" asked Billy.

"Overruled," said Dorfman.

"It is not FDA-approved for anyone under eighteen, if that's what you're asking," answered Drummond.

"Do you know or are you aware if pediatricians out there do prescribe it to children, regardless of FDA approval?"

"Again, Your Honor, I object," said Billy. "What's the relevance of this testimony? Mr. Ray was not a child and nor were the other victims that day."

"The door has been opened, Your Honor," countered Spearman. "Doctor Drummond testified earlier that the pharmaceutical sales reps are trained to push Zerevrea for ADHD, which is something that affects children. I should be allowed to explore those areas . . . this is coming from their 'so-called' expert."

"Objection to the sidebar!" cried Billy.

"I'll allow it," Dorfman said, "move along counsel, and please refrain from the sidebar comments."

"Yes, Your Honor," said Spearman, as he resumed his cross-examination of Drummond.

"I know that we would like pediatricians to recommend it to parents because, again, we believe Zerevrea is a good drug. So, that is why we train our sales reps to educate doctors on the wonderful benefits. Now, whether or not pediatricians do prescribe it, I couldn't tell you. I have no knowledge of that. If they do, then that would be under the 'learned intermediary doctrine,' which I believe your laws here in Texas allow."

"How many clinical trials were conducted on Zerevrea?" Spearman asked.

"Three."

"Were all of these studies published?"

"Yes . . . in the *Journal of the American Academy of Child and Adolescent Psychiatry.*"

"All of the studies?" Spearman pressed further.

"No, only the first study," admitted Drummond.

"And the other two . . . were they ever published?"

Drummond looked over at Billy, then at Spearman and finally at the jury. "No, because it was not necessary."

"Why did your company withhold publishing the other two?" By asking this question, Spearman wanted the jury to infer that BostonMagnifica had something to hide. "Any particular reason for that?"

"BostonMagnifica felt the results in all three studies were consistent. So, there was no need to publish the other two."

"Is that the real reason?"

"That's it."

"Isn't it true that there were some discrepancies between the studies? Your Honor, may I approach the witness?"

"You may."

"Dr. Drummond, I'm showing you Exhibits 20, 21 and 22, the three studies in question. They're already in evidence. Can you tell this good jury why the results are different in 21 and 22 when compared to Exhibit 20?"

Drummond took the studies from Spearman's hand. He put on his reading glasses and glanced at Exhibits 21 and 22. "Well, yes, I see," he mumbled, studying the documents. "Here it is . . . the differences can be attributed at the variances between the different subject pools. At least that's what we found."

"What were those discrepancies, or differences, as you called them?"

"One study showed Zerevrea worked on depression and another study found no significant effect, while the last one was inconclusive," replied Drummond.

"Your Honor," cried Spearman, "I want defense counsel to tender for inspection all the clinical data supporting these two studies that Doctor Drummond just talked about. We asked for all of that in discovery but never got it. What are they hiding?"

"Objection!" shouted Billy, jumping up from his chair. "Sidebar, Your Honor. No one is hiding anything. Doctor Drummond already explained the discrepancies, Judge. He has no reason to lie; he's here under oath. Besides, had counsel been more specific in his discovery requests, maybe we would have been able to identify the documents he was looking for. It's not my fault he doesn't know how to formulate a simple request for production. We produced over one hundred boxes of documents, as requested."

"Move along, counsel," instructed Dorfman. "The witness has already answered."

Spearman was shaking his head. "With all due respect, Doctor, no one is talking about depression. We're talking about suicide. What was the difference in the studies on that issue alone?"

"The difference was so small that it was negligible. All studies have some margin of error, plus or minus and the difference was within the margin," said Drummond, covering his tracks. "All attributed to the difference in subject pools."

"But, shouldn't the public and the scientific community have access to all your studies, the clinical data and then let them decide? Let the FDA decide?"

"Well, I'm sorry it didn't get done in this case, but that's what happened. There was no malice involved, no intent to defraud, no trickery or underhanded chicanery, nothing like that," explained Drummond.

"What's the recommended starting dose for Zerevrea?"

"Ten to twenty milligrams, once daily, with weekly increases of ten milligrams per day up to sixty milligrams."

"What happens if the patient doubles up on it?" Spearman asked, "Let's say because of a missed dose?"

"Slight agitation, that's all," Drummond answered, shrugging his shoulders, "a very slight form of akathisia."

"Any other known side effects?"

"Nausea, fatigue, weakness, sweating, loss of appetite and sexual dysfunction."

"And less common side effects?"

"Insomnia, anxiety and, in some cases, shaking or tremors."

"Doctor Drummond," said Spearman, switching gears, "how do you know if a particular individual is suffering from an imbalance of serotonin in the brain?"

Dr. Drummond looked at the jury, took a deep breath and then went into his explanation. "No one really knows for sure," said Drummond. He focused on the jury foreman as he testified. "Remember, there is no test that allows us to get into the brain and see how it works or what's missing or misfiring."

"So, there is no test for this?"

"No."

"Then how do you know it works?" Spearman asked, sounding confused as he looked over to the jury. "Aren't you guys just speculating, then, since you admit no one really knows?"

"Scientific theory. We believe that studies have shown that Zerevrea increases the levels of 5HT, which is a byproduct of serotonin. People that commit suicide, most suffering from depression, I might add, have extremely low levels of it."

"So, you equate low levels of the byproduct with low levels of serotonin, am I right?"

"That's the scientific assumption," Drummond said. "What Zerevrea does is increase the levels of this byproduct, at least that's what the testing has shown."

"So the theory is, basically, if there's an increased presence of the byproduct, then there's got to be an increase of serotonin in the brain, correct?"

"Yes. Zerevrea works by blocking the reuptake of serotonin, in essence preventing its escape so more of it stays in the brain where it is needed."

"In simple terms, Doctor," said Spearman, "that's how you *think* Zerevrea works, but no one really knows. Is that a fair statement?"

"Zerevrea increases the byproduct, which, we believe, indicates an increase of serotonin."

"Answer the question, please," admonished Spearman. "We don't really know how it works, is that a fair statement?"

"We choose to believe there is an increase. That's what the tests show," Drummond answered, trying to be cute.

"Your Honor," cried Spearman, "would you instruct the witness to answer my question?"

"He's answered the question!" replied Billy from counsel's table. "Counsel's beating a dead horse, Your Honor."

"Answer the question," Judge Dorfman said. "Do you really know if Zerevrea can prevent the loss of serotonin?"

"No," admitted Drummond, "there's no way to get into the human brain and measure or test for it. No one knows for sure, but the tests show it works that way."

"Thank you, Doctor," Spearman replied, shaking his head.

"Doctor," continued Spearman, "would it surprise you to know that Tommy Ray had high levels of 5HT consistent with high levels of serotonin?"

"Well, there can be other explanations for those high levels. High levels do not necessarily mean the patient was on selective serotonin reuptake inhibitors, or Zerevrea in this case."

"What do you mean?"

"A high level or unusual levels of serotonin metabolite, what you and I call 5HT, can be the result of renal insufficiency or can even be attributed to diet. Bananas, avocadoes, pineapples and even walnuts have been known to affect levels of this metabolite."

Seeing that he was not getting anywhere with this witness, Spearman decided he'd heard enough. It was obvious Billy had prepared the witness. To a certain degree, the guy had come across as very honest and credible. "I pass the witness," said Spearman, disgusted.

"Mr. Bravo," said Judge Dorfman, "your witness."

"Thank you, Judge," replied Billy as he picked up where Spearman had left off. "Dr. Drummond, can you tell this good jury if the appropriate testing was done in this case that could conclusively prove that Tommy Ray had Zerevrea in his system?"

"Not that I've seen. No, no one tested for it. We can't say if Tommy Ray had it in his system or not."

"Can you tell us to a reasonable degree of medical certainty and in your professional expert opinion from everything you know about this case, if Tommy Ray had Zerevrea in his system the day he pulled the trigger?" asked Billy, seeking to pound the nail into Spearman's coffin.

Drummond turned around and locked eyes with the foreman. "No, he did not. There's not a scintilla of evidence—nothing—that proves he had it in his system. There were no brain tissue, liver, kidneys, no blood samples, nothing tested that would indicate the presence of Zerevrea. The increase in 5HT could be attributed to anything, really."

"Thank you, Doctor," said Billy, again looking toward the jury foreman. "Oh, one last thing . . . "

"Yes?"

"Is Zerevrea an unreasonably dangerous drug as Mr. Spearman would like this good jury to believe?"

"Of course not. If it was, it wouldn't have FDA approval. And, like any other drug, sure there are some minor, temporary side effects, but it is safe and effective when taken in the right amounts and under a physician's care."

"Pass the witness."

"Nothing further," Spearman replied, sounding quite depressed himself.

"Let's break for lunch," ordered Judge Dorfman, "the jury is excused. Be back at one-fifteen, and we'll resume after lunch at one-thirty PM."

CHAPTER 47

ONDAY AFTER LUNCH, Riley Spearman called as his next witness Dr. Richard Maxwell, PhD, a professor of economics from the University of Texas at El Paso. The expert was called to explain to the jury that Mrs. Ray, her children and the Ray estate had suffered damages at least to the tune of one hundred million dollars. When the expert mentioned the gigantic figure, the jury members (who, for the most part, looked bored and possibly were even falling asleep after having had lunch) did a double-take.

According to Billy's jury analyst, the highest paid member of the jury had been the manager of Delphi Components, a *maquiladora* plant in Nuevo Laredo. The manager came close to making six figures, but the rest of the jury members made between fourteen thousand and forty-five thousand a year.

As soon as Spearman had solicited the astronomical figure, Billy noticed three of the jurors looked down at the floor, disgusted at the prospect that someone had the gall to even ask for such an award. Three others had shifted uncomfortably in their chairs. As the jury analyst had predicted, it appeared as if most of the Laredo jurors would have a mental block to awarding anything over half a million. The other six jurors had continued to stare in disbelief, as if they had run out of memory and their mental computers had frozen. Nothing was clicking or registering.

The expert continued to testify that Tommy Ray's lawfirm brought in from ten to twenty million dollars in fees per year. On the average, Mr. Ray received a salary from his firm of two to five million dollars a year. Tommy would also receive compensation for being on the board of directors for Ray's Appliance Stores. That was another million, when one computed and added dividends, bonuses and salary. Since he was expected to live another twenty years, his family's loss could be estimated to be between forty and seventy million. Those were Tommy Ray's actual economic damages after taking into consideration inflation and the dollar's present and future value. For noneconomic damages, the expert added, such as mental anguish, loss of companionship and loss of consortium for Gina Ray and the children, one could easily factor in an additional fifteen to thirty million dollars and that was on the low side. The expert broke down for the jury how he'd arrived at all the figures with scales, graphs and pie charts.

Billy tried to force the expert to concede that if he'd been hired by the defense, his projections would probably have been much smaller. When confronted with such allegations, Professor Maxwell countered that his services were not for sale, that he was testifying in accordance with the economic evidence before him and that he had, in no way, shape or form, manipulated the numbers. The hundred-million-dollar mark, he sustained, was pretty accurate, no matter the accusations leveled against him.

Billy wasted no time in pulling stacks of Maxwell's prior depositions and copies of trial transcripts from other legal proceedings in which the professor had testified and proceeded to slice-and-dice Spearman's expert testimony. In another case involving an even more famous attorney, a forty-something from Houston whose family also owned gas- and oil-producing wells, Billy was able to show that Maxwell had downplayed the widow's damages to about fifty million. In that case, the expert had testified for the defense after the attorney died in a highway zone construction accident. In another case involving a forty-one-year-old CEO of an Internet company, even when the CEO owned the majority of stock and the company's IPO had brought in close to one billion dollars, Maxwell had testified that the loss to the victim's parents (the victim was still a bachelor at forty-one) amounted to no more than ten million dollars.

Billy spent the remainder of Monday afternoon showing the jury that Professor Maxwell's testimony could not be trusted and that he was going to say whatever it was they wanted him to say as long as they paid his fees.

"Let's break for the day," interrupted Judge Dorfman, as if telling Billy to stop the carnage. "We'll resume first thing in the morning at nine AM. The jury is excused until then. We'll be in recess."

"Let me see all counsel in chambers," the judge called out, "at once."

CHAPTER 48

U.S. DISTRICT JUDGE Kyle Dorfman was standing by the large window in the back of chambers, right next to his desk. Off to one side was a wall covered in antique law books and old collectible maps. The judge was scratching his head and looked concerned.

"Gentlemen," said the judge as he pointed to Spearman and Billy to take a seat. "I'm seriously considering doing either one of two things: granting the defense an instructed verdict on the issue of proximate cause or their 12b Motion to Dismiss. So far, I haven't heard anyone conclusively establish that Mr. Ray had Zerevrea in his system or that he pulled the trigger because of the Zerevrea circulating in his system."

"Your Honor," Spearman chimed in, "again, the burden of proof in a civil case is not clear and convincing or firmly conclusive, with all due respect. My burden is to prove to the jury, by a preponderance of the evidence, that what we're saying occurred did probably happen—that it was more likely than not that Zerevrea made Tommy Ray commit suicide. And we've met that burden, Your Honor. It was more likely than not that Mr. Ray took those two Zerevrea pills."

"Yes," replied the judge, "but *was* it more likely than not that Zerevrea made Mr. Ray pull the trigger? I haven't heard evidence that he even had it in his system."

"My burden is not," continued Spearman, "and never has been, to prove my case beyond a reasonable doubt. This is not a criminal case, Your Honor! You can't grant them a directed verdict

311

. . . just like that." Spearman was now several shades of red, wiping his forehead with his silk tie.

Unfortunately for Spearman, not only could the learned judge throw Spearman and his client out, but he could also award Billy all of his defense costs, down to the last penny. It had happened before in cases where the federal judge felt the plaintiffs had filed a frivolous lawsuit without any merit. In one famous case out of McAllen, Valeria Allende, then sitting as a visiting judge, had allowed Pfizer Pharmaceuticals to recover more than three hundred thousand dollars from the plaintiffs after she had granted Pfizer's motion for summary judgment. This, even though the court was at fault for the increase in costs when it sat on the motions for two and a half years. It granted them at the last minute, just thirty minutes before jury selection. Had the judge granted the motions two and a half years earlier, the estimated amount of attorney's fees and court costs spent by Pfizer would not have amounted to more than fifteen thousand dollars. Since the judge just sat on Pfizer's motions, the parties had continued to prepare as if they were going to trial, hiring experts, deposing every witness to hell and beyond and spending huge amounts of money.

"I don't know," replied the judge, "I'm not convinced. I'm surprised you didn't hire your own forensic doctor or a lab to test the tissue samples or Mr. Ray's blood."

Billy and Spearman looked at each other with disdain while digesting the judge's words.

Dorfman continued, "I would think that would be the first thing one did. If I'm going to claim Zerevrea did this or that, I need to show the victim had it in his system. How could you overlook the obvious? Unless you meant to file a frivolous lawsuit?"

"There was no chance to do further testing, Your Honor. Mr. Ray's Last Will and Testament called for his body to be cremated. His ashes were spread over the Gulf of Mexico. You must remember, I did not get involved with the case on the day Mr. Ray died. By the time I got the call and was explained the details, time had passed. No one, not Mrs. Ray, not Dr. Dahm nor anybody else thought of saving tissue for additional testing down the road. All

I had to work with were the findings of the coroner, the spinal fluids they initially obtained and saved and a few blood samples, which were mostly used and spent to test for illegal substances. There was nothing left for further testing."

"Well, then, I'm surprised you even took the case without making sure you could prove first that the evidence existed and that Mr. Ray had Zerevrea in his system." The judge looked over at Billy. "What's your position, Mr. Bravo?"

"I'm with you, Your Honor. But my client wants a defense jury verdict, once and for all. If you give us a directed verdict, we're afraid it will send the wrong message."

"Oh, yeah? Why is that?" asked Dorfman.

"That we got lucky or we got a friendly judge. The trial lawyers will think that maybe it's worth another try in another court with another judge. The plaintiff's Bar will keep trying to get into a favorable courtroom. A jury verdict for the defense says, 'Don't even try it, or you're gonna get spanked.' That's the message we want to send."

"Is that what you want, Mr. Bravo? You'd rather roll the dice and let the jury give you a defense verdict?"

"Yes, Your Honor. I would like to try. I feel pretty good about this jury. Their body language says they're with us. I know Riley has tried a hell of a case, but with all due respect, I think the jury is with us on this one, Your Honor."

"Okay, but if you change your mind and you want a directed verdict to dismiss their lawsuit, you better make sure you raise that motion before you start putting on your case, Mr. Bravo," said Judge Dorfman. "Otherwise, it might be too late."

"I still have witnesses to put on," interjected Spearman. "I'm not finished with my case-in-chief."

"How many more?" asked Dorfman.

"Gina Ray's eleven-year-old daughter. She's my last witness."

"And you, Mr. Bravo? How many witnesses?"

"One witness at the most, Your Honor. We won't take very long, and I don't plan on wasting the court's time."

"Good. The jury is already half asleep. To tell you the truth, I think they're bored as hell. They probably made up their mind the first day of trial," said Dorfman.

"I agree with you, Your Honor. I don't think it was wise for Mr. Spearman to mention that Mr. Ray killed two others."

"I'll try my case," yelled Spearman, "the way I please . . . got it?"

"Okay, that's enough of that!" yelled the judge, "or both of you will spend the night in the holding tank. I don't care if you have to try the case in those same clothes. Novices! Get the hell out of my chambers before I change my mind."

CHAPTER 49

"**A**RE WE READY to proceed?" asked Judge Dorfman as he looked over at the jurors sitting in their respective places. The trial was starting a little later than usual since Judge Dorfman had summoned Spearman and Billy back to chambers in order to review their jury charge samples prepared in anticipation of the upcoming charging conference. The clock on the wall showed it was precisely ten AM, Tuesday morning.

"Yes, Your Honor," replied Billy and Spearman at the same time, now standing at their respective counsel's table.

"Call your next witness."

"We call Erika Ray to the stand," announced Spearman.

The entire courtroom, including Judge Dorfman, the jury, both legal teams and the remaining spectators, turned their focus to the back of the courtroom and awaited the entrance of the next witness. A security officer cracked the door open and called out the name of Erika Ray. After a few minutes, the door opened a bit more and the room suddenly got quiet as everyone waited for the young witness to come forward.

Billy knew that putting a child witness on the stand could have adverse consequences for his case. On the one hand, it could be a big turn-off if the jury felt that Spearman was desperately trying to win the case, no matter what the cost, even to the point of subjecting a child to such an unpleasant experience. On the other hand, a defense attorney who pounded on the child while cross-examining him or her could easily turn the jury against him and

315

the client. Any form of abuse on the child witness from either side, and the jury was going to take it out on the client.

Eleven-year-old Erika Ray walked in, looked around and eventually picked her mother out from the crowd in the courtroom. They smiled at each other. The jurors' eyes followed the pretty young girl as another U.S. Marshal helped escort her over to the witness stand. Erika took her place in the witness chair, turned and looked at the jury, then smiled at the judge.

"Please raise your hand, young lady," instructed Judge Dorfman in a playful tone, "and repeat after me. I, Erika Ray, swear to tell the truth . . . "

The young witness went along and started repeating the words, slowly.

"The whole truth, and nothing but the truth, so help me God," finished Judge Dorfman.

Erika finished taking the oath and sat up straight, paying close attention to her mother's attorney.

"You may proceed," continued Judge Dorfman, looking over at Spearman.

"Erika, good morning," said Spearman.

"Good morning, sir," replied the girl shyly.

"Have you ever testified before in a courtroom like this?"

"No, sir."

"You understand what it means to tell the truth?"

"Yes, sir."

"Can you tell us your full name?"

"Erika Nicole Ray."

"Erika, are you nervous this morning?"

"Yes, sir, a little."

"Tell us a little about yourself," prodded Spearman. "Where do you go to school?"

"Laredo Christian Academy, sir."

"What grade are you in?"

"Sixth grade."

"What's your favorite subject?"

"Science, but I'm also in band."

"Oh, yeah? What instrument do you like to play?"

"I play drums," said Erika.

"Really? When did you start to play the drums? Why the drums?" asked Spearman.

"Daddy had a favorite band, Boston, a rock band from the seventies. He always listened to it. He said it reminded him of his first high school dance when he and Mom first slow-danced together to 'More than A Feeling'."

"Really?" asked Spearman. "I remember Boston. Too bad they're no longer around. They were a great band. So that's how you came to play the drums?"

"Well, no, not exactly. I started listening to his album collection, and pretty soon I discovered 'Long Time,' another Boston song, and that's when I decided it would be kind of cool to play drums. So, Daddy got me a drum set. He was thrilled I also happened to love the same band he loved. It brought us close together."

"What else can you tell us about your dad. What kind of daddy was he?"

"He also coached our kickball team. He loved to take us out to the ranch. Whenever he wasn't working, we would go horseback riding, camping or to the movies. He loved the movies. He could sit with us and watch all the *Home Alone* movies, one after the other. He loved to see us laugh."

Tears started running down Erika's cheeks. Spearman approached her and handed her tissues from the Kleenex box that had been sitting at counsel's table. She patted the moisture away.

"You tell us if you need to take a break, all right?" indicated Spearman in a tender tone.

"It's okay. I'm okay."

"What else did your dad like to do?"

"He was happiest when he grilled outdoors and we played and swam in the pool. Boston music played in the background, maybe a little Steely Dan or Bruce Springsteen. He also loved those bands. He'd go all out. Sometimes I wanted hamburgers, my brother wanted chicken and Mom wanted shrimp. Dad would cook for all of us. He didn't mind . . . whatever we wanted."

"Do you miss him?"

"Terribly." More tears began to flow. She blew her nose into a tissue.

By now, Billy noticed that two of the females in the jury were also misty-eyed. The testimony was tugging at their heartstrings.

Erika continued speaking. "It breaks my heart to see my little brother . . . he still thinks Daddy is away on a trip. We haven't told him the truth. He thinks he's coming back."

Gina Ray was now sobbing at counsel's table, too. All of the female jurors were now crying, getting choked up and holding back or sniffling.

"I'm so sorry about your baby brother," said Spearman, sounding completely insincere. The male jurors were not buying any of it. Neither was Dorfman, who by now was looking at his computer screen sitting high on top of the bench, probably surfing the ESPN website, checking out the latest baseball scores.

"Will your life ever be the same without daddy?" asked Spearman.

Billy knew opposing counsel was milking it for all it was worth. Soon, it would be his turn to cross-examine little Erika. Except he had no plan, no questions prepared, no outline to follow. As a matter of fact, it had never occurred to him that Spearman would sink that low, that Spearman would try every trick in the book, even using a child to sway the jury. And now, it was happening. What was he to ask of this little girl that would not offend the jury and make them turn on him or his client?

He was deep in thought when Spearman suddenly and without notice passed the witness. It had been the shortest, but probably the most effective direct examination Billy and Judge Dorfman had witnessed in their entire careers.

"Mr. Bravo," said the judge covering his mouth with his large hand as he fought the urge to yawn. "Your witness."

"Thank you," uttered Billy and briefly paused for a minute. He took a deep breath, thinking of what to ask. But there was nothing. He drew a blank. He pretended to look for his reading glasses until he found them in his coat pocket. Twelve pairs of eyes from the jury box were now focused on him. Charlie Jensen was looking at him, and so was Hector. Gina Ray was now leaning forward, waiting to see what kind of tough questions Billy Bravo, the trial master, was going to ask of her little girl . . . the real victim in this game that Spearman and Bravo were playing.

"We're waiting, Mr. Bravo," followed Judge Dorfman as he tapped the bench with his pen.

Billy looked down at counsel's table, shook his head, fixed his reading glasses and searched for the right words. Then, without notice, from somewhere in his subconscious, the words began to flow freely, effortlessly. "Your Honor, this little girl has suffered enough already. She's been a victim once when her daddy died and again at the hands of her mother's attorney, and this good jury has heard enough. I will have no part in subjecting this little girl to any more suffering. I have no questions for Miss Ray."

"You may step down," said Judge Dorfman, impressed with Billy Bravo's kindness. That had been the smartest thing either one of the lawyers had done during the entire trial. "Call your next witness."

"We rest, Your Honor," announced Riley Spearman.

"Okay, then," said Dorfman, "let's break for lunch. Mr. Bravo, have your witnesses ready. You're on next, after lunch. This court is now in recess. Back at one-fifteen, folks."

"WHERE WERE WE?" growled Dorfman after coming back from lunch and having taken his place at the bench. He was looking at both Spearman and his associate, Hanslik.

"We had rested, Your Honor," declared Spearman.

"Very well," answered Dorfman, and, looking over his reading glasses, proceeded to turn and address BostonMagnifica's counsel. "Mr. Bravo, before you go on for two to three days putting on your case, presenting evidence and testimony, should the court excuse the jury and entertain certain motions outside their presence?"

Dorfman wanted to know if Billy was ready to urge his Motion for Instructed Verdict. Was Billy Bravo willing to push for an outright dismissal since Spearman had not been able to show that Tommy Ray had Zerevrea in his system? Without such evidence, there was no way to prove Zerevrea had triggered the suicide. By the tone of his voice, it sounded as if Dorfman's mind was made up, and all Billy had to do was ask that the court find for his client and dismiss Spearman's lawsuit for failing to establish a causal link between BostonMagnifica's drug and Tommy Ray's suicide. The downside, Billy knew, was that if Dorfman dismissed the case on such grounds, then the next plaintiff's lawyer taking a shot at BM would just need to test tissue and find the presence of Zerevrea to survive an instructed verdict in order for that next lawyer to get his or her case to the jury.

"We'd like to recall Sergeant Detective Marks," announced Billy as he looked over at the jury.

"Are you sure, Mr. Bravo?" asked Dorfman, giving Billy an icy stare, as if pleading with him to reconsider. Spearman apprehensively looked down at his yellow pad and scribbled some notes. Dorfman continued looking at Billy Bravo, waiting for the appropriate response; a request to excuse the jury so that Billy Bravo would urge the court to dismiss the case at once. And all the while, as Dorfman and the jury waited, Billy was wondering if his instincts were right. Was he going to thumb his nose at Dorfman, shun his little gift and instead gamble that the jury would come back with a verdict for the defense? What if the jury was with Gina Ray? What if all they wanted was for the attorneys to wrap up their presentations so that they could start awarding figures with six zeroes attached to them? What if after years of not losing a single jury trial, things were going to turn out differently today? He had to admit things had not been going well these last couple of months.

There was a long silence, but when Billy finally spoke, he spoke with courage and conviction. "Your Honor, it will be brief. The defense recalls Sergeant Detective Marks."

Judge Dorfman was shaking his head, amazed at the fact that Billy Bravo had rejected, for all intents and purposes, a solid, non-reversible, appeal-proof judgment on behalf of his client. "Very well, suit yourself. Marshal, please recall Sergeant Detective Marks . . . he should be outside in the hallway, as I haven't excused him yet."

"Yes, Your Honor," replied the young marshal.

Sergeant Detective Marks walked back into the courtroom, past the jury box and counsel's table and took his place on the witness stand.

"Detective," said Dorfman, reminding him, "you're still under oath. Proceed, Mr. Bravo."

"May I approach the witness?" asked Billy as he was making his way over to the witness stand, a folded newspaper under his right arm.

"Go ahead," answered Dorfman.

"Detective," started Billy, "do you recall that last week I asked you about some rumors floating around about Tommy Ray having some involvement in a money laundering ring?"

"Yes, sir. I recall."

"Have you had a chance to read the *Houston Chronicle* this morning?"

"I'm sorry?"

"Have you had a chance to read the *Houston Chronicle* this morning? The Houston newspaper?" asked Billy, again. Hector had gone out to buy the paper after Miguel Celia had left a message in his voicemail saying that "something major" was coming down . . . to run and get the newspaper.

Spearman was looking intently at Billy, not knowing what kind of rabbit Billy Bravo was about to pull from his top hat. This was the first time the seasoned plaintiff's lawyer had noticed the newspaper in the courtroom.

"Here," said Billy as he unfolded the paper and handed him a few pages. "Take a moment and read this back part . . . starting right here." Billy was pointing at the bottom, right-hand corner of the page.

"'Houston,'" began the detective, "'federal authorities announced publicly the indictment of fourteen suspected drug traffickers and money launderers accused of working with the notorious Gulf cartel out of Laredo, Mexico.'"

"Objection," cried Spearman as he bolted from his seat, "this is all hearsay, Your Honor. There hasn't been a proper foundation established in order for Mr. Bravo to introduce the contents of the newspaper into evidence."

"Denied," shot back Dorfman, "it's a newspaper, Mr. Spear-man, and in case you missed it, it's the government having a press conference regarding the 'unsealing' of indictments, which are now public record. It comes in."

"Keep going," added Billy, "please continue."

"The indictments were unsealed Friday in Houston," continued the witness, "and accused the suspects with conspiring to distribute cocaine, conspiring to launder money, racketeering and other related charges."

"Keep going," said Billy, "just keep reading."

"'Robbie Ferguson, head of the U.S. Drug Enforcement Administration in Houston, said the investigation disrupted a cell of the Gulf cartel, which is now being run by Jose 'El Chango' Cárdenas after taking over from Victor Montalvo. Other names revealed in the previously sealed indictment included Tomás Alberto Reyes, aka Tommy Ray, for allegedly having used his appliance stores up and down the border to launder the organization's drug profits.'"

"Are you finished, Detective?" asked Billy, as he turned around and looked at the jury box and the few spectators in the courtroom. Their eyes were glued to the detective.

"No, there's more."

"Please continue."

"'According to Ferguson, Cárdenas has been Mexico's most-wanted man since he broke out of a high security prison in 2001. He has been accused of spearheading the cartel's renewed efforts to increase profits by adding a new line of products such as black heroin, methamphetamines and a more powerful and cheaper marijuana.'"

"Go on."

"'These are big fish, indicated Rick Ponce, DEA Special Agent, who helped coordinate and plan the operation by the code name *Tourniquet*. 'By shutting down their ability to launder drug profits through legitimate businesses,' said the agent referring to the chain of Ray's Appliance Stores, 'we've disabled the cartel's ability to move millions and millions of dollars all the way up and down the Texas-Mexico border.'"

"Go ahead . . . finish," Billy said, who by now had returned to counsel's table and was sitting next to Jensen, who looked completely surprised, scratching his head in total and utter disbelief.

"'Authorities,'" continued Marks, "'say the group smuggled cocaine, heroin, meth and marijuana into the United States via tunnels between Brownsville-Matamoros, Reynosa-McAllen and Nuevo Laredo. The drug shipments were later stored in San Antonio, the cartel's distribution center, and from there shipped to groups in Atlanta, Miami, New York and Chicago. Authorities believe the drug proceeds were laundered through the appliance stores belonging to the Ray family. The case broke open last January when agents received a tip dealing with a shipment of fifty million dollars in cash located at an appliance warehouse in Laredo. Authorities say the group packaged the bundles of cash in large Igloo ice chests for transport. The year-long investigation has resulted in sixty-four arrests over several months in Laredo, San Antonio, Round Rock, North Carolina, Chicago and Miami. Five of the indicted suspects were arrested Thursday in San Antonio. Tommy Ray, the alleged mastermind behind the laundering portion of the operation, died of an apparent self-inflicted gunshot wound a few days after authorities seized millions stored in a Laredo custom broker's warehouse last January. Authorities believe the custom broker's warehouse was a storefront for the cartel'." When Marks finished reading the article, he looked dumbfounded, even shocked.

"Is it possible," asked Billy from counsel's table, "and based on your law enforcement experience and everything else you've seen as a twenty-five-year veteran with the force, that Mr. Ray chose to exit life rather than face shame and disgrace from being in prison?"

"Objection!" shouted Spearman, "calls for speculation. How can this witness know what Tommy Ray was thinking?"

"Counsel is not asking whether Detective Marks knew what Mr. Ray was thinking, but rather if Detective Marks believes it's possible that the threat of incarceration is sufficient to trigger a suicide response in some individuals," explained Dorfman. Then, turning to the witness, he said, "Detective, do you know?"

"It's possible. Yes, sir. Folks do all kinds of things in order to avoid going to prison, so maybe Mr. Ray figured this was a way out."

"I renew my objection," cried Spearman. "This witness is speculating."

But before Dorfman had a chance to respond and rule on Spearman's objection, Billy Bravo announced, "Nothing further from this witness."

"You want to cross him?" asked Dorfman, this time looking at Spearman over his reading glasses.

"No, sir, he may step down."

"You're excused, Detective. Call your next witness, Mr. Bravo."

"The defense rests," replied Billy, "and we close."

"What says the plaintiff, Mr. Spearman?" asked Judge Dorfman.

"We also rest and close."

Gina Ray was looking as if the wind had been knocked out of her. Spearman looked pretty bad too.

"Okay, ladies and gentlemen of the jury," said Dorfman, this time addressing the folks in the box, "this means both sides have finished presenting all of their evidence. I am going to excuse you until tomorrow morning at nine, and then the attorneys will deliver their closing arguments. Soon thereafter, you'll start your deliberations. We're in recess."

CHAPTER 50

RILEY SPEARMAN DELIVERED perhaps the most gut-wrenching closing argument of his meteoric legal career. In Billy's humble opinion, Spearman's closing argument had been nothing short of brilliant.

Despite Billy having warned both Jensen and Hector to avoid looking in awe at Spearman while he delivered his closing argument, Billy sensed he was getting to a couple of the jurors, the females mostly. The males, it seemed, were not that impressed. The foreman and two other males were actually yawning and looking down at the floor, avoiding making eye contact with Spearman. They would not be convinced to come around and line up behind Gina Ray. Their minds were made up and probably had been since day one.

While Spearman paced back and forth in front of the jury box arguing his case with his arms flailing and asking for all kinds of figures with zeroes, zeroes and more zeros, Billy Bravo ignored him and kept busy scribbling notes on his yellow pad. After Spearman thanked the jury in advance for the one-hundred-million-dollar verdict of his dreams, he quickly returned to counsel's table and sat down next to Gina Ray.

"Mr. Bravo, you're up."

Billy stood up and nodded to Judge Dorfman, found his reading glasses on top of his head and grabbed his yellow pad and pen. He made his way over to the podium in front of the jury box.

Billy looked up at the bench and then slowly made eye contact with each member of the jury, and then spoke. "May it please

325

this Honorable Court, ladies and gentlemen of the jury, Mr. Spearman, Mrs. Ray."

"It's easy to play the blame game." Billy looked intently at the jury foreman, the plant manager for Delphi Electronics in Nuevo Laredo. He casually leaned on the jury box rail with his right hand in his pant pocket. He then brought both hands together, as if praying, slightly pushing up his horn-rimmed glasses and paced toward the female juror at the end of the first row. "Especially when we're confronted with questions we don't have the answers to. It's human nature, and it's normal. We're always looking for an explanation, a solution, a way out. And when that doesn't happen, when we can't get those answers, we play the blame game."

Billy now walked to counsel's table and picked up the newspaper, the one that had the story about the indictments coming down from Houston. He now focused on Juror Nine, in the back row.

"You see it every day. Democrats blame Republicans. Republicans blame Democrats. We blame the lack of jobs and high unemployment rates on the undocumented immigrants because they're easy scapegoats . . . easy targets. No one is willing to admit that all the good-paying jobs have been sent overseas because we want cheap prices. We blame our kids failing high school on the teachers, on the principals, when in fact no one is at home helping the child learn. Dad's in prison, and Mom's busy holding down two or three jobs and is unavailable. Our children are raising themselves alone at home.

"Our nation has a serious drug problem. And what do we do? We blame Mexico, Colombia, Bolivia, Jamaica and everyone else but ourselves. Oh! *They're* the drug producers! If *they* would only stop producing so much dope! We fail to recognize that we're a society full of addicts and alcoholics, and we also happen to be the largest drug consumers in the world.

"And it doesn't stop there. We blame high gas prices on the oil companies, claiming that they're making too much money. We blame the Middle East for not enough output. Yet we refuse to drive less, trade in our gas guzzlers or find alternative fuels. Let somebody else suffer. Why should I carpool to work or give up my freedom, my Hummer, my Escalade, my Expedition?

"We get into debt, and it's those damned credit card companies. They're out to get you, gouge you at every turn! But we won't admit that we love those credit cards and we run them up past their limits."

Billy paused. A few of the jurors were nodding their heads, completely in agreement with what Billy Bravo was saying. The remainder of the jurors were spellbound. Two female jurors in the back row were giggling about the last comment.

"We find ourselves even making excuses for child molesters, rapists and murderers. It was their upbringing, they came from a broken home. The parents were entirely too strict or not strict enough. It's either this or that. We even say they were bullied or grew up fatherless. Whatever . . . you fill in the blank.

"And so Tommy Ray turns a gun on himself after killing two innocent bystanders because he knew his time had come . . . he was about to have his 'come to Jesus' meeting with the federal justice system, and what do we say? What does Gina Ray and her smooth-talking lawyer want you to believe?"

Juror Number Nine, the young man in the back row, surprised everyone when he sat up straight and blurted out, "Zerevrea made him do it!"

Billy turned around and stopped pacing. He looked at Spearman and then faced Gina Ray and then proceeded to unfold the paper.

"If, in my heart of hearts, I knew that Zerevrea had pushed Mr. Ray over the edge, I myself would join Mr. Spearman and ask you to award Mrs. Ray a monetary award. *No importa qué cantidad de dinero.* Whatever amount of money that was."

He waited to let his Spanish words register in the jurors' minds, for the words to sink in, resonate, ring true. He could feel them opening their hearts, their minds. They were hanging on his every word. He had them.

"Use your common sense, ladies and gentlemen of the jury. You know why Tommy Ray pulled the trigger that Saturday morning? He knew the feds were onto him. The gig was up! This case has nothing to do with Zerevrea or black box warnings. You and I know that. When Tommy Ray realized the gig was up, he made a decision. He was not going to take it lying down. No . . . he was going to exact revenge on the lead agent building the case against him. How, you ask? By taking out the one thing near-and-dear to Sammy Guerra's heart. And that would be the fiancée and his daddy. Both were killed at the same time, and both were federal employees. You do the math.

"So, you've already heard Mr. Spearman—how he wants you to answer the court's verdict form. Let's look at it. Let me read it to you. It reads:

> We the jury, duly empanelled in the above entitled action, unanimously find the following answers to the questions propounded by the Court.
>
> 1. Do you find by a preponderance of the evidence that Zerevrea can cause some individuals to commit suicide/homicide?
> Answer "yes" or "no."
> Answer: _____

"I submit to you, ladies and gentlemen of the jury, the answer to Question No. 1 is simply NO. *La respuesta es simple y sencillamente NO.* You won't need to answer anything else once you've answered 'No' to question one. You stop right there. You're done. All you have to do is notify the marshal that you're done, and that's it. He'll take it from there.

"It's up to you, me and every one of us to do our part and help end the blame game. Because, ultimately, that's what Mr. Spearman wants you to do. Gina Ray wants you to blame Zerevrea for Mr. Ray's troubles, and we know Zerevrea was never the real reason Tommy Ray pulled the trigger. We know it wasn't Boston-Magnifica who pulled the trigger that fateful Saturday morning. BostonMagnifica did not help Tommy Ray launder money or gamble away his family's future and security. Zerevrea didn't do any of those things. Tommy Ray created this mess, and now he wants you to bail him out. He's screaming from the grave for you to award his widow millions. But, in fact, Zerevrea had nothing to do with his demise. The truth of the matter is that Zerevrea is safe and effective when used as prescribed.

"Friends, we cannot blame the medication for Tommy Ray's troubles. Put blame where blame lies. Tommy Ray and Tommy Ray alone is responsible for his own suicide. Not you, not me, not society, not BostonMagnifica Pharmaceuticals and certainly not Zerevrea. You know it, and I know it. Thank you."

CHAPTER 51

"WHY AREN'T YOU getting your promotion?" asked Hector. "I was there . . . I saw you kick Spearman's ass. You got BostonMagnifica its defense verdict!"

"I did not win the case," explained Billy. "Spearman threw the case. That's different."

Hector took a swig from his coffee mug. "What are you talking about? I saw you kick his ass during the trial. We all did. I've never heard a better closing argument, honest."

Billy was going around his office, boxing up all his belongings, clearing his desk. "I, we, BostonMagnifica, our client, put fifty million dollars in his secret bank account so we could have a defense verdict. We bought the verdict. Spearman also helped me put some 'hush' money into Andarza and Guerra pockets, to get them to go away, quietly."

"What?"

"We did it to send a message to the trial lawyers across the nation that these cases cannot be won . . . to just go away. To leave Zerevrea very much alone," continued Billy.

"Wait, wait, wait . . . I've never heard of such a thing!" Hector was scratching his head, looking bewildered. "In all my years of working in and around attorneys, I've . . . never . . . "

"It's true. Tommy Ray had traces of Zerevrea in his system, but Spearman agreed to keep the existence of his forensic pharmacologist, Dr. John Patterson, a secret. Dr. Dahm testified as to what he knew and Freemont was there to fool Dorfman and the observers. Spearman could have called Patterson to testify about

330

the traces. You see, Spearman called the lab Dr. Dahm used and instructed them to save some tissues for further testing. Those tissues were sent to Patterson for testing. We agreed not to call him as a witness."

"But . . . but Gina Ray . . . you, yourself, said she would not back down. That you had never met such a plaintiff, pissed, angry, ready to eat BostonMagnifica for lunch."

"We paid her off, too," explained Billy. "No one can ever find out, you hear. Otherwise, we'll all lose our licenses or worse . . . go to prison."

"What?" Hector plopped down on one of the client chairs in front of Billy's desk, completely blown away by the latest revelation.

"Look, Spearman helped me convince her to take twenty million and go away. It was a tough pill to swallow, but we did promise to put improved black box warning labels on Zerevrea, admonishing the consumer of the fatal results if taken while suffering from PTSD. I got BostonMagnifica to commit to raise public awareness on the risks of suicide. We also came through and took care of the Andarza and Guerra families, like she wanted. That's what we agreed to do in exchange for a secret settlement."

"You mean when you got into the courtroom, the first day of trial, the case had been fixed already behind the scenes?"

"Yes. Can you imagine what Dorfman would do if he found out we wasted his and the jury's time? I'm sorry, but we needed a defense verdict. A settlement, even if it had been confidential, would have sent the wrong message. The public would know that BostonMagnifica settles these cases. And as soon as the trial lawyers hear the word 'settlement,' the feeding frenzy starts. A settlement would have sent the trial lawyers scurrying, lining up plaintiffs down the street and around every corner and filing lawsuits left and right, as we speak. I don't have to tell you. Remember Vioxx? Hell, Tommy Dykeman in east Texas had already signed up thirty potential Zerevrea cases . . . he was ready to go."

"I still can't believe Gina Ray went for that. There's gotta be more."

"There is."

Hector finished his coffee and put the empty Dallas Cowboys cup on Billy's desk. "What else is there?"

"Remember the indictments on money laundering, how Tommy Ray was mentioned as a target defendant? Well, the feds were going to seize everything that was his, including his businesses, his law firm and all the receivables. Gina Ray was gonna end up on the street. With the money we paid her, she could start her life anew, put the kids through college and have money left over. What made the deal attractive for her is that this money would not have come from any illegal activity. Thus, the millions would be out of reach from the feds. That's how we sweetened the pot. It was that or nothing."

"So, that's how you convinced her to take the millions and keep quiet," Hector figured. "The stuff I got from Celia, copies of the sealed indictments, helped to put pressure on Mrs. Ray?"

"Absolutely. Had it not been for you talking to Miguel Celia and following that lead, we would have never gotten the case settled. Once Gina Ray understood that her husband had probably committed suicide—not because of Zerevrea but because an indictment was coming down. Tommy was finished and was probably heading to prison. She changed her tune."

"You have to admit, Tommy was pretty smart," said Hector, still reeling from the news. "He knew the feds would take everything, but being the attorney that he was, he knew that a jury award or settlement paid to the wife from a wrongful death lawsuit was off-limits to the government. Do you think he set it up like that?"

"Don't really know. Maybe Gina was looking for answers, figured Zerevrea was an SSRI and decided to roll the dice. There's been considerable litigation against the makers of these drugs, you know."

"So, how did you come up with the idea and get Spearman to play along and let you win?" asked Hector.

"Once Mrs. Ray understood the impact of mentioning the sealed indictments was going to have on her case, she had no choice but to accept my offer. Otherwise, she was going to end up without a penny to her name."

"And how did you convince Falcone to part with the millions?"

"The guy's a businessman. He understood that even seventy-five million bucks for a defense victory was cheap. He knew that if we lost the test case, within weeks there would be thousands of other lawsuits filed. In the end, it was going to cost billions to clean up the mess. But in order to convince him, I had to lie and tell him and Hughes that Spearman also had the memos and Croutoux's unpublished studies."

"Which he didn't have because we had those, right?"

"Yes, but Falcone didn't know that Spearman had nothing. But once he believed Spearman had them and that he was about to leak the studies, he went ape-shit and found the money for me to buy their silence."

"But there's one thing I don't get . . . " said Hector. "If you had Gina Ray on the ropes and she wasn't going to win her case because of the indictments, why offer her money? Why waste money? I mean, she wasn't going to win her case anyway. Why give her so much money?"

"Because she needed an incentive to go through with the exercise. After she found out that I was going to reveal the existence of the indictments, she advised Spearman to dismiss her lawsuit. She wanted no part of it, but I needed a warm body in the courtroom. Think about it this way. What would have happened if she had just dismissed her case and walked away because she realized she couldn't win?"

"Guys like Dykeman would have filed their cases the very next day," answered Hector, "trying to take a crack at it."

"Exactly! More litigation, more headlines and more bad publicity while the trial lawyers attempt to get that first plaintiff's verdict . . . and then the floodgates of litigation would be wide open."

"So this way," Hector said, finally understanding, "Boston-Magnifica gets the favorable jury verdict, and that stops everyone in their tracks."

"Right. Even Judge Dorfman dismissing Spearman's lawsuit in the middle of the trial would never have been the same as getting an outright defense jury verdict."

"Don't you think," followed Hector, "that the trial lawyers might say 'Billy Bravo got lucky because he used the indictment to beat Gina Ray over the head'? And maybe that was the real reason BostonMagnifica won?"

"Yes, I've thought of that. But you know what?"

"What?"

"I don't care. Hey, if somebody else wants to take another shot at BostonMagnifica, let them. I did the best I could with what I had at the time. For the time being, BostonMagnifica gets to live another day. And don't forget we forced BostonMagnifica to add stronger black box warnings, addressing the post-traumatic stress disorder issue and we also got them to agree to better educate the medical profession . . . all thanks to the Tommy Ray litigation."

"So, that's how you did it, eh?"

"Yep. I wanted Mrs. Ray to come out ahead on this deal and make a difference. But she needed to go through with the trial despite the indictments, despite everything else that might come up. BostonMagnifica needed a very visible, very public win and that was worth some money."

"So, you played them both?"

"I had to."

"Jesus Christ!" cried Hector. "I never saw it coming . . . *no lo puedo creer*. Unbelievable! Keep going . . . don't stop. How much did the whole thing cost?" He was anxious to hear how his boss had masterminded one of the biggest legal ploys in courtroom history.

"We offered her twenty million to go through the exercise. Spearman was against it, obviously. He hated my ass, Falcone's ass and everyone else at BostonMagnifica . . . and he was advising her against it. He wanted to try the case because he really believed that he could keep the indictments out and away from the jury. He finally came around. In the end, we had to put another forty in Spearman's pocket to buy his silence and his performance."

Hector got up from his chair and walked to the window. "But Spearman must have known that even if he kept the indictments out, the fact that Tommy Ray blasted two people to death . . . was not going to sit well with the jury."

"That was a whole other issue," explained Billy. "Spearman knew he'd be fighting an uphill battle and that it was going to be extremely hard to convince a jury to award money to the fucker who nailed two federal employees, even with the indictments thrown out, even if Tommy Ray had had Zerevrea in his system. Who would want to reward a murderer?"

"So, he took the money?" asked Hector.

"Wouldn't you?"

"Sure . . . of course. I've got to hand it to you, Billy. The whole thing was brilliant! And you used the threat of a *screaming jury verdict* for Gina Ray to make those things happen."

"That, plus remember . . . Falcone was extremely worried about the juries down in South Texas . . . we live in a judicial hell-hole."

"When did you think the sham trial might be the ticket?"

"In the old days, Big Tobacco would always pay off the plaintiffs behind closed doors. Then, the plaintiff's lawyers would pretend to try their case, put on some evidence, purposefully fail to present the smoking gun memos and the defendants would win and walk away. It was all staged in order to send the signal that they were invincible. It went on for decades. That's why Big Tobacco always won."

"Pure evil genius!" cried Hector. "I still can't believe it. The witnesses, the trial, Mrs. Ray on the stand . . . all a setup."

"Yep."

"And you're an ethics professor?"

"Not anymore," conceded Billy. "I'm embarrassed, if you must know the truth. I had a hand in subverting justice . . . the judicial process, everything it stands for . . . I made a mockery of it."

"I just never thought . . . "

"Look," interrupted Billy, "I'm not proud. But my daughter needed this win, too. She deserves to live, Hector. Short of giving one's life, how far would you go to save your child?"

"I'd give my life for my kids," he answered.

"Well, then, there's your answer. I had to think of something to save Ale and make sure she had a shot at life. In the end, BostonMagnifica avoids more litigation and imminent bankruptcy,

Gina Ray walks away with money, and Fledkort continues to be available, while Zerevrea and the public get better black box warnings."

"What do we do about the sealed indictments?"

"They're no longer sealed. Remember, I asked Marks to read the newspaper article in open court? They've been unsealed, and I don't think it matters much now."

"So, things worked out after all."

"No, not really. Bates said the committee voted against my promotion and instead voted to terminate my sorry Hispanic ass . . . *en pocas palabras*, immigration issues, you know? I embarrassed the firm, not to mention I threatened a client, which translated into a major business loss to the firm. In the end, even though we won for our client, Falcone gave Bates and our firm the boot."

"Screw them!" Hector said, fuming as he looked around to make sure the door to Billy's office was shut. "Bates and the others—they're a bunch of morons."

"Anyway, I've made arrangements to surrender my Bar card and my license until I can figure out if I'm a U.S. citizen or not."

"What are you going to do next?"

"Don't know. But, whatever it is, it'll have nothing to do with the practice of law."

"I'll miss you," said Hector, extending a hand.

Billy gave Hector a hug goodbye.

"Here . . . " said Hector, "before I forget."

"What is it?"

"Tommy Ray's suicide note," said Hector as he handed Billy a small, sealed envelope, "I think."

"How did you find it?" Billy now remembered the conversation with Fay Hendry, the professor. She had said that most suicide victims leave a note, although not always.

"When we were getting ready for trial, I'd gone by the hospital to see if they still had his robe, his slippers—anything that we could use at trial. They gave me the robe in a plastic bag. I never checked it until a few days ago when I was putting everything away. It fell out of his robe pocket."

"Did you read it?"

"No, because it's addressed to Gina Ray," explained Hector. "It says so, right here, 'To my Gina.' I just couldn't."

"Leave it with me," instructed Billy. "I'll get it to Spearman; he'll know what to do with it."

CHAPTER 52

DOCTOR IVÁN GONZÁLEZ pointed Billy Bravo to a brown leather chair in the corner of his downtown Reynosa office. Billy had phoned his old friend, wondering if he could come by and talk. Iván handed Billy a glass of Bressia Profundo red wine. The over-sized Sommelier-style glass felt light and delicate in Billy's hand. He stretched on the chair, pulled a box of cigarettes from his shirt pocket and offered one to the doctor.

"No, thanks, Billy," said Iván, "I never knew you smoked?"

"Started about a year ago. Remember, I consulted you on a case?" He said as he contemplated lighting up in his friend's office. Besides, there were no visible ashtrays anywhere. "Can I smoke in your office?"

"I'm sorry," said Dr. González, "I don't allow smoking in here, Billy. Why did you start?"

"Something to do with the Tommy Ray trial," answered Billy.

"Yes, I remember now. Has it been that long?"

"Yes."

"So, what's happened since then, Billy?" asked the doctor.

"Well, I got my client his victory, but in the process I came close to losing everything."

"Why?"

"It's a long story. I had to come clean and admit I had a son out of wedlock."

"You screwed around behind Yami's back?"

"One time many, many years ago. Can you believe it? I never knew that the woman had gotten pregnant. One day, out of the blue, I get a phone call from the mother saying she's got only a few

338

months to live. She'd been diagnosed with cancer. She wants me to take care of our son, William."

"No? ¡Dios mío!"

"Yes. Then, right around the same time, just a few months before the Ray trial, Ale falls ill with leukemia. She almost died on us."

"Are you serious? Is she okay?"

"Yes, her leukemia is in remission. She's starting college, soon, thank God. She's been admitted to Rice University in Houston. She wants to study marketing to help me run my father-in-law's cigar business."

"You're no longer practicing law?" asked Iván, sounding surprised.

"Not right now. I'm rethinking my options. Yami thinks I should take over my in-laws' business. She always wanted me to run the operation from their hacienda down in Veracruz."

"And?"

"I don't know. I thought for sure a victory in the Ray case would give me the push I needed to make name partner, but that wasn't the case. That's all I ever wanted."

"And? What happened?"

"After my dad died, I came to find out I wasn't even a U.S. citizen. My old man had bribed a *partera* to lie and say I had been born in the United States."

"Wait!" yelled Iván, shaking his head, "you're not an American citizen?"

"Well, yes and no. Do you have time? It's kind of a long story."

"Go ahead," replied Iván, "I'm dying to hear this."

"Remember Hector, my investigator at the firm?"

"Yes. . . you mentioned him before."

"Well, he looked into it and helped me out without my asking. It turns out I'm a U.S. citizen and have been all along, but I still need to untangle the mess my dad created."

"How so?"

"Hector came to find out that my dad had been married twice, something I never knew. My sister Lucía and I were born to his first wife, Laura, who happened to be a U.S. citizen. She died while giving birth to me in a Mexican clinic."

"Okay," nodded Iván, "and?"

"Saddled with two small children and no wife to help raise us, my dad quickly married a girl named Eva. They had a girl together, Aracely. Naturally, I grew up thinking Eva was my mother and that Aracely was my blood sister."

"You don't say!"

"Yep. Since Dad lost his mind the day his wife died—my birth happened on a weekend trip down south to visit Laura's parents—he surmised he'd bribe a midwife to lie and say that I had been born on U.S. soil like Lucía, my sister. Due to his lack of education, he didn't know that despite the fact that I was born in a Mexican clinic, I had derived my citizenship from Laura, my mother, after all since she was a U.S.-born citizen."

"Wow, wow, wow," exclaimed Iván, "un-freakin'-believable!"

"Oh, and get this . . . from the Mexican Civil Registry, Hector managed to track down my original Mexican birth certificate where my real mother, Laura, is listed as a U.S. citizen. After that, Hector scored a copy of my mother's own birth certificate along with baptismal records showing that she had been, in fact, born and raised in San Benito, Texas, a small farming community on the American side."

"So, how do you fix the mess?"

"All I had to do is fill out and file the N600 form with copies of the documents uncovered by Hector. Isn't it funny, the whole thing? In the end, it didn't matter that my dad—in his desperation—had bribed a midwife. I was a U.S. citizen after all."

"I'm glad to see things worked out. When are you going back to live in the U.S.?"

"I don't know. I've been living down in Veracruz, with my in-laws. I come up to Reynosa every other week to see Mauricio. He's enrolled at the Marine Military Academy in Harlingen. On weekends, my sister Aracely picks him up and brings him to visit with me."

"Wow. All these changes, simply amazing."

THE NAME PARTNER 341

"And don't forget Hurricane Emily. Do you remember that?"

"How can I forget? Thank God my office is on the second floor. The office suites down on the first floor flooded with six inches of water. It was a mess, even here in Reynosa."

"Well, I was so busy with all kinds of shit at the office that I asked my old man to go and board up my beach house. He had a heart attack and died. But get this . . . "

"What?"

"As if having one's old man die wasn't bad enough, we also lost our beach house and then the insurance company didn't want to pay. *Un verdadero desmadre.*"

"I'm sorry about your old man. I had no idea that's what killed him."

"It was all my fault," muttered Billy.

"Don't beat yourself over it, Billy. Those things happen. He could have died taking a shower at home, no? When it's your time to go, it's your time to go. No one can change that. Not you, not I, *nadie.*"

"I'm trying to accept it . . . it's been really hard."

"And Yami? How's she handling all this?" asked Iván, changing topics.

"She almost divorced my ass! It was too, too much. Ale in the hospital, my health insurance not wanting to pay for her treatment, our credit cards maxed out. We had to sue our homeowner's insurance company to get them to pay for the beach house. Then she freaked out when my old firm gave me the boot because they found out there were issues with my citizenship. My son out of wedlock didn't help things either. . . . "

"I see. But you're recovering, right?"

"Yes, Yami and I have started talking again. We're trying to focus on the positive, you know . . . still adjusting. The funny thing is that William, Wicho and Ale get along just great."

"So, if you're not working . . . who's paying the bills? I mean, Rice will be expensive, and MMA is not cheap. What gives?"

"My lawyer, Hugh Collins, sued the insurance company for bad faith and for refusing to pay on my beach house. He popped them for a couple million. The guy's aggressive as hell. He's also handling my whistleblower lawsuit against BostonMagnifica for price-fixing. I have coming a 20 percent cut from the five-hundred million dollar settlement being hammered out between Collins, the government and my old, piece-of-shit client."

"No love lost there, eh?"

"None whatsoever," said Billy, as he finished his wine. "Besides, I've already made twenty million off the Tommy Ray lawsuit."

"Come again? How?"

"Spearman, the guy suing BostonMagnifica, pitched me half of the forty million I got him. Let's just say we had our own secret arrangement, *por debajo del agua*, on the side."

"Really?" muttered Iván, scratching his head in amazement.

"Sure. Never before would I have considered such an arrangement, but after I learned certain things about my client, it was easy. *Como quitarle un pelo al gato, por ojetes.* Sure enough, my suspicions were later confirmed with the arrest of BostonMagnifica's CEO. It was Falcone who ordered the hit on his most vocal opponent, Doctor Croutoux."

"Holy crap! *Qué despapaye.*"

"Tell me about it. In any event, BostonMagnifica's not hurting for business and Gina Ray came out okay. Her husband somehow managed to take care of her and their kids. It was all spelled out very subtly in his suicide note. All you had to do was read between the lines."

"Can I get you another glass of wine?"

"Please," said Billy as he handed the empty wine glass to his friend. "Anyway, I didn't make name partner, but things turned out okay in the end. And as long as my Ale continues to live, continues to have her health, and my three children, William included, become well-adjusted, productive members of society, I'll be fine."

"Sounds to me like you've got it all figured out."

"Did I tell you Yami started the Bravo Foundation to help all the children left behind in the United States after their parents get deported? It's keeping her very, very busy, flying back and forth. I've started a sister foundation here in Mexico to work with displaced parents in order to help them reconnect with the children and relatives left behind in the U.S. via tele-conferencing. The Guillermo Bravo Foundation for displaced children and families —named after my old man—operates three such communications centers in Mexico City, Guadalajara and Ciudad Juárez. All equipped with video-conferencing equipment. All free of charge."

"That's great!"

"I've got to do something, otherwise I'll go crazy. I'd figured it was time to put my money where my mouth is. It was time to help *mi gente*."

"Your dad would be proud, Billy."

"*Gracias*, Iván. Thanks for listening."

"Anytime."

"Anyway," started Billy, "I've got to get going. I'm taking Wicho to the movies. It was good seeing you again."

"You're always welcome to drop by, if only for a visit or a consult . . . whatever you want. It's good to talk to you."

"*Gracias*, Iván."

Billy got up and started heading for the door. He reached for the door knob, paused and turned around. "Hey, did I tell you I'd finally figured out what the stingray nightmares meant?"

"Really?"

"Yes. Make sure you don't get stung while reeling in your dream fish," explained Billy.

Dr. González followed up, "you mean it comes with a big price tag?"

"Yes . . . it does."

Dr. González got up from his chair. "*Pues sí. Estoy de acuerdo,*" said the doctor as he wrapped an arm around Billy's shoulder escorting his childhood friend out the door. "I completely agree . . . but what a ride, huh?"

"Ha, ha," chuckled Billy, while nodding his head in complete agreement. "That's for sure."

"I'm glad things turned out okay for you and your family. At the end of the day, what good is it to snag the American Dream, if you don't have anyone to share it with, right?"

The two friends shook hands and said their goodbyes. Dr. González remained standing in the hallway outside his clinic and watched a much transformed Billy Bravo exit the office building and vanish into the sweltering Reynosa afternoon.

Also by Carlos Cisneros

THE CASE RUNNER